THE TALLOW IMAGE

Also by Jane Brindle

Scarlet
No Mercy

The

TALLOW
IMAGE

Jane Brindle

ORION

First published in Great Britain in 1994 by
Orion
An Imprint of Orion Books Ltd
Orion House, 5 Upper St Martin's Lane, London WC2H 9EA

A CIP catalogue record for this book
is available from the British Library

ISBN 1 85797 245 7

Typeset by Deltatype Ltd, Ellesmere Port, Wirral
Printed in Great Britain by Clays Ltd, St Ives plc.

For Rosie
(who could coax blood from a stone)

Foreword

The lunatic asylum in Fremantle and now featured in *The Tallow Image* is a formidable place, built by the convicts themselves and today preserved as an art and craft museum.

What initially happened to Matt and Cathy is an actual reconstruction of what happened to me and my husband; though what followed, thank God, is created only within a storyteller's mind.

The memory I have of that vast and aged building will stay with me for ever. To stand in that tiny padded cell, to see the narrow iron bed and to imagine the many wretched souls who may have wept themselves to sleep there, was an experience that gave me many a sleepless night. When I put my hand inside that crumbling wall where Cathy finds the tallow doll, a feeling of icy cold came over me, a feeling that someone unseen was watching me. It wasn't long before I was hammering on the door, desperate to be let out.

That night in the hotel I couldn't sleep. The name Rebecca Norman seemed to haunt me. And though my husband and I had thumbed through many convicts' names during the researching of this book, neither of us could recall the name Rebecca Norman. Even on our return, when we retraced our steps to Liverpool docks and searched the records again, we could find no mention of such a convict ever having been transported.

Her name, and the experience I felt in that cell, induced me to write *The Tallow Image*. Rebecca Norman is not real. She is only a figment of my imagination. *I have to believe that!*

Acknowledgements

The receptionist at the old lunatic asylum; Lorraine Stevenson (Archives), Town Hall, Fremantle, W.A.; Mary Faith Holloway (Custodian), Prison Museum; Sunita A. Thillaineth (Librarian), Fremantle, W.A.; The Port Authority officials, Fremantle, W.A.; Chamber of Commerce officials, Fremantle, W.A. *And Rebecca Norman, who insisted that her story should be told.*

PART ONE

———

1880
Fremantle
Western Australia

———

Through the flames
Eye to eye
Only then
The curse will die.

Chapter One

'They say I should watch out for that one. I'm told she's bad . . . evil.' The warder's curious gaze was drawn to the dark-haired figure below in the prison kitchens. 'What a woman, though,' he murmured, lapsing into deep thought, 'have you ever seen such a beauty? How can anyone who looks like that be so shockingly wicked?' Shaking his head, he murmured, 'Even when I suspect it to be true, I still can't believe it of her.'

Below them, Rebecca Norman applied herself to the laborious task of drawing the dark, coarse loaves from the blackened ovens. Captivated, the two men watched her every move.

'You'd better believe what they say, matey!' returned the other man sharply. *'Unless yer ready to trade souls with the divil!'*

With stern expression he quietly regarded the young officer, at once being cruelly reminded of how different were the two of them: himself approaching the age of fifty, a weathered and red-necked fellow with drooping jowls and a drinker's pock-marked nose, while his companion was no more than . . . what . . . twenty-seven . . . twenty-eight? Brown eyed and handsome, and cutting a dash with his tall, uniformed figure. Prime meat, he thought with crushing fear and not a little envy, prime meat for a particular woman who would swallow him up and suck the life blood out of him.

'Mark my words,' he warned the young man now, 'if you value your sanity, you'd best stay clear o' that one.' He regarded his colleague closely. 'You're on loan to the prison, ain't you? . . . A minder at the lunatic asylum, ain't you?' He sniffed and wiped his hand along the flat uninteresting contours of his face. 'Since the

3

'flu took two of us off sick, we've been dangerously short-handed. How long is it before you're sent back to your duties at the asylum?' He softly laughed, then pressing his palm against the side of his nose he squeezed a trailing dewdrop between finger and thumb. 'I couldn't look after crazy folk,' he remarked sourly. 'Is it right you have to wipe their arses?'

For a long uncomfortable moment the young officer gave no reply. Instead, he watched the woman, seeming bewitched by her. Mirrored in his warm brown eyes was a degree of compassion, and a dangerous admiration for the convict woman; a woman of volatile character, a stunningly attractive woman, a secretive woman who during her twenty years' imprisonment had made no friends but nurtured too many enemies. In the authorities' records she was listed as Rebecca Norman, known to some as 'the silent one', and feared by others as 'the devil's messenger'.

'She's magnificent!' whispered the young officer. 'The most beautiful creature I've ever seen. Such dark, soulful eyes.' When suddenly the woman boldly smiled at him, perfect white teeth flashing in an olive-skinned face and black laughing eyes appraising him, he was visibly shaken. Looking quickly away, he turned to the older guard, saying in a harsh whisper, 'She doesn't look dangerous to me.' He gazed at the woman again. 'Well, not unless you count her dark beauty as being a wicked temptation.'

Amusement over-riding his deeper fears, the other man chuckled. 'Fancy 'er beneath the blankets, do yer?' he taunted. 'Long for the feel of a divil woman underneath yer, is that it, eh? You horny bastard!' It pleased him to see how his words brought embarrassment.

Suddenly, though, his mood was serious. 'Yer ain't used to hardened convicts, Ryan,' he warned. 'You'll find they ain't so tame nor manageable as them poor soft-headed inmates in the asylum. Still . . . there'll be time enough for you to know what you've let yerself in for, I reckon. Time enough to find out the badness in this place.' His expression was grim. 'Until then, you'd best listen to them as knows!'

Disgruntled now, he swung himself round to face the convicts

4

who were using the lapse in discipline to indulge in a flurry of whispering; all but the one known as Rebecca Norman, and she was standing upright, legs astride and her black eyes beseeching the young officer. At once the old guard sprang forward, flailing the leather bullwhip in the air as he yelled, 'Back to yer work, afore I lay the whip across yer shoulders!' In an instant the whispering stopped, the woman lowered her dark gaze, and an ominous silence descended. Above it only the occasional clatter of metal was heard as the convicts' leg-irons chattered to one another.

Ralph Ryan took up a strategic position, surveying the scene from a curve in the upper level. All was well. He tried not to gaze on the woman, but she was strong in his mind; the bold, slim figure, the way her sack-dress had slipped on one shoulder displaying the tantalising rise of a plump firm breast; the idea of long slender legs beneath a brown, shapeless convict gown; the short-cropped hair that was like a black skull cap over a proud handsome head, *and those secretive dark eyes*! Powerful and hypnotic, they put him in mind of a moonlit ocean. Even now, though his gaze was deliberately averted, he could sense her eyes playing on him, burning his thoughts, erupting the pit of his stomach and exciting him deep within himself. He could see no evil in such rare beauty. Neither did he feel threatened. Instead, he was exhilarated by the experience; acutely aware of her nearness, yet afraid to turn his head and look on her, being deeply conscious of the turmoil she had wrought in him.

For the remainder of his duty, Ralph Ryan deliberately concentrated his attention on the other convicts – four in all, three men and one old hag. To his mind, it was the *men* who demanded extra vigilance; surly of mood and devious in mind, they were already labelled as troublemakers. Down here in the kitchens, shackled in leg-irons and closely guarded, they presented little threat, but their dark resentful moods infiltrated the air, creating a brooding atmosphere. As the convicts went sullenly about their duties – fetching and carrying and generally following the well-practised routine that went into the preparation of food for many inmates – Ralph Ryan allowed his secret thoughts to dwell on the one known as Rebecca Norman.

He was not yet fully briefed on her background. All he knew was that she was some thirty-four years of age, although to his mind she looked younger. In 1860, at the tender age of fourteen, she was transported to the shores of Australia to serve out a sentence of twelve years. She might have long since been released, but she had proved rebellious and violent; numerous clashes with both prison guards and inmates had brought severe punishment. Time and again her sentence was extended, until now it seemed she would end her days incarcerated here: *or dancing on the gibbet from the end of a rope.*

'The witch has got to you, ain't she?' The voice of the older guard hissed into Ryan's ear, startling his thoughts and bringing a deep red flush to his face. When he slewed round, it was to see the weathered face crumpled in a sardonic smile.

'Got the hards for her, have yer . . . can't wait to mate with her?' Suddenly the smile slid away and in its place came a look of impatience. 'Like I said, yer a bloody fool! Don't be fooled by dark smiling eyes and a promise.' He cast a scornful glance towards the woman, whose knowing gaze was instinctively uplifted. For a brief second their gazes mingled; his accusing, hers bold and challenging. In the moment when he surged forward, the fear within him erupting in fury, the woman quietly smiled and turned away, deliberately busying herself before the open ovens, her handsome face blushing pink from the intense heat they generated.

Frustrated, the guard fell silent, his brooding eyes intent on her face. 'There's a witch if ever I saw one,' he mumbled. 'If yer ask me, Rebecca Norman shoulda burned, alongside her grand-mother!'

'What's that you say. . . ?' Ralph shifted his weight. It had been a long day and his feet ached. 'Was her grandmother *burned?*' He had witnessed the conflict between his colleague and the woman. Now he was excited and further intrigued by the snippet of information grudgingly imparted. 'What was her crime?' he asked

6

quietly. 'Lord knows, there's plenty gets strung up, and plenty as deserves it, but the gallows seems a harsh punishment for an old woman.'

'Save yer sympathy, matey,' the other man replied gruffly, his small shifty eyes surveying the scene below. 'Rebecca Norman's grandmother weren't no "old woman" . . . no more than forty-eight year old, they say, though o' course there's them as *is* ready fer the knacker's yard at that time o' life.' He grinned broadly, flicking the tip of his tongue in and out of the many gaps between his blackened teeth. 'Look at *meself*,' he prompted, 'the tail end o' forty-nine and in the prime o' life, wouldn't yer say?' As though to press home a point, he drew himself up to full height and sucked in his belly. ' 'Tis a handsome fella I am,' he chuckled, 'though I do say so meself.' Reaching up, he took off his hat, straightened his hair and replaced the cap with a flourish. 'Oh, aye, there's many a woman would be delighted of a night in my company.'

Amused, Ralph Ryan roved his gaze over the other man's physique, at the pot belly straining beneath its broad black belt, the red neck that now grew purple from the effort of suppressing that mighty mound of blubber, and he was obliged to smile. 'You're certainly in better shape than many a man at your age,' he remarked.

'Ain't that the truth, eh?' the older man rejoined, thankfully deflating a little and grinning at a certain realisation. 'Especially when yer consider that most old cronies my age are already worm's meat!'

Impatient now, Ralph persisted. 'You were saying the woman was burned?'

'Yer mean the grandmother?' When the young guard nodded sombrely, he went on in a quieter voice, 'Aye. Her crime was recorded as *murder*, so they say.' His suspicious gaze darted to where Rebecca Norman was laying out the shapeless mounds of dark-baked bread. '*Murder*, that's what, but there was talk o' witchcraft and diabolical acts. The old trout was sentenced to be hanged, but local folk had other ideas. They took her from under the nose of the authorities, and they burned her to death.'

7

'Was there ever any evidence that she committed murder?'

The older man appeared not to have heard, and he gave no response. Instead, he shifted uncomfortably. Grabbing the crotch of his trousers, he complained, 'These bloody uniforms'll be the death of me!'

'I asked was there any evidence,' Ralph reminded him.

'Oh aye! Evidence enough, so they say. Evidence that led the authorities to the place where that one and her grandmother were hiding. They were holed up in some filthy shack aside the Liverpool docklands. Candlemakers they were, the two of them. A strange, unsociable pair, I'll be bound!' Undoing the buckle of his belt, he sighed noisily. 'Christ almighty, me belly's near cut in two!'

'When you say "diabolical acts", what d'you mean exactly? And *who* was murdered?'

'I don't know, do I?' came the impatient reply. 'All I know is what's been told me over the years. Some say the fellow were known to the witch and her brat.' When Ralph asked about the Norman woman's parents, he explained what had been detailed to him down the years. 'By all accounts, the father ran off with some floozy. Ain't that what allus happens?' Agitated, he loosely fastened his belt.

'And the mother?'

'By! Yer do like to know the ins and outs of a cat's arse, don't yer, eh?' He licked his rubbery lips and went on with the story; if the truth were told, he was enjoying telling the tale, especially when the listener was so impressed. 'Well now, from what I can make of it, the poor bugger was struck down by a terrible illness . . . died, I expect.' He had no more to tell, which to his mind was a sin and a shame. 'The crux of it all is that the brat's father deserted her and her mother, who took it so bad, well, she just upped and died. The poor girl was deserted by *both* her parents in a manner o' speaking. The father going off that way . . . he med her an orphan, that's what! The young 'un grew up under the influence of the old witch. Soon after there was a body found and the old candlemaker were charged with his murder.' He suddenly chuckled. 'Wouldn't surprise me at all if it were the brat's own daddy that was bumped off.' The idea took his fancy, although it had never been said, as far as he could recall.

'What else?'

'Nothing else!' The guard eyed Ralph Ryan with puzzlement. 'If yer mean the witchcraft, well, there was talk aplenty, or so the story goes.'

'Talk, eh? But was there *proof*?'

'When was such a thing *ever* proven, eh? If yer ask me it's true enough. You've only to look at that one . . . at them black witch's eyes.' He glanced down, half-smiling.

Ralph's inquisitive brown eyes followed the other man's intent stare. 'What was *her* crime?'

'I'm surprised yer need to ask!' came the retort. 'She may have been only fourteen year old, but no doubt she were a full partner to what took place. The grandmother swore to the end that the young 'un were innocent . . . never changed that likely tale neither, the old bugger. Not even when the flames were sizzling her eyeballs.' He smiled, delighting in the images brought to mind.

'And if this one *was* innocent,' Ralph continued to look on the prisoner below, her dark head bent to its task, 'yet sentenced to twelve years and transported to these far shores; wouldn't that be enough to bring out the worst in any of us?'

'Innocent? Not that one! If yer ask me, she were every bit as guilty as the old woman. Mebbe even *more* so. Guilty o' murder an' foul practices that don't bear thinking on.'

'There's many an innocent been wrongly accused.'

'Aye! And there's many a bad 'un slipped through the net. But not *this* one, no indeed. *This* one's in the right place, and if it were up to me she'd never again see the light o' day!' When he saw Ralph regarding him with curiosity he became cautious. He must be careful not to give away too much. It wouldn't do for Ralph Ryan to guess the real reason for his loathing of Rebecca Norman. It would be a bad thing if the truth were to get out.

It was a well-known fact that now and again a desperate guard

9

would press himself on a female convict, especially if she weren't old and withered by the passage of time in this place. As for himself, the old guard mused, he'd never risk catching a dose o' the scabs on a cell floor, not when he had a fat belly at home to squash up against; his own woman was not the *prettiest* thing you ever saw, but at least he were the only one to get beneath her petticoats. Oh no, he'd never taken such a fancy to any inmate – at least, not until Rebecca Norman's black eyes fell on him with a particular purpose. Thinking on it now made his blood run cold. It were fifteen years since, during a shocking night of storms and gales that lashed mercilessly through the dark hours. His colleague was laid low with an injury, leaving that particular duty shift short-handed. There was no trouble, the storm seemed to exhaust and frighten every manjack behind bars. He recalled the night now. Wild, it were, the wind howling like a wolf, the sky black and heaving, except when the lightning tinged everything blue, and it seemed like the end of the world. On that night he had seen Rebecca Norman dancing in her cell. Like a dark, flitting shadow she was, magnificent, and naked as the day she were born. Like a moth to a flame he was drawn to her. Even now he could recall every detail like it was only yesterday – her young warm body merging with his, the delicious feel of her nakedness, the way she seemed to weave herself round him, *inside* him, her shocking, primeval beauty and those eyes, those dewy fathomless eyes that watched him even while he was in the throes of the deepest ecstasy.

Later, he was in no doubt that she had deliberately bewitched him. When the rush of pleasure was over, she had begged him to help her escape. When he refused, she turned on him like a wildcat, tearing at him with sharp, jagged nails and leaving him with scars he carried to this very day. Worst of all, she had spat out a terrible curse on him and his family.

Within hours of ending his shift, he was stricken with a mysterious fever which raged for days and kept him at death's door. His wife, too, contracted the illness. He survived. She did not. In his heart he knew it was Rebecca Norman's curse, but he dared not voice his suspicions for fear of punishment. Guards had been severely reprimanded, badly punished, and even dismissed for fornicating with an inmate. These days, a man in his work was more secure than he used to be – trade unionism had come a long way since the leader of the shepherds' strike was given five hundred lashes for daring to demand higher wages. Even so, a man had to be wary, observe certain rules, and sleeping with prisoners was only inviting trouble. It went on, 'course it did, even to this day, but always with the utmost discretion. Now, once more he had a woman to call his own, again not pretty, but homely and eager to please him in every way. He had learned his lesson the hard way.

Sneaking a look at his young, handsome colleague, he hoped history was not about to repeat itself. 'I'm not one to give advice as a rule,' he told him, 'but, where she's concerned, I'm telling you for your own good. She's every bit as bad as they say. There! I've warned you, matey. The rest is up to you.'

He had seen how Rebecca Norman looked at Ralph; and he was afraid. But he was not his brother's keeper. All he could do was warn of the dangers. This he had done. Somehow, though, he didn't believe his warning would make any difference. Looking at Ralph now, at the glint in his dark eyes, he believed it was already too late.

The day's work was done. Like the wail of a banshee the weird lament of the siren pierced the air, telling one and all that prisoners should now be secure under lock and key. It was the moment when warders gave a sigh of relief, and convicts began to shuffle under guard to the dank, dismal cells where they would remain, incarcerated, until the grey light of morning, when the long, monotonous day would begin again.

'Move along, move along!' The older guard, the one they called Jacob, cracked the bullwhip behind the line of convicts, urging them on, defying them to stumble, wishing they would. As they edged forward, up the steps and along the darkened, narrow corridor, the stench of damp, oozing flesh was rancid.

Bringing up the rear, Ralph Ryan kept his eyes skinned and his every nerve-ending on edge. He had reluctantly accepted the temporary transfer from the lunatic asylum to Her Majesty's Prison; the pay was better for working shifts, and what with Maria fat with their new child, every extra penny came in handy. Besides, he had been given little choice in the matter. When men went down ill at either establishment, it was common practice to make temporary transfers of staff from one to the other. Still, he hoped it would not be for much longer. Demanding though it was, he preferred his job at the asylum.

Still, he had accepted this temporary transfer knowing all the risks. If he should falter in his judgment, or betray any sign of weakness, then his credibility would be dangerously undermined. There were desperate men here, wicked creatures of the worst order – although there were others whose severe punishment did not fit the paltry crimes committed. Sadly, once a man of lesser crime was sent to this place, his character could change overnight; he would grow bitter and resentful, aching with revenge, and more often than not he would become a more dangerous animal than his hitherto more violent counterpart. Ralph Ryan knew this and as he ushered the convicts to their cells, his expression was grim, his manner unbending.

Realising the strength and iron-like determination of their guards, and always wary of the penal back-up system that was there to crush them, the convicts went quietly, if grudgingly, to their cells.

Rebecca Norman, though, had a message to impart. Being one of only two females left wasting in Fremantle Prison, she was spared the overcrowding and the fraught atmosphere to which the men were subjected. Instead, she and the old hag were assigned to a cell whose small iron-barred window looked out over the cobbled courtyard. It was a bleak area all the same, surrounded by high walls, and seeming always to be immersed in shadows, even on the brightest day. Strangely, the song of birds was never heard in this part of the yard.

Now, as she filed past him, following the old hag into the cell,

Rebecca Norman deliberately and deviously brushed against the young guard, sending a shock through every corner of his being. When he made a slight gasp, instinctively drawing back, her wide dark eyes searched him out, smiling, delving deep into his soul. In the moment before he swung the heavy cell door into place, her whisper bathed his ears, causing him to tremble. '*Tonight . . . in the dark hours I'll be waiting.*' Her voice was soft, enticing as a summer's breeze. It haunted him.

As he walked away, he could hear her laughter. Suddenly she was quiet and the old hag's voice could be heard taunting her. 'Want him, d'you? Want to squeeze him dry, d'you? Think he'll be the one to set you free from this 'ere cage, is that it?' Her laughter was cruel.

The old one's voice dipped low, out of Ralph's earshot. 'You'll *never* be free, dearie! D'you hear me? You'll never again see the light o' day. You'll grow old like me . . . old and ugly. Nobody's gonna want you then, are they? Think on that, me beauty. You're stuck here till the end of your days, just like me. But then it's no more than you deserve. They say as how you helped kill some poor unfortunate! There's also them as say you're a witch.'

Incensed but incredibly calm, Rebecca walked towards her, her eyes opaque and deadly, like the shark's. She made no sound.

Outside in the corridor, Ralph listened. The silence was unnerving. Suddenly the old hag screamed out. There was terror in her voice. 'Get away from me! Dear God above, help me. *Somebody help me!*'

Her cries went ignored. It wasn't the first time she had raised the alarm in such a way. In their cells the prisoners settled down, stretching out on the narrow iron beds, exhausted and miserable. The guards went about their duties, checking the inmates, logging the events of the day and making preparations for the changeover of the shift.

After a while, the old woman was silent. The sound of snoring began to infiltrate the claustrophobic corridors. Soon the remaining daylight would be swallowed up, darkness would creep over the land and all would be still – save for those tortured souls who dreamed of home, and love, and freedom. And one particular soul that craved only revenge, a terrible and exacting revenge, the like of which filled her every waking moment. Rebecca Norman had not forgotten how they had hanged her grandmother; nor how they had sentenced her to this dismal place. She had not forgotten that. Neither had she forgotten *him*. Nor had she forgiven. She never would.

The sounds that echoed along the corridors were familiar. Hushed voices, jangling keys and smart, hurried footsteps. The guards were changing shift. As he left the building, Ralph bade the duty officer goodnight. Strange, he mused, how his voice and manner were so normal, even while his insides were fluttering like so many butterflies. She had got to him, the black-eyed beauty, and – try as he might – he could not thrust her from his mind.

Outside, he paused a while, drawing in long, refreshing gulps of unsullied night air. The tang of salt was carried on the freshening wind. It tasted good. Filling his lungs and mentally dismissing the dark, clinging atmosphere of the prison, Ralph Ryan lingered a moment, his sharp, busy mind assessing the day's events. Today the prison had been every bit as suffocating as every day in the previous two weeks, but uniquely satisfying also. He felt right in his prison warder's uniform. It stamped him with a degree of authority. He liked that. Also, to his surprise, he had discovered a certain awareness in himself, a kind of quiet respect for some of the milder-mannered convicts. Like almost every other citizen in Fremantle, he had entertained small regard for the convicts on the hill. They had earned imprisonment. There were few feelings of mercy or compassion for these hapless creatures. From many quarters was nurtured a measure of deep resentment towards them. This bitterness went back a long way, some thirty years or more. During the period from 1850 to 1868, nearly ten thousand convicts were transported from Britain to Western Australia, a considerable number arriving in Fremantle itself. Cheap labour for a young and growing colony, they were employed on the ships and on the land, loading and off-loading cargo, constructing new roads and erecting new buildings; even raising their own places of incarceration. Now, some twelve years after the last incoming shipment of convicts, many of these unfortunates had earned tickets-of-leave, and even pardons. Most had settled in Fremantle; some had moved on to make a new start elsewhere. Others, like Rebecca Norman, had constantly rebelled against the system, consequently lengthening their years in custody, and ultimately jeopardising the day of their release.

'Can't wait to get home and out o' these bloody trousers!' came the older warden's voice. 'Like bleedin' strait-jackets, they are!' He ambled past, still fidgeting with the crotch of his trousers. 'G'night,' he called.

'G'night.'

Beset by sharper and more tantalising images of Rebecca Norman, Ralph headed homeward. As he followed the route along by the tramway and on down William Street, he found himself smiling at the words she had murmured to him . . . 'Tonight . . . in the dark hours. I'll be waiting.' Did she really believe he could be tempted? The smile slid from his face when back came his own answer. He *was* stirred by her, by the way she sensuously brushed against him, and by the enchanting look in her sultry eyes.

Deeply disturbed, he quickened his step. The night was closing in, hot and humid, sucking a man's resistance. The sweat trickled down his back, melting the shirt to his skin. Agitated, he loosened the neck of his shirt and nervously glanced about. This week he was working an eight-hour shift, two p.m. until ten p.m. Normally, at this hour of night people were still walking the streets, younger ones making for the coolness of the beach, more senior citizens hurrying home, ready for their beds. Tonight, though, the streets were deserted. The quietness and absence of other living souls heightened his pensive mood.

As he turned into the High Street, the sound of a woman's laughter startled him. He slewed round. There was no one to be seen. Swallowing hard, he went on his way, his footsteps pushing faster and faster until they were almost running. Down the High

Street and into Henry Street, towards South Bay and the tiny terraced house that was home to him, his wife Maria and their three-year-old daughter, Agatha. Soon there would be another child. A son, maybe? The thought of his family had a sobering effect on him, lightening his heart and causing him to smile. 'Pull yourself together, you bloody fool, Ryan,' he said through clenched teeth. The older warden's words came to mind and he laughed aloud. 'Happen *your* trousers are too tight an' all . . . squeezing what little sense you have.' The thought had not occurred to him before, but suddenly he tugged at the crotch of his pants and felt the better for it.

Hurrying along Henry Street, his quiet gaze scouring ahead, Ralph let out a delighted chuckle when he saw the familiar figure of Maria silhouetted at the door. At this late hour he was surprised to see little Agatha there, a fidgeting, laughing bundle who, until now, was restrained by her mammy's hand.

The child rushed forward on seeing Ralph, her little legs running fast, until, with a whoop of joy, she was caught in her daddy's arms and flung high in the air. Maria watched from the doorway, her own delight obvious in the wide smile that shaped her pretty face.

'You're late, sweetheart.' Maria looked up at his weary face. 'Tired?' Her love for this man shone from her eyes.

He nodded his head, wincing when the excited child bit into his ear. 'Hey! Haven't you had your dinner yet?' he cried laughingly as he gently put her to the ground.

'We waited for you,' Maria explained.

Placing his hands on her small shoulders, he gazed down at her. 'Sorry,' he said simply, 'I was a bit late getting away.' How could he explain why he was reluctant to leave his place of work? Maria wouldn't understand how Rebecca Norman's eyes had touched his soul.

'Well, you're home now,' she said, reaching her face up to him.

When in a moment Ralph bent his head to kiss her, she made no mention of the feeling of dread which had invaded her day – a strange, lonely kind of feeling that even now, with his

16

homecoming, had not altogether left her. Her need to confide in him was strong. She resisted. There would be time enough later, she told herself. Her man was home, no doubt eager to relay news of his day at the prison.

Unhurried and with remarkable calmness, Maria set about fetching the meal to the table while, with his jubilant daughter hanging on his coat tails, Ralph went into the scullery, where he took off his jacket and peaked cap before washing his hands and returning to the tiny parlour.

It was a cosy room, with an open fire-range that was daily polished to a high shine. From the picture rail hung many small portraits of long-departed relatives. There were numerous brass artefacts lovingly placed around the room – a trivet in the hearth, a jardinière on the small oak sideboard, two matching candle-sticks on the mantelpiece and a marvellous old oil lamp standing proud in the centre of the table. The sideboard and table were constructed in the same light-coloured oak, its texture mellowed warm by Maria's daily polishing; the sideboard was no more than four feet long, with a centre run of three deep drawers which were flanked either side by a spacious cupboard. The three drawer fronts and the cupboard sported sturdy wooden knobs, large and perfectly spherical in form. The table was also circular, small, but boasting the same handsome wood and reflecting the same loving care. It had one central leg, a thick bulbous thing which spread out at the base like the webbed feet of many frogs. For most of the time its surface was covered in a heavy green tablecloth, but for meal times, like now, the cloth was folded away and replaced by a pretty pink gingham square.

The only other furniture in this tiny parlour consisted of four straight-backed dining chairs positioned round the table, and two beech rocking chairs, one either side of the fireplace, each dressed in deep, squashy cushions. Over by the window stood a narrow table with tall legs and a lower shelf containing bric-à-brac; situated on its upper surface was a magnificent pair of brown and white pot dogs. These were Maria's pride and joy. The window was bedecked with fine lace curtains and many bright coloured

17

flowers, springing from the numerous brass plant pots. The view from the window swept towards the beach and, by straining her neck whilst squashing her face close to the windowpane, Maria could just see the South Bay and the jetty there.

'It's good to be home.' Ralph settled his long, lithe figure into the chair, the child clambered on to his knee and his warm, brown eyes observed Maria's every movement. When she paused in her task to smile at him, his heart leapt; it had always been that way – the very first thing that had attracted him to her was her lovely shy smile. They first met on the steps of St John's church. Later, their paths crossed again and he was bold enough to speak. Having each lost their closest relatives – any others still alive were not of these shores and consequently not known to them – a bond soon formed, love blossomed and marriage followed. Neither had ever regretted it and they were as much in love now as on their wedding day.

'Will you be glad when they no longer need you at the prison?' Maria dished out the broth, its warm, delicious aroma filling the room and making Ralph realise just how hungry he was. 'Come away from your father now, child,' Maria told little Agatha, at the same time pulling out a chair and pointing to it. 'Come and sit here,' she said, waiting for the child to scramble from its father's knee and climb obediently into the chair indicated. Shaking her head, Maria explained how the child 'has been restless all day' – much like myself, she thought curiously. When all were ready, a short thanksgiving was uttered by Ralph, after which they began their meal. Presently, Maria's question was answered when Ralph admitted that although he had suffered certain qualms about serving as a warder at the prison, he was now convinced that the experience was most useful. He was very careful not to mention the name of Rebecca Norman.

Throughout the meal of broth, cheese and newly baked bread, he remained unusually quiet, not unaware of his wife's curious glances, and acutely conscious of the excited feelings alive in him – excited not by his own adored Maria, but by another, a woman some six years his senior, a woman whose reputation was of the worst possible kind – sinister and evil, a convict, by all accounts destined to end her days behind bars or, worse, on the gallows.

Rebecca Norman was all of these things and yet, *and yet* . . . He hardly dared let loose his thoughts. All the same, he could not deny her magnificence, nor that beguiling way in which she had come to him, laughing at him, bewitching him with her persuasive eyes and silvery tongue. He recalled Jacob's warning, and though his every instinct told him to be wary of her, he indulged instead in the pleasure she stirred in him. He felt strangely uplifted, outside of himself . . . like a man drowning.

When the meal was finished, Ralph sat in the rocking chair, gently pushing to and fro, sucking intermittently at his briar pipe, his handsome face set in a grim, thoughtful study. From the scullery he could hear all those homely sounds that normally filled his heart to brimming: the unmistakable clatter of crockery being washed and stacked, the busy chatter of the irrepressible Agatha and, in between, his wife's soft, melodic voice uplifted in song. All of these sounds filtered through his uneasy mood, but, where they normally brought calm and great happiness, on this evening when he most needed peace of mind, the sounds brought only guilt, and a strange kind of pain.

Outside, the wind rose with a vengeance, and the heavens opened to spill a deluge over the land. Like many quick fingers, the rain began relentlessly tapping at the windowpane, shivering over the rooftops until it seemed as though the house itself was alive.

Astonished at this sudden, vicious weather in the height of summer, Maria came bustling into the parlour, hurriedly unrolling the sleeves of her blouse and glancing nervously at the window. 'It's like all hell let loose,' she told Ralph, at the same time sweeping the child into her arms and going towards the narrow doorway which led directly to the stairs and the upper floor. 'There hasn't been a cloud in the sky all day . . . blue as cornflowers,' she said quietly.

'Not as blue as your eyes, though, I'll be bound.' Ralph came to her side, his loving smile gently searching. In this moment of awful uncertainty he needed her more than ever. For a long, wonderful moment they enjoyed each other, their hearts together, gazes mingling, he smiling deep into the blueness of her lovely eyes. Darkest blue, they were, like the ocean itself; and something else – they were refreshingly innocent, almost childlike in their starry quality. It suddenly occurred to him how different from another's they were, different from the eyes that had looked on him earlier, dark and exquisite, murmuring with secrets and timeless things, incredibly beguiling. He visibly trembled.

'Are you ailing?' Maria was at once concerned that he might have caught a fever. After all, it was well known that the prison harboured more undesirable parasites than convicts.

'No, no . . . just a slight chill, I expect,' Ralph assured her. His gaze fell to the child. Satisfied that her daddy was home, and being content and warm with the small amount of broth she was allowed at this late hour, little Agatha was already heavy with sleep. 'Here, let me take her,' Ralph whispered, gently lifting the child into his arms. His reward was a quick, sleepy smile from a small, round face, and two twig-like arms wound round his neck. It was a good feeling, soothing the turmoil within him.

On slow, sure footsteps he carried his daughter up the stairs and into the smaller of the two bedrooms. Here he laid her tenderly into the wooden cot which he himself had taken great pleasure in making. Gingerly, he tucked the thick grey blanket about her, afterwards stealing quietly out of the door, which he carefully closed; it was always a fear of Maria's that the child might wake in the night and tumble down the stairs. Ralph's answer was to move the door-sneck to a higher point, beyond little Agatha's reach. He had it in mind to construct some suitable obstacle over the mouth of the stairs to prevent any possible accident, but so far his first measure had proved more than satisfactory.

When he returned to the parlour, it was to find Maria relaxed in the chair, with two mugs of steaming hot cocoa standing in the hearth. This was the moment he loved best, when the child was sleeping peacefully and he could sit here, quietly rocking in the chair, gazing across at Maria and counting his many blessings. He did so now, his gaze reaching out to the figure of his wife. Tired and growing heavier with child, Maria had laid her head back against the chair, her eyes were closed, her breathing low and rhythmic as though any moment she would succumb to slumber. Ralph's gaze grew tender, taking in every detail of the woman he loved.

Dressed in long dark skirt and pretty cream blouse, with neck ruffles and pearly buttons, Maria made a handsome sight; the now obvious bulge of child across her midriff only enhanced her beauty. With almond-shaped eyes of darkest blue, and thick rich brown hair that wound into a shining coil at the nape of her neck, she was a woman any man could be proud of. In nature she was kind, loving but firm, and, above all, she was a wonderful wife and mother. Ralph counted her as his greatest blessing. Then came Agatha, and in four months' time, he instinctively believed, his next blessing would be a son.

'Oh! Goodness me!' Maria's eyes suddenly popped open and stared at him. 'I'm sorry, Ralph . . . I didn't realise how tired I was,' she exclaimed, leaning forward to collect the two mugs from the hearth. With a small laugh she handed one to Ralph, before settling back in the chair and carefully sipping at the hot liquid.

'It's a fine thing,' Ralph said with humour, 'when a man comes home to find his wife bored with his company.'

Her answer was a smile. 'I could never be bored with you,' she told him sincerely. 'You can't know how much I miss you when you're not here.'

When Ralph made no comment, she regarded him quizzically, saying, 'You would tell me if the work at the prison was too depressing, wouldn't you?' Anxiety betrayed itself in her voice.

'You know I would,' Ralph quickly assured her, absent-mindedly rolling the mug in his large, tanned hands and making no effort to drink from it. 'Wouldn't do no good though . . . I'd still have to put up with it.' He sensed her heightened apprehension and quickly assured her, 'But no, Maria, I can handle it fine.'

'But there is . . . *something* on your mind,' she insisted. 'Won't you talk about it?' She might have imagined it, but in that moment she sensed a fear in him, that was not unlike her own.

'Nothing to talk about,' he told her, taking a deep gulp of the smooth, dark cocoa. 'I do feel at odds with myself, though,' he finally admitted, in the hope of putting her mind at ease. 'I've no doubt it's because of working shifts . . . never worked such late hours before. I'm used to starting early of a morning, and being home before little Agatha's bedtime. Don't worry, though, it won't be long before I'm back at my duties at the asylum. One of the blokes who took ill from the prison is said to be reporting for work within the week. So you're not to worry yourself. Everything's just fine.'

'You're sure now?' she insisted. When he nodded, a thoughtful look on his face, she persisted, 'And there's nothing else troubling you?'

Avoiding the need to lie, he gave no answer, other than to rise from the chair and stretch his hand out. 'If you've finished with your cocoa, I reckon we'll be off to bed, eh?'

Nodding in agreement, she put the half-empty mug into his outstretched hand. 'I don't want any more,' she said, with a grimace, 'or I'll be in and out of bed all night.' Patting the rise of her tummy, she laughed. 'Lately, my bladder refuses to hold more than a cupful. There's not much room in here for anything but the little one.'

Ralph smiled with her. 'I'm glad I wasn't born a woman,' he said thankfully. Taking the mugs into the scullery, he put them into the deep pot sink and came back into the parlour. Maria was waiting at the door of the stairs, candle in hand. 'Funny,' she said quietly, smiling up at him, 'but I don't feel tired now.'

'Really?' His voice was teasing, his expression suggestive. 'And neither do I,' he murmured, bending his head to kiss her. Afterwards, they mounted the stairs together, she in front, he behind; and a well of love between them.

In the bedroom, Ralph stood by the window, his quiet gaze looking towards the ocean. The wind had abated, the rain still evident, though, on the small puddles that had formed within the dips of the window ledge, and in the occasional prick of raindrops which disturbed their black, shiny surface. He stayed a moment longer at the window, his brown eyes looking out yet unseeing, his thoughts captured in a strange kind of daydream. The sound of his name being called, softly, prompted him to look round. What he saw was Maria, already in bed and wanting him to lie beside her.

'You dressed in a hurry this morning,' she said with a twinkle in her eye.

'Oh? And how do you know that?' he asked.

'Because you're wearing odd socks.'

He came towards her. In the flickering candlelight, her eyes appraised him as he undid his belt and laid it over the iron bedstead at the foot of the bed; then came his trousers, shirt and undergarments. Unashamedly he stood before her in all his glorious nakedness, his need for her so obviously proud in him. Drinking in his manhood, Maria's blue eyes darkened, dulling with passion. The flush of embarrassment coloured her face. Coyly, she turned away, hiding her confusion in the depths of the bolster.

Laughing softly, and loving her all the more, Ralph slid in beside her. A moment before, he had grown chilled, even though the room was stiflingly hot, with only the half-hearted breeze from the window to cool it. Now, with his bareness against her soft, silky skin, the warmth spread through him. As always when his need for her grew strong in him, he made himself be patient, wanting to please her also. He could never understand a man who was selfish in love.

Gently, his fingers probed her body, moving slowly, teasing and tantalising, raising all manner of delight in her. Now, the flat of his hand traced the mound of her midriff, wonder rushing through him when he realised that it was his child curled safely there, his son, *their son*. The thought was like a giant fist squeezing his heart. 'Oh, Maria,' he moaned, wrapping his arms about her, pulling her trembling form into him. His mouth closed over hers; thrills raged through him like the fiercest storm. All restraint gone, he

23

pulled himself up, leaning over her, instinctively pushing in anticipation. Returning his fervent kisses, she clung to him, softly moaning. When with a cry of elation he thrust himself into her, she groaned, half-laughing, half-crying; instinctively she opened her thighs, wound her arms over his thick firm waist and snatched him deep inside her, arching to him, sharing his passion, wanting him with the same deep-down urgency. He was her man, her beauty, her joy. And the unborn between them was a part of it all.

Later, when all passion was spent and they lay contented in each other's arms, a feeling of shame came over her. It was always the same. She was a woman, and women who shared such violent emotions were frowned on; the things of night, and passion, and wantonness, were these things not condemned in harsh, trembling voice by the preacher in his sermon? And yet, the shame she felt was only a small, passing shame, because Maria believed that God had joined her and Ralph in the eyes of heaven and would not brand her a hussy for keeping good the vows she had made her husband. If he awakened such raging passion in her, it must be right. It could be no other way. In the half-light she glanced at him. Shame ebbed away. Pride and profound love flooded her heart. When she stirred in his arms, he held her closer. Soon she drifted into a sound sleep.

Ralph could not sleep. He also felt ashamed. In those moments of heightened passion when his thoughts were glorious, something else had spiralled into his mind. It was an image, a face, a pair of eyes. Not Maria's but the convict woman's. And, far from disgusting him, he had been elated by the experience, imagining Rebecca Norman to be the nakedness in his arms, wanting it, enjoying it. Now, though, the disgust infiltrated every corner of his being.

Agitated, he slid softly from the bed and collected his clothes from the bedstead; he took the lighted candle, tiptoed out of the room and down the stairs. In the parlour, he placed the brass candleholder on the sideboard and quickly dressed. In a matter of moments he was out of the house, standing forlornly against the closed door and wondering at his own actions. Nothing he had

24

ever known before had disturbed him so deeply as he was disturbed now. He felt incredibly lonely, like a lost soul, and yet there still remained in him a strange and gripping excitement. *And a very real sense of terror.*

The streets were eerily silent. Only the faint moonlight relieved the darkness, creating shadows that flitted and danced, going before him like so many phantoms. On slow, deliberate footsteps he went to the top of Henry Street, feeling dangerously hemmed in on all sides, the tiny terraced houses standing shoulder to shoulder in a packed and colourless line, seeming to him like an army of sentries, spying on him, reading the ugliness in his mind, waiting for a vulnerable moment when they would seize and punish him. He shivered within himself, though the heat of the night was suffocating. On and on he went, trudging the deserted streets, deliberately distancing himself from the prison, *from her*, desperately trying to rid himself of her, yet knowing he could not.

Down the High Street he went, then along Cliff Street, past the Custom House and towards the beach. For a while he wandered aimlessly from North Jetty to South Bay, pausing a moment near the jetty, his troubled gaze scouring the many vessels that bobbed up and down, creating their own weird lament as the water slapped the hulks and occasionally pushed one into the other. The port of Fremantle and its thriving colony relied on these vessels and the trade that had built up here. A busy seaport always gave a feeling of security and pride.

Ralph felt that now. He had often thought to be a sailor and roam the world's great seas, but the fire was never really kindled in him, at least not to the extent that he ever followed his earlier intention. Now, he was content to keep his feet on firm ground and leave the sailor's life to those who craved it most. All the same, although the sea itself was not in his blood, Fremantle was. A jewel in any ocean, with long stretches of fine, bleached sand, an ever-growing community and ambitious plans for the future, Fremantle was a fine place; what was more, the Fremantle to Guildford section of the railway would soon be opened. It was an

25

exciting time – especially now the convict ships no longer brought their unhappy cargoes to these shores.

Inevitably, a certain convict loomed large in Ralph Ryan's mind at this moment. In restless mood he skirted the beach, the sharp, salty smell of the sea in his nostrils and a fine spray of sand kicking up from the toe of his boots; at one point he squatted to his knees, clutching at the sand and letting it trickle through his fingers like silk water. A lone seagull screeched at him, its brilliant beady eyes watching his every move. From somewhere along the jetty a man's voice was raised in anger, the sharp invasive tones cutting the still night air and startling a scavenging mongrel, who shot out in front of Ralph's striding figure, fleeing into the darkness, its tail between its legs.

Not mindful of any particular destination, but urged to seek a degree of solitude, Ralph was astonished to find that he had gone up the High Street, past his own home on Henry Street, and was now standing at the mouth of the short walkway that led to the prison itself.

Almost without realising it, he had brought himself back to within a stone's throw of Rebecca Norman. It was a sobering thought. One that raised all kinds of chaos in him. Staring up at that imposing building, he could not help but admire its awesome dimensions. For a place that contained within its great heart the most wretched of mankind, it stood proud, almost noble in its beauty. Ironically, it was the convicts themselves who had constructed this formidable place, having quarried the stone that formed its impregnable walls, floated the timber from Woodman's Point and, with the aid of stout, broad-muscled horses, hauled the timber along the beach, before delivering it to site. Parts of that timber were used to build the gallows, and many a hanging had taken place on them; there would no doubt be many more in the years to come.

Suddenly, Ralph saw what he must do. Tomorrow morning he would explain his intention to Maria; only the intention, though – being most careful not to betray the real reason behind his decision. Afterwards, he would report for duty at the prison, ask for an appointment with the Governor, and request an urgent transfer back to his former duties at the asylum. The reason he would give was surely obvious, because wasn't his wife heavy with child? And wouldn't it be sensible for him to work a normal day, instead of arriving home so late of an evening? It was a feasible excuse, and one which would serve his purpose.

With lighter heart and a merry tune whistling from his lips, he turned about and began his way home. The convict woman had somehow touched him deeply; *too* deeply. But he prided himself on being a strong-minded man who saw what he must do and did not shirk from doing it. He had misgivings about his decision, of course he did, if only because it seemed as though he was begging out of harsher duties. As a rule he would not succumb to rash decisions, preferring instead to weigh all the options. This time, though, he was urged to follow his instincts. Strange and new instincts. Unsettling instincts. Instincts that murmured of danger, and things he did not fully understand.

As Ralph Ryan quickened his step homeward, his mind alive with the day's events, there was another, not too far away from him in that moment, whose thoughts fired the blood in her veins. In the darkness of her prison, Rebecca Norman stood with her beautiful eyes raised to the outside world. She was smiling, soft laughter on her lips. It was a chilling sound. Now she grew quiet, her head tilted to one side, her small exquisite ears strained for the slightest sound. In the distance she heard the firm, determined steps that took Ralph Ryan home, that carried her quarry away. Bitterness stabbed her heart as she waited for the last echo of his footsteps. A vicious curse fell from her lips. But then, suddenly, she was smiling. All was not lost. The image of his tall, attractive frame came into her devious mind. Charmed, she caressed it. *He was no stranger to her.* When she looked on him, the years fell away and the pain became unbearable. At first she had not fully understood. But she understood now.

From that moment when she had first felt his gaze on her, Rebecca Norman had been drawn to the young guard; she had sensed his inner turmoil and been strengthened by it. His handsome face had stirred a dark memory deep inside her, churning something that had lain dormant all these years. There was no going back now. She wanted him, needed him, his body and mind, *his very soul*. And, beside his strength, she had sensed his weakness, a weakness that scarred his serious brown eyes whenever they looked on her. *That weakness was her*. His only weakness. A weakness she would not hesitate to exploit for her own ends. A weakness he may well come to regret. Her dark, beautiful eyes closed in a smile. Ralph Ryan's weakness would be his undoing.

Chapter Two

The child's merry laughter echoed along the beach, mingling with the screech of swooping seagulls and causing passers-by to pause and smile; there was always something uniquely satisfying in seeing a happy family at play.

'You're a rascal, Agatha Ryan!' Maria told her giggling daughter.

'Mammy, play!' The child was too full of energy to be quietened. Stooping, she clutched the elusive sand between her tiny fingers. 'Play,' she insisted, looking up with mischievous eyes, as she ran towards them.

Laughing aloud, Ralph and Maria fled hand in hand, feigning horror when the child bore down on them with two fistfuls of sand; they were mindful, though, not to make too long a distance between themselves and the delighted little girl.

When in her haste Agatha tumbled to her knees, Ralph seized her into his arms and, raising her high in the air, perched her securely on the broad span of his shoulders, where she wound her skinny legs round his neck and tugged at his thick brown hair until he protested in mock yells and pleas for mercy; her answer was to collapse in a fit of infectious giggling.

Presently, all three were content to pause awhile; Agatha still bubbling with energy and eager to resume their game, Maria flushed and breathless, with her two hands spread over the bulge beneath her shawl, as though in attempt to calm the turmoil there. When, in her great joy, she looked up at her husband whose face was turned out to sea, she thought she had never seen him more handsome. His strong, clean-cut features made a proud study; the sea breeze played with his unruly hair, flicking it every which way, and causing him to narrow his brown eyes as they gazed out to the horizon, entranced by the beauty of the ocean. Quietly, yet with immense feeling, she slid her small hand into his. Without a word he turned his gaze from the sea, his heart full with love for this woman who was his wife. For what seemed an age, he looked on her uplifted face, half-smiling, half-serious. Between them lay a precious silence. A silence too wonderful to break.

It was time to go home. The day was almost over. Soon the sky would begin to darken, and thoughts of tomorrow would busy their minds. Slowly, still holding hands, they sauntered along the beach, heading homeward. Together, the three of them made a rewarding sight – Ralph who was tall, with slim, upright figure and tousled hair, starched white collar and long black jacket, and Maria, dressed in her Sunday gown of blue taffeta and the pretty white shawl which was crocheted by her own hand. The wide-brimmed blue bonnet was not exquisite or of the best quality, but it had a deep-blue extravagant ribbon that made an elegant bow beneath her chin, enhancing the blueness of her eyes and lending a delicate aura to her lovely face.

Their route took them by way of the old lock-up, known as the Round House and occupying an elevated position above the cliffs; beneath were the great caverns and tunnels excavated around 1837 by the Fremantle Whaling Company, who used the tunnels as a convenient and direct route by which they could transport their goods from the beach to the warehouses along Cliff Street. From the sudden, lopsided weight on his shoulders, Ralph realised that his daughter had fallen asleep; gently he took her into his arms and cradled her against his breast. Maria began to hurry on ahead, over to Cliff Street and into High Street, then home to the tiny house on Henry Street. Along the way both she and Ralph exchanged pleasantries with neighbours and acquaintances who also enjoyed the habit of a Sunday evening stroll along the front.

The call of the sea was strong in a place such as Fremantle. For many years the Aborigines had lived on the bounty of the seas, and sailors made up a good deal of the population. The smell of the ocean was pungent to the nostrils; by day and night the sea thrashed and talked, always moving, heaving and breathing, 'like the heart of a man', some said, 'or the milken breasts of a woman'. Lingering awhile, Ralph roved his eyes over the blue and gold lines of the distant horizon, so vivid and powerful, so evidently made by a mighty hand; the vast silvery-blue of the ocean, going on as far as a man's eye could see, and the sky – huge, daunting, beyond human perception. It was a splendid and awesome sight. One that never failed to make him humble.

As he walked away, the wonder of it all stayed with him, but the closer he came to home, such admiration was cruelly lost in a surge of misgivings – misgivings which he had deliberately suppressed all day, and which now were rising through the joy and laughter his family always brought him. Misgivings that suddenly were paramount to his mind, dulling the day's enjoyment and harbouring doubts that wouldn't go away. Was he right to ask for a transfer back to the asylum? Surely he was stronger than the woman they called Rebecca Norman. Why had she got under his skin, riling him until he couldn't think straight? It seemed incredible, but she had. She had!

'Are you all right?' Maria had seen how troubled he was.

At once he was on his guard. 'Never more so,' he lied, and she seemed satisfied.

'What do you want for your tea?'

'I don't mind.'

'You never do.'

'Are you complaining, woman?' he demanded in mock authority.

'No, but just for once I would like you to say what you fancy.'

'Really?'

'Really.'

'You.'

'What?'

'I fancy *you*.'

'How?' Now she was playing the game.

'Oh . . .' He eyed her up and down, stroking his chin and quietly smiling. 'Naked, of course.'

'Of course! And on satin sheets?'

She was smiling at him and he adored her.

'You're shameless,' he said.

'I know. But you wouldn't change me?'

'Not for the world.'

'I'm glad,' she said. And as they made their way home, there was no more need for words.

The following morning, Maria seemed troubled. Now, when she spoke her voice was low and her blue eyes looked to him anxiously. 'Are you sure, Ralph?' she asked. 'Have you done the right thing?' She had faced him with the same question many times during the past week. 'You mustn't be swayed by my condition; if you really want to stay at the prison until you're no longer needed, then it's up to you. Don't worry about the shifts. Elizabeth is never far away.'

Ralph had been standing with his hand on the half-open door. Closing the door, he placed his two hands on her shoulders, gently shaking her and replying in chastising voice, 'Maria . . . oh, Maria! I've told you that I have already given it a great deal of thought. I'm not altogether happy working at the prison.' Images of Rebecca Norman came into his mind. Suddenly all his doubts vanished. 'Yes, I've made the right decision,' he told her firmly. But then he kissed her. 'Now then, let that be an end to your nagging, woman,' he said, good humouredly.

'If you're sure.' Maria did not relish the thought of him working either at the prison *or* the asylum. She would rather he had stayed at the warehouse on Cliff Street, where he was employed when they first met. It was true the pay was more, in Her Majesty's establishments, but she felt he was not happy.

'Trust me,' he said, then, suddenly, he was gone.

Coming out to the pavement, Maria watched him go down the street. He seemed lost in thought, head bowed, his footsteps less jaunty than usual. When he reached the bottom of the street, she waited for him to glance back as always. When he did not, she went back into the parlour. For some inexplicable reason, she was suddenly filled with a fearsome premonition of danger, of something beyond her control. When a small voice cried out from an upper room, Maria hurried upstairs, anxious that her daughter might begin fretting. She called to her. 'It's all right, sweetheart . . . Mammy's here.' For the moment, the deep murmurings that had so disturbed her were forgotten.

In her innocence, Maria could not know of the dark forces already unleashed, nor of the awful consequences they would avenge on her and her family.

Coming up the rise of land that led to the lunatic asylum, Ralph Ryan indulged in thoughts that had already steeped him in a mood of uneasiness. He had not lied when he told Maria that his transfer back to the asylum was for the best, nor had he regretted making that particular request. His only deception was when he had allowed Maria to believe he preferred his work here. He did not. It was true that the asylum was a splendid feature of architecture, being a vast and striking building of character built in the 1860s by the convicts and making an impressive sight, with its distinctive gables, fortress-like structure and far-reaching views over land and sea. And it was true that there were less pleasant surroundings. But, while in the prison there were undesirable and dangerous criminals, there were worse things here – *least of all, madness.*

But then again, while there was madness here in the asylum, there was Rebecca Norman in the prison. Madness was a terrifying thing. It made him nervous. *She* made him nervous, creating a yearning in him that terrified him even more than did these poor, mindless creatures. For some time now, he had come to believe that the Devil had walked with him, whispered to him, tempted him in the form of Rebecca Norman. When faced with a choice of the two evils, he was convinced that he was now faced by the lesser of them. Relief washed through him. A smile whispered over his mouth. All that was behind him now, thank God, he promised himself. And yet, the more he tried to convince himself of it, the more he felt threatened. Even after this past week back at the asylum, it was hard to thrust her from his thoughts. There were even moments when he truly enjoyed her nearness to him . . . deliciously dangerous moments when he actually called her to him, beckoning her magnificence into his senses, letting her toy with him, allowing her to invade every corner of his being, wanting her there, the longing in him almost like a physical pain that took away his very reasoning. But these moments had grown few and far between of late. And, as he grew stronger, the yearning in him grew weaker, until now at long last she was no more than a memory, growing ever dimmer, fading like a bad dream in the sunlight.

'You're in fine spirits, ain't you?' Mr Bullen was a kindly man. Tall, large boned and cumbersome of movement, he had a most unpleasant habit of staring at a body through bright, green eyes that were slightly out of focus, and squeezing them into glittering narrow slits that glared out of fleshy bulges with unnerving directness. With his smooth, bald head and slow methodical movements, he had the look of an inmate, rather than the authority of one who minded them. When he smiled now, it was to display an astonishingly beautiful set of straight, white teeth. 'Been a strange sorta night,' he told Ralph, who had just come into the small office adjacent to the main ward; at that time of the morning the lunatics were already congregating for their first meal of the day. They began shuffling past now, flanked on either side by their minders, and occasionally grinning through the office window; they made a rare and strange assortment – young and old, male and female, a collection of lost souls, some quiet and helpless as newborn lambs, other dangerous in their madness, violence ever simmering beneath the surface. Yet they were not criminals, never totally responsible for their own actions. They were sadly demented. Warped and twisted beyond repair. More to be pitied than blamed.

Ralph was regularly reminded of this very fact by Mr Bullen, who had minded such unfortunates long before this building was erected. For nigh on twenty-five years he had watched over them, even during the early days when they were temporarily housed in an overcrowded, ill-ventilated and damp warehouse, alive with the overpowering stench which crept up from the beach and the putrescent jellyfish, seaweed and other decay there. Other minders had come and gone, only a few stayed for any length of time. But Mr Bullen stayed. He would stay until the day they carried him out feet first, or so he told Ralph. And Ralph had not the slightest doubt that Mr Bullen meant every word.

'You're assigned to the laundry this week,' Ralph was informed.

'I could have done without that.' The laundry duties were among the worst.

'Sorry, matey,' Bullen apologised, again consulting the duty roster. 'I know what you mean, but that's it, I'm afraid.'

Laundry duties were not well received by any of the minders. In the large wash-house situated out in the yard, the female lunatics laundered an average five hundred pieces of clothing each week. It was a tiresome task, hard and grinding, made worse by the heat and steam from within, and the scorching hot sun beating down relentlessly on the outside. Tempers were quick to flare, and on many occasions in the past it had been necessary for the minders to break up what might otherwise develop into a dangerous situation – in fact, some two years ago, there had been a strangling. Done out of sight and in the midst of a deliberately planned 'uproar', it was all over by the time the minder realised. From that day on, a contingent of four were on duty at any one time. Since then, there had been little trouble, although it remained the most unpopular duty in the asylum, both for minders and inmates alike.

All the day long there was no respite from the debilitating heat that sapped a body's strength. The sun's rays beat down mercilessly, the slight breeze that had cooled the air in the morning hours suddenly sped away before noon turned. In the rising steam from the cauldrons the women visibly wilted; like zombies they continued in their work, their thin, shabby garments clinging to the film of sweat that coated their bodies. The overpowering odour from flesh and laundry alike billowed into the air. It was fetid, offensive. For minder and inmate alike there was no escaping it.

'Christ almighty . . . it's a bloody scorcher!' The tall, bony man peered at Ralph from beneath unusually hairy eyebrows, the beads of sweat breaking open on his forehead and trickling down the weathered skin to be absorbed by the thick, greying brows that were drawn tight together in a frown. 'We'll get no trouble today, and that's a fact,' he told Ralph, 'it's too hot to *work*, let alone squabble.'

'At least we're outside, and not cooped up,' Ralph pointed out. He had not forgotten the grim interior of the prison, the darkened corridors and the confined work areas; a stark contrast to the lofty, spacious rooms in the asylum.

'Huh! If you ask me, we'd be a bloody sight cooler inside,' came the retort. When Ralph gave no answer, merely nodding before turning his attention to the women at their work, the man wandered away, skirting the walls of the wash-house and occasionally stopping to chivvy one of the inmates.

Ralph had been standing in the wide doorway, legs astride, his back to the yard and his thoughtful brown eyes skinned in observation of the women. He could never remember a time when he had been so physically uncomfortable. The stiff jacket with which all minders were supplied felt like a metal tube over his body, the sharp-peaked cap pressed into his skull and forehead, sticking to the sweat that lay like a band round his head, and, even as he stood there, he could feel the rivulets trickling down his spine, fusing the shirt to his back and creating a dull irritation to his senses. Now, when the sweat erupted on his face, running down his neck and into his shirt collar, he reached up, and taking off his cap, he wiped the cuff of his jacket across his forehead and promptly replaced the cap. Taking a deep breath, he prepared to begin a tour of the wash-house.

Something held him back. A feeling, an awareness, a strange excitement that rippled through him, riveting him to the spot and compelling him to look behind, *look behind*.

Slowly, he turned, his brown eyes suspicious and curiously

afraid. The sweat was like a torrent now, bathing his whole body; he could feel himself trembling. A glance told him there was no one behind him, nothing in sight at all; the yard was normally deserted at this time of day. It was deserted now. Strange, he thought, *he had the feeling that someone had come up behind him.* More than that, he could have sworn that he'd heard the sound of laughter, low and soft in his ear; pretty, silvery laughter, yet cruel and taunting.

'Are you all right, matey?' The bony man with the hairy eyebrows stared hard at Ralph, whose face was drained of colour and whose brown eyes were wide with fear. 'Bugger me, if you don't look like you've seen a ghost!' he chuckled, seeming both surprised and amused by the sudden change in his colleague's countenance.

Quickly composing himself, Ralph forced a small laugh, though it clogged his throat. 'It's nothing,' he said, in a matter-of-fact voice, 'the heat, I expect . . . it has a way of getting to a man.'

'Aye, well, it's bloody uncomfortable, there's no denying it.' He grabbed Ralph by the shoulder, and shook him good humouredly, at the same time dipping into his jacket pocket and taking out a round silver fob-watch. Flicking open the case, he stared at it with narrowed eyes before announcing, 'Almost four o'clock. Nearly time to march this lot in and get 'em fed.' Swinging round, he stuffed the watch back in his pocket, saying, 'Matter of fact, there's Jim now . . . look . . . y'see.' He pointed to the far side of the wash-house, to the stocky minder who was signalling to them. 'That's it, matey,' he sighed, smiling at Ralph. 'Pack the buggers up . . . let's get 'em outta here.' Dipping into his pocket again, he withdrew a whistle, which he promptly put to his lips, the ensuing shrill sound the signal for the lunatics to make orderly file towards the door. This they did, and in a surprisingly short time, the same tired and straggling file was making its way along the spacious walkway and on into the heart of the asylum.

'Phew! I reckon that bugger's shit himself.' The other man brought Ralph's attention to the old bent figure as it went by.

37

'Dirty buggers, some of 'em,' he added, wrinkling his nose and momentarily pressing the flat of his hand to his mouth. Angered, he stuck the tip of his truncheon in the old lag's back. 'Get on!' he urged. 'Get on, yer stinking sod!'

Ralph took little notice. He had more important things on his mind. There were times, like now, when he was able to lift his thoughts from what was going on around him. He did that now, and found comfort in his family.

It was while he was in the washroom, splashing cold water over his face and neck, that Ralph heard the unearthly uproar outside in the corridor. Rushing out to investigate, and fearing some kind of trouble, he was not surprised to see the small party of uniformed men already going out of sight towards the cells reserved for violent lunatics.

What he saw was a new inmate being brought in. The guards were desperately struggling to contain the woman; her unnerving screams echoed in the air long after she and her captors had gone from sight. Shaking his head sadly, Ralph made to turn away, pointing his footsteps in the direction of the office. His shift was finished; he was eager to make his way home to Maria. Suddenly, he was filled with the same inexplicable feeling that had disturbed him earlier that afternoon.

Curious, he paused, the sweat once more breaking out all over his body, creeping through his skin like icy fingers. He shivered, cold yet hot all at the same time. *There it was again!* The same silvery laughter, teasing, beckoning. A deep compulsion took hold of him. He didn't even want to fight it; it was uniquely pleasurable, exciting, almost like making love.

Like a man in a dream, he turned, changing direction and following the same route that the other uniformed men had taken, back along the corridor where the sun came in through the fanlights and chased away the shadows, then on, deeper, to where the light grew dimmer and the corridor narrowed to a walkway flanked by eight tiny, grim cells, places of darkness and despair, places that were designed to incarcerate the most disturbed and violent of all the lunatics; places of safety, and hopelessness.

As he rounded the bend in the corridor, he was at once confronted by the three officers; each haggard yet determined face told a story. The one whose nose and cheek were laced with fresh jagged scars spotted with crimson droplets and scored deep in his flesh, was the only one who spoke. 'Don't go near her,' he warned Ralph, mindful also of the fact that this particular corridor led only to the padded cells. 'Not unless you want your eyes ripped out!'

'Who is she?' An unholy realisation had taken hold of him. He had to know.

The other man paused, regarding Ralph with inquisitive eyes. The other two men pushed past and hurried away. 'You mean you weren't told?' When Ralph shook his head in answer, a dark and serious expression on his face, the man asked, 'Have you just come on duty?'

'No. My shift has just ended. I was in the washroom when I heard the commotion . . .'

'Hmh! Commotion, you say? Commotion!' He jerked his head towards the direction of the cells. 'We've just brought her in . . . mad as a hatter. Evil bugger, too.' He rang his fingertips along the edge of his torn skin. 'The bastard!' he hissed, wincing with pain. 'I'd give a year's grog to teach her a lesson.'

'You'd best get that seen to. Looks like it needs stitching.'

'Damn her eyes!' He began striding away, but then he half-turned, saying, 'I wouldn't mind, but I've only been back at work a few days . . . been badly . . . germs breed in this awful heat. Fetched her from the prison, we did. She's allus been a troublemaker, but this time she's gone too far. Murdered her cell-mate, she did. Strangest bloody thing! They reckon she killed the old hag without even laying a finger on her. Strangest thing . . . weird.' He made the sign of the cross on himself. 'Don't bear thinking about!'

For a long, heart-rending moment, Ralph stood there, a great turmoil alive inside him. Just like before, he had the feeling that someone was near to him. He could feel the warm breath against his neck, and was he imagining those soft, caressing whispers fanning his ear? The trembling started deep inside him. In a moment it had spread through every inch of his body, until it took all of his control to stop his limbs from visibly shaking.

'Take hold of yourself, Ralph Ryan,' he muttered, a wave of anger coursing through him. What the hell was the matter with him? He didn't even know whether it *was* Rebecca Norman back there in the cell. But if it *was*, it should be of no more consequence to him than if it were *any* madwoman. He had always prided himself in his ability to do a job with singlemindedness. He was always a man known for his common sense. Why, then, was he made so jittery by this woman? What did it matter to him whether she was the one in that cell? . . . 'Mad as a hatter' . . . a murderess who had 'killed the old hag without even laying a finger on her'. If all of that were true, then she really was a dangerous and unstable creature. That's all. A maniac. Nothing more sinister than that. And he would do better to spend his sympathy on more deserving causes.

Having all but convinced himself, he had half a mind to turn back; the padded cells were not a pleasant duty at the best of times, and to go near of a body's own accord was downright asking for punishment. All the same, he was curious as to whether the woman committed here really was Rebecca Norman. Why not find out? What was there to be afraid of? Don't be a fool, man . . . satisfy your curiosity and be done with it, he told himself. The best way to deal with a dilemma was to face it full on.

Determined, he pushed onward, his face set like granite. Going past the line of stout panelled doors, he raised the heavy observation panels one by one, peering in, his heart beating so loud it echoed in his chest. The first four cells were empty. As he came to the next one, he heard soft, low singing coming from inside. He paused, his two hands on the hinged panel. Doubts filled his mind. The singing stopped. Gingerly, he slid out the metal pin which secured the panel, then, with his heart in his mouth, he lowered the heavy wooden square just enough for him to peer over the top.

Looking inside, he saw nothing to tell him that it was occupied.

He lowered the panel all the way down. The cell was not unlike the other seven – painfully small, with high ceiling and tiny barred window positioned some safe way up the wall; a narrow iron bed, walls and floor covered in a crude padding of stuffed canvas and secured by wooden battens. It was a soulless, dismal place, made by man to contain fiends, and often the last place where hapless souls might lay their poor lonely heads before having their necks stretched on the gibbet.

It was dim in the cell, the only light coming in from the tiny window being insufficient to illuminate any corner of it. Ralph's searching gaze was drawn to the bed. His heart almost stopped when something stirred there. He instinctively stepped back. *It was her!* Like a silvery shadow she rose from the greyness of the bed, her black luminous eyes bathing his face, holding him to her, mesmerising him. With deft and enchanting movements she raised her slim white arms, gracefully crossing them above her head, where with long sensuous fingers she plucked at the shoulders of her shapeless garment and drew it from her body. With a tantalising smile she dropped the garment to the floor and, in a sinuous dancing movement, she came forward. She was the epitome of womanhood, slim and lithe, supple and perfectly formed; she knew her power, and she used it to hold him.

Watching her was like being woven into a dream, *or into a nightmare.* Unable to draw his gaze from her magnificence, Ralph felt helpless, lost in admiration of her timeless beauty. Greedily, his eyes travelled her body, from the delicious rise of her breasts, with their stiff upturned nipples, to the dark and bewitching triangle between her milk-white thighs. As she danced towards him, her shining eyes making silent promises, her whole body reaching out to him, he knew at last beyond any doubt. *He wanted her!* Never in all his life had he ever wanted a woman so badly; so much that he could hardly breathe with the longing in him; so much that the blood in his veins burned like molten fire. A crazy urge sped through him; a driving impulse to tear down the door and to take her, to take her savagely, to have her for himself.

Suddenly, her face was only inches from his, her dark eyes

smiling into his very soul. 'It was for you,' she murmured in a voice that was black silk. 'I did it for you . . . to be near you.' He was like a man drowning in his own senses. In his mind's eye he could hear another voice, whispering. Now he was making wanton love; images that put him in turmoil. God almighty! Was that really him? *No! No!*

With a cry he slammed shut the panel. His hands were shaking, his insides boiling. Frantic, he fled from there, not stopping until he was within sight of the office near the main door. From behind he could hear her singing, a plaintive song, unearthly.

'She'll hang, there's no doubt about it.' The duty officer regarded Ralph with passing curiosity, at the same time indicating the direction from which Ralph had emerged. 'Been checking on our new inmate, have you, Ryan?' He saw Ralph's stark, wide eyes and the profusion of sweat teeming down his face. Without waiting for an answer he went on, 'That's a bad 'un we've got there . . . a real bad 'un. Oh, aye, she'll swing from the end of a rope afore long, you mark my words. They found the old hag cowered in a corner of the cell. By all accounts the Norman woman killed the old 'un just by staring at her!' He shook his head, his eyes intent on Ralph who had taken off his cap and was vigorously wiping the flat of his hand over his face, as though wiping away something that clung to him, something suffocating. Something that would not be so easily wiped away.

'Can you imagine that, eh?' the other man went on. 'She stared the old 'un to death!' He shook his head again, his gaze shifting towards the direction of the padded cells. Then, in a hushed voice, he murmured, 'Only a witch could do such a thing.'

'It's not possible!' Ralph did not want to believe, and yet . . . and yet . . .

'Oh, it bloody well is!' protested the duty officer. 'I'm telling you that's exactly what happened. It were the old hag's terrible screams that brought the warders running . . . oh, she's yelled and screamed afore, right enough, but this time it were different, so I'm told. Terrible, they said. Anyway, when they burst into the cell, they found that one –' he flicked his anxious gaze back and forth from the direction of the padded cells to Ralph – 'the Norman woman, was standing over the old hag. Stripped bare, she was. Naked as the day she were born. She were staring right through the old 'un – staring black eyes burning like coals. The old 'un wasn't screaming by this time. She were whimpering, curled into the corner and whimpering like a terrified babe. When they pulled the Norman woman away, it were too late. The old hag were dead as stone. Oh no! There's no doubt at all. The old 'un were yelling and screaming murder, and that's exactly what happened.' He shivered loudly. 'Unless you're unfortunate enough to be put on guard over that one, I should keep your distance.' He chuckled, hissing through the many gaps in his yellow teeth. 'Or she might put the evil eye on you an' all!' He laughed aloud, prodding the air with two fingers, as though laying a curse on him.

When Ralph gave no answer, but instead began walking away, he called after him. 'We can all rest easy in our beds, because afore the week's out that neck of hers won't be so lovely when it's stretched a measure.'

His loud guffawing followed Ralph from the building. It also echoed down the empty corridors to where Rebecca Norman was softly singing. For a moment the singing stopped. Magical black eyes looked towards the cell door. Her laughter was soft, beautiful. In her heart she felt all manner of emotions – wickedness, loathing for the other man, the man who bore an uncanny likeness to this tall handsome warder . . . the father who had long ago deserted her. Loathing also for the woman who had given birth to her, then later died. In a different way that woman had abandoned her also.

Fonder, more painful memories murmured deep inside her, and a love so strong that it would never die. The love of a girl for an old woman, the grandmother who had cherished her when no one else would. There were shadows in her heart now, long dark shadows that flitted and shifted, never resting, never peaceful, always driving, demanding to be let loose; dark, excruciating memories of how they had burned that dear old woman, an innocent candlemaker, whom they labelled a witch.

But it was not the old one. No. It was not she who was the witch. And yet they were merciless. In their fear and superstition, they had done wrong. The old one was burned, and they believed it was over. Oh, how wrong they were. *Maybe it would never be over!*

Chapter Three

Maria opened the door, wondering who it could be so late in the evening. The cold night air took her breath away as she peered into the darkness. 'Oh, Elizabeth, come in,' she said, being relieved to see that it was one of her neighbours. Knowing Elizabeth, it was more than likely an errand of kindness.

The woman stepped inside, slipping the blue-fringed shawl from around her neck and letting it slip to her ample shoulders. She was not a young woman, yet not old, possibly in her early forties. There was still a handsome strength about her; in the depth of her hazel eyes and the firm lines of her face was portrayed a measure of suffering, but also an admirable determination. Elizabeth Manners was a woman who made the best of what the Good Lord had given her, the worst of which was a husband who had drunk himself into an early grave, leaving her as a widow with three growing sons. Fortunately, the Good Lord had given her a talent for 'dressing' those wretches who departed the human race, and welcoming those who had seen fit to struggle into it. For these service she made a small charge. Her expertise was much in demand, and though her three sons were now self-sufficient grown men, she still coveted her work and her fiercely held independence. Besides which, the money would all go to helping her when she travelled back to England to live with her ageing sister. The older she got, the more determined she was that this would happen.

'I thought I'd best pop in before taking to my bed,' she told Maria, boldly scrutinising the now considerable bulge beneath Maria's ill-fitting dress. 'Evening, Mr Ryan,' she called, seeing him relaxed in the chair, supping his cocoa and staring deep into the flames of the fire. 'I was just saying to your wife, I wouldn't feel right if I went to my bed without checking on her condition. In my experience, you can't be too careful, not when a woman's so close to birthing as Mrs Ryan here.'

At once, Ralph's mood was brightened by the woman's observation. 'It's comforting to know that you're only as far as next door, Mrs Manners. You're on a wasted journey *this* night though. As you can see, Maria has never been more content.'

'So I'm not wanted, then?' She rained her smile on Maria.

'Not tonight, I'm thinking,' Maria replied, smoothing her hand over her belly and startling the other woman by gently blushing with pleasure. 'It's not due until the *end* of May . . . more than two weeks yet,' she reminded her.

'I'd best be away, then.' Elizabeth Manners patted Maria on the shoulder. 'But you mind you don't overdo,' she warned. 'We don't want no complications, do we now, eh?'

Ralph twisted himself round in the chair, his handsome face looking pale and drawn in the firelight. 'I don't know what we'll do when you leave for old England,' he said, adding with a laugh, 'Suppose Maria takes it in mind to have another dozen?'

'God forbid!' remarked Mrs Manners, looking at him aghast.

'We'll have what comes, I expect,' Maria quietly interrupted, 'but, for the moment, my only concern is with the one I've got, and the one on the way.'

'Quite right, m'dear,' rejoined Mrs Manners, casting a cursory glance in Ralph's direction. 'Bringing a child into the world is a serious business . . . drains a body's energy . . . another dozen indeed!' she remarked in mock horror. 'What would men know?'

'It's kind of you to keep an eye on my wife,' Ralph told her, resisting the urge to explain the lightheartedness of his comment. A dozen children may very well drain a body's energy, but they would also drain a body's purse. The very idea of twelve or fourteen children was too overwhelming, although he suspected there were many such families living here in Fremantle.

'It's what my job is, Mr Ryan . . . keeping an eye on your wife,'

Mrs Manners said. 'And how are you yourself today? Has the fever left you completely?' She eyed him dubiously, clucking her tongue. 'So long as you're on the mend, that's all that matters, wouldn't you say?'

'I'm fine, thank you.' His voice was tired, and she was not convinced.

'He's well enough, Mrs Manners,' Maria intervened. 'We both are.' Maria knew how Ralph hated to be questioned so. She moved towards the door. 'You can rest safely in your bed tonight.' She inched the door open, wincing as the cold breeze rushed in. 'Baby Ryan doesn't seem in too much of a hurry to venture into the wide world.'

'You'll call me if the birthing starts?'

Maria nodded. 'Of course.'

'Mind you do.' Mrs Manners brushed out of the house without another word. Thankfully, Maria closed the door and returned to the chair opposite Ralph, where she resumed her darning. After a while, when the silence grew too heavy and she sensed the trauma of her beloved husband's thoughts, Maria raised her dark blue eyes to him, discreetly observing this man whom she adored more than anything in the world. But he had changed.

Over these past three months, and during the awful fever that had struck him down without warning, there had been times when her husband was a stranger to her.

On that night in January when he came home from his work at the asylum, he had the look of a man possessed.

Maria's heart lurched at the memory of it. Wild eyed, he was, the sweat oozing from every pore of his body, like a tap had been turned on somewhere deep inside. She had wanted to call a doctor then and there, but he would have none of it. Instead, he had struggled up the stairs and into his bed, straight away falling into a deep and fretful sleep. For weeks he hardly knew anyone, passing in and out of consciousness and, in his more lucid moments, insisting that she must not summon a doctor. 'We can't afford to, Maria,' was his reason and, to tell the truth, it was a sound enough one. Maria, however, rarely left his side, nursing

47

and loving him, bathing and reassuring him, spoonfeeding the rich hot broth that kept him alive, and softly talking him through the frantic nightmares that constantly plagued him.

Elizabeth Manners had been a godsend throughout, helping with Agatha and occasionally relieving Maria whenever she would allow it. Now, as she watched her husband, a wave of despair washed through Maria. With his head bowed, and the forlorn gaze in his quiet brown eyes, Ralph was a desolate man. Not for the first time, she wondered for his sanity.

'She's a good woman,' he murmured, without drawing his gaze from the dancing flames. 'You don't think I was harsh with her?' he asked.

'Of course not.' Maria lightly laughed. 'When were you ever harsh with *anyone*?'

An answering smile played at the corners of his mouth, but never blossomed. The silence descended, cradling them, drawing them together, then pushing them apart. Maria sensed the chaos in him. She knew the cause of it, and she prayed he would not be too hasty in his decision. Presently, he spoke, and the bitterness showed. 'A man is nothing without his work!' She could never imagine the anger in him, and the terrible feeling of hopelessness.

At once she was by his side, cradling his dark head, murmuring to him, comforting him like a mother might comfort a child. 'You're not ready yet. You know that, don't you?' she pleaded. He gave no answer, but she felt him stiffen in her arms, and she knew.

'A man has to work. I'm strong enough, Maria, and I'll grow even stronger when I'm at my work.'

'Don't let money force you back before you're ready,' she told him. 'We've managed well enough these long weeks, and we'll manage for as long as it takes to get you really well.'

Far from pacifying him, her words seemed to antagonise. Twisting round, he grasped her two small hands in one of his fists, gripping them so tightly that she was made to gasp. 'Look at me!' he ordered, pushing himself into a tall, upright position. 'Tell me, Maria, do I look like a man who could be idle when his wife takes in washing and mending so he can be fed?' His face was set like stone, the small muscles in his jaw working furiously. His strong brown eyes glittered with anger and the slightest suggestion of tears.

'You mustn't think like that,' she said, helpless in the face of his despair.

'But I do!' Roughly releasing her, he stood up, taking a moment to stare on her lovely face before going to the window, where he lifted the curtain just enough for him to see along the street. He saw a street deserted, only a stray dog strolled by. The sky was dark, menacing, a striking backdrop for the skyline of chimneys, each drawing a smoky signature across the cold stars.

Maria remained silent, her anxious gaze intent on the familiar figure at the window. Certainly, he did seem stronger in himself, still the same tall, proud man, though thinner now, his handsome features sharply etched by the illness which had nearly taken him from her. 'I can't tell you what to do, my darling,' she said in a whisper, 'but don't be too hasty.' She felt in her heart that he still had a long way to go before he was strong enough to resume his work.

Coming to the fireplace, Ralph stood gazing down on her, loving her for the woman she was, and knowing deep inside himself that she was right. It was true that his strength was not yet fully recovered, and that there was still a fever raging in him. Yet, the fiercest fever was his own impatience to return to his work. These past few days he had been determined that he should report for duties within the week; he had stubbornly refused to lie wasting in his bed.

'You heard what Mr Bullen said?'

'Yes.' Maria had resented Ralph's work colleague for coming here a week ago and unsettling Ralph the way he had. 'But he said nothing that should concern you.'

'Oh, Maria! You know as well as I do that he came here for one reason, and for one reason only – to warn me that my post would not be held open indefinitely.'

'He did not say that.'

'Not in so many words, no. He didn't have to! But I could read between the lines.'

'There's always the warehouse.'

'The warehouse!' Disgust filled his voice. 'For God's sake, Maria, I *have* a job!' He had not told her how he had already arranged to return to work. When Mr Bullen called a week since, Ralph knew his own job was on the line, so he had informed Mr Bullen then and there – and out of Maria's earshot – to include his name on the duty roster, as from tomorrow, when, he had assured the man, he would be fit and ready to resume his work.

'So, your mind's made up?' Maria knew him more than he realised. 'You've told him you're going back?'

He nodded. 'I'm to report for work in the morning.' He was outwardly cool, with determination set in every muscle of his face.

'Then I pray you're doing the right thing,' Maria told him, a deal of sadness in her gaze, but resignation also. She knew how stubborn he could be. Bidding him goodnight, she went slowly up the stairs. She felt uncomfortable, the unborn weight pulling on her. For some reason she could not fathom – but which she put down to her own imminent birthing, and her husband's insistence on returning to work before he should – she felt greatly troubled, as though a deluge of misfortune was about to be unleashed on them.

Downstairs, Ralph watched his wife until she was gone from sight. Now, alone, he sank into the chair, a sudden weariness on him. He was *not* fully recovered – every bone in his body told him that, every aching muscle, every step he took that felt as though he carried another man on each shoulder. And those dreams . . . those nightmarish images that swam through him night after night, washing away his strength and using him up. There had been times when he felt as though the dark angel of death had taken him by the hand and was leading him away. But three months! Three long, wasted months. Where had the summer gone?

Sadness settled on him. He must fight this parasite that drained him. Incredibly tired, he closed his eyes. Like before, like so many times before, *she* came to him. Dark and sensuous, always smiling, ever beckoning. For a while he was lulled by her beauty. But then he remembered. She was only a woman. He knew, now, that it was the onset of the fever that had blinded him, confused him into believing that she had somehow bewitched him. He smiled, he actually laughed aloud. It had been the fever. Nothing else, not her, a lunatic, a murderess. No, not her. It had been the fever boiling his blood, churning his mind. The fever. Only the fever. Now the fever was all but gone, only the tiredness in his bones remained, and soon *she* would be gone also. According to Mr Bullen, Rebecca Norman would 'hang by the neck until she was dead'. The sentence was passed. Ralph felt only a passing regret.

'Well, I must say, Ryan, you look like a man who's been through the wringer, and no mistake!' The duty officer cast a discerning glance over Ralph. 'Hmm . . . let's see now.' He lowered his attention to the ledger resting on the desk before him. Whilst he perused it he made the comment, 'So, you decided to fetch yourself back to work, eh? Feeling strong again, eh? Raring to go, you say? Best thing too.' He observed Ralph again, thinking how pale and unwell the fellow looked. 'A very wise move, if you don't mind me saying so . . . getting back to your work,' he remarked, while musing that if it was *him* that had been struck with the fever, he would not be in a hurry to leave his warm bed.

After a moment the officer stubbed a chubby finger on to the page. 'Here we are.' Keeping the place with the tip of his finger, he looked up. This time his voice took on a more serious note. 'It's a good job you're fighting fit; you *are*, aren't you?' he insisted.

When Ralph assured him of it, he nodded with satisfaction. 'Good! That's all right, then. You're assigned to duties with Morgan.' He scrutinised Ralph from beneath raised brows. 'It's a quiet enough duty, right enough.' He chuckled. 'Quiet as the grave, you might say.' Pointing in a particular direction, one which Ralph vividly recalled, he told him, 'The Norman woman!' He made a cutting gesture across his throat. 'They'll be coming for her soon. You know she's condemned?'

When he saw Ralph's stony face, he studied him thoughtfully.

51

Eyeing him with a curious look, he said in a serious manner, 'It's no more than she deserves.'

Ralph made no comment. Instead he asked, 'Will she be hanged from here?'

'No. She'll be taken to Her Majesty's Prison, where she'll spend her last night. Then it's the gallows at first light tomorrow.'

As though suddenly afraid that there but for the grace of God go I, the duty officer quickly made the sign of the cross on himself, afterwards informing Ralph, 'You know the ropes, Ryan. Morgan's there already. They'll be coming from the prison to collect her later today.' He frowned. Never a happy man and easily frustrated, he dipped his head to scrutinise the duty roster one more time. 'On your way, then,' he snapped. And Ralph, who believed for a moment that the other man had been about to impart other information with regard to the morning's duties, hesitated a moment before moving away. He was used to the curt, impatient nature of the duty officer, a man not readily liked and whose changeable moods were best ignored.

On realising the duty to which he was assigned, Ralph had suffered certain misgivings. The apprehension he felt was tempered now by a deal of regret that the woman known as Rebecca Norman had come to such a sorry end. So violently insane that only a padded cell could safely contain her. It was a sad and cruel world that harboured such creatures. His regret was countered only by the knowledge that the Norman woman had shown small mercy to the victim whom, by all accounts, she had 'scared' to death. It was a bad thing, there was no denying. A bad, evil thing that, despite his determination to remain objective in his views, clutched at his heart like a relentless fist.

As he approached the row of padded cells, his thoughts turned to Maria. The merest suggestion of a smile lit up his serious brown eyes. These days he lived with constant anxiety, financial strain, the inner weariness which was a legacy from his illness and which had not altogether left him, the nagging worry that Maria would go into labour and him not by her side to aid and comfort her – although he was not unaware of the staunch belief among women that birthing was 'woman's business', with the menfolk being sent as far away as was humanly possible. Such had been his fate when Agatha was born; even though he strayed no further than the downstairs parlour, from where he heard every sound . . . Elizabeth Manners' urgent footsteps, her constant demands for the hot water which he duly kept supplied and, in between, Maria's heart-rending cries of pain. He would never forget the absolute relief when, after a quiet lull in the procedure, there burst into the air a loud and piercing yell, the tiny bairn that was their beloved daughter. Such an experience would never leave him. On that day he had been overwhelmed by it, filled with awe. Now, the mere recollection of it all flooded every corner of his being with great pride and joy. The same pride and joy uplifted his expectations of the imminent birthing of their second child, which he secretly hoped would be a son to himself and Maria, and a brother for little Agatha.

A strange and sudden mood took hold of him the nearer to the cells he came. Thoughts of Maria remained paramount, and he found himself clinging to them like a drowning man clinging to a life raft. Rebecca Norman spiralled through his thoughts. Deeply disturbed, he mentally turned away. Compared to his lovely Maria, the root of his life and all his delight, that dark-eyed bewitching creature was no more than a passing vessel to him. Determined, he thrust all thought of her from his mind. In his heart, though, there lingered a degree of compassion, of curiosity, and of sadness. He convinced himself that these emotions were for *all* such creatures everywhere, the wretches of this world who were more to be pitied than blamed.

Morgan was overjoyed to see him. 'Thank Christ you're here!' he greeted Ralph in a harsh whisper. 'Gives me the bloody shivers, it does . . . I ain't ever watched over somebody who's soon to be strung up.' He stared at Ralph, his piggy blue eyes bloodshot and marbled with fear. Ralph suspected that Morgan had spent the previous evening seeking comfort in the bottom of a whisky bottle.

'Relax, man,' he told him, discreetly taking stock of the fellow.

53

Morgan was a round, stocky build, much like a bull terrier, red faced and square of features, some three years younger than Ralph's twenty-eight years.

'I ain't kidding. It gives me the bloody creeps, I tell yer!' His nervous glance flitted to one side, to the adjacent cell where Rebecca Norman was incarcarated.

Impatient, Ralph pushed past him, coming into the padded cell, which was temporarily seconded as a duty room for the two men, sparsely furnished with a small wooden table and two upright chairs with arms. The long iron bed was stripped bare of its thin mattress and grey blanket; it made a formidable reminder of their purpose here. Resting on the table was an open ledger and a writing instrument, for the purpose of making notes during the hours of observation. There were also two enamel mugs, one drained dry except for a few remaining dregs floating in the bottom. There was also a *News Chronicle*, depicting the most recent and hair-raising accounts of Ned Kelly, Australia's most infamous bushranger.

'Sleeping, is she?' Absentmindedly running his glance over the news page and the headlines which screamed, 'NED KELLY: POLICE CLOSE IN', Ralph suspected it was more likely Ned Kelly's exploits that had so greatly excited and terrified Morgan, and not his own adventures on this day, however grim and unpleasant they might be. He discreetly slipped the newspaper underneath the ledger, where it was less likely to divert attention from their actual purpose here. Watching over a woman who would soon be taken to the condemned cell and from there to the gallows, was no more pleasant for him than it was for Morgan. But it was a duty that had to be done, by them or by someone else; it made no difference. At least he was not one of those who would walk her to the gallows, thank God. Tomorrow it would all be over. And as far as Ralph Ryan was concerned, tomorrow could not come soon enough.

'Sleeping, you say?'

Morgan shook his head vigorously, nervously. 'Dunno. I ain't looked. She's been quiet, though, real quiet. I reported here about ten minutes since . . . took over from the night duty. By all accounts they'd just took her breakfast in. That's all I know.'

'You haven't checked her at all?'

'Naw. But like I said, I ain't heard a peep outta her.' He fell back into the chair, seeming to shrink visibly as he pressed himself deeper into it. 'D'you reckon you oughtta take a look?'

Ralph stared down at the man and opened his mouth to speak. He thought better of it. Instead he turned and strode out of the room. At the door of the adjoining cell he paused, his hands on the panel. All was deathly silent on the other side. In the eerie quietness he imagined the palpitations of his heart to be loudly echoing from the corridor walls. He had been impatient at Morgan's obvious discomfort, angry with him, disgusted. Now, though, the disgust was for himself. In his mind's eye he saw her as she had been on that day . . . naked, enticing, the most beautiful woman he had ever seen. He recalled the deep yearning she had caused in him. He felt it now. His glance fell to his hands, still poised to open the panel; they were trembling. 'What the hell's the matter with you, Ryan?' he muttered, gripping the panel until the knuckles bled white. Hadn't he already convinced himself that he was safe? It was the *fever* that had torn his insides apart! The *fever* that had whipped his imagination into a frenzy. Not her. *Not her!*

After a moment, a sense of reality came over him. His composure now regained, he drew in a deep relaxing breath and raised the panel. Outside the daylight was strong. In the gloomy confines of that tiny cell, it might have been midnight. Thin shafts of light filtered in high up through the window, its thick iron bars splitting the light and making harsh patterns against the opposite wall. Only the shadows drifted down, dark shadows that settled into the corners and hid themselves away. At first glance, Ralph could see only the shifting gloom, and in the foreground the narrow iron bed, its blanket crumpled into a heap, at its foot a battered slop-bucket. There was no one in the bed and, as far as he could see, there was no one in the cell at all. Alarmed, he pressed his face close to the opening, his searching gaze reaching all four corners of the cell.

On preparing to open the door in order to satisfy himself that

Rebecca Norman was still secure inside, he was suddenly startled when her face appeared within inches of his own. With a cry he reeled back, the panel slamming down when his hands fell away. Behind it, her laughter was soft, invasive to the ear, a floating unreal sound. In spite of his determination not to let her affect him as before, he could feel himself sweating, shivering from inside to out.

'What the hell were that?' Morgan dashed from the safety of his closet, but only as far as the door.

Feeling his companion's eyes on him and realising that, of the two of them, it was he who must be the stronger, Ralph straightened his back, squared his shoulders and told Morgan sternly, 'Nothing to be alarmed about. The panel slipped, that's all.'

'Oh?' Morgan eyed him curiously. 'What about . . . her?'

'No problems.'

Glancing at the large round-faced clock at the end of the corridor, Morgan made the comment, 'Seven-fifteen. We have to make the entries every quarter.' He paused, closely observing Ralph, reluctant to venture away from the doorway.

'Make the bloody entry then, man!' Ralph felt irritated. Inside he was all churned up.

'All right, all right!' Morgan was surprised. Ralph Ryan was normally a mild-mannered man, not known for his temper. 'What entry shall I make . . . "no problems", like you said?'

Seeing the consternation on the other man's face, Ralph was at once apologetic. 'Sure . . . just that,' he said, 'seven-fifteen . . . no problems.' The other fellow nodded eagerly, obviously relieved. He quickly returned to his place, leaving Ralph staring at the open panel.

The face was gone. Only the shadows stared back. On surer footsteps he went forward, taking the panel into his hands, peering into the cell, not knowing what to expect. She was there, a proud, defiant figure in a posture of prayer, yet not praying. She was sideways on to the door, facing the east wall, her dark head bent forward, her hands spread outwards on the ground, palms

56

upwards, long slender fingers splayed out in rigid formation. She was chanting, or singing, or was she crying? Ralph wondered. He was intrigued, mesmerised.

Suddenly she stopped, jerking her head round to stare at him, her black eyes playing into his. Then, in a low resonant voice that was dangerously caressing, she murmured, 'You won't forget me. I won't let you.' Rising graciously, she came to the cell door, all the while her eyes smiling, her power all around, drawing him to her, arousing his curiosity, toying with his senses. 'When will they come for me?'

'Soon.'

'They mean to hang me.'

Reluctantly, he nodded. He did not like what she was doing to him. But then, it was an enriching experience.

'Isn't the condemned man allowed one last request?' She was smiling, teasing him.

'Not here. They'll see to that in prison . . . tonight, I expect.'

The smile slid from her face. Her mood darkened. 'No. Not "at the prison" . . . here, now.'

He shrugged. 'I can't see as it makes any difference.'

'It would,' she laughed softly, 'if they really did agree to my last request.'

'Which is?' All the while she was looking at him, his heart was in his mouth. She was real enough, and yet it seemed to him as though she had no substance. Somehow she got right inside him through those dark, glittering eyes, as though her very soul was pouring into him. His instincts urged him away, but a deeper compulsion kept him there.

'My freedom. Will they grant me that?'

This time it was he who smiled. 'No, but you can have anything within reason.'

'*You?*'

'What are you saying?'

'I want *you* . . . heart and soul.'

'This is a time to be serious,' he reminded her.

'Oh, but I *am* serious.' She laughed, and it was music to his ears.

57

'*I will have you, you know.*' Her voice was like silk. 'That's all I want.'

Excitement coursed through him. Their gazes mingled. 'Nothing else?' he asked with amusement. It gave him pleasure to tease her. *He could not know how he had increased her loathing of him tenfold.*

The moment seemed for ever, and her dark gaze never left his face. When her sinuous fingers crept up to the panel and stroked his skin, he was shocked to the core. Stepping back, he told her, 'If there really is something, I can ask on your behalf. I'll do my best, that's all I can promise.'

Going to the far wall, she spoke to him in an arrogant voice. 'When I was a child, my grandmother taught me her skill. She was a candlemaker.' Her eyes shone with tears. 'It's been so very long. It's time now. Time for me to resurrect her skill, time to use the talents she taught me.' She watched him, enjoying his curiosity, heightening his confusion. 'My request is not excessive, I think,' she said softly, 'some wick, and a quantity of tallow.'

'You want to make a candle?' He could not hide his astonishment. 'That's what you're asking . . . that you be given materials to make a candle?'

'You may call it a "candle",' she said with a devious smile, 'but you'll see. You'll see.'

Ralph thought it little to ask. He nodded. 'I'll do my best.' He began to close the panel, pausing when she addressed him with a question.

'Are you a good man, Ralph Ryan?' He was momentarily stunned. She knew him by his first name!

Panic first, then realisation, and with it came a surge of relief. Of course! Names, first or otherwise, were no secret in this place. Minders addressed each other all the time within earshot of the inmates. At the prison also, the officers did the same. There was nothing unusual in that.

More importantly, he told himself, there was nothing unusual in Rebecca Norman. He must keep reminding himself of that. Of course, she *was* different from most other women – in her beauty, in the reputed evil make-up of her character, and in the very fact of her being here in the first place. There could be no denying that she was 'unusual' in these ways. In the back of his mind a small voice murmured persistently – 'In other ways too . . . in other ways you would rather not think about.'

Looking her directly in the eye, he replied, 'I hope I am a good man, yes.'

" 'A good man, a family man, a man like all other men, yet *not* like all other men?'" *Only like one man, long ago.*'

Her words stirred a fear in him. The intensity of her gaze unnerved him. The smile had gone from her eyes, and there was a deeper mood on her. A feeling rippled through him, a sensation of what was running through her mind. *Hatred.* A deep crippling sensation of loneliness, and dark wicked loathing. It touched him, as real as though she herself had lain a cold hand on his heart.

'*You remind me of my father,*' she whispered. In the hidden crevices of her tortured mind all the memories lurked – long-ago memories, hidden away, quietly festering. One by one she drew them out. She was a child again, happy with the old woman who doted on her, who taught her the moods of the sun, the moon, of all nature with its dark and glorious secrets. Her grandmother, who had been everything to her – her saviour, her mentor – she was not of this world now. Hanged by suspicion and fear, hanged by those who were not possessed of the true spirit, nor of that unique gift which shaped her grandmother's soul, and which that old woman had passed on to the child.

These memories were agony to that child, who was now a woman and who, like the grandmother, was to hang by the neck until the last breath was drawn. The thought did not strike terror in her. It made her smile. What did these fools know? How could they realise that far from ending her miserable life here, they were instead releasing a captive soul to greater heights? Could they not see how they were giving her the very freedom she had so long been denied? But no, how could they? These unfortunate creatures would never understand. Nor would they ever know why. Only she knew. Only her grandmother knew the awful loneliness, the cries that echoed through the long endless nights, heartfelt, anguished cries that might bring a father home to his own child, a child cruelly robbed of its mother. Cries that went on for ever, that went on even now in those dark, painful corners of the mind. But they went unheeded then – and now. The pain never stopped. It only grew, until there was nothing else.

From the depths of one particular memory, the dark eyes looked out, looked at the father, looked at Ralph Ryan. *The image was the same.* The loathing, the love, the longing, the desperate need of a child. It mingled in the heart. It was all still there, a deep and terrible craving. It had long ago transcended all things normal, possessing the mind, the heart, the soul. Now, it was focused on Ralph Ryan. And there was no escape.

In those wonderful eyes he saw it, and was strangely troubled, elated beyond belief, yet filled with a premonition of something awful, something . . . hideous.

'I'm not asking too much, am I?' she coaxed.

He shook his head. 'No. Like you say, a quantity of tallow and some wick, no, it isn't much to ask . . . considering.' He raised the panel to shut those eyes from his sight. The panel felt like a lead weight, resisting. 'Okay, I'll see what I can do,' he promised.

She gave no reply. As he slid the metal pin through the bolt-holes, he heard her laughter. It was true. At first he had doubted it. Not any more though, because he knew now that she was mad. Knowing that, and being aware of the fearful manner in which she had scared that old hag to her death, he was shocked. Shocked, too, by his own emotions. Against his every instinct, there still lingered in him a certain sympathy. A certain fascination. It was inexplicable. Beyond his experience.

'What the 'ell does she want wick an' tallow for?' The duty officer's sour mood had not improved with the passing of the hours. He glared at Ralph, waiting for an explanation, and mentally preparing himself to refuse the request anyway.

'She says she wants it to make a candle.'

'A what?' He wasn't sure he had heard right.

60

'A candle,' Ralph repeated in a firm voice. He had no particular liking for this fellow, nor did he himself understand the reasoning behind the prisoner's unusual request. All the same, he defended her right to ask for the materials. 'Apparently, it was her grandmother's trade . . . the old woman taught the child. I suppose it will bring back happier memories, make her feel less afraid of the gallows.' To his mind, it was a reasonable enough request.

'Strange, that. She could have any number of creature comforts on her last day on earth . . . a priest, a tub of hot water, even a hearty meal, but you say all she wants is "wick and tallow"?' The duty officer stroked his chin, deep in thought. 'All right,' he said at length, at once reaching into the top drawer of his desk and drawing from it a slip of paper which he hastily scribbled on. 'Send Morgan to the stores with this chit.' He stretched out his hand and gave the slip of paper to Ralph. 'I'd rather you remained on duty at the cell.' He made a snorting noise; Ralph wasn't sure whether he was sneezing or laughing. 'If the Norman woman took a mind to throw a fit in there, that fool Morgan would like as not take to his heels and be half-way home before anybody else knew about it!' This time he chuckled and leaned back in his chair. 'Sometimes I reckon Morgan's dafter than a lot o' the bloody inmates! Still, it's difficult enough to get staff who'll work in this place. We've to make the best use of what we can get.'

Suddenly impatient and embarrassed by his own un-characteristic good humour, he waved his hand in a dismissive gesture. 'Don't forget, Ryan . . . send *Morgan* to the stores. You keep a close watch on her. Although, o' course, she won't be going nowhere till they come to fetch her away.' Surprisingly, he actually smiled, but it was more malicious than friendly. 'Wants to make a candle, eh? Tell Morgan to get a bloody move on or they'll be taking her away before she gets a chance to start it. Happen she'll put a curse on him then, eh?' His smile became a grin. 'You tell him that, Ryan. Tell him to get off his arse and hurry back with that there stuff, or she'll put a curse on him!' The grin broke into a hearty chortle.

The chortle became a loud unpleasant guffawing when the duty officer saw that even Ralph was amused by the thought of Morgan having to cope with his charge 'throwing a fit'. Though he was reluctant to agree, he had to secretly admit that at times Morgan really did seem dafter than the inmates. When the duty officer began laughing aloud, though, Ralph took the opportunity to be on his way. Already, it was seeming an unusually long day, fraught with all manner of unexpected things. He would not be sorry when this particular day was over and done. No, not sorry at all.

As he strode down the narrow gloomy corridor which led to the padded cells, it was merciful that Ralph Ryan's uneasy thoughts took him no further than the end of this day. For when this day ended, morning would never break.

It was four thirty p.m. when they came for Rebecca Norman. Morgan had been nervously watching the clock all day. Ralph lost count of the number of times his colleague went out yet again to see how many minutes had ticked by on the clock which hung high on the wall at the end of the corridor. He had been to the ablutions at least a dozen times, each time staying for no longer than a minute, and returning in highly nervous state, redder in the face and wringing his hands as though to wear away an invisible and nasty affliction from his leathery skin. 'Ain't they been yet?' he asked on each occasion. 'Ain't they fetched her?'

Whether it was because he was highly nervous, or insatiably greedy, he had spent the hours stuffing himself with whatever food he could lay his hands on. He paced the floor, noisily expelling gases, and making no apology for it. 'Christ almighty, I wish it were over!' His wide frightened eyes plucked at Ralph's face. 'How can you be so bloody calm? They *ain't* fetched her, have they? Have they, eh?'

Ralph refrained from answering, if only because the sounds of the prisoner could be heard emanating from the padded cell next door. Since the quantity of wick and tallow had been passed through the panel earlier that morning, Rebecca Norman had

62

stripped herself naked and hidden herself in the darkest corner, swaying back and forth like a soul in a trance, chanting out a low rhythmic and strangely intoxicating drone, while feverishly kneading and fashioning the now pliable tallow in the blood-warm palms of her hands. Completely engrossed in her labours, she had ignored all offers of refreshment.

The stone floor struck cold to her legs, charging her whole body with a chill. Yet her soul was on fire, burning with the grandmother long gone. In her fevered mind she imagined that old lady. She felt herself being dragged through the streets to the blackness of the woods. In her imagination the woods came alive with the awful flames that engulfed the wizened old figure. She heard the old one's cries, and her heart was broken. 'Wait for me,' she murmured. 'One day soon, we'll be together, you and I.' The tallow moulded softly in her deft fingers. 'One for you, and one for me,' she whispered, pressing her lips to the tallow dolls. 'They should have burned me with you. But they will. One day they will, I promise you. Until then, let them suffer. Let them know my anger, and my loathing.' Holding the two dolls face to face, she chanted softly,

> Through the flames
> Eye to eye
> Only then
> The curse will die.

'God almighty! If she don't stop that awful wailing, I think I'll go out o' my mind!' Morgan cried while pacing the floor with his two hands pressed tight over his ears. 'I can't stand it no longer!' he screamed at one point, and if Ralph had not barred his way, the poor haunted fellow might have fled the building there and then.

Even the duty officer was haunted by the unearthly, nerve-splitting chanting, rushing down the corridor to hammer on the door of her cell, threatening its inmate with all manner of punishment, 'if the caterwauling don't stop this bloody minute!' His punishment, though, could not be more exacting that the one already conferred on her.

Rebecca Norman paid no heed to his threats. Maybe, in the throes of her evil work, she did not hear them. Eventually, she was left alone, her captors uneasy, frustrated and reluctantly resigned to their unenviable task. And so they waited.

The hands of the clock moved round, relentlessly ticking away the seconds, the minutes and the hours. Until, when it seemed as though the shift would change before the condemned woman was taken, the four burly men came down the corridor, making a formidable sight in their dark stiff uniforms, thick wooden cudgels swinging from their belts, and every man with his features set in grim expression. Like participants in a funeral procession they advanced, one man leading, two centre and the fourth officer bringing up the rear; the formation was precise, it had a purpose and, as they came, so they would leave, but with the woman at the heart.

Ralph and Morgan stood ready to receive them, Morgan visibly relieved at the prospect, and Ralph less so, but purposely deliberating his thoughts on to his beloved family. As though to comfort himself and, almost in unison with the continuous chanting which even now throbbed into the air, he murmured his woman's name over and over. 'Maria . . . Maria . . . Maria.' It had a soothing effect on him.

Silently, he perused the letter of authorisation that was handed to him. With a brisk nod, he delivered the keys and went to stand by the door of Rebecca Norman's cell; the four men followed. Morgan remained a distance away, his piggy eyes wide and alert, and, for the first time that day, he boasted the look of a man in charge.

'Do you really need that?' Ralph saw one of the other officers had pushed his way forward. In his hands was a grubby hessian garment, shapeless in appearance, but with many long tabs hanging from it. Ralph knew instantly what it was; he knew its purpose. He also knew that strait-jackets of this kind were sometimes necessary in order to restrain vicious and destructive offenders. He had always considered such measures to be offensive and dehumanising, although, by the same token, he knew there were times when the proper use of the strait-jacket could prevent serious injury.

'There's no other way we're taking that hell-cat outta here!' the officer told Ralph, with an accusing, hard stare. The moment he spoke, the chanting from within abruptly ceased.

The ensuing silence was ominous. Ralph's watchful gaze went from one man to the other. He saw the look of fear in their eyes, and the look of arrogance. He felt the awful tension, and the hatred born out of terror. He saw the strait-jacket made ready, the cat-o'-nine-tails gripped tightly in another's fist. He read the grim stone-like expressions on each face. While he accepted the situation, he could not really come to terms with it, feeling, as he did, oddly distanced from it all, as though he played no part in it, as though he was on the outside looking in. In spite of himself, his thoughts were with the woman on the other side of that door; in his mind's eye he could see her so vividly it was unnatural, *and yet the most natural thing in the world*. He imagined her fear, her defiance, her innermost thoughts. For a shocking moment it was almost as though he was one with her.

Inside the cell, she had heard the gaolers at the door, and she knew her time was close. Soon, too soon, it would be over. Her dark eyes were not without fear as they looked once more on the tallow images which she had fashioned through the long telling hours. As the key fumbled in the lock, she hurriedly rose from the kneeling position. Her legs were sore from pressing into the cold hard ground, but not for one moment did she relax her straight, proud stance.

Quickly now, before they burst in and dragged her away, she furtively glanced about. Where to hide it? Where to hide it? Ah! The dark eyes gleamed. Softly she went to the wall-panel, her deft fingers lightly groping there. Yes. The padding was not too resistant, yielding to the touch. Tentatively the long sinuous fingers probed into the seam between the padding and the narrow wooden batten that secured it to the wall. Swiftly she eased the smallest area into a deeper slit; further probing told her that it was just as she suspected ... inside it was cavernous, safe.

Withdrawing her fingers, she glanced down to the two tallow images clutched in her other hand. It took but a second to separate them, one being thrust deep into the wall-padding, which was then cleverly made to seem as though it had never been tampered with, and the other laid reverently on the ground, nestling into the discarded convict garment that had earlier clothed her nakedness. One more furtive whisper, one more knowing glance at the effigy, and then she was ready.

When the door was flung open, the intruders were not prepared for the stunning sight that awaited them. Before their shocked and avaricious stares, Rebecca Norman was a proud, challenging figure, her trim gently rounded lines making a rich and rewarding contrast to that grey mundane place. With her head held high and the dark hair already grown to small attractive curls which coiled to her head like sleeping vipers, she met their unbelieving stares with smiling eyes, her lips slightly parted and the perfect teeth glinting white in the half-light from the corridor. As they gazed on her, there was not one man there whose heart didn't beat that much faster, and who would not have eagerly bedded her there and then.

'Blatant hussy!' The one in charge was the first to speak; he too had been taken aback. Now, though, he quickly realised the situation and promptly defused it by flinging the strait-jacket over her nakedness. At once the others rushed forward. Within minutes the strait-jacket was in place. It was a stiff, abrasive thing, reaching to the prisoner's knees, its long winding tapes tied round her body and securing her folded arms tight across her breast. While they made rough with her, pulling and pushing her this way then that, and callously bruising her, she made no cry, nor did she resist. Her reticence surprised and confused them. They were not unaware of the manner in which she was reputed to have murdered her cell-mate, and so they hurried all the more, deliberately averting their eyes, lest they too should suffer the same fate.

Ralph, though, had not cringed from looking her in the eye. In his own well-meaning manner he thought his quiet discreet smile might bring her a measure of comfort. He was shocked when she did not return his smile, but instead stared long and hard at him. He wondered at her thoughts in that moment, he felt her great strength. Such was the force of her emotion in him that he had to look away. And so he stood, his back to the cell, his shoulder resting against the door jamb and, like the others, he now cast his gaze elsewhere.

Soon, they brought her out, one officer in front, one behind, and – being manhandled through the door between the two other officers – Rebecca Norman, head high, defiant as ever. And then something happened. In the instant that she drew level with him, she turned to Ralph; her smile was exquisite, her proud beauty never more bewitching. In a hoarse whisper, she told him, 'I made it for you. The tallow image. Take it. Cherish it.'

Before he could reply, she was whisked away, her bare feet making a pitiful sight amongst the heavy boots that resounded a menacing march against the hard ground beneath. In a moment they were gone. Only the chaos lingered, and then the silence, the unbearable inauspicious silence. For a long aching moment, Ralph stared after her. He shivered. It was suddenly cold. A whispering cold that crept right into a body's bones and numbed them.

It was gone five p.m. The shift was over. Morgan lost no time in gathering up his various paraphernalia: his coffee mug, the belt from his trousers – which he had draped over the back of his chair – his cudgel, the ledger and newspaper from beneath. 'Thank God this day's over,' he told Ralph as he hurried away. He did not look back. Ralph suspected he would not be in this work for very much longer; in fact, he doubted whether the poor fellow would ever report for duty here again.

It was deathly still. There were no occupants now in the padded cells. In the far distance, Ralph could hear a whistle being blown, then the muted sounds of many movements, voices raised in authority, the low drone of a multitude of noises, not too far off. He felt oddly isolated.

Sighing deeply, he turned and strolled into the cell, *her cell*. A chilling, pleasurable sensation came over him. She was still here. *The essence of her was all around.* His glance fell to the garment, straw-like, crumpled. In its folds lay what looked like a doll. He bent, stretched out his hand to retrieve it, and her words throbbed in his mind. 'I made it for you . . . the tallow image.' He hesitated, but did not know why. An instinct, a small persistent voice cautioning. 'Take it,' she had implored, 'cherish it.'

Grasping the doll in his fist, he raised it to the fading daylight. He gasped aloud. *It was her!* Fashioned in the image of Rebecca Norman herself, it was incredibly beautiful. Its gown was a threadbare remnant torn from her convict dress. It was crudely made, drawn over the doll's head and reaching to the calves of its trim, shapely legs; the garment was drawn in at the waist by means of a slender thread; the sleeves were short and ragged, the hands and feet perfect in every detail. Altogether a primitive thing, though cleverly created. The face, though, was unbelievably exquisite. Perusing the strong classic features – the slender throat, the mass of dark hair and those latent hollowed eyes where the shadows mysteriously flitted – he was overawed. With loving fingertips he stroked the moulded features; they felt unexpectedly silken to the touch. In that moment he had never felt more alive.

With the likeness of Rebecca Norman burning the palm of his hand, Ralph wondered at the pathos inside him. All caution had left him. His heart was uniquely calm. Taking a moment longer to enjoy her beauty, he then slipped the doll into his pocket. At the door he turned and smiled into the room. He could not know how alike their smiles were, his and Rebecca's – secretive, *sinister*.

Now, as he swung to shut the heavy wooden door, the vibration trembled round the cell, along the wall and to its very heart. Here lay the duplicate likeness which Rebecca Norman had malevolently fashioned from the depths of her black vindictive soul. A likeness, *yet not a likeness*! In the wake of the reverberating din, the doll trembled, shifting slightly, its empty eyes looking towards the source of the noise. As it slipped deeper into its hiding place, it made a soft rushing sound, a sigh. The silence settled once more.

*

'What is it, Ralph? Why can't you tell me about it?' Maria had woken to find that Ralph had left his place beside her in the big iron bed they shared. On sitting up, she had seen him in the far corner of the room, seated in the wicker chair, the incoming moonlight from the window bathing him in its hazy yellow glow. He was bent forward with his head down, looking like a man who had the world on his shoulders. He was not a man at peace – Maria had known that since the previous evening when he had returned from his place of work. There had been something about him that troubled her, a sense of loss . . . a strange mood that had taken him far away from her. It was on him now, that uneasy, oddly tranquil mood which she had never seen in him before. It frightened her.

Climbing from the bed, Maria shivered in the cold night air. There was a chill in the room, sharper than she could ever remember. Yet, by the same token, the air was sultry, a clinging stillness, almost claustrophobic. Taking her shawl from the foot of the bed, she wrapped it about her, clutching the ends together over the mound of her stomach. The child kicked, making her smile.

'No, Maria. Go back to bed.' Ralph was looking up, pleading with her. He made as though to rise from the chair but Maria was already there, standing before him, her anxiety reflected in the way she reached out to place her hand on his face, gently stroking the thick tousled hair and, after a while, drawing him to her, burying his face in the warm uncomfortable bulge that was their unborn. For a time no word passed between them, only love, and comfort, and a great sense of belonging.

No sense of peace passed between them, though, no re-assurance that all was well. No answers. Only unspoken ques-tions. Presently, Ralph moved away, leaning back into the chair, sighing deeply. 'Please, Maria. Go back to bed,' he implored. His voice was low, no more than a whisper.

'No. I won't do that,' Maria replied softly, falling to her knees and searching that familiar face, all the love she felt for him strong in her eyes. 'I know you're troubled. Please, Ralph, let me help you.'

'You're imagining things,' he lied, 'there's nothing troubling me, as you say.' Ashamed, he could not bear to look on her.

'Is it money?' she persisted. 'Oh, you mustn't worry, because we're managing well enough.' When he did not reply, she went on, 'There *is* something! If it isn't money, then what?' She slid her hand in his. Still he could not bear to look on her. 'Are you still plagued with the fever, then? Is that it?' Still he was silent. 'Or is it your work? Has something there caused you anxiety?'

Now, when he turned to gaze on her, she was startled by the anguish in his brown eyes. Suddenly, she recalled something she overheard between Elizabeth Manners and another of the neighbours. They had stopped outside her front door in the moment before that good woman had made one of her frequent checks on Maria. The other neighbour had made mention of a hanging. Poised to open the door and admit Elizabeth, Maria had been shocked to learn that the one to be hanged was a woman. It was not too rare an occurrence for a man to be taken to the gallows, but, for a woman to be hanged, that was not a regular thing. Maria had thought it a sad and terrible fate for any human being, let alone a woman. She had said as much to Elizabeth Manners soon after, but that dear woman would not be drawn on such a horrendous subject, especially with Maria, who was so close to her time.

All the time, it played on Maria's mind, so much so that she had been tempted to mention it to Ralph in that quiet time after the evening meal, when Agatha was sleeping and the two of them happily exchanged news of the day. But Ralph had come home in such a quiet unreceptive mood, that Maria had thought better than to depress him with matters that neither of them had the power to alter. And so, she had gladly pushed the whole issue from her mind. Now, though, it had bounced back with a vengeance, illuminating her mind and answering so many questions there. 'It *is* to do with your work, isn't it?' she persisted gently. 'It's the hanging in a few hours' time, the woman known as Rebecca Norman.' She squeezed his fingers, leaning in to him, desperate to share his troubles.

'I don't want you to talk of such things,' he said, looking her directly in the eyes and with such vehemence that Maria was shocked. He saw her reaction and was mortified. 'Oh, Maria . . . Maria!' He reached out and tugged her into his embrace. 'Forgive me.' He kissed the top of her head and stroked one hand down the long loose tresses of her silky brown hair. 'You're so good for me, such a good, fine woman. I don't deserve you.' He laid his head against hers, a measure of peace entering his agitated spirit. 'You're wrong, though,' he lied again, 'work isn't playing on my mind, not Rebecca Norman . . . not money, and nor am I still plagued by the fever.' Only fever of a different kind, he thought. Instinctively, his sorry gaze was raised to the window, to the garish moon and its incandescent halo of light, to the dark mysterious sky and the twinkling specks high, high up, beyond all human dimensions. Thoughts of *her* came into him. Was she also gazing at the night, those wide black eyes uplifted, their magnificence shaming even the heavens? Soon, those eyes would be dulled for ever, devoid of life, empty of light. In a few more hours, when the dawn began to chase away the darkness, *she* would be immersed in darkness for all time. From somewhere beyond his own perception a soft laughing voice called to him. She was not afraid, he knew that. She entertained no terror of the fate that awaited her. *But he did!* In turmoil he drew his gaze from the world outside his window. It was a cold, unfeeling night. He shivered.

'I believe you're worrying unnecessarily about me and the child,' Maria gently chided him.

'Yes, that must be it.' In all of their time together he had never deceived Maria, yet, on this night, he had deliberately lied to her three times. Why was he not more ashamed? Why could he not tell her of these alien feelings that made him a stranger to her?

'We'll be all right, me and the infant,' Maria assured him, 'you'll see.' She smiled into his face. 'Come to bed.' Stroking the goose-pimples on his arms, she told him, 'You're icy cold.'

Her smile was returned, but it was not a smile to reach his heart. 'I'm a foolish man,' he confessed.

71

'No, not foolish, my darling,' she protested. Clambering to her feet, she groaned, then laughed when he helped her up. 'Soon the baby will be born, and things will get back to normal,' she promised. *She did not realise it was not her promise to make.*

When they were lying side by side and quiet with the onset of sleep, together once more, his arm embracing her, and she nestling into his broad shoulder, Maria was at peace with the world. Before too long her weary body succumbed to a deep slumber.

After a while he tenderly eased her from him and got quietly out of bed, before quickly dressing. Going downstairs, he went into the passageway and towards the front door. He took no candle-light, knowing the way well and beckoned by the brilliance of the moon, which gentled through every window to penetrate the shifting shadows.

Every evening on his return from work, it was his habit to hang his jacket on the nail behind the front door. It was there now, one side dipping slightly from the weight in its pocket. As he withdrew the tallow image, his fingers were trembling, his heart palpitating. The touch of it spread through him in a warm glow.

On silent footsteps he returned to the parlour, to the window and the moonlight. He held the doll up, watching with pleasure when the soft translucent light bathed the features, highlighting the deep hollowed eyes so that they came alive. A melody came to his mind, one he could not recall, but which now whispered to him in its entirety – a haunting, lovely melody that hummed on his lips and flooded his heart with joy. And all the while he could not take his eyes from her face, no longer a fabrication, no more an inanimate thing, but real, alive, pulsating with life. He could hear her calling him, her eyes dancing with fire, laughing, making love to him. There rose in him such passion, such longing, that all of his strength went before it. *Rebecca Norman was here.* Here in this very room! She wanted him. *And he had no power to resist.*

'Ralph!' Maria had been awakened by the rush of cold air into the bedroom and now, on realising that she was alone, she had got out of bed, flung on her shawl, and was already hurrying down the stairs, the lit candle in her hand. The sound of the front door, banging to and fro in the wind, struck the fear of God into her. 'Ralph!' Each time she called his name, it was with greater urgency. A swift glance into the parlour told her there was no one there, all was exactly as they had left it on retiring to bed; her attention was only momentarily diverted by the trinket on the floor, a doll of sorts, probably one of Agatha's.

She looked at the clock on the mantelpiece . . . three thirty in the morning. Soon it would be dawn. *'Ralph!'* Panic filled her voice. She rushed along the corridor, the palm of her hand shielding the flickering candlelight from the inrush of wind. At the door she stepped over the threshold; the hard pavement shocked bitter cold through her feet. The candle was blown out, shadows leaped from every corner. Up and down the street she looked; there was no sign of him. 'RALPH!' Her voice startled the night. She recalled how strange of mood he had been last evening; she remembered the anguish in his eyes. It had frightened her then, it frightened her now even more. She tried to reason with herself. He must have gone for a walk . . . the sea was always a source of comfort to him. But no, she was not convinced. There was something wrong, every instinct in her being told her so.

'Mammy! Mammy!' Agatha's voice sailed from bedroom. Maria was frantic. She strained her eyes towards the ocean. There was not one living soul out on this hostile night, not a soul but Ralph, she told herself. She had to find him! Going to her neighbour's door, she banged her two fists against it, the ensuing noise sounding like a death knell. All along the street nervous faces appeared in the bedroom windows.

Elizabeth Manners flung open the door, gasping in horror when she saw Maria there, barefoot, still in her nightgown and only the thinness of her shawl to keep out the night chill. 'God above, child!' she cried, sheltering the candle flame with the crook of her arm. 'You'll catch your death!' Her frilly nightcap was askew, strands of greying hair blew about her shoulders like cobwebs in the wind.

73

Convinced that Maria had started in childbirth, and wondering why it was not Ralph who had come for her, she would have pulled Maria into the shelter of the passageway, but Maria resisted.

'It's Ralph!' she told her in a rush. 'I have to find him . . . please, see to Agatha!' Even now, the child's voice could be heard screaming for its mammy.

Before the other woman could reply, Maria took flight, desperation filling her with strength, fear stripping her of all reason. Behind her, she could hear all manner of noises – doors clanging shut, shouts, hurrying footsteps. She took no mind, but ran on, now and then calling his name. Her shawl was gone with the howling wind, and the bitter chill had penetrated her every bone. Tears sped down her face; cold wet rivulets that clung to her skin, chafing it. The breath was caught in her throat and her heart felt as though it might burst wide open, but still she ran, the weight of her unborn child pulling her down, crucifying her. Some inner terror drove her on, a deep certain knowledge that her man was in mortal danger. In that fearful moment, nothing else mattered.

Now, as she rounded the corner, Maria saw him, only a dark distant shape but unmistakably her man; tall and straight, broad of shoulder, the familiar smart manner in which he strode away. That same determined stride was taking him along the beach, but there was something horribly wrong. Maria's heart leapt. *He was going towards the ocean!* She called his name. The sound was caught in the thresh of the wind. It was howling now, wild, whipping at her hair, numbing her face, clawing at the hem of her nightgown.

Screaming his name, frantic, she stumbled on, the night playing tricks, the moonlight silhouetting him, *and another*, the figure of a woman close beside him, her naked skin glistening in the half-light. Disbelieving, Maria blinked her eyes. When she opened them the ghostly figure was gone. 'Ralph . . . stop! For God's sake . . . *Stop!*'

She came on to the sand; it sucked her down. Behind her she could hear people shouting; the sound of running footsteps. The

74

child lurched inside her, shifting, agitated. And the pain! Doubled up, she fell to her knees, her stricken eyes holding the image of her man. Now she could see only the upper part of his familiar figure, now the waters were lapping over his shoulders and still he went on, unseeing, not hearing, like a man entranced.

Ralph Ryan did not feel the rush of water about his body, nor the cold wet grave that gently devoured him. Maria's desperate calls never reached his ears, nor at any time did he sense the danger he was in; all he knew was that *she* was calling. Rebecca – now before him, now beside him, ever constant, beckoning him onwards, her dark mysterious eyes compelling him to follow. There was pleasure in him, and a great longing, and such peace, oh, such peace that he had never known before. There was nothing else, no other sensation, no fear. *Only Rebecca.*

When she took him by the hand, a warm memory fled through him. His mouth shaped the name 'Maria', but then it was gone.

The sultry black eyes burned into his; the silvery laughter was a haunting melody. His senses were lulled. He went with her, willingly, gladly. She caressed him, the touch of her hands feeling like the gentle lapping of the ocean, pulling him down, floating him away. He knew no pain. He felt no sorrow.

They had all seen Ralph Ryan drown. Only one other, besides Maria, saw the ethereal figure that went beside him to his watery grave. Elizabeth Manners had been distraught when Maria fled into the night. Taking only a minute to pull on her gown, she had raised the alarm and sent a neighbour to Maria's house where the child could be heard loudly sobbing. At once she had pursued Maria, whose very real terror seemed to have lent wings to her feet. When Elizabeth came upon her, Maria fell into her arms, exhausted, bleeding and beside herself with grief. In that moment, when Elizabeth cradled the devastated young woman in her arms, she raised her eyes to the ocean, to the spot where he had gone from sight. There was nothing to be seen. Not now. *But she had seen the apparition in the same moment that Maria had seen it.* The chilly night air made her gasp aloud. She clung to Maria, drawing her in to the warmth of her own body. 'You'll be fine, child,' she whispered, the image of Ralph Ryan strong in her mind. Had she imagined the figure of a woman? No! She had never been one to see things that were not there. Making the sign of the cross on herself, she clung all the more tightly to Maria.

It was Mr Leyland the blacksmith who carried Maria home. He laid her gently beneath the blankets on the big iron bed, where only a short while ago she had been warm and safe in the arms of her man. 'I'd best fetch the doctor straight away, Mrs Manners,' he said grimly, 'but I don't think it'll do any good.' Before departing the room, he looked once more on the crumpled sorry mess that was Maria. 'If you ask me . . . there's nobody can help that poor creature now.'

Elizabeth Manners' answer was to chase him from the room with the harshly whispered warning, 'Every second you waste, her life ticks away! Go as fast as you can, and don't stop until you're sure the doctor is out of his bed and making haste for Henry Street!' When, flustered, he hurried from the room she then recruited the urgent assistance of a large busy-faced woman by the name of Ada Reynolds, who promptly cleared the room of all those who had congregated there – the anxious, and the curious, who had been roused from their beds by the terrible events of this night. Satisfied that Maria's daughter was now soundly sleeping and watched over by a kindly soul, Elizabeth lost no time in attending to Maria. 'There are logs downstairs in the hearth,' she told Ada Reynolds. 'Be so kind as to fetch them up and get a fire going in the grate there.' She pointed to the small fireplace. 'We must keep her warm at all cost.' While the other woman hurried about her task, Elizabeth turned her whole attention to Maria. It was obvious that the birthing was imminent. Half-conscious, Maria struggled between life and death. 'Don't let my baby die,' she pleaded, her wretched gaze never once leaving Elizabeth's face.

'I won't, child,' she was promised, 'with God's help . . . I won't.'

During the next thirty minutes or so – when Elizabeth feared more than once that the doctor would not make it in time and that God had deserted them – Maria slipped further and further away. 'Keep your senses, child,' Elizabeth pleaded. 'You have to help. I can't do it without your help!'

She wondered how she herself might have been, lying there, her heart broken by the sight of what she had witnessed. Deliberately thrusting it from her mind, she worked with desperation to bring a small new life into this world.

She could not push it *all* from her mind, though. Not *all* of it. Not the lingering image of a woman, naked in all her glory . . . a woman? Or just a figment of hallucination, born out of fear and terrible panic. Elizabeth did not know. All she *did* know was that it was the strangest and most unnerving experience of her life. And, for all of her life, she would never forget it.

They found Ralph Ryan just as the dawn broke through, a magnificent dawn that split the night asunder, marbling the sky with fingers of brilliant reds and gold. When they stretched him out on the sands, silently gathering round him with bowed heads and huddled shoulders, there were those who wept unashamedly. There were those who said, later, that they would not forget this day, nor the look on Ralph Ryan's face as he stared blindly towards the sky, a look of wonder, they said, a look of disbelief. *A look of horror*. No, they would not forget. In that very same moment, when they uttered a prayer over Ralph Ryan's soul, the trap-door was slung back beneath the gallows, and Rebecca Norman plunged to her death.

A heartbeat later, Maria's own fight for life was sadly lost. At first it was feared that the son born to her would not survive either. Weakened and exhausted by his struggle into this world, it seemed as though he was destined to go the way of his mother and father. But, against all the odds, he survived. The doctor said it was because he had been blessed with the unique strength and determination of his mother; Elizabeth Manners believed that it was because, in those final moments when she had almost despaired, the Good Lord above had answered her prayers and spared the child.

Ada Reynolds tied the bonnet strings beneath the girl's chin. 'There you are, Agatha,' she said, straightening up and taking the child by the hand, 'you're as pretty as the day's long.' When Agatha made no response but to cast her soulful gaze to the ground, the woman sighed and turned to Elizabeth Manners, who was in the process of making herself ready. She asked, quietly, 'Do you think the authorities will let you keep the children after all?' Looking round Elizabeth's homely little parlour, and knowing the exemplary character of that dear soul, Ada thought the children would be safe here.

'I don't know,' Elizabeth replied, going to the sideboard and opening the small wooden chest that was Maria's. She had it in mind to place into it the unusual tallow doll which she had found in Maria's parlour. 'You know how the authorities like to take their time, my dear. I shall just have to be patient.'

She was greatly saddened at the objects which were lovingly placed in the Ryans' wooden chest and which was now in her keeping – none of them items of any value, but each one a part of Maria and Ralph's life: the small butterfly-shaped brooch of silver filigree; a box of hairpins and a mother-of-pearl slide; the badge from Ralph's work jacket which bore the name and place of the establishment where he was employed; a small enamelled pill-box into which Maria had proudly hidden one of little Agatha's first curls, and beside it a thin dark strand of hair from her son's head and which Elizabeth had now thoughtfully put there.

There was also a small blue notebook. On its face, in perfect longhand, was the name Maria Ryan. Elizabeth suspected it was a diary. Of course, like any other woman, she was curious as to its contents, but her respect of Maria was such that the very idea of perusing its contents would be both unthinkable and unforgivable.

Keeping back the tallow doll, she closed the lid over these private and personal articles. Ralph and Maria were at peace now, side by side in the churchyard. Their belongings would go to Agatha, small consolation though it was. 'You go ahead, my dear,' she told the other woman, 'and pray that they agree to me keeping the children and raising them as my own.' She had been allowed to keep them for over a week now, while decisions were made as to their future. The prospect of parting with them was daunting to her. If she was fortunate enough to keep them, she would call the boy Matthew, after her own father. 'Look, Agatha,' she called, going to the child and holding out the doll, 'look what I found . . . it's yours, isn't it?'

The girl shook her head. She had never seen the doll before.

Elizabeth was surprised, and yet on all the occasions when she had called on Maria and played with little Agatha, she herself could not recall ever seeing the doll before.

'Oh? . . . Not yours?' She smiled. 'Perhaps later, eh? Till then, I'll put it safely away in the chest. Shall I do that?' When the child eagerly nodded her head, she bent to kiss her firmly on the mouth. 'That's what we'll do, then, sweetheart,' she said.

Going across the room, she examined the doll, a strikingly beautiful thing, with exquisite features, long dark tresses and vivid black eyes, which were really deep hollows etched into the tallow. Although it was clothed in a coarse grey gown, it had the look of a princess. Made of tallow though, mused Elizabeth, it was not really suitable for a child to play with. It occurred to her now that it may well have belonged to Maria. 'We'll put it away in the chest,' she told Agatha, 'where it will be safe.' Then, collecting the infant boy from his cradle, which she had previously arranged to be brought from next door, she wrapped him warmly in a shawl, and followed the other woman and Agatha out of the door. Today, the children's fate would be decided. And, consequently, her own.

It was darkly silent in the cramped interior of the chest, where the tallow doll lay unmoving, nestling down amongst the things that were once so cherished.

Yet it was not so dark, or lonely, as the place where its mirror

79

image lay, secreted deep within the padded wall of a cell, the cell where Rebecca Norman had devised her merciless vengeance.

Though made with the same hand, and in the same material, the two images were not so alike. Where one was young, the other was old – one being incredibly beautiful, the other repugnant to the eye. One was fashioned in Rebecca Norman's own likeness, the other a model of her aged grandmother. Each was of tallow, each was clothed in remnants plucked from her own garment, and the blood from her torn fingertips were speckled in one as in the other.

To the unknowing, these two were more different than alike. Only their maker could tell. Only their maker knew of the sinister quality woven into each one – an unspeakable quality that bound one with the other for all time. An intangible thing, a merging of evil that would grow and fester down the years; sleeping now, patiently waiting. All things were in the heart. *And the heart was secret.*

PART TWO

1988
Bedford
England

. . . a dark
Illimitable ocean without bound,
Without dimension, where length, breadth, and highth,
And time and place are lost; . . .

Milton, *Paradise Lost*

Chapter Four

'Let me see!' Laughing, Cathy grabbed at the envelope, her grey eyes alight with excitement.

'Oh no you don't!' Keeping her at bay with one arm encircling her tiny waist, Matt stretched his other arm above his head, teasing her by waving the envelope out of reach. 'If you can guess what's in it, you can have it.'

'I *know* what's in it,' she cried, tiptoeing against him and throwing her arms about his neck.

'No, you don't.' He looked into her upturned face and his heart swelled with love.

'Yes, I do,' she insisted. 'You've booked a honeymoon for us.' Pointing to the envelope she observed, 'And don't think you've been clever, Matt Slater, because you forgot to cross out the travel agent's stamp . . . see?' She giggled as he clumsily placed his thumb over the agent's bright yellow logo. 'So you might as well own up.'

He sighed. 'All right then. I've booked us a honeymoon.' Even when she squeezed him, gazing up with wide bright eyes, he kept the envelope out of reach. When she knew, he hoped she would understand. Their destination would be part honeymoon, and partly a search for his ancestors' history, and consequently his own. He thought of his father, Abel, and he knew it was right to go.

'I thought you said we couldn't afford a honeymoon . . . what with the new costly stable block and our business only now breaking even?'

'I lied.' His dark eyes danced with mischief.

Playfully digging him in the ribs, she demanded, 'Let me see, then.'

'No.'

'Oh, Matt!' she cooed, snuggling closer, nuzzling into his broad chest and licking at his mouth with the tip of her tongue. 'Where are we going?'

'Guess.'

She winced, biting his lip until he cried out. 'You'd better tell me,' she threatened, pressing her body into his, 'unless you want me to seduce you here and now.' She was well aware that one of the stable hands could walk in at any minute.

'What . . . *again*!' he groaned, rolling his eyes to the ceiling and feigning boredom. 'When does a man get any peace round here?'

She began to undo his trousers, all the while rubbing against him and softly moaning as though in the throes of lovemaking.

The voice of a woman called from the outer hallway. 'Hello! It's me . . . Laura.'

With his trousers loose about his hips and Cathy's hand fumbling for his growing member, Matt didn't flinch. 'I don't mind if you don't,' he told Cathy mischievously.

'Cathy, are you in there?' Laura's footsteps were coming down the passage.

'You monster, Matt Slater!' Cathy hissed, snatching away. 'I do believe you'd charge her money to see us at it.'

'I would!' he lied. 'Oh, I would!' He grinned as she hurried from the room, carefully closing the door behind her and leaving him both dishevelled and fully aroused. 'You little sod!' he muttered, then in a softer voice, 'But I love you. Aggravate me all you like, and I'll just love you all the more.' Cathy and he were soon to be wed, and she was his life. As hard as he had worked to build up the successful livery here, he would let it all go tomorrow, rather than lose her.

A valued employee, Laura was a superb horsewoman and trained instructress. She was skilled in dressage and blessed with a natural ability to take on a yearling and school it into a fine showjumper. A handsome woman in her thirties, she possessed a ready smile and an abundance of auburn hair. 'Nervous, are you?' As they walked to the stables, she glanced sideways at Cathy. 'The big day looms nearer,' she teased, 'I think I'd be losing my courage right about now.' Taking a piece of ribbon from the pocket of her jodhpurs she tied her long hair back. As they hurried down the lane, she was glad Cathy couldn't read her thoughts, because they would betray how she wished it was her and not Cathy who was soon to walk down the aisle with Matt.

'To tell you the truth, I'm scared stiff!' Cathy confessed. 'I've been watching my weight so much that I'm worried the dress won't look right on the day. I'm concerned about the reception and whether the cake will be everything I hoped. I'm having nightmares about the service . . . will it be too long or too short, and whether people will like the hymns I've chosen. And on top of all that, I *still* haven't been able to persuade Dad that Matt and I would like to pay half the bill.' She chuckled. 'He's a stubborn old bugger, my dad!'

'You're lucky to have a father like that.'

The sadness in her voice didn't escape Cathy, and she was mortified that she might have sounded ungrateful. 'I know,' she answered, 'and I wouldn't want you to think for one minute that I don't appreciate everything he's done for me. I *do*! More than he'll ever know. It's just that the wedding is proving to be more expensive than I first thought. Matt and I can afford to chip in, but Dad won't hear of it.'

'Let him have his way,' Laura suggested. 'It's natural that he wants to pay for his only daughter's wedding.'

'I know you're right,' Cathy admitted, 'but Matt and I reckon it will amount to about two thousand pounds. It's such a lot of money, and though he's built his business up to a thriving concern, he's not a wealthy man by any means.'

'Enjoy your wedding. Worry about the cost afterwards.'

Cathy laughed. 'I seem to be looking for things to worry about! I dare say he wouldn't insist on paying for it if he couldn't afford it.' She always felt relaxed in Laura's company. Not for the first time, Cathy wondered about her. Though she was an exemplary employee and a lovely person, Laura never revealed anything of her background. There were times when she seemed lonely. It was during these times that Cathy would try to draw her out of herself. That was why she had asked Laura to fetch her the minute the kittens were born. To tell the truth, she wouldn't mind having Laura as a friend.

'They're real beauties, aren't they?' Laura told her now, as they came into the tack-room and peeped into the deep wooden box. The big ginger cat was licking the newborns all over as they struggled to stand on their fat little legs. There were three of them, one ginger, another black as coal, and one tiny little thing, multi-coloured with a snow-white nose. 'I don't think that one could make up its mind which colour it wanted to be.' Looking fondly on the kitten, Laura explained, 'It's a bit of a mongrel.'

'I think they're *all* lovely,' Cathy said, leaning down with the intention of lifting one.

Laura stopped her. 'Sometimes, if the mother smells the touch of humans, she'll kill the kittens and eat them.'

Cathy was horrified. 'I've never heard that before.'

'It's true. Not so much with domestic cats. But these are part wild . . . unpredictable.' She looked at Cathy and realised why Matt had fallen in love with her. She was not only beautiful, but she had a warm, trusting nature that made her unusually vulnerable. 'You can stay here if you like . . . watch the mother feed them.'

'I'd like that.' Cathy had been won over by the multi-coloured one. 'I think we'll keep him at the house,' she said. The mother cat's tongue had left a deep wet shine on his long coat, giving him a sleek, darker appearance. 'He's beautiful, don't you think?'

Laura agreed. Then, leaving Cathy convinced that she had said something to offend, she quickly went out of the tack-room and made her way to the top of the yard. A feeling of loneliness had come over her, and she needed to shake it off. The sooner she got started on her work, the better.

Concerned, Cathy came to the door of the tack-room and watched as Laura's figure disappeared out of sight. Her instinct was to follow and offer to lend a hand with the work. But she got the feeling that Laura wanted to be alone, so she went back inside the tack-room and watched the kittens for a while. Later, she would make herself useful.

A few minutes later, Matt found her. She was seated on a bale of hay with her knees drawn up to her chin and a thoughtful look in her grey eyes as she watched the kittens sucking on their mother's laden teats. Her face lit up on Matt's arrival. 'I've guessed where you're taking me for our honeymoon,' she told him as he strode across to her. 'We're going to Devon.' She had always liked Devon. He knew that.

'Wrong.' He eased himself on the bale beside her and draped an arm round her small shoulders. 'We're not going to Devon.'

'Jersey, then?' He shook his head. 'France?' she asked. Again he shook his head, and her patience snapped. Lunging at him, she pushed him backwards into the hay, her two hands plunging into his pockets in search of the envelope.

'Want to play rough, eh?' he teased, drawing her deeper into the soft bed of hay. His mouth found hers, and now there was no turning back. 'You've only yourself to blame,' he told her, unzipping her dress. 'You've riled me, and I can't muck out stables when I'm aching to make love to you.'

She struggled, but not too much. 'Mrs Leatherhead will be here in half an hour. You'd best feed and groom her horse. You know what the old battleaxe is like if her horse isn't champing at the bit by the time she arrives.'

'I pity the poor horse. Fancy having that great lump hoisting itself up on you!' The thought horrified him.

Cathy smiled. 'Well, I don't think it's any different than you hoisting yourself on *me*!' she teased, fighting with him.

'Okay,' he said, smiling back and slyly removing her dress. 'How about if I lie here and *you* get on top? I'm not fussy either way.'

'Show me the letter first.'

'Take it.'

First she kissed him, then she opened his shirt and undid the zip on his trousers. Taking the folded envelope from his pocket, she quickly opened it, shivering with delight when he toyed with her nipple.

When she read the contents of the envelope, her delight erupted in a scream. *'Australia!'* She stared at him through shocked grey eyes. 'Oh, Matt! Are we *really* going to Australia for our honeymoon?' She could hardly believe it.

'Only if you put me out of my misery, and let me have my wicked way with you right now,' he murmured, grabbing her to him.

'You deceitful devil!' she cried. 'You must have known for ages and you kept it from me.' Lying down, she kissed him full on the mouth. Then she tossed the letter aside and lovingly opened herself to him.

Neither of them realised that Laura had returned to collect a harness from the tack-room. As she came in the door, she heard the rustling noises coming from the hay bales. When she saw that it was Matt and Cathy deep in the throes of making love, she tiptoed out. Going to the farthest barn, she took a harness from there and hurried to the top stable where the grey was ready to be taken to the field. She thought of Matt and Cathy, and their forthcoming marriage. 'You're a fool!' she told herself. There was nothing here for her. And the sooner she realised that, the more content she would be.

Cathy's father was thrilled. 'Australia, you say?' Bill Barrington had been invited to dinner at Matt's home. The occasion was to tie up any loose ends with regard to the wedding arrangements. But Cathy was so excited about the honeymoon that she couldn't wait to tell her father. Bill Barrington was a tall well-built man in his mid-fifties, not handsome, but possessed of strong, homely features and a warm smile. His light brown hair was beginning to recede from the front, though his neatly trimmed beard was thick and bushy, and his kind brown eyes could still sparkle with youthful enthusiasm. They sparkled now as he addressed Matt. 'Mind you, I shouldn't be surprised you chose Australia for your honeymoon. You have links with that country, don't you?' It did his heart good to see this young couple so excited about their future together; especially when he could see no future of his own.

Cutting a piece of steak, Matt left it lying on the side of his plate. Bill's words brought back a multitude of memories. 'There are things I need to find out about myself,' he said thoughtfully, 'and there are other things I've never told a living soul.' He cast his eyes downwards, staring at the pattern on the lace tablecloth. Even now, after all this time, it was still too painful for him to remember.

'You don't have to talk about it, Matt.' Cathy reached out to cover her hand over his. The tragic death of both his parents was well known hereabouts. Matt was an only child and it was natural that he was devastated.

'No. I need to get it out in the open.' He squeezed her fingers affectionately, then took his hand away and clasped his fists on the table. 'I know I've been reluctant to talk about it before, but now that we're to be man and wife, I don't want to keep anything from you.' Glancing at Bill, he added, 'From *either* of you.' When Bill nodded sympathetically he went on, 'You both know how my parents died . . . everyone knows how they died. Most people have forgotten now, and rightly so. But *I* can't forget.'

'Well, of course you can't, sweetheart,' Cathy was quick to reassure him. 'I don't suppose you ever will.'

He smiled at her. 'For months after, I couldn't get it out of my mind . . . the *manner* in which they died. That day, when my father plunged to his death from the train . . . eyewitnesses said there was no weight on that door to make it fly open . . . no one near it but my father, waiting for the train to stop, just as he had done many times before. One man said it was "almost as though a hand reached inside and plucked him out".'

'Some people have vivid imaginations.' Bill had seen how the memories were affecting him.

Matt smiled, but it was a sad smile. 'It seems such a waste, to die like that. At first, it broke my mother's heart. But then she rallied round and seemed to be picking up her life. Then all of a sudden she suffered a breakdown and was dead within weeks.' He shook his head. 'I can't help but feel it was all too quick . . . too evil.'

Cathy couldn't bear to think of him still hurting inside. 'I can't pretend to know how much you miss them,' she told him softly. 'But what do you mean when you say their deaths were "evil"?'

'God only knows!' He laughed cynically. 'It's just that one minute they were healthy and enjoying life to the full. Then one is sucked out of a train to a grisly end, and the other is struck down by some illness the doctors couldn't seem to agree on. In the end, they said my mother had simply lost the will to live.'

Bill spoke then. 'It has been known to happen,' he revealed, 'partners who are devoted to each other. Sometimes, when one dies, the other can't face life alone.'

'Maybe you're right,' Matt reluctantly conceded, 'but I still think the way they died was "evil".' For months after his parents' deaths Matt had wondered about it. None of it made any sense.

'There's something else on your mind, isn't there?' Cathy sensed there were still things left unsaid.

Turning to her, he smiled. 'It's a pity you never knew my father, sweetheart. He would have adored you.'

'I've often wondered what he was like, but you've never spoken about him.' She wanted to know everything about his family, but she respected his grief, and knew the time would come when he might confide in her. It seemed the time had come now.

'Abel Slater was a good man. Fifty years old when he died,' he began, glancing at Cathy's father. 'You remind me of him, Bill . . . hard working and respectable.' Pushing his plate away, he folded his arms and relaxed. Suddenly he felt more at ease with himself. At last, he was able to talk about his family without experiencing that crippling pain which had clawed his insides for so long. 'He was thirty-five when he came to England, full of ambition, he was. He'd always loved the land, he told me that.'

'He came from Australia, didn't he?' Bill asked.

'That's right. Perth . . . had a parcel of land there.'

Cathy was intrigued. 'You never told me your father came from Australia.'

Bill interrupted. 'I saw the report on the accident, but they never mentioned he was Australian.'

'That's because I never told them.'

'So *that*'s why you want to go to Australia for our honeymoon?'

'Not if you don't want to, sweetheart.' He wished now he hadn't sprung it on Cathy like that. 'I'll cancel it if you like? We could go to Devon . . . or a cruise. Whatever you want.'

Cathy knew now – he really needed to retrace his father's footsteps, in order to lay the ghost. 'There's nowhere else I'd rather go,' she said simply.

'It would be wonderful to see where he grew up,' Matt admitted, 'but there are *other* reasons for wanting to go. Reasons I've never told another living soul.'

'Go on?' Cathy inched her chair nearer to him.

Matt was silent for a moment, seeming to gather his thoughts. 'I have to go back to my father's beginnings, to try and discover more about him. You see, he was brought up in an orphanage. As soon as he was able, he made extensive enquiries about his background. When he came to England he was following a clue that led nowhere. For years he never gave up, until, in the end, he was exhausted. Right up to the day he died, his one regret in life was that all his enquiries had come to nothing. He was driven by the need to know his roots: Who were his parents? What was his background? He had to find the answers.'

'Were there no records?' Cathy could understand why Matt needed to go to Australia, and now she, too, was keen to uncover the truth.

'Apparently not. But when he first started making enquiries, he did discover that he had a rich aunt somewhere.'

'How did he find that out?' Bill was fascinated.

'When my father reached the age of eighteen, he received a letter from a solicitor, instructing him that he had inherited a trust fund. Apparently, it was set up for him when he was an infant.' Leaning back in his chair, Matt mentally pieced together the story his father had told him. 'The solicitor gave him as much information as he could. My father learned that a wealthy aunt

91

had put him in care, and it was she who had set up the trust fund for him. There was a letter, in her hand, stating that the boy's name was Abel Slater, and that his parents had perished in a bushfire.'

'Was that all he knew?'

Matt nodded. 'Apparently the solicitor who actually met with the aunt had died long since. The letter and the trust fund details were kept safe in the firm's offices.' Scraping back his chair, he went to the Welsh dresser and took out a long brown envelope. 'Here it is,' he explained, 'everything that's known about my ancestors is in there . . . in my great-aunt's handwriting.' Giving it to Cathy, he told her sadly, 'Not much to pass on to our children, is it?'

Opening the envelope, Cathy read it aloud:

To whom it may concern. This child is my kin, and recently made an orphan. Sadly, I am unable to keep him, and regretfully commit him to the authorities.

His name is Abel Slater, and his parents perished in a bushfire. Being his only living relative, I have set up a trust fund for him, to mature when he reaches the age of eighteen. Beyond that, I want nothing more to do with the child. As I intend to make my home in England and do not yet know what my address will be, it is better to sever all ties now. To this end, I do not wish to be kept informed of his progress, and require that my identity remains unknown.

The letter ended abruptly. Cathy was shocked. 'No wonder your father was driven to find her. She's probably the only one who knows the entire story, then?'

'Did he never find her?' Bill could imagine how desperate Abel Slater must have been.

Matt shook his head. 'At first he stayed in Australia, trying every which way he knew to find her. He tried to trace her through the trustees of the fund, but they knew very little. Every enquiry drew a blank. It was just as though she had vanished from the face of the earth.'

'She meant what she said in that letter,' Cathy remarked. 'It was obvious she didn't want to be found.'

'Anyway, in 1968 Dad sold his farm in Australia and came here to England with me and Mum. He tried everything to contact his aunt, but he never did find her. Eventually, he conceded defeat and abandoned the search – just as she had abandoned him so long ago.'

'Then, of course, there was always the possibility that she might not be alive,' Bill suggested. And, of course, Abel Slater had also been forced to consider that same possibility.

The meal was ended in subdued silence, each deep in their own thoughts: Matt feeling that he had done the right thing in explaining his reasons for wanting to go to Australia; Bill putting himself in Abel Slater's shoes, and thinking how that man must have sometimes been driven to desperation. And Cathy, loving Matt for having confided in her and, as much as she enjoyed her father's company, aching to be alone with her future husband.

It was eleven p.m. when Bill nosed his van out of the drive. Cathy had decided to stay over for another night. She and Matt stood by the gate arm in arm, waving to Bill as he went away down the lane. Afterwards, they strolled back to the house where they sat beside a log fire, sipping chocolate and talking of things closest to their hearts. Cathy had never felt closer to him than she did then.

Chapter Five

The sound of organ music reverberated through the old church. Today was Cathy and Matt's wedding day. As she came to the altar, all eyes turned to look at the bride. Dressed in a simple white gown, she looked stunningly beautiful. The gown was fitted at the waist, with a straight skirt and sweetheart neckline. Cathy had chosen a garland coronet, studded here and there with tiny pink rosebuds. Her bouquet hung with carnations and lilies, and her veil touched the ground as she walked.

Bill Barrington made a splendid sight as he walked beside her, his arm linked with hers, and the smallest hint of a smile on his face. Conscious of the admiring glances, he felt as though he would burst with pride, while at the same time he was filled with bittersweet regret that Cathy's mother was not here to see this day.

As she approached the altar, Matt turned to smile on her and Cathy's heart skipped a beat. This day had seemed so long in coming. She had been nervous and worried that it might all go horribly wrong. But now that it was here, she felt incredibly calm and relaxed, almost euphoric. Soon she would be Matt's wife. It was all she had ever wanted.

The service was short but moving, and as the newlywed couple came out of the church, they were showered with confetti.

'You look lovely.' Laura's eyes were bright with tears as she kissed Cathy on the cheek. She merely smiled at Matt, saying, 'We'll all miss you while you're away.' But she would miss him more than most.

The guests numbered twenty in all. Cathy's only relative was her father, and Matt had none, other than his new wife. But the stable staff were there, as were Edna the housekeeper, and Joseph, her husband, who was also manager of the stable yard. Edna cried buckets, and Joseph couldn't wait to get to the Bedford Arms in Woburn, where the reception was being held. He had a thirst that only a pint of beer would satisfy.

In no time at all the photographs were taken, and the sun shone as though to order. Amidst laughter and yet more showers of confetti, Cathy and Matt left the delightful old church in Ridgmont, and were carried in style to the ancient inn by means of a very costly but sleek black Rolls. The guests followed, some in hired cars and others in their own transport.

The distance from Ridgmont to Woburn was five miles. Matt held Cathy's hand all the way. 'Happy, sweetheart?' he murmured.

'You can't know how much,' she answered. Her heart was full of love, and, not for the first time, she realised how very lucky she was.

The manager welcomed them into the banquet room. 'I hope you approve?' he said anxiously, gesturing towards the long white-clothed tables. They looked a splendid sight, bedecked with flowers and groaning with the most wonderful spread of food. There were several hams, beautifully dressed with pineapple slices, enormous salmon, pink and plump, and laid in beds of various salads. The cake stood in the centre, a two-tiered creation, with the bride and groom standing in pride of place on top. Altogether it made a splendid sight. 'It's lovely,' Cathy told him, and his face beamed from ear to ear.

The festivities began and the time seemed to fly away. 'If we're to catch our plane, we'd best make a move.' Matt had been watching the clock like a hawk.

With the farewells over, they travelled back to the farm, where Cathy and Matt quickly changed. Bill went with them, and in no time at all the three of them were on their way to the airport in Matt's car. The arrangement was that Bill would bring the car back and collect them on their return.

95

The motorway was unusually quiet, so they arrived at the airport in plenty of time. 'Take care of yourselves,' Bill told them, 'and mind the spiders don't bite,' he teased.

Cathy laughed. 'You're the one who's afraid of spiders, not me!' she reminded him.

When their flight was called, Matt shook Bill's hand. 'See you in a fortnight.'

Cathy hugged him. 'Thanks for everything, Dad,' she whispered. 'Love you.' Choking back the lump which had risen in her throat, she realised that these men were all the family she had. And she could not imagine life without them.

Bill watched them go through the departure gates, and for the briefest moment he was afraid. Australia was a long way – the other end of the earth. 'God bless,' he murmured as they disappeared from sight, 'and bring you safely home.'

Emily manoeuvred the wheelchair through the doors of the Golden Egg café. 'A cup of tea and then we'll make our way home,' she told the old lady. It was Saturday afternoon and Bedford High Street was teeming with traffic. The market had been packed with shoppers, and it was difficult winding a way through the crowds and trying to balance bags of shopping on the handles of the chair. She was hot and tired, and her feet were throbbing. 'I don't know about you,' she sighed wearily, 'but I won't be sorry to get back to my own kitchen.'

Maria appeared not to have heard. She had seen how other customers were staring at Emily, curious about her slight limp and attracted by the mark on her face, a dark meandering blemish which, after years of consultations and tiresome examinations, all of Maria's money had failed to remove. The ugly stain curved in a long thin line from her right ear, and upwards over her cheekbone, to within an inch of her eye. Emily was pretty, but without that mark – which had plagued her for many years – she might have been exceptionally lovely. She had a small heart-shaped face, with clear skin, good white teeth and the brownest eyes; her short bobbed hair was the same deep-brown colour as her eyes and, for a woman of fifty, her skin was remarkably unlined. Dressed in a blue blouse and floral printed skirt, she made a pleasant sight, attractive in spite of the imperfection that marred her face.

Seeing how everyone's eyes were turned towards them, and realising yet again how brazen and unfeeling people could be, her blood was fired. It was always the same! And Emily, lovely creature that she was, either didn't see the rude stares, or she chose not to notice. 'Leave the wheelchair here,' Maria snapped, unwittingly venting her anger on the younger woman. 'I'm quite capable of walking a few steps to the nearest table!'

'Can I help?' The manager was of Italian origin, handsome and attentive. But it had been a long day and Maria was in no mood to be patronised. One shrivelling look from her sent him scurrying back behind his till.

Emily couldn't help but smile. 'You're incorrigible!' she said, helping Maria out of the chair and leading her to a table by the window. 'He was only offering his assistance.'

'I'd rather be offered a cup of tea,' Maria said, a smile creeping over her aged features. 'Oh, and a slice of that jam sponge in there.' She pointed to the dessert counter. 'And tell him not to be stingy with it!' When Emily began her way towards the counter she called out, 'And don't you apologise on my behalf either. If I feel an apology is necessary, I'll give it myself.'

'I wouldn't dream of apologising on your behalf,' Emily retorted, smiling as she turned to face the manager. 'I'm sorry,' she said, 'she really doesn't mean to be rude, but she's old, and she can be difficult at times.' Still peeved, he nodded politely but made no comment. Then he went stiffly into the kitchen, leaving Emily to order her refreshments from the amused assistant.

A few moments later Emily rejoined her. Carefully emptying the tray, she placed the teapot where Maria could reach it, and the plate containing a huge slice of cake beside it. 'There you are,' she said, pushing the tray on to the next table and pouring out her own tea. 'Drink it while it's hot, then we'll make our way home.' Glancing out of the window, she noticed that Goldings Iron-mongers were due to have a sale on the following week. 'I must remember that,' she said, sipping at her tea. 'We need some new curtain rails for the dining room. The old ones are sagging in the middle and the curtains don't hang right.'

Maria had been closely watching her companion. She thought Emily appeared tired and pale. 'Are you all right?' she asked, always concerned, always guilty.

Emily returned a bright smile. 'I'm fine,' she answered, 'it's just that I can't stand this heat. It wears me out.'

'Hmph! You don't know anything until you've lived in Australia. What! You could fry an egg on a dustbin lid.'

Emily was surprised. It wasn't often the old lady spoke of her origins. 'You miss living there, don't you?'

'Whatever gave you that idea?'

'I often wonder, that's all.'

'Well, you can *stop* wondering.'

Emily gave no reply. Instead, she picked at her slice of cake and hoped she hadn't revived bad memories in the old lady's mind. After all this time, she knew even less about Maria Hinson's background than she did her own.

Maria regretted her sharp tongue. Whatever happened in the past was no more Emily's fault than it was hers. She might do well to remember that, she told herself angrily. There were many things she would have changed in her life if she had been able to. But adopting Emily was not one of them. Even though Emily's parents had left their wishes clearly stating how, in the event of their early demise, they would want Emily placed with their 'dear friend, Maria Hinson', the legalities had been long and drawn out. In the end, Maria believed it was her wealth – accrued from sheep-farming in Australia and boosted by her late husband's insurances – that persuaded the authorities how she would be a 'suitable choice'.

When Emily first came to her over thirty years ago, Maria had found it very hard to come to terms with the girl's physical handicaps. It became clear that surgery was not the answer – a course on which Emily herself had been reluctant to embark. She knew what Emily's parents had told the girl . . . that the twisted bone in her leg and the scar on her face were a legacy of birth. Maria knew differently. Yet, like Emily, she had wisely learned to live with the explanation. And, even now, after all this time, the secret she kept caused Maria a great deal of anguish. It was the guilt again. It was never to do with any sense of disgust or revulsion at those awful physical reminders. She loved Emily more than anything in the world. But it was the guilt. Always the guilt!

Suddenly she felt ill. 'I'm ready to go home now,' she told Emily. She had a vigil to keep.

'But you haven't drunk your tea! And what about that cake you fancied?' Emily was used to Maria's strange mood swings.

The walk back along the embankment was a pleasant one. The unusually hot April sunshine which had sapped Emily's strength had now weakened with the onset of evening. 'See there,' she told the old lady, pointing to where two swans were nuzzling each other. Maria loved to see the ducks on the river. Often, in the cool of a Sunday evening, the two women would spend many an hour feeding the ducks or listening to the band playing in the arena.

But for now, Emily wanted to go straight home. She had a pile of ironing to do, and the back windows to clean. And then there was Maria to be got ready for her bath before bedtime. Mentally exhausted by the work still awaiting her, she decided she might just leave the window cleaning until tomorrow.

Maria Hinson sat by the long casement window, her aged face turned towards the fading light of an April evening, her dark blue eyes dulled by the sadness which had haunted her down the long, lonely years; years marred by tragedies, cruel inexplicable tragedies that, one by one, had robbed her of those she loved. Even now, though it was almost a lifetime since she had fled Australia, Maria was never at peace. Fear stalked her every waking moment, murmuring through her deepest slumbers. *Why?* So many times she had asked herself that question . . . Why? *Why?* She did not know. She suspected she may never know. But then, some secret part of her was afraid to know, terrified of the evil influences that had so long shaped the path of her ancestors. 'It still isn't finished,' she murmured.

Generations had come and gone, and, throughout, the evil had persisted. Yet somewhere there was a man, probably the only male descendant of Ralph and Maria Ryan. 'He's out there somewhere, not knowing the full horror of his past,' she recalled. I pray to God he has somehow survived.'

Lowering her gaze to the opened book resting on her lap, Maria thoughtfully perused the writing there. The book was a large black Bible, old and dog eared, but more cherished by Maria than anything else she had ever owned. Now, she gazed lovingly at the names written there, names of those whom she had never known . . . such as her grandparents, Ralph and Maria Ryan, so long gone, and other names – names with faces which were etched in her mind for all time. The first two entries were made in the meticulous flowing longhand of her own mother, Agatha; the remaining ones written there in Maria's own thin, dainty scrawl.

Through the years, the family Bible had been a great source of comfort to Maria, and also a painful reminder. She gazed a moment longer on the details recorded there. Every name, every word, every awful happening was as familiar to her as the lines on her own face:

On the first day of January, in the year of our Lord 1896, I, Agatha Ryan, being the eldest child of Ralph and Maria Ryan, have made the first entry in this Bible. God willing, from this day on, the details of the Ryan lineage will be recorded by the eldest surviving child in each generation. All that remains of our heritage is contained in the chest, which is to be handed down with this Bible.

Ralph Ryan
Died 1880, aged 28 years – mysteriously drowned

Maria Ryan
Died 1880, aged 24 years – died in childbirth

Two children survive the above – Agatha (4) Matthew (infant)

Matthew Ryan (son of Ralph and Maria)
Died 1900, aged 20 years – stabbed in a brawl

Lou Baker (Agatha's husband)
Died 1910, aged 32 years – died of the fever

Jack Baker (Agatha's son)
Died 1914, aged 4 years – crushed to death in an accident

*On the 19th of July, in the year of Our Lord 1924, I, Maria Baker, being
the eldest child of Lou and Agatha Baker, herein dutifully record the death
of my beloved mother. In accordance with her wishes, I cherish this family
Bible, and accept the responsibilities now entrusted to me.*

Agatha Baker
Died 1924, aged 48 years – lost the will to live

Two surviving children – Maria and Lizzie

Thomas Hinson (husband of Maria)
Died 1934, aged 36 years – thrown from his horse

Lizzie Slater (Agatha's third child)
Died 1938, aged 27 years – trapped by bushfire

and her husband Abel Slater
aged 29 years – died with his wife

Two surviving children – Abel (5) and an infant girl

Maria thought of all those who had gone before, and her heart was
heavy. It had been fifty years since the last entry was made in the
Bible, but then, on the day following the funeral of her sister Lizzie
and Lizzie's husband, Abel, Maria had realised with a shock she
and the two children were all that remained of the bloodline
directly descended from Ralph and Maria Ryan. It was a chilling
thought, and one which made her examine the past, with a deeper
purpose.

Even more chilling were the discoveries she made. Firstly, the family name itself had not survived. The only male who might have kept the name of Ryan alive was Ralph and Maria's only son, Matthew. Tragically, he was only a very young man at the time of his death. There were other intriguing things also, each with a bearing on the male descendants of Ralph Ryan. No male child born had been christened Ralph, while the name of 'Maria' had been lovingly passed on.

There had been only seven children born through the generations – two to Ralph and Maria, three to Agatha and Lou, and two to Elizabeth (Lizzie). Of these, only three were male, one meeting a violent end before he reached full manhood, and a second crushed to death when little more than an infant. Lizzie's son, thank God, had escaped the bushfire that took his parents.

It occurred to Maria that if indeed there was an evil and terrifying influence stalking the descendants of Ralph Ryan –who himself met a strange and particularly sinister end while yet a young man – then its purpose was to wreak its revenge on the males in the line.

It was disturbing, also, that of the females who had married, each of their husbands had been struck down in a cruelly unnatural manner. Firstly, Maria Ryan's husband – drowned; then Agatha's husband – taken by the fever; Maria's own husband – whose neck was broken when he was thrown from his horse. And, in 1938, Lizzie's husband was encircled by a raging bushfire. Sadly, Lizzie also lost her life going to his assistance.

Now, there was only one male descendant. This was Lizzie and Abel's son, also named Abel, after his father.

'Abel . . . Abel Slater.' Maria murmured his name aloud. Was he still alive, after fifty years? Had he perpetuated the line, with his own sons and daughters? Oh, she hoped and prayed that this was so. Fifty years! Almost a lifetime, and there had not been one day when she had been able to rid herself of the guilt. But then, she hadn't really deserted the boy, she told herself. By leaving her nephew there in that orphanage, putting as many miles between them as was humanly possible, Maria convinced herself that she was giving him his only chance of survival.

She had long suspected that somehow the evil that haunted the Ryan breed was hosted by herself. It was a disturbing and terrible thing, but the more Maria thought on it, the more she had come to believe it. And after a certain eerie incident on board the great liner that carried her across the oceans from Australia to England, she had lived in the shadows, afraid to be with other people, fearful that she might in some way cause them harm, although she knew instinctively that it was primarily the Ryan descendants who were in real danger . . . especially Abel – and any sons he may have begotten. Maybe he would be safe enough, though, as long as she kept away. As long as *it* kept away! A certain image crept into her mind, awakening all the terror that had lain dormant these many years.

On impulse, she moved her gaze along the garden to the dwarf apple tree, a wizened, misshapen thing that lived, but never blossomed. Her eyes grew round, flickering with the fear that whispered through every corner of her being. *It was there, beneath the ground. Biding its time.* Clutching the Bible to her breast, she began whimpering. It knew! It always knew.

'Cold got to you, has it? Let me move you. You've been sitting by the window for too long!' Emily's voice was chiding, yet soft with affection. No one was closer to Maria than Emily. With the passing of time the two had grown ever closer, until now they were more like mother and daughter than mere companions. Maria's influence had had a profound effect on the girl. Always a quiet creature and being long to recover from the trauma of losing her parents she, like Maria, had shunned the company of others, preferring instead the emotional security and solitude that Maria provided.

Seeing the other woman approaching with the intention of helping her away from the window, Maria raised her hand in protest. 'No, no . . . leave me awhile. I have some thinking to do.' Her uplifted eyes appraised Emily's small, slim figure – too slim to be fifty years old, too shapely, and, in spite of the slight limp that was more pronounced when she hurried, the kind of figure that any young girl might envy.

Oh, how Maria would dearly have loved to confide the burden she carried, but she must never reveal it, not ever, particularly not to Emily. It would be far too dangerous, even after all these years. Instead, Maria consoled herself with the knowledge that she had done all that was within her power. She had buried the evil that might have destroyed them, and she had used her wealth wisely, justly. No, there was no one with whom she could share the awful secret. And so it must remain locked inside her; a secret she may even have to take to the grave with her.

The thought was a terrifying one. Because of it, Maria feared for her very soul. If only she had regained her faith in God, she might have sought comfort in His Church . . . confessed all to the priest. But she could not bring herself to forgive. Like those she had loved, her faith was lost to her. It was a sad and lonely thing which Maria truly regretted, but there was so much disillusionment and mistrust in her heart. Too much. All else was diminished by it.

'All right, then,' Emily agreed, 'but only for a short while. The evening is drawing in, and I don't want you overtiring yourself.' She placed her hand on Maria's bony shoulder when, leaning forward, she followed the old woman's gaze. She knew how much Maria must love the garden, for she spent many hours looking out from the window, and yet, strangely enough, she rarely, if ever, actually ventured into it.

In fact, the only time Emily could recall Maria ever going into the garden was when she had seen the gardener preparing to dig up that small, deformed apple tree. Maria was almost inconsolable at the thought of it being uprooted. On pain of being instantly dismissed, the gardener was made to promise that he would never again attempt to dig up the tree, although he protested, 'It's an eyesore, miss . . . puts a blight on the whole garden!'

'It is a delightful place,' Emily murmured now, lovingly slipping her arm round the old woman's shoulder, and the two of them looked out over the large expanse of ground that spanned beyond the old Victorian house. The garden was a large, beautifully tended place, with high walls all around making it both secluded and a pleasant sun-trap. Set with various trees and flowering shrubs, meandering crazy-paved walkways, and with the walls smothered in a profusion of climbing plants, it was a little paradise. Soon it would be May, and the buds would burst open, the flowers would be a riot of colour, and the heady scent of blossom would overlay the garden like a perfumed blanket.

Unlike Maria, Emily spent as much time out there as she could, but, what with being responsible for the day to day running of this big old house, and with only a local girl coming in two hours a day to help, she had little time left for leisure activities, although, of course, the evenings were not so demanding and did allow Emily to indulge herself. As she had never been one for going out and about, or mixing in the social sense, she was contented to sit in the garden and read a good book, or perhaps to push Maria in her wheelchair along the embankment.

'I'm ready for my evening drink, though,' Maria said, looking up into Emily's pretty brown eyes.

'Really?' Surprised, Emily glanced at the mantelpiece clock. 'But it's only seven thirty,' she pointed out.

'I'm tired, my dear,' Maria explained. 'I won't be too long before I go to my bed.' She watched Emily hurry away in that slightly dipping manner. Again the guilt rippled through her. And yet she knew it was not really her fault.

Suddenly, she felt bone weary. Sometimes, like now, Maria felt she could no longer go on. That feeling would come on her suddenly, without warning. Weeks might go by, months, even years, when she could push it all to the back of her mind, but it never really went away. Then, one day, for no obvious reason, it would all come flooding back, tormenting her, making her fearful that somehow the evil had found her.

She had woken this morning with a terrible mood of foreboding on her; a kind of premonition, a sense of danger pressing her down. The feeling had been with her all day. Because of it, she had stayed by the window, watching, her eyes rarely leaving that particular place where, fifty years ago, by the light of the moon, she had dug a hole deep enough to bury a man. The thought made her inwardly shiver. It was no man that she had put deep into the earth. No man. No creature. Nothing that had ever possessed a soul. Unless it was a soul that was dark and awful as hell itself.

The hours had passed. She slept, she woke. The sun rose high in the sky; the morning was gone and the daylight lost its lustre, and still she watched. Nothing had moved, only the leaves being blown gently in the breeze. Nothing had changed, save for the buds that were surreptitiously pushing themselves out on the branches and thrusting through the earth, towards the sun. There was no outward sign to warn her of impending tragedy. *Yet Maria knew it was closing in.*

It was some short time later that Maria allowed Emily to help her up the broad handsome stairway. At the top, she looked down, her serious gaze encompassing the splendid ebony hallstand, the old grandfather clock and the deep rich carpet that lay like a crimson sea before them. The gilt-framed oil paintings hanging on the walls represented a small fortune, as did the dark wood antiques that furnished each one of the ten rooms in this grand old house.

'Soon it will all be over. Eighty-three years is a long time to live,' she murmured, feeling Emily's anxious gaze on her, yet not wanting to meet that gaze, in case her own eyes gave away too much.

'Don't talk like that,' Emily pleaded. 'Eighty-three years *is* a long time, of course it is, but you still have your health and strength . . . and you still have *me*.' Emily laughed, but it was a nervous, frightened laugh. Emily's worst nightmare was that Maria would die, and she would be all alone. 'Come on, now, let's get you to bed. It's been a long day.'

The old lady had sensed Emily's fears, so very different from her own, yet just as awesome to Emily. She spoke to her now, her voice quietly reassuring. 'You know you'll always be taken care of, my dear, don't you?' she asked.

'Please . . . you know I don't like you to talk this way.'

'Oh, but I must!' Maria insisted. 'And when I'm gone, you must sell this mausoleum and make a new life for yourself.'

106

Frantic, she grasped the other woman's hands into her own gnarled fingers. 'You must not stay here!' she told her in a chilling voice. 'Do you understand? You must get away from this place . . . far, far away. You will, won't you? Promise me, Emily. I want you to promise me.' She had made a clause in her will, but it suddenly occurred to her that Emily might want to buy back this house where she had been so content.

Emily had been astonished by the old woman's outburst. Firstly, because until this moment Maria had never discussed the possibility of Emily inheriting the house, and, secondly, because of her insistence that it must be sold. Such a beautiful house. Maria had lived here these past fifty years, so why would she be so against Emily remaining here? After all, the two of them had found friendship and solace in this house.

Emily could not fathom Maria's thinking, but then, she *was* very old, and lately her mind had begun to wander. 'Whatever you say,' she assured her. 'Now, please let that be an end to it.'

Emily was further astonished when Maria told her, 'I'll make sure you're well taken care of. You, *and him*. Everything I own will belong to you both one day.' As though she had said more than she intended, she then lapsed into a deep silence.

Emily, though, was greatly intrigued. Was Maria's mind wandering? If not, then who was she referring to when she said, 'you . . . *and him*'? Not the gardener, because Maria had little to do with him. In fact, she had little to do with anyone, and, as far as Emily knew, there was no family – or at least, Maria had never spoken of them. Besides which, in the thirty-six years that she herself had lived here, there had been no letters or communication of any kind, apart from the usual traders and the occasional hawker.

But then again, the old lady was a secretive soul. Look at that old wooden chest that she kept locked in her wardrobe! No doubt it contained papers and belongings of a personal kind – besides that old Bible which Maria loved to peruse but would hide away whenever Emily came near – so maybe there *was* a relative somewhere. Emily thought not, or why had he not kept in touch

107

with such a kindly and delightful person as Maria? No. Emily suspected this 'him' was a figment of her friend's imagination. Still, if it gave her comfort, there was no harm in it. No harm at all.

Unrolling Maria's grey hair, Emily took up the silver-backed brush. 'You're in a strange mood tonight,' she told her.

'Tired, that's what I am,' came the reply. She had said too much and hated herself for alarming her dear companion.

'You do have lovely hair, Maria,' Emily commented. 'Such a shine, and so very soft.' Her own hair was boringly straight, and not so easily manageable.

Maria laughed. 'At my age I might as well be bald!'

'Shame on you!'

'It's true, and you can't deny it,' Maria insisted. 'I'm ready for the knacker's yard.' Inclining her head to one side, she studied herself in the mirror. 'Every day another wrinkle . . . my skin resembles a dried prune. I've got varicose veins and swollen feet, and look!' She pointed at the image in the mirror. 'The bags have fallen so far over my eyes, I can hardly see out.'

'Away with you!' Emily retorted. 'You might be old, and you may have a few aches and pains, the same as the rest of us, but you're certainly not ready for the knacker's yard.'

Shocked to hear Emily say such a thing, Maria turned to stare disapprovingly at her. 'I hope you're not picking up any of my bad habits?' she queried sharply.

Emily made no reply, but when Maria turned away again, she too was smiling. Happen the old lady would think twice before saying such a thing again, she thought fondly.

Friday mornings heralded a special treat for Maria. It was the day when Emily went into Bedford town centre to do whatever shopping had accumulated over the week, and to place the usual grocery order, which was duly delivered later in the day. Before Emily went on her way, she would run a bath full of hot water and help Maria along the landing from her bedroom. Then, with the old lady complaining that 'I'm quite able to wash myself!' and insisting that once Emily had helped her into the bath, she should

'Leave me be . . . come and fetch me in twenty minutes,' and knowing it was useless to argue, yet being always wary of Maria hurting herself, Emily would do as she asked, but leave the door slightly ajar and stand quietly outside until her name was called, or until she felt instinctively that Maria had been in the water long enough.

After the hot bath, when Emily would wash the old lady's iron-grey hair and dry her thoroughly with a large soft towel, Maria would be dressed in a clean wincyette nightgown and warm bathrobe, with fleecy slippers on her feet and a rosy glow to her once handsome face. When the ritual was over, Maria allowed herself to be happily propped up against the feather pillows in her double bed, waiting for Emily to return from the kitchen bearing a large tray, which carried a cup of tea, a lightly boiled egg, two thin slices of toast, and a local newspaper . . . namely the *Bedfordshire Times*. Her spectacles were placed within reach, and Emily would then go about her business in town, waiting only for the arrival of the daily help, in order to issue precise instructions – which were exactly the same as the ones issued the Friday before, and the Friday before that: 'Be sure to keep an eye on Miss Maria. I'll be back as quick as I can.' The girl always did, and Emily always was.

Maria heard the front door bell ring. It was the milkman, come to collect his money. Maria liked to have her bedroom door open. It was open now, and she could clearly distinguish the conversation taking place on the front doorstep. 'Morning . . . nice day.' There was always a pause while he consulted his little notebook. 'That'll be one pound fifty . . . you had two extra pints on Monday.' Mr Barker had a habit of forgetting when Emily ordered less, but he always recalled when she took extra. Another pause while Emily searched in her purse for the loose change. 'I reckon the world's gone mad!' he went on. 'Week before last we had Gorbachev signing for peace in Afghanistan . . . today the newspapers are full of how the US have bombed the Iranian oil base.' Taking the money from Emily's outstretched hand he slipped it into his pocket. 'Ups and downs!' he remarked wisely.

'Can't have one without the other, I suppose.' With that philosophical comment he took his leave.

Upstairs, Maria couldn't help but smile. Mr Barker – who by his own confession had never read a book in his life and accrued all of his knowledge down the pub of a Saturday night, was always putting the world to rights.

A few moments after the milkman had departed, so did Emily. Maria waited for the sound of the front door closing. She heard the tap of Emily's footsteps going down the path and, leaning sideways in her bed, she watched for Emily to come to the edge of the kerb where she could be seen, merrily waving. When Maria waved back, she went quickly on her way.

Today, the sun was glorious. All along the embankment the recently planted flower beds made neat regimental patterns in amongst the decorative street lamps and the lovely overhanging willows, whose branches teased the surface of the water and provided shade for the many ducks and swans that graced the river at this particular stretch. The river and the broad embankment had been one of the reasons why Maria had chosen to settle here. The other reason was that, according to Elizabeth Manners – who had raised Maria's mother Agatha and who had passed on information gleaned from Agatha's late parents, Maria and Ralph – their forefathers had originated from this county.

Arriving here at the age of thirty-eight, recently bereaved, alone and afraid, and pursued by some malign force beyond her understanding, Maria had found a small measure of peace, albeit a shallow and uneasy one.

'Good morning.' The chirpy voice drew Maria's attention. It was the young woman whom Maria had employed to help out with various duties about the house. 'I'll be in the back garden,' she told Maria. 'There's a pile of clean washing needs pegging out. If I put them out now, they'll be dry before I leave.' She was a chubby little thing, with a broad smile and a mass of blonde hair piled up on her head and tied with a gaudy pink ribbon. She had on a pair of low-heeled shoes and a dark ankle-length dress which was oddly old-fashioned. Emily had been unsure of her at first, but domestic help was hard to find, besides which, Sally had proven herself to be hard working and always prompt on reporting for duty. 'I thought I'd best tell you, because it's no good you shouting or knocking the floor with that there stick.' She pointed to the walking cane which Emily insisted Maria should keep beside her bed in case she needed to summon her companion from the drawing room directly beneath. Maria had scorned the idea, saying, 'I'm not so old and senile that I can't find my way down the stairs, or raise my voice if needs be!' She had never used the stick. She had no intentions of ever doing so.

'Don't you concern yourself about me, young lady,' Maria remonstrated with a firm expression. 'Just get on with your work and leave me in peace. I shall be out of my bed within the hour,' she declared, before adding, 'when I will expect a fresh brew of tea, and the kitchen to be sparkling clean.'

The girl gave no answer, but frowned slightly, making a wry expression as she turned away. Unperturbed, Maria enjoyed her breakfast, before pushing the tray to one side and opening the newspaper, which she spread out in front of her and perused in great detail. She enjoyed the local news. She did not use her spectacles as Emily had directed. Maria believed that once you began to rely on such things, it was only a matter of time before you became totally dependent on them. Presently, you wouldn't be able to see your hand in front of your face unless it was through a pair of spectacles!

It was the heading that caught her eye. She looked closer, reading: 'LOCAL MAN TAKES NEW BRIDE TO THE FAR SIDE OF THE WORLD.'

Intrigued, Maria began reading it, a smile on her face; it was always a joy to hear of a young couple starting out in life together. But, as she read on, the smile slid from her face. Every word seared itself into her mind, heightening the terror there.

The article showed the wedding picture of a young man and his bride. The bride was in her wedding gown, the groom in his formal suit. They made a striking pair, she being small, fair haired and exceptionally lovely . . . he, a tall handsome man with dark eyes and a mop of unruly black hair.

The heading referred to their planned honeymoon, which was to be in Perth, Australia. The young woman's name was Catherine. Her new husband was called Matthew Abel Slater. *Matthew Abel Slater*!

At first, Maria was too numb with shock to rationalise her thoughts. All she could think of were the two people she had seen buried in a churchyard in Australia fifty years before – her own sister and brother-in-law, caught in a bushfire that killed them both . . . Lizzie and her husband, Abel Slater . . . *Abel Slater*! Dear God. Could it be a coincidence that this young man's name was also Abel Slater? And that his first name was Matthew, the name of her own uncle? She reminded herself that the name was not uncommon. Yet, her instincts told her that this young man may well be part of the awful legacy handed down to her. A legacy created by forces beyond her understanding.

Suddenly the years sped away. The panic was back, the terror of it all. In her mind's eye she saw three children playing around the gravestones whilst their mother, Agatha, placed flowers on her husband's grave . . . and the children, two girls and a boy, a small boy, hiding behind the headstone. The youngest girl ran away to hide. The other was the seeker. She, Maria . . . was the seeker. For some reason she would never understand, she was meant to see the tragedy unfold.

The horror was as real in Maria's mind now as it was all those years ago. She could see it all now through the same eyes, *the eyes that had seen the headstone fall in that moment before it actually did.* Eyes that had stared into the boy's own terrified face and seen it all . . . *even before it happened!* She could hear herself screaming, yet even as the headstone came crashing down she was powerless to move. She had willed it! *She had made it happen!* She knew it then; she knew it now. At the time she did not know why. But later, it had all become clear.

On the liner she had tried to dispose of the evil thing that had been placed in her care. With her own eyes she saw the tallow doll sink beneath the waves and drown. Yet when she opened the chest on arriving at this house, *the doll was there* . . . nestling in amongst the precious items that had been her grandmother's! Horrified, Maria had thrown it into the fire; watched it melt as the flames licked about it. The next morning there it lay in the ashes – whole, unblemished, seeming to smile at her. That was when she had gone into the garden and buried it deep, afterwards planting a sapling over it, hoping the invasive roots would spear the doll's venomous heart.

Fifty years – fifty long years – it had lain dormant. But now . . . what now? This young man, Matthew Abel Slater? According to the article, he lived some thirty miles from Bedford. Maria wondered why she had never heard of him before. But then, why should she? He lived in the country. She lived in the town. It was only natural their paths had not crossed. Could he possibly be the son of Maria's own nephew, whom she had left in the Perth orphanage? Yes, it could well be. All things were possible. All the same, she would not rest until she knew for sure one way or the other.

In her heart, Maria feared the worst. She knew also that there was another who would not rest. *Not while there were males of the Ryan lineage still breathing.* Oh, but wait! Wait, Maria . . . think! *How could it know?* 'Because it watches!' she told herself in shocked tones. It may be entombed deep in the dark, clammy earth, but it watched, and it listened. It read her mind. It was reading her mind now; it knew her thoughts, sensed her terror. Shh . . . shh! Don't let your fear show, Maria. *Don't let it hear you think!*

Sally had pegged out the washing and was crossing the hallway to fetch the vacuum cleaner from the big understairs cupboard, when she was startled by the commotion – first the stick being frantically pounded against the floor and then the old lady's voice, feeble, desperate. In a moment the girl was racing up the stairs. She did not stop until she went bursting into Maria's bedroom. The sight that greeted her turned her heart over. Maria was standing by the bed-head, oddly stooped as though two unseen hands were pressing her down. She was clinging to the bed-head, the walking cane at her feet, her face drained white and a look of abject terror in her surprised eyes.

She was violently trembling, making small unintelligible sounds in the back of her throat.

Shocked, the girl rushed forward, wrapping her arms round the frail shivering figure and easing her into the bed. 'Come on, now, gently does it,' she coaxed.

Inside the girl was in turmoil. She had never before come across this kind of situation and the prospect of seeing someone die before her eyes was terrifying. Yet, as she enticed the old lady into the bed, her voice was surprisingly calm. She felt Maria resisting. 'No, no, sweetheart . . . you must get into bed. Then I'll go and call the doctor,' she told her gently. She didn't reveal that the doctor's number was always placed in a prominent position on the hall stand, whenever Emily went out.

At that point, Maria drew on every last ounce of strength. 'There must be no doctor!' she said quietly. What ailed her was not of this world. 'I want you to do something for me, child,' she said, her vivid blue eyes intent on the girl's face.

'Only if you get into bed,' replied the girl, astonished that the old lady had so determinedly regained her composure. Maria's face was still white as chalk and she was still trembling, but her speech was lucid now, and she had a certain authority that must be acknowledged. 'Into bed,' the girl insisted, 'then I'll listen to what it is you want me to do.'

'Has she been all right, Sally?' Emily asked, putting her shopping bags to the floor and taking off her jacket.

'Oh yes. No trouble at all,' lied the girl. She had strict instructions to say nothing about the earlier incident, and Maria had rewarded her well for her silence; even now the wad of notes could be felt, warm and secure, in Sally's pocket. She had given her another set of instructions also. Sally had been astonished on reading what Maria had written down. She thought it a strange and unusual request, but she would carry out the instruction to the letter. After all, she had been generously paid, almost a month's wages, and who knows what little titbits might be offered if she was to worm her way into the old biddy's affections.

All the same, what the old lady had asked her to do was odd. *Very* odd, and it occurred to the girl that she would have to be careful not to get caught up in things that might bring trouble to her own front door!

Upstairs, Maria could not take her eyes from the wedding picture. The longer she looked on the young man, Matthew Abel Slater, the more she was reminded of how her mother Agatha described her own father, Ralph Ryan . . . 'tall and lithe of limb . . . dark hair and eyes . . . a proud upright bearing.' Elizabeth Manners had kept alive Agatha's memory of her father. Now, when Maria gazed at the picture, it revived all that she had learned about her grandfather. Her every instinct told her that here . . . here was the last remaining male link in the Ryan chain. With every bone in her body, she knew that the young man was in mortal danger. But she couldn't be certain. She *had* to be certain! Perhaps she was just confused. After all, she was very old, and lately she was prone to imagining things.

Hearing Emily coming up the stairs and calling her name, Maria quickly folded the newspaper, tucking it beneath her pillow. Suddenly a strange feeling came over her; she felt dizzy, light headed. It seemed as though she was moving out of herself, not in the room at all, but outside, looking in. A cold hand grasped at her heart. She recalled the same sensation only once, many many years before . . . on the day her young brother was crushed to his death.

Maria opened her mouth to speak. She heard herself call Emily's name, but the voice was not hers. She was compelled to look towards the doorway. Relief surged through her as Emily came into the room. *But then something happened to make her question her own sanity.* The familiar figure of Emily began to change. It became taller, slimmer, the brown bobbed hair was now rich and dark. She came forward; there was no limp, no blemish on the face, only the most stunning beauty, *and an aura of terrible evil.* Maria could hear herself crying out, calling for Emily. The apparition kept on gliding towards her – it was as though she was seeing everything in slow motion. The full inviting mouth opened, laughing, and then it spoke!

When Emily reached her side, Maria was quiet but visibly shaken, staring at her with wild, frightened eyes. Later, when the doctor left and his patient was calmer, Emily made up a bed in the same room. She would not leave her friend's side – not until she was certain the old lady was fully recovered.

It was in the dark early hours when Maria woke. Her first fears were for Emily. Had the evil discovered that she, too, carried the Ryan blood in her veins? The thought was chilling. In her mind's eye she saw it all. *The apparition . . . the tallow doll.* Its mocking words hummed in her head, swimming into every corner of her being . . . '*Through the flames . . . eye to eye*'. What did it mean? *What did it mean?*

Exhausted and alone in her terror, Maria glanced lovingly towards the narrow bed and Emily sleeping there. 'At least you won't come to harm,' she murmured. 'I believe you will be safe . . . as long as you don't know the truth about me . . . about yourself. I pray to God you will *never* know.'

The cold clammy air pressed in. With a shock, she realised again. It was all around. Possessed of the power to move in and out of her senses at will. Don't let it know your thoughts, Maria. *Don't let it know your thoughts!*

Chapter Six

'Oh, Matt, I do love it here!' It was the day before Cathy and Matt were due to fly home. They had seen and done everything, and now they were on the train going to Fremantle. The journey from Perth took approximately half an hour, according to whether they encountered any stray animals on the line.

'I'll certainly be sorry to leave,' Matt replied. 'It's so different to anything back home.'

'I'll be glad to see Dad, though,' Cathy remarked. 'I miss him.'

'No doubt he misses you.' Shuffling along the wooden seat to make room for two young people carrying surf-boards, Matt promised, 'We'll come back, though. And when we do, we'll try and persuade your dad to come along.'

Cathy laughed at that. 'You won't persuade him out of England. You know how he's always saying he travelled the world when he was in the Navy? And all he wants now is to sit in front of an English fireplace, with his pipe and slippers.'

Matt didn't argue. He knew it would be the devil's own job trying to bring Bill to the other side of the world. 'Pity,' he teased, 'the two of us could have tried our hand at surfing.' He winked at Cathy and she giggled. Then, much to the amusement of an old woman with a smoking pipe and a big straw hat, he kissed her full on the mouth.

'Honeymooners, ain't yer?' Her wide grin revealed a mouthful of rose-pink gums. When Cathy blushed to the roots of her hair, she chuckled and puffed at her pipe, blowing out the smoke until it billowed all around and hid her from view. When she saw Matt smiling, she winked a cheeky eye. 'Mek the most of it,' she said wisely, peering through the smoke. ' 'cause young love don't last too long.'

The train pulled in and the passengers clambered out. Cathy and Matt went towards the town centre hand in hand. 'The receptionist at the hotel said they'd spruced Fremantle up since the Americas Cup was run from here.' Fishing the camera out of her shoulder bag she clicked open the shutter and took a picture of Matt close up. 'I can see right up your nostrils,' she laughed, quickly replacing the camera in her bag before he could snatch it from her. He had an aversion to having his picture taken, especially close up.

The little square was another picture. There were shops selling all manner of wares, raised flower beds and cafés with colourful blinds over the windows, and the whole delightful area was teeming with people. 'Let's sit here.' Dropping her bag to the ground, Cathy sat on one of the many chairs situated around numerous tables. 'An ice-cold drink, then we'll explore. What do you say?' Shielding her eyes, she glanced up at him. The sweat was running down her back, and it was such bliss to throw off her shoes and stretch out her legs. Matt and she had covered many miles since arriving here. The first three days had been used up in pursuit of his father's origins. All of his enquiries had come to nothing, and he had been bitterly disappointed. Yet he had not allowed his disappointment to overshadow his and Cathy's honeymoon.

Matt didn't need asking twice. 'My tongue's stuck to my throat,' he confessed. 'I have to admit I can't stand this heat.'

'That's 'cause yer a bloody pom, and yer ain't used to it!' The old man had watched them approach and now he shifted his chair a little nearer. 'If yer ain't used to it, the heat can shrivel you up,' he warned. He was shrivelled himself, brown and leathery, with blue eyes that twinkled with merriment. His shirt was open to the waist and his broad-brimmed hat was bedecked with corks – 'To keep the bloody flies off,' he explained, when he saw Cathy admiring it. 'Here! Try it on,' he suggested, snatching it from his head and holding it out to her. The brim was stained with oil and the inside had a thick grimy ring round it. But Cathy tried it on anyway. 'Suits yer!' he chuckled. 'Yer should get yerself one.'

Returning the hat, Cathy told him they were going home tomorrow, but that, 'We intend to come back some day.' The old fellow thought they should drink to that, and Matt ordered them each a long, cool lemonade.

'Have yer been to the lunatic asylum yet?' the old fellow asked. When they said no, he shook his head, saying solemnly, 'Yer can't go home without seeing that.' He explained how the early convicts had built most of the buildings in Fremantle . . . 'The warehouses and the prison . . . all of it.' He chuckled. 'Don't seem right, does it? Especially when a lot of the poor buggers went mad while helping to build their own asylum.' He told them how the building had fallen into dilapidation, but then was restored some years ago. 'It's an art and craft museum now. A beautiful building. It'll be a real pity if you go home without seeing it.'

When the old fellow had gone, Matt went to pay for the drinks. 'Off home, then, are you?' The waitress was a chatty soul. Seeing how Matt was surprised that she knew they were going home tomorrow, she laughed. 'I'm nosy by nature,' she explained, nodding towards the table where Cathy was waiting. 'I overheard you talking to the young lady.' He looked puzzled, thinking she meant Cathy. 'She's right, you know. You ought to see the lunatic asylum before you go back.'

Matt smiled, not fully understanding. 'Oh, we will,' he assured her, 'but it was the old fellow who told us about the asylum.'

'Old fellow?' Her eyebrows drew into a frown as she glanced at where Cathy was seated. 'What old fellow?'

Matt nodded. 'The one who was sitting with us when you brought the drinks to the table.'

She didn't reply for a minute. Instead, she stared at him, then she glanced again at Cathy. 'Aw, right, matey!' she said, her face opening with feigned enlightenment as she pretended to recall the old man. She gave him his change and watched him walk away with Cathy by his side. Turning to her colleague, she shook her head in exasperation. 'If you ask me, they should keep *him* in that asylum.'

119

'Oh, why's that?'

'Because there weren't no old fellow sitting at their table. I've had my eyes on them all along.' She pursed her lips and made a sucking sound. 'You know me. I just thought he was a big handsome hunk, that's all. But he's not right in the head, I reckon . . . 'cause there weren't no old fellow . . . just him, with that fair-haired sheila, and another woman. A real looker, that one was – jet-black hair and dark sinister eyes! It were *her* that told him about the asylum.' She nodded towards Matt's figure as it went away. 'If you ask me, the sun's fried his brains.'

Her colleague laughed. 'And if you ask *me*, I'd say you were at the grog last night.'

The other woman looked round. 'I know what I saw,' she said firmly. 'There was him . . . and two women. And I ain't touched a drop o' grog since I fell over that garden wall and split my arse open.' At that they both burst out laughing and the incident with Matt was already forgotten.

The receptionist was fresh and pretty, and eager to help. 'Oh, no,' she said in reply to Cathy's question, 'There's little left of the old asylum.' She went on to describe exactly what the old fellow had told them, that the asylum had housed many convicts who had 'gone over the edge'. She explained how all manner of bad and pitiful creatures had gone to the gallows from there. 'Mostly men,' she said, 'but there *were* a few women. The one who comes immediately to mind was a young woman by the name of Rebecca Norman . . . a wild and spirited creature, by all accounts, darkly beautiful and mad as they came.'

Cathy was fascinated. 'What was her crime?'

The young woman got out of her seat and walked across the spacious reception area. There were shelves all around, laden with books and leaflets. Choosing a particular brochure, she handed it to Cathy. 'According to this, Rebecca Norman and her grandmother were accused of witchcraft and murder. Her grandmother was sentenced to death. Because of her age, the girl escaped the death sentence.' Pointing to the brochure, she went on, 'It's all in there . . . the history of this place, and a few sketchy stories taken from the old ledgers.'

'Is there nothing left of the old asylum, apart from its shell?' Matt was intrigued.

'Oh, yes.' Gesturing towards an opening at the far end of the reception area, she said, 'There are things to see through there. And right at the end of the corridor you'll find that one of the cells has been preserved. Some say it's the very cell where Rebecca Norman was held, the night before they took her to the gallows.'

All along the corridor, encased in glass-fronted cupboards, artefacts from the Asylum's history were displayed: inmates' uniforms, kitchen utensils, leg-irons, strait-jackets and other horrendous instruments of punishment. And, just as the receptionist had described, one tiny cell, untouched for over a hundred years. Even the door was formidable. Thick and heavy, with a small window covered by a trap door, it swung open to reveal a tiny room. Matt peered inside, but made no effort to go in. 'God! It smells rank in there.'

Cathy went inside. Matt was right. It *did* have a strange smell. She couldn't quite put her finger on it. 'I expect it's damp,' she told him, going deeper into the room. A strange feeling came over her, a feeling of being isolated, totally and utterly alone. The air in here was incredibly chilling; it made her catch her breath. Wrapping her arms round herself, and hunching up to ward off the cold, Cathy looked around.

The cell was tiny. There was a small window in the far wall, and a soak-away grating in the floor. Against the nearside wall stood a narrow iron bed, and beside the bed was a bucket. The walls were covered in a trellis of thin wooden slats, most of which had rotted away to reveal what looked like wattle and daub beneath. Cathy ran her hand over the wall. It struck oddly warm. The warmth pulsed through her, shocking her to the core. In that moment she was compelled to slide her hand between the wooden slats. There was something there! She drew the object out, wiped the cobwebs from it and what she saw made her gasp with astonishment. 'It's a doll!' A strange feeling of elation came over her. Standing there in that cell which was unchanged after more than a hundred years, where she had been shivering with cold only a minute before and now she was warm, Cathy almost believed she had gone back in time. It was the strangest thing.

'What in God's name is it?' Matt stared at the object with disgust.

'It's a doll.' Stroking her fingers over the coarse features, Cathy told him, 'I think it's beautiful.' She pressed it to herself, afraid that he might suddenly snatch it away.

'*Ugly*, that's what it is.'

'Well, you'd better get used to it, because I'm keeping it.'

'Shouldn't you show it to the curator?'

'No. He'll only put in a glass case.' Hugging it close she pleaded, 'It's a wonderful memento of our honeymoon. You won't really mind if I keep it, will you, Matt?'

'And if I did, would it make any difference?'

'No.'

'All right. Let's get out of here. This place gives me the creeps.'

Outside in the brilliant sunshine he shivered.

'You're not cold, are you?'

'No.' He chuckled. 'But I think somebody's just walked over my grave.'

The hotel was a short walk from the station. A lovely place, with a cool spacious foyer decorated with abstract paintings and adorned with pink velvet drapes, it was a welcome oasis after the searing heat outside. A short exchange with the blonde-haired girl behind the desk, then Cathy and Matt went straight to their room.

'God, this heat!' As they came into the room, Matt plucked the shirt from his back. 'A drink first, then a shower,' he said, picking up the bedside phone. 'What do you want from the bar?'

Cathy was so engrossed in examining the doll, she didn't hear him at first. When he repeated his question, she looked up, startled. 'Oh, a jug of ice-cold water, I think.'

'I hope you're not going to let that thing come between us,' he teased.

While they were waiting for the drinks to arrive, Matt decided he'd have his shower right away. 'I feel like I've been in a Turkish bath.'

Cathy too was hot and uncomfortable. 'We'll shower together,' she said. And they did. They also made love right there beneath the running water. It was exhilarating.

Later, after collecting the drinks from outside the door, Matt had his arm round Cathy, and Cathy had the doll near by. 'I'm sorry you couldn't find out anything about your father's background,' she said sincerely.

'So am I, sweetheart,' he replied thoughtfully. He had hoped to discover at least something, but, like his father before him, he had been disillusioned.

'What now?' Cathy asked.

'Home, that's what,' he replied light-heartedly. 'I'm taking you home, Mrs Slater.'

Cathy snuggled up to him. 'Mrs Slater,' she murmured, contentedly smiling, 'I'm still not used to it.'

They talked and they planned, and the evening wore on. 'Bed!' Matt looked at the clock and was surprised to see that it was almost midnight. 'We need an early start in the morning.'

It had been a long day and Cathy was bone tired. 'And I haven't even started to pack,' she said sleepily. When Matt suggested they could do it in the morning, she was happy to climb into bed beside him, safe in his arms and deeply in love. 'Goodnight, Mr Slater,' she whispered, turning out the light.

'Goodnight, *Mrs* Slater,' he returned, kissing her tenderly on the mouth. To tell the truth he wasn't sorry to be going home.

It was in the dark early hours when Matt was woken. He hadn't felt Cathy get out of bed, but when he reached out and she wasn't there, he was filled with a feeling of dread. 'Cathy!' Calling her name, he clicked on the light and swung his legs over the bed-edge. He was still half-asleep when out of the corner of his eye he saw her.

With a look of sheer terror on her face, she was standing in the darkest corner of the room, pressed hard to the wall, her arms up

123

over her face and head as though protecting herself from an attacker. When he slid his arms round her, murmuring words of endearment and assuring her she was safe, she resisted at first. Then she sobbed as though her heart would break. Somehow he coaxed her back to bed, but it was a full hour before she fell asleep, a full hour during which time she clung to him with such terror that he was desperately afraid for her.

In that time when he held her close, she stared at the open window, her stone-grey eyes brilliant with fear, her whole body gripped in a violent fit. Later, Matt recalled how the breeze through the open window fluttered the net curtains and cooled the room. The air-conditioning was full on, causing him to shiver, yet Cathy was bathed in a river of sweat, her body burning in his arms, the awful nightmare still on her. Now and then he gently called her name, but she made no response, her eyes still turned to the window, transfixed in horror. After a while she was comforted and reassured by his voice, secure in his embrace.

When at last she was limp and still in his arms, he laid her gently back against the pillow and covered her over. She never spoke to him, never once looked at him while she was in the throes of what he took to be a nightmare.

In the morning it was as though it had never happened. 'I must remember to get enough magazines for the journey,' she said. 'I'll get them from the airport, they always have a good selection there.' She bustled about, stuffing yesterday's dirty washing into a carrier bag before laying it in the suitcase. 'I'm glad we had our washing laundered each day,' she told him. She sang while she emptied the toiletries from the bathroom, and while she was rushing about, she occasionally took time off to hug and kiss him.

Matt was amazed. Cathy was her usual bright cheery self, teasing and tormenting. And he was loath to raise the issue of what had happened in the dark hours. When he asked her whether she had slept well, she hesitated and, just for a brief moment, he thought she would recall the nightmare. But then the frown went from her eyes and they were once again clear and untroubled. 'I am a bit tired,' she admitted, 'but I can sleep on the plane.'

Relieved, he said nothing. But it bothered him.

Chapter Seven

Matt shifted uncomfortably in his seat. He was tired, aching to be home, wanting to resume his everyday life and looking forward to the future, now that he was a married man. Not a great traveller, he was secretly afraid of being strapped in an aircraft many miles from the surface of the earth, with only clouds, fresh air and unpredictable engines to keep them from plummeting to the ground. He had told no one of his fears, not even his new bride. He was ashamed to admit it. Men were not supposed to have fears.

'Are you comfortable, sir?' The air hostess smiled down on him, her small firm breast rubbing against his shoulder when the plane lurched.

'I'm fine, thank you,' he lied. He watched her as she moved away, his dark eyes always appreciative at the sight of a lovely woman. His gaze swept her from head to toe, from the burnished sheen of her coiled hair, to the slim shapely ankles. In that moment before she went into the cabin and drew the curtain behind her, she turned her full magnificent smile on him. Embarrassed, he grinned and turned away.

The flight from Perth, Australia was a long and tiring one. Already they had been in the air for over nineteen hours, not counting the hour's stopover in the airport at Singapore. As though reading his mind, the captain spoke through the tannoy, his distorted nasal tones advising the passengers that the plane would be landing at Heathrow, London in forty-five minutes. 'Thank God for that,' Matthew muttered beneath his breath, 'it can't be too soon for me!' He would not completely relax inside until his feet touched firm ground.

He turned his head to glance on Cathy's lovely face and a deep sense of pride surged through him. He knew how fortunate he was. From the very first moment he had set eyes on her, he was lost. He vividly recalled the day. It was a wet and windy afternoon in November, some three years ago. Still shocked and deeply angered by the accident that had recently taken his father's life, he might himself have walked straight underneath a lorry, had it not been for Cathy's warning shout. Certainly he had neither seen nor heard the articulated lorry as it thundered towards him. He had thought then how ironic it would be if he, too, met with a grisly end, just like his father.

Cathy had been his saviour. She had come to be everything to him, and he could not envisage life without her. Now he gazed on her loveliness, his great need for her rising inside him. He thought how like a child she seemed, so small in that wide, encompassing seat, with her rich corn-coloured hair smoothly falling to the slim, straight shoulders, and the attractive classical features of her face so exquisitely lovely in repose. He imagined her eyes looking up at him, grey and striking, speckled with black; eyes that could turn his heart over, sometimes fiery with the rush of passion, sometimes softly enchanting, sometimes grey-steel with anger and impatience, but always uniquely beautiful. Like all women, Cathy was a creature of many moods. She was funny and serious, she was arrogant, impossible, engaging and often hard to understand. She was infuriating and wonderful. She was all he desired in life, and he thanked God for her. Suddenly, he could not resist the urge to reach out and touch her. Tenderly he traced his finger over her lips. When she stirred and opened her eyes, he smiled down on her.

'All right, sweetheart?' She nodded, her eyes still glazed with sleep, her senses not yet fully awakened. 'Won't be long before we land,' he told her in a quiet voice.

'*How* long?' She fidgeted and closed her eyes again. It had seemed like an endless journey.

'Forty-five minutes, the captain said.' Matt saw that she was not listening. He grinned and shook his head.

Cathy shifted, making herself more comfortable. Her face was lifted to the window. The afternoon light streamed in, her hair shone like gold and the suntanned skin was smooth, soft as velvet. Matt could not draw his gaze from her loveliness, nor could he resist the urge to kiss the full soft lips that were partly open, always inviting. In the instant he pressed his mouth to hers, she pushed up to him, winding her arms round his neck, pulling him down. He drew away, gently laughing, acutely aware of the man seated to his right, and whose curiosity was evident by the way he reached across Matt and feigned to look out of the window. Turning away to settle into sleep once more, Cathy also chuckled. She knew how best to tease him. He was easily embarrassed, and she loved him for it.

As she let the weariness ebb over her, Cathy's foot touched against the small vinyl bag lying on the floor. Heeling it beneath the seat, she was pleasantly reminded of their trip to Australia. She would never forget the marvellous sights they had seen there, nor the experiences they had encountered. *There was one particular experience that would stay with her to the end of her days.* Thinking on it now ... the brooding atmosphere in that tiny cell ... a strangeness came over her, a kind of deep euphoria ... just like when her probing fingers had closed around the tallow doll which was hidden in the emaciated wall padding. She smiled. *The doll was hers now.* Her smile deepened. She glanced sideways at her unsuspecting husband. *He did not see how Cathy's grey eyes seemed to change, growing darker, blacker, infused with long-ago hatred.*

Settling back in his seat, Matt closed his eyes. He was curiously lulled by the monotonous drone of the engines. It had been a wonderful honeymoon, everything he had hoped for, and more. His thoughts were drawn back to Fremantle and Perth. He had no recollection of his early years in that amazing land; he knew it only through his father's memories. Matt had always vowed that one day he would go to Australia and see for himself the places his father had described so vividly ... the orphanage where Abel Slater was raised, and the land he had first farmed, the round house overlooking the beach, the grand awesome buildings which

128

the convicts had erected so many years ago . . . the prison, the old lunatic asylum.

Cathy and Matt had visited them all, and they were overawed by the splendid sights and excursions which had enriched their time there. The whole experience had given Matt a deeper sense of his own family history. Yet, while he would always be thankful that he had seen these places where his own father grew from boy to manhood, Matt, like his father before him, was saddened by the fact that all knowledge of past generations was lost for ever. It had been his father's greatest regret. It was his also. And it was a strange disturbing thing, because it seemed as though someone had deliberately obliterated all evidence that might have allowed a wider and more thorough investigation into the past; even the orphanage records were 'lost' many years ago. There was no explanation. The records were simply missing.

All of Abel Slater's enquiries, and now Matthew's, had come to a dead end. There was nothing else now but for Matt to cherish his father's memories, and to pray that he and Cathy would produce a son to carry on the name. Matt consoled himself with the fact that his *own* son, God willing, would at least have two generations of history to draw on. The thought gave Matt a great deal of comfort.

'Sorry, mate, I can't stay and talk today,' Bill apologised. 'I'm collecting my daughter and son-in-law from the airport.' He swung the parcel into his van and slammed shut the doors. 'See you next week,' he called, clambering into the driver's seat. The engine had been left running, so he shifted it into gear and drove away, keeping his speed down to a steady ten miles an hour through the industrial estate.

Once out on the main road, he pointed the van in the direction of Bedfordshire, and put his toe down. He would soon be home, washed and changed, and on his way to the airport, 'If you don't kill yourself first!' he muttered, when a lorry pulled out in front of him, forcing him to slow down. But the traffic wasn't heavy, and he quickly picked up speed.

In less than two hours after leaving the industrial estate in Birmingham, Bill drew up outside his modest little house. Letting himself in, he dropped the van keys on to a shelf near the front door. After making himself a cheese sandwich and wolfing it down with a mug of tea, he bathed and changed, and was on his way out, this time driving Matt's car, which had been parked in the garage the whole time Cathy and he had been away.

Groaning when a sharp pain stabbed at his chest, Bill chuckled wryly. 'Serves you right, you silly old bugger! You should have taken your time eating that sandwich, you know how prone you are to indigestion!'

It seemed an age before he arrived at the airport, but once there he had little difficulty in parking, though there were people with trolleys pushing and shoving their way in and out of the airport, and taxis by the dozen queuing up on the kerbside.

Rushing into the arrival lounge, he saw from the overhead screens that the plane from Perth had been in for almost an hour. Pushing through the crowd, he searched the many faces, hoping he hadn't somehow missed Cathy and Matt, and cursing himself for taking on that last job. 'Shouldn't have done that last delivery,' he muttered, still frantically searching. 'But if you hadn't done it, they'd have found somebody else.' He was the first to recognise that the competition on deliveries was fierce. Let a company down just once, and they would probably never ask you again.

His eyes lit up on hearing Cathy call out, 'Dad! . . . Dad!' He swung round. In the surging throng he had missed them.

Now, when Cathy left Matt's side and came running towards him, Bill Barrington hurried to meet her. Two weeks his daughter had been gone; two long weeks when he had missed her far more than he had anticipated. Since Doreen had walked out on him and their darling daughter some ten years before, he had tried so hard not to lean too heavily on the girl. He liked to think he had done a good job of raising her. Now, as she threw herself into his arms, it was like a flood of sunshine had brightened his life.

'Did you miss me, Dad?' she asked, curving her arm into his, her mischievous grey eyes smiling up at him.

'Of course not!' he exclaimed, a returning twinkle in his eye. 'What makes you think I'd miss you, eh?' She would never know how much, he thought. 'You've deserted your old dad now . . . Mrs Slater!' he teased. 'You've your own man to take care of.' He added in a more serious voice. 'I expect I shall have to find myself a good woman now, somebody to fill the space you've left behind.'

For a moment, and in spite of his ready smile, Cathy sensed the very real loneliness in her father's words, though she knew he would deny it to the end. She had never really understood why her mother had walked out on them. A letter had arrived a few days after, but as soon as he read it, her father threw it into the fire. That same night she heard him crying himself to sleep. She suspected the letter might have mentioned a lover. Cathy had never forgiven her mother. She never would. Her father was a fine man; he had been a good husband as far as she could tell, an excellent father and a conscientious provider, having run his own modest delivery service for as far back as she could remember.

'Welcome home, Matt.' Cathy's father kept one arm round his daughter while extending his other arm to shake his son-in-law by the hand. 'Look at the pair of you,' he laughed, glancing from one to the other, 'brown as berries and looking disgustingly healthy. Married life suits you, that's for sure.' An expression of confusion shaped his face. 'I thought May was coming up to the *winter* season in Australia?' He began manoeuvring the cumbersome trolley along, still holding Cathy, and his eyes on Matt, who was helping to keep the trolley in a true direction.

Matt nodded. 'You thought right,' he confirmed, 'the weather was beginning to deteriorate when we left. But it's still in the eighties.'

'Did you have a good time?'

'Fantastic. You wouldn't believe it.'

'We'll talk later,' interrupted Bill as they joined the queue at the parking-ticket desk. People were jostling for space, and in the background could be heard the intermittent announcements. 'It's like bedlam here!' he groaned, digging into his back trouser pocket and withdrawing a small folded ticket which, together with a ten pound note, he handed to the clerk. 'Let's get the cases loaded first.' He looked at Cathy. 'Hungry, are you?'

'No, I just want to get home and soak in a hot bath,' she replied. Suddenly, she felt exhausted and curiously depressed. She supposed it must be the long flight. The airport was so crowded. She was surprised to feel herself beginning to panic. When her father pushed on ahead, she pressed closer to Matt.

'We'll be home soon enough, sweetheart,' Matt told her. He had seen Cathy nervously glancing about. That was not like her. It worried him. In fact, he had been concerned about her more than once in these past few days. But then, they were not used to the searing heat of Australia, and it was likely Cathy may have been affected by it. Still, in a couple of hours they should be home, providing the motorway was not too congested with traffic.

It was six thirty p.m. by the time Cathy's father nosed the car down the motorway slip road. 'Looks like we've missed the tail end of the rush hour,' Matt commented. He was glad that Cathy's father had refused his offer to drive. It was far more agreeable just to lean back in this big comfortable car, relax and stretch out his long legs. A glance in the back seat told him that Cathy had already curled up in the corner, her eyes closed and a look of contentment on her face.

He smiled when he noticed how she was cradling the small vinyl bag to her chest. He knew she had the doll in there. He didn't like the thing, and he could not understand what possessed Cathy to want the wax image of an old woman. He thought it the ugliest thing he had ever seen. Memories came pouring back. Recollections of the day when Cathy discovered the doll. Now, when Bill enquired about the places they had seen, Matt spoke the first thing that came to mind. 'One place I would rather *not* have seen was the old lunatic asylum.'

'Oh, why's that?' Bill swore under his breath when a red Porsche overtook him on the inside. 'Bloody yuppies!' he snapped. 'We've *them* to thank for the soaring house prices . . . greedy grasping buggers. Thatcher's got a lot to answer for.'

'Aw, she's not all bad,' Matt remarked.

'Aye, well.' The older man glanced sideways at Matt. 'You were telling me about the old asylum. Not one of your favourite memories, I take it?'

'The lunatic asylum used to house mad convicts years ago,' Matt explained. 'Now it's been turned into a museum and craft centre.' Matt was relieved the subject had moved on. He sensed his father-in-law was about to embark on a long tirade about the woman he loved to hate. Bill Barrington made no secret of his belief that it was Prime Minister Margaret Thatcher and her financial policies that had created this new breed of the 'grab now and pay later brigade'.

'Convicts, you say? How old is it, then, this lunatic asylum,?' Bill's attention was wandering. Intrigued by a dark hatchback that had been behind them all the way from the airport, it occurred to him that the driver seemed to keep exactly the same distance all the time – even when he himself either slowed down or accelerated. Agitated, he wanted the car to overtake, but it sat behind him, like a shadow on his tail.

Matt saw his father-in-law glancing into the wing mirror, a look of irritation on his face. Inquisitive, he turned in his seat and looked at the car behind. His glance met that of the driver, who seemed surprised and oddly embarrassed. Suddenly, the hatch-back gathered speed and went by them at an alarming rate; in a matter of seconds it was out of sight.

Turning off the motorway, the driver of the hatchback pulled into a layby and took out a pack of cigarettes. Lighting one up, he puffed on it for a while. He was annoyed, angry with himself. Flicking the stub out of the window, he coughed and grumbled, 'You'd best give these buggers up, before they ruin your lungs!' Taking a notepad from the glove compartment, he scanned the instructions there. 'You're a bloody fool, Tomlinson! The old lady warned you not to arouse their suspicions!'

After a while, he dropped the notepad on to the passenger seat, nosed the car back on to the motorway and drove like a maniac until he caught sight of Matt's car. He then slowed down and kept a discreet distance between them. 'If you blow this one, you blow next month's mortgage!' he muttered, darting behind a lorry when he feared he might be seen.

Bill half-turned to Matt, reminding him, 'You were saying?'

In as brief and concise a manner as possible, Matt went on to explain how the lunatic asylum . . . 'a grand old building' . . . was built in the 1860s by prisoners transported from England. 'It was a huge task, by all accounts,' he said, repeating the curator's words and describing how the vast building was of Gothic design, having two wings with steeply pitched roofs, Dutch gables, and a central section linked by two arcades. 'The limestone was quarried on site, and all ironmongery, hardware and even nails were made in the prison workshop.'

'Is any part of it *still* used as an asylum?' Bill wanted to know.

'Not since the turn of the century. In 1900 the asylum was condemned. New premises were built shortly after and the old asylum was left to fall into disrepair. At one stage they even considered demolishing the place, but it was of architectural interest and eventually there were moves to restore it.' Matt had been deeply fascinated by the old asylum. 'The place is steeped in history. During the war, it was occupied by the US Navy as a headquarters.'

'And now it's a museum, you say?'

'Arts centre and museum, yes. But they've kept a stark reminder of the original purpose of the building.' Matt felt his blood run cold as he went on to describe how one padded cell had been left exactly as it was over a hundred years ago. 'It's grim, I can tell you,' he said, shuddering at the memory. 'It's like every tormented soul that was ever incarcerated there has left some-thing of themselves behind. I'm not kidding you, Bill . . . the atmosphere in that place really gets to you.' He hadn't forgotten how the cell made him feel as though he had been there before.

Glancing round, he saw how Cathy appeared to be sleeping. Gingerly, he reached and stole the vinyl bag from beneath her arms. Balancing it in his knee, he dipped his hand inside. His fingers touched the cold hard surface which he suspected was the wax doll. Drawing it out, he held the doll up where Bill could easily see it; even the touch of it was deeply unpleasant to his skin. 'What d'you think of that?' he asked quietly.

In a series of fleeting glances while still keeping his main attention on the road ahead, Bill examined the tattered object. 'What the hell is it?' he asked at length, an expression of disgust on his face.

Matt lowered the artefact, turning it over in his hands. 'It's a *doll* of sorts . . .' Fingering the coarse ugly hair over the misshapen head, he stared into the deep hollows that were its eyes. A feeling came over him. An eerie, uncomfortable sensation.

Wondering at Matt's abrupt silence, Bill glanced at him. 'It's *hideous*!' he exclaimed. 'Where did you get it from?' When Matt gave no answer, he nudged him hard. 'Don't *you* fall asleep on me. It was a lonely drive coming to the airport. A bit of company on the way back would be much appreciated. That . . . *thing*, where did you get it?' He was shocked to see how chalk-white was Matt's face. 'Are you all right, son?' he asked, instinctively slowing the car.

'Yes, I'm okay. Just a bit queasy.' He smiled half-heartedly. 'The heat, I expect . . . too much sun.' He answered Bill's question. 'Cathy found the doll in the padded cell and she wouldn't be persuaded to leave it behind.' Certainly she seemed curiously fascinated by the repulsive little doll she found there, but for some inexplicable reason, Matt was deeply disturbed by it.

'Do you reckon the doll had been left there by some kiddie?' Bill asked, quietly intruding on Matt's deeper thoughts. 'Although it doesn't *look* like the kind of doll a child might have.'

'I can't think how else it was left there,' Matt admitted, 'although the place does sell all manner of curios and local craft. I expect it *was* left by some mischievous child.'

'Hmm!' Bill stared at the doll. 'And Cathy thinks it's a treasure, I expect. Women are funny creatures and no mistake. As for me, I wouldn't give that thing house room!' He wrinkled his face in repugnance.

Matt laughed. Cathy valued this little doll more than anything

135

they had bought on their travels. His love for her spilled over, submerging all his superstitions. 'I expect I'll have to live with it,' he grinned, 'but if it was up to me . . . I'd fling it out here and now!'

He and Bill were still chuckling, neither of them aware that Cathy was awake, disturbed and angered by Matt's good-humoured threat to 'fling it out here and now'.

What happened next occurred with such speed and ferocity that it took them both by surprise. With a strangled cry, Cathy lunged forward, intending to snatch the doll from Matt's hands. When he instinctively clung to it, jerking his head round in astonishment, it was to see Cathy wild eyed and frantic. Making another desperate grab at the doll, she tore it from his grasp, scoring her nails along the soft flesh of his wrist, and seeming not to notice the fine spray that spattered across the windscreen like crimson rain.

'Christ almighty!' Bill yelled, pushing his foot to the brake and swearing at the ensuing melody of car horns that told him how close he was to causing an accident. By the time he had manoeuvred the car across the lanes and on to the hard shoulder, he was still shaking. One look at his son-in-law told him that Matt also was clearly shocked.

Matt was the first to speak. Turning in his seat, he was taken aback to see how Cathy was totally unruffled by the incident. In a firm, controlled voice he told her, 'That was bloody stupid, Cathy! You might have got us all killed.' Inside, he was trembling, but his instincts told him not to make too big an issue of it. While he waited for Cathy's response, Matt was aware of her father's eyes on him. He felt the other man's horror at what Cathy had done.

For a moment it seemed as though Cathy did not recognise either man. She stared first at Matt, and then at her father. Slowly, she smiled, a curious, unattractive smile. And then she was laughing, harsh, wicked laughter. Suddenly silent, she grabbed the doll to her breast and began singing a lovely haunting melody that was strange to them. There was a madness about her.

'Cathy?' It was her father who spoke. She gave no answer. 'What in God's name made you do such a thing?' Still no answer.

With a calmness that belied the fear in him, Matt climbed from the car. His intention was to sit in the back with her, to cradle Cathy in his arms until they reached home, where he would summon the doctor. She was ill, he knew that now.

On opening the rear door, he was astonished to see Cathy quietly curled up in the corner of the seat, fast asleep, the gentle deep rhythm of her breathing suggesting that she had not moved or awakened since the minute she had first closed her eyes, soon after leaving the airport. Puzzled, he glanced at the other man. Bill was visibly trembling.

'Get back in the front,' he said. 'The sooner we get her home, the better.'

For the remainder of the journey, the atmosphere was painfully subdued. The two men were reluctant to speak, for fear of waking her. Still shaken by his daughter's frenzied outburst, Bill concentrated all his attention on the road, eager now to deliver Cathy safely home. Occasionally he would glance at his son-in-law, secretly wondering what could possibly have made Cathy behave in such a spiteful way. A small suspicion rose in his mind, but almost at once he thrust it out. Matt was not to blame in any way. He had been a good match for Cathy, and his love for her was obvious. Besides, apart from that unfortunate skirmish with the tallow doll, Matt and Cathy had seemed idyllically happy.

The only other explanation was that Cathy suffered too much sun. After all, sunstroke did have an unpredictable effect on some people. It could have been a bad reaction on waking . . . all the same, it would do no harm for Cathy to get a check-up. 'She'll be fine,' he murmured, glancing at Matt. 'A storm in a tea cup.' He smiled, but was not too surprised when Matt did not return his smile.

Reaching out, he slid a cassette into the player; instantly the soothing orchestration filled his senses. Visibly relaxing, he kicked the car into a higher gear and surged forward. Another hour and they would be home. With the music playing on his senses and Cathy peacefully snoozing in the back, it was suddenly easier to believe that it really *had* been no more than 'a storm in a tea cup'. Matt's grim expression reminded him how totally weird it had been.

Matt had wiped the blood droplets from the windscreen and was now holding the crimson-stained handkerchief to his throbbing wrist – Cathy's nails had gone deep. Now, in the ensuing calm, he could not believe that she had actually launched herself at him in such a way, snarling, lashing out, *wanting to hurt him*! In that moment when he had swung round to look into her face, it was almost as though he was looking at a hostile stranger.

He glanced at her now, at the corn-coloured hair that tumbled attractively about her face, the serenity of that lovely face, the innocence there . . . almost childlike. Even the way she was curled into the corner was reminiscent of a child. *This* was Cathy; this was how he knew her. So how could he explain the way she had viciously attacked him, her eyes fired with such loathing? He could not explain it. It was almost as though she'd suffered a brainstorm. He turned away.

For a while, Cathy moved not a muscle. Then her eyes slowly opened. She watched Matt through half-closed eyes, black, glittering eyes alive with murderous intent. Inside her furtive mind the voice whispered, enticing, persuasive. In her heart she knew the darkest evil. *Matt, like his forefathers, would have to die.* But first he must suffer pain, torture. He had to know what it was like to see someone he loved being destroyed. He must be relentlessly pursued beyond all human endurance. He must know that there can be no hope, no reprieve, no salvation, *not even beyond the grave*!

Growing suddenly fretful in her sleep, Cathy began to fidget this way and that. The doll slid to the floor. Soon a great sense of inner peace overwhelmed her. Presently she was sleeping contentedly, the nightmare subdued, for a while. Only for a while. The seed was sown. There could be no turning back.

'Here we are. Home at last.' Bill followed the snaking traffic from the motorway, but when the four or five vehicles continued along the main road towards Bedford, he turned the car into the wide country road which ran in the direction of Holden, and Slater's Farm. *As they wended their way along the lane, neither man saw the hatchback which followed at a discreet distance.* 'Best wake Cathy,' Bill told Matt. His voice was calmer. Somehow the incident seemed unreal.

'I'll wake her when we get there.' Matt also felt distanced from what had happened. After two long weeks, they were back on familiar territory. He was eager for signs of home; the house on the corner with its huge sign outside, which told passers-by of the 'Flowers for sale'. Beneath the sign was a small tray and a black plastic bucket crammed with bunches of tulips; propped up against it was a smaller sign that instructed purchasers, 'Fifty pence a bunch, please leave the money in the tray'. Further along Safford Lane was a large farmhouse of Edwardian design, and in the front paddock stood a huge spherical building, reputed to have a sliding aperture through which the farmer studied the night sky. The lane was mostly flanked by high-reaching hedges and, beyond, rolling pastureland with intermittent spinneys.

On the horizon could be seen rows of long low buildings, erected to house the many thousands of battery hens . . . 'a shame on those who built them', Cathy had often claimed. She detested the thought of God's creatures being denied the light of day and freedom to run about. There were many who shared her views, but for every farmer who abhorred such practices, there were others who were always willing to put profit above all else.

The narrow meandering lane that led to Slater's Farm was just ahead. Bill eased the pressure on the accelerator, allowing the car to slow to a crawl. In a moment the lane was in sight. Cautiously, and mindful of the fact that this lane was the only means of exit from the two cottages and the stables, he turned in from the road. Almost immediately the red-roofed stable blocks came into view; tall and regimental in design, they were constructed of tongue and groove planking with lofts over, and housed a total of forty top bloodstock animals. In the lush paddocks could be seen a number of horses contentedly grazing, then, as the car drew closer, it became obvious that the schooling ring was occupied, with some twenty children under tuition.

'Laura's working late, isn't she?' Matt remarked, his eyes picking out the tall, slim figure of a woman who stood in the centre of the formation issuing instructions and occasionally rebuking either rider or mount. No sooner had he spoken than the school began to lead away in an orderly fashion towards the stables. In that same moment the floodlights came on. The daylight was almost gone. Bill had been driving on sidelights since turning into the lane; they were sufficient now to see him to the cottage. As the car cruised past a group of riders, Laura raised her arm in greeting.

'I envy you this place, Matt,' Bill Barrington told him now, when the main cottage came in sight. The evening light was a perfect complement to the old thatched dwelling. With the sun going down behind its chimneys and the lights twinkling from the downstairs windows, it made a picturesque vision. History told that the cottage was built in the mid-seventeenth century; its crooked walls, beamed ceilings and inglenook fireplaces all bore testimony to that. The windows were tiny but many, each criss-crossed with lead-light and lending the cottage a unique pretti-ness. Having four large bedrooms, two reception rooms, two bathrooms and a spacious farm kitchen, it was considered to be unusually large and, though many interior alterations had taken place, they were always in character, retaining the timeless essence and easily blending with all original features.

Cathy was awake. With a sleepy 'Home already?' she uncurled and sat forward on the edge of the seat, leaning between the two men and laying her head on Matt's shoulder. 'Sorry, I slept all the way,' she said, nuzzling her nose against his face. Suddenly she noticed the blood-soaked handkerchief pressed over his wrist. 'What's that . . . what have you done?' Clearly shocked, she sat upright, her anxious grey eyes staring at Matt and waiting for his explanation.

It was her father who answered, his voice low and incredulous.

'You mean you don't know?' He felt oddly out of his depth, unsure and apprehensive. He did not turn to look at her but, instead, he glanced into the overhead mirror, seeing her reflection there and thinking how distraught she seemed. Maybe she *did* know, after all.

'Well . . . no! I *don't* know how Matt did that.' Cathy stared from one man to the other. 'I can't remember you cutting yourself,' she told Matt. When she saw how Matt and her father exchanged furtive glances, she was inexplicably afraid, searching her mind, trying so hard to recall when it was that Matt cut his wrist. But she could not recall the incident, and yet both Matt and her father seemed not to believe her. She knew instinctively that there was something wrong, something horribly wrong. Not for the first time since embarking on the journey home, Cathy sensed a strange lull in herself; not a peaceful, contented lull, but an awful sensation that deeply unnerved her. Panic now. 'Matt, how did you cut your wrist?' She was reaching forward, clawing at his turned-back cuff, wanting to see the wound more clearly. It was then that she saw her own blood-stained fingers and the ragged blobs of what looked like skin wedged beneath her fingernails. 'Me? *Was it me?*' she gasped. 'Did *I* do that to you?' In the mirror her father could see the disbelief in Cathy's wide-open eyes.

Sensing her rising panic, Matt quickly wound his long, strong fingers round Cathy's small fist. Drawing her to him, he kissed her mouth, saying when she abruptly pulled away, 'You lashed out in your sleep. It was my own stupid fault. I wanted to show your father what you had found in that padded cell. When I pulled the bag away, it must have frightened you.'

'What are you saying?'

'Just that you lashed out in your sleep, that's all.' He grinned, that handsome lop-sided grin that always won her over. 'Serves me right,' he said, 'but it might be a good idea to get your talons trimmed.'

He smiled nervously, slipping a corner of the handkerchief beneath her nails, teasing out the torn remnants of his skin and telling her, 'It's just a scratch. I bleed easily.' When he turned now to look at her, he could see she was not altogether convinced. 'I'm not about to die,' he said, showing how his wrist was no longer bleeding, though still raw and angry, and patterned with a series of deep gashes now turgid with congealed blood. 'Like I said,' he teased, 'it wouldn't hurt to get your talons clipped.'

He had sensed the uncertainty in her, and it hurt him. It frightened him too. So how could he tell her the truth – that she had not merely lashed out in her sleep, but had in fact viciously attacked him? And yet she remembered nothing of it! What was he to think? What was he to do? This was not the first time something like this had happened, though. He recalled the night before leaving Perth, when Cathy had woken from that awful nightmare.

'Look! There's Edna, and the dogs.' Cathy brought the two men's attention to the far paddock and the well-trodden footway that led from the field gate to the rear of the cottage. Silhouetted against the evening sky, and heading for the cottage, was a large ambling figure in black wellington boots and a dark duffle coat, the hem of which fell below the cuff of her boots. She had on a headscarf and carried a long stout branch which she now discarded, propping it up against the gate post, where it would no doubt remain until she passed that way again.

Almost before the car had ground to a halt in the gravel driveway, Cathy was clambering from the car. 'Bonnie . . . Shandy!' she called, her laughing face betraying her utter delight as she fell to her knees on the rose lawn. Her arms opened wide when the two black Labradors came bounding towards her. In a minute they were on her, heavy cumbersome beasts, long pink tongues licking her face while the three of them rolled over and over, joyful in each other's company.

'Hey! That's enough!' Fearful that Cathy would be swamped, Matt slipped his hands one under each of their collars and pulled them back. 'One of these days, sweetheart,' he warned the laughing Cathy, 'you might be sorry you let them rampage all over you.' The two dogs were Matthew's. Shandy was found wandering along Safford Lane some nine years ago, bedraggled, hungry and in pup. It was Matthew's opinion that she had been abandoned, so he took her in and cared for her. Soon after, she gave birth to eight fat healthy pups, seven of which he gave to good homes, and the one remaining he kept back. Bonnie was the weak runt in the litter, and Matthew feared she would not survive, but, under his constant care and supervision, not only did she survive, but she outgrew her mother, making a proud-looking animal with an instinct for hunting. Unfortunately, both dogs were past their prime, Sandy being the wrong side of ten years old, and Bonnie only a year younger, yet in spite of the fact that the whiskers on their faces were now greying with age and they were more easily tired after a walk across the fields, the dogs were bursting with health and still full of high spirits. Now, when Edna deliberately clattered the spoon against their feeding bowls, the two dogs raced away to enjoy the main meal of the day.

After collecting the luggage and paraphernalia from the car, Matt and Bill followed, with Cathy in pursuit, protectively clutching the vinyl bag that held various gifts and little treasures, not least of which was the tallow doll.

Edna was a woman in her late fifties, 'salt of the earth', Matt's mother always used to say. She had been coming to the house every weekday since as far back as Matt could remember. When his parents were alive, Edna and her husband Joseph had been invaluable to Slater's Farm . . . Joseph being Abel Slater's right-hand man and knowing all there was to know about breeding, buying and training good horse stock. And Edna, who could turn her hand to whatever duties Mrs Slater required of her.

Since the tragic death of Matt's parents, he had come to rely on Joseph and Edna Tully – Joseph was manager of the yard, and Edna seemed happy to spend her days at the house, doing all the things that a man may not do quite so well. Now that Matt had taken a wife, Edna was looking forward to retiring, when she would 'visit my sister in Bedford a bit more often', but she had assured Cathy, 'Whenever you want me, child, you've only to let me know.' Cathy liked her. She and Edna had become firm friends and certainly each seemed to fill a need in the other, with Cathy not having a mother to confide in, and Edna never having been blessed with children.

'That was good of Edna to prepare a meal for us,' Cathy told Matt now, as the two of them relaxed in front of a small log fire. Normally, at this time of year they wouldn't dream of lighting a fire but, after returning from the heat of Australia, the May evening seemed surprisingly chilly. Now, after the delicious ham salad and apple pie with cream, Cathy felt wonderfully contented. The table lamps gave off a soft warm glow, the firelight flickered and danced, creating weird fascinating shadows all around the room, and, with Matt's arms about her as the two of them lounged in the squashy comfort of the settee, Cathy thought herself to be the luckiest woman in the world. It had been an unforgettable honeymoon, a wonderful homecoming, and the half-hour spent lazing in the bath seemed to have melted away that deep sense of fear which had troubled her these past few days. There had been times when she had wondered whether it stemmed from a deeper anxiety, a long-held insecurity that had started when she had been deserted by her mother. Since then Cathy had been almost afraid to commit herself to a close relationship; always terrified that it would never last. She had felt that way with Matt, not daring to hope that things would come right for them, yet loving him so much that she lived in dread of losing him.

'It's good to be home.' Matt bent his head towards her, touching his mouth against her neck, raising all kinds of longing in her. Her answer was to turn her face to him, reaching up to meet his lips and shivering with delight when his mouth came down on hers, his long fingers feeling their way into her pyjama top, caressing the softness of her breast. He knew how to please her, to arouse her. Eagerly she twisted her body towards him, the tip of her tongue tracing his lips, her two hands undoing the belt of his bathrobe. Slithering the palms of her hands across the hard expanse of his chest, she teased his nipples, loving the sensation she felt when the thick dark hairs touched her fingertips.

What had been a tender kiss now became more ardent, she felt her need for him growing inside her. Softly moaning she pulled away, uncurling from the settee and standing before him. Slowly she undid the lower buttons of her pyjama top, afterwards letting it slip down her shoulders and fall in a rumpled pile at her feet. Next came her pyjama bottoms. Her dove-grey eyes never once left Matt's face; his passion was obvious as he roved his gaze over her slim shapely figure, sensuously silhouetted in the golden glow of the fire. For a moment he made no move, choosing instead to enjoy her nakedness, his love for her flooding every corner of his being, raging through him and firing his desire until only the feel of her in his arms and the taking of her in a way that only a man could know, would satisfy him.

Now, when Cathy came towards him, he rose to his feet, his fingers clumsy in their eagerness to shed the bathrobe. There was nothing between them now. In the quiet solitude only the crackling of the logs disturbed the brooding atmosphere. Tenderly, he laid his hands on her shoulders, pushing her down into the soft rug-pile, pressing himself on to her, his fingers rippling tantalisingly over her skin, feeling out the places he had come to know as her most sensitive . . . that soft indentation at the base of her neck, the curve of her spine, the dip in her soft inviting thighs. 'Oh, Cathy . . . Cathy!' His mouth murmured against hers, moving along the creamy whiteness of her throat, down to the hard, erect peaks of her small, round breasts. Her closeness was intoxicating to him. Thrills ebbed in and out of his heightened senses, and the desire within him hardened until he could wait no longer. Keeping his mouth over hers, his tongue playing, exciting, thrilling her to impatience, he reached down. She stirred, softly moaning. When she opened to receive him, he arched away, teasing, making her want him all the more. And then he felt her – glorious, aching for him.

Savouring the moment he slowly entered her, laughing softly when he felt himself being sucked in as her legs came up to wrap around him. There was great love in him as he pushed deeper inside her, the sensation was powerful, all consuming. In his delight he murmured her name, raising his face to gaze on her.

Parting his lips he sought her mouth, sighing inside when the kiss was more exquisite than he had ever known before. A frenzy took them both, he making long invasive inways deep into the soft moistness of her flesh, and she pushing up to meet him, now and then crying out, pulling him into her, her head tilted back, her mouth open, and her face a study in rapture. Seeing her that way gave him pleasure. Thrill after thrill engulfed his senses. His need grew stronger and in the instant when his desire soared within him, he glanced up, the thrills burst inside him, cascading through him, sapping his strength.

But with the ecstasy, came riveting shock. *The shock of looking not into Cathy's face, but into the face of a stranger!* Dark eyed and stunningly beautiful, she smiled at him, and then the eyes were bitter, black with loathing . . . simmering with evil. The face was real, and then it was not.

Rolling away, he dared to look once more, a terrible confusion reigning in him. Cathy's soft grey eyes gazed on him. She leaned up on one elbow, her face brushing his. 'Love you,' she murmured. One fleeting kiss before she rose and then she was gone into the kitchen, leaving him bewildered. Was he going crazy? As he pulled his bathrobe on, Matt convinced himself that it had all been a trick of the firelight. There was no 'stranger'; how could there be? It was *Cathy's* eyes he had seen smiling back at him, a trick of the firelight, nothing more. *Just a trick of the firelight.*

It was almost midnight. Cathy was soundly sleeping, but Matt was too disturbed to sleep. For a while, he paced the bedroom, his anxious eyes watching Cathy's sleeping face. He could not rid himself of the feeling that there was something eerie happening to him. He had no way of knowing what it was, or whether in fact it really was all in his imagination, but there was fear inside him. Real, crippling fear. A fear he had never known before. An awful terror he could not explain. Long into the early hours he paced the floor. There was no sleep in him this night. And no peace of mind.

Outside, some way down the lane, the hatchback was parked in a position from which the occupant could see the cottage. He watched now, his eyes intent on the shadow of Matt walking up and down. He watched until the bedroom light went out and all was still. In the light from the glove compartment he made an entry in his notebook. Beneath the heading 'Mrs Hinson' it read: 'Watched the house until dark. Nothing untoward.'

Chapter Eight

It was a strange sort of day for mid-July . . . overcast and unusually cool, without even the lightest breeze to stir the air. On this day – when Matt's fears were diminished by the quiet contentment of the past two months – it seemed that nothing could ever again destroy his peace of mind. But something did. Something so strange and horrifying that it struck at the very heart of him, threatening everything that he held dear.

Throughout the stable yard there was great excitement; six o' clock on this Saturday morning saw an army of young grooms, boys and girls alike, all busily engaged in feeding the horses, mucking out the stables and generally preparing for an enjoyable day of horsemanship and competition.

Opening the gate, Matt waited for Cathy to come into the stable yard, his dark gaze running appreciatively over her slim figure. She had a particular energy about her, a glow that outshone everything round her. Dressed in thigh-hugging denims and a loose emerald-green sweater, with her corn-coloured hair tumbling in disarray to her small straight shoulders, she had the look of a child, possessed of a certain innocence and fresh beauty. Now, when she smiled on him, making extravagant gestures, bowing in mock servile manner and telling him with wide mischievous eyes, 'Why, thank you, sir,' his heart spilled over with love and he wondered how he had ever lived without her, for she filled his life with sunshine.

'Get to work, wench!' he replied in a grim voice, pointing towards the stables while she slunk away, trying not to laugh, especially when she saw how the stable-hands were watching, thoroughly enjoying what she and Matt had believed to be a little private entertainment.

The yard was a happy place, bristling with people all going about their work. All the day long the air echoed to voices uplifted in song, in accompaniment to the transistor radio which blared through the speakers from the tack-room. Now and then a burst of merry whistling could be heard emanating from the inside of the stables; everybody knew everybody else and they were all part of the same happy family. The horses were already out of the stables, each one tethered to a ring by the individual stable doors, and each animal standing patiently, knowing the routine and being resigned to it. Some were having their flanks scrubbed, others were being curry-combed and brushed, some were having their manes plaited or their hooves picked. While all this was going on, they would stand like gentle giants, unperturbed, uninterested. The noise did not bother them, nor did the less experienced grooms who noisily hurried into the stables with empty wheel-barrows and hurried out with the barrows piled high with still-steaming horse-droppings and soiled straw.

Skilfully separating the two commodities with the long fine-pronged pitchforks, the youngsters threw the straw on to one mound and the droppings on to another. Later, the trader would transfer the rotting mountains to his lorry, paying good money for the privilege. The stench was overpowering, thick and warm, it spread over the yard like a creeping blanket, permeating every nook and cranny with its unique fragrance; it was not unpleasant to those who had grown accustomed to it, but it clung to everything and everyone like a second skin.

Most of the horses here were privately owned, the owners paying upwards of two thousand pounds a year to keep their expensive mounts stabled, and exercised to peak fitness. Abel Slater had been a farmer here, but over the years his agricultural interests were sold out. His great passion was horses. Matt had inherited his father's talents and had built on the excellent reputation enjoyed by Abel Slater, by carrying on the same traditions, breeding and selling valuable event horses. More often

149

than not, these same horses remained at Slater's Farm, because the new owners were more than happy to let Matt and his well-qualified staff train and stable them. In a single season a horse might be entered in only a dozen events, yet it must be kept fit and ready at all times.

Today, most of the horses were being made resplendent before Matt's fleet of six horse-boxes would transport them some twenty miles away to Soulbury, where the biggest annual event in the horse owner's calendar was due to begin at ten a.m., and would go on until late afternoon. The competitions were open to anyone, and already the huge number of entries in each class indicated that this would be the biggest show yet.

Normally Matt and Cathy, who were both accomplished riders, would not miss the opportunity to take part in such a competition; besides which they were always eager to see how the horses performed – a clutch of trophies taken by the animals trained at Slater's Farm was always a good advertisement. On this occasion, however, they were expecting a potential buyer for two particular geldings which showed excellent promise as top showjumpers. Matt had placed a very high price on them. He knew their value.

'I can never get used to the yard when it's quiet like this.' Matt stood by the gate, his arm round Cathy and his curious gaze travelling the deserted stable yard. It was eight a.m. The last of the horse-boxes had disappeared down the lane and on to the main road. Now there were only the two of them left, amid a strange calmness that seemed all the more unnerving after the earlier bedlam.

'Afraid I'll take advantage of you?' Cathy murmured threateningly. 'Do you think I'll have my wicked way with you?' Her grey eyes shone with villainy as she looked up at him.

He laughed aloud, walking on towards the tack-room and taking Cathy with him. 'You're a bad one,' he chided playfully, 'but I think I'll keep you all the same.' He thought he would never be more contented than he was right now. These past weeks had been heavenly; Cathy's awful nightmares had stopped and only this morning she had told him of her growing eagerness to have a child. Previously when he mentioned how he would love a family, Cathy had not been quite so enthusiastic, always telling him, 'Not yet, Matt, we're only young. There's plenty of time.' And then this morning her attitude had changed. She had given him no indication, and he was both astonished and thrilled.

There had always been a deep need in him, a strong belief that he must build on the slender history left to him by his father. On the day of his father's funeral, when he alone represented what was left of their history, the need to create the seeds of a whole new dynasty began to grow in him. But it was not so great a compulsion that it dictated his life. When, later, he fell in love with Cathy, he made no mention of his deeper feelings. He adored her, even though she showed no enthusiasm for having children. He quietly hoped the day would come when she might change her mind. Today was that special day. Tonight, he would wine and dine her in that lovely restaurant along Bedford embankment, and later they would make love. His heart lurched at the thought. Tonight, a whole new life might be conceived . . . a son, God willing, to carry the name of Slater down the ages. A son, to right the wrongs of the past and create a new beginning.

'Penny for your thoughts.' Cathy had never seen him so lost in thought. Somehow it disturbed her.

'Oh, they're worth much more than that, sweetheart,' Matt told her, opening the tack-room door and ushering her in. Once inside he caught her roughly in his arms, looking down on her uplifted face, his hunger for her bright in his eyes. 'You haven't forgotten what you told me this morning?' he quizzed.

'I haven't forgotten.' She had been smiling at him, but now the smile fell away. A darkness came into her senses, a strange and overwhelming feeling of malevolence. Suddenly she resented him. Confusion and chaos split her emotions. Reluctantly she pulled away; the surprise on his face was hurtful to her. 'And *you* haven't "forgotten" that we have a very important visitor coming here this morning?' She glanced at the big round clock on the wall over Laura's desk. 'He's due at ten o' clock. That's less than two hours,

I hope you realise?' Going to the harness rack, Cathy collected two head-collars. Throwing one to Matt, she reminded him, 'There's a great deal to be done . . . Sergeant and Copper to be put out in the paddock, their stables to be mucked out . . . the horses warmed up so he can see them at their best and . . .'

'Hey! Woah! I *do* know what has to be done.' He was puzzled by her abrupt change of mood. Now, as she hurried out of the tack-room, he detected something odd about her, something different. He had been close to Cathy long enough to know when she was acting completely out of character. He prayed it was not starting again; the nightmares, the fear. He had hoped against hope that it had all gone away. Now, he was desperately afraid that it had not. His bubble of happiness cruelly punctured, Matt went in pursuit of her. He had to know that all was well between them, or there would be no peace for him this day.

The day went well. The geldings were sold for four thousand pounds each, and after, Matt had suggested they should saddle Sergeant and Copper and go for a brisk canter. The new cross-country course over their land had proved to be a marvellous asset, not only for exercising their own horses, but also bringing in revenue from other owners. Cathy's dark brooding mood had thankfully lifted. The ride was invigorating. Matt's big bay was pulling at the bit and Cathy drove her horse like a demon, flying the hedges and galloping over the fields like a thing possessed. Several times Matt called out to her, cautioning her, fearful for her safety, especially when an overhanging branch sliced into her temple, causing a small gash. But she was a good horsewoman, and soon his spirit was as wild as hers.

It was nearly evening when Matt and Cathy returned to Slater's Farm, hungry, dirty and exhausted, but contented, and greatly exhilarated. 'I didn't realise we'd been gone so long,' Matt shouted to Laura, who was emerging from one of the stables.

When Laura saw Matt and Cathy she hurried forward, eager to tell how well the horses had done at the show. She also looked dishevelled, her hair untidy about her long thin face, and her jodhpurs stained black by the horses' sweat. 'It's been a long day,' she said, subconsciously tapping the leather riding crop against her boots. 'All the horses are fed and stabled.' She glanced up and down the yard – deserted almost, except for themselves and the curious horses who now poked their heads out of the stable upper doors to watch them with large, soulful brown eyes. 'Young Joanna's still here, though. Her horse has a nasty kick on the knee. She's attending to it now.'

'Should the vet see it?' Matt was always careful about such things. His motto was 'better safe than sorry'.

Laura shook her head. 'No. Joseph checked it over. He's explained to Joanna what she must do.'

Matt cast his glance to the far end of the yard. 'Where is Joseph?'

'Gone home to get cleaned up. He'll be back to lock up and check that all's well.'

Matt nodded. Joseph was a man to be relied on. He and Edna lived only a short distance from the main cottage, in a pretty little place that belonged to Slater's Farm. 'He'll be pleased to know the yearlings were sold,' Matt told her. Then, while Laura and Cathy had a brief exchange of words, Matt walked Sergeant up the yard and into his stable. The horse was still in a sweat. He didn't want it catching a chill.

Some time later, Matt was coming out of the stable when he saw the familiar grey-headed figure crossing from the direction of the cottage. Joseph was no longer a young man, but he was fit and strong, though his broad shoulders were now slightly stooped and the lines in his rugged face were deep and meandering. Matt often wondered what he would do when the time came for Joseph to retire. Over the years he had served the Slater family well, and it would be a hard task to find a man experienced enough to replace him.

Matt went to meet him. On the way past the tack-room where Cathy was just finishing off, he peered in to tell her, 'I'll just have a quick word with Joseph. Make your way home if you want to. I'll be along shortly.' When Cathy made no response, but turned to

153

stare at him, he was taken aback by the glint of hostility in her eyes. 'Cathy?' He peered into the shadows where she quickly retreated. Again that awful murmuring deep inside him. 'Did you hear?'

'Yes.' Her voice was low, and different.

'Are you all right, sweetheart?'

'Yes. Why shouldn't I be?' There was impatience now, and anger.

'No reason.' And there *was* no reason, he told himself, except in his own imagination. 'I won't be long, just a few minutes.' He made a small laugh. 'We could both do with a bath. But don't bother getting a meal. I'm taking you out.' He had been looking forward to this evening with Cathy. He hoped she might be thrilled that he had planned a surprise dinner. She made no comment. 'Like I say, I won't be long,' he said, lingering a moment. When she turned away from him, he went on his way, not understanding, hurt and disillusioned. But it had been a long day, and no doubt they would both feel better after a hot bath and a meal.

From the depths of the narrow dark room, Cathy waited, listening to the sound of his boots against the concrete, waiting for it to die down. *That man was her enemy*. He was dangerous. Cathy knew that, because the voices told her so. They had been with her again today. She could hear them now. 'Kill him, Cathy . . . kill . . . him.' Over and over they whispered, like hypnotic music inside her, flooding every corner of her being. 'Kill him . . . *kill him* . . . KILL HIM!' The voices were so beautiful. They were her friends. *He* was her enemy. Yet something held her back. She knew he must die, but somehow the thought gave her no pleasure. Matt was a good man. She loved him. No! No! Not love. *Hate*. The loathing rose in her until she could taste its bitterness. Yet the conflict was still there. Something bad was happening. '*Go away!*' Her shout echoed from the walls, then another voice, familiar, terrifying. '*Kill him!*' The voice was a silent one, inside her, compelling.

Desperate, she fought against it. 'No! Leave me be!' And then she saw it, the figure, opening the stable door, coming towards her. Shadowy, silhouetted against the brightness, the grey shawl draped round its body, wisps of hair oddly floating as it moved, thin bony arms stretched out, the mouth opening and closing, calling her name. 'Kill him.' The voice soared through her, drowning every instinct.

'No!' Spinning round, she grabbed the axe from the wall, blindly hitting out, the need to kill strong in her. She felt the blade find its mark. She heard the soft sickening thud, saw the red bubbles spurt into the air like a gushing fountain, splattering her face, warm and sticky. Again and again with all her strength the blade swung up and down. The sky was red, the screams were deafening. The figure was gone, but she kept on lashing out, eyes closed now, the screams one long unearthly sound.

Spent and terrified, she crumpled into the corner, blinded by the light, crazed by what she had done. She opened her eyes and peeped out. Blood was everywhere – on the walls, the ceiling, running down her arms. Chaos welled up in her; the tears sped down her face. Then the voice calling. 'Cathy.' Soft, laden with love. It was *his* face. Thank God, oh thank God. She was sobbing now, her arms outstretched.

'Help me . . . please . . . help me.' Tears blinded her.

Matt leaned down. 'It's all right . . . all right.' Strong tender arms plucked her from the darkness, held her close. She was safe now. Safe. Whatever she had imagined, it was inconceivable to him. To Cathy though, it was as real as if it had actually happened.

'It wasn't my fault, Joseph. Honest to God, it wasn't my fault!' Joanna was not yet sixteen, a quiet serious girl with short fair wispy hair and a painfully thin immature figure. She moved in a slow lazy manner, and had a habit of slinging her horse's rug over her shoulders. Now, she stared at Joseph. Her eyes were wide with shock. 'I just heard her yelling, "Go away", at the top of her voice. I was coming down to put my things in the tack-room and . . . oh . . .' The girl was sobbing now, deeply shaken by what had happened. 'She went crazy when she saw me. She just went crazy!' She put her head down and fell silent, her narrow shoulders trembling.

'I know, lass. It were a terrible thing to see and no mistake.' He patted her on the shoulder. 'None of it were your fault.' In his mind he could still see Cathy cowering in the far corner, a broken, terrified soul. 'You get yourself off home. She'll be fine. The doctor's on his way. She'll be fine, I promise you.' He walked with her to the door, in time to see Matt and Cathy going on slow tortuous steps towards the cottage . . . Cathy a tragic little figure, clinging to her man, and he wrapped protectively about her, his head bent to hers, whispering words of love, assuring her, giving her his strength.

Joseph's gaze moved round the tack-room, scrutinising everything, from the desk and the much-used telephone to the meticulous line of polished saddles and bridles, the row of tools hanging neatly on the wall . . . the spades, pitchforks and the two axes. Everything was in order. *Exactly as Laura and the grooms had left it earlier.* Satisfied, but deeply concerned for Cathy, he locked the door and followed the path home to his own humble cottage. The whole incident had unnerved him. Life was a strange thing. Like a will-o'-the-wisp it came and went, ever surprising, sometimes cruel, sometimes kind, but always unpredictable.

Chapter Nine

'It's such a lovely day, I thought you might like to go for a short walk.' Emily breezed into the drawing room. She was carrying the old lady's shawl. 'Just as far as the paper shop.'

'I've already told you, I don't want to go out.' Maria was sitting by the casement windows in the drawing room. From here she could see the apple tree. In her mind's eye she could see what lay beneath. 'I don't feel well,' she lied.

Emily was used to her tantrums. 'Feeling ill' was a regular ploy. 'Please, Maria,' she urged, 'it's a beautiful day. The sun and fresh air will do you a world of good. Besides, didn't you say you wanted a local newspaper?'

'Yes. But I didn't expect to have to fetch it myself.'

'But you *will*, won't you?'

'I shall have to, or I won't hear the last of it,' Maria answered sulkily. 'But I'm not going in that blessed chair!' She set her mouth in a tight line and continued to stare at the apple tree.

'Maria?' Emily had come to stand beside her.

'What?' She didn't look up.

'Why don't you ever go out into the garden?'

'You've asked me that before!'

'And you've always given me the same answer.'

'And I'm giving you the same answer now. I don't feel easy out there.'

'I've been giving that some thought.'

'Oh?'

'Yes. I think it's because there are no comfortable seats for you to sit on.' She pointed to the rustic bench. 'Even *I* can't get comfortable on that.'

'Maybe. But I've no intention of paying out good money for seats and suchlike, when I can sit here and see the garden just as well.' She could have explained how she was terrified to set foot in that garden. But she let Emily satisfy herself that she had found the reason. 'Come on, then!'

Deep in thought at the old lady's words, Emily was visibly startled out of her reverie. 'Oh, I'm sorry – what did you say?'

Maria sighed. 'For goodness' sake! Didn't you just keep on at me to go for a walk? Well I'm ready, so make your mind up, either we're going or we're not!' When she saw the light fade in Emily's brown eyes, she touched her on the hand. 'I'm sorry, my dear,' she said affectionately, 'just an old woman's bad temper.'

As they went out of the door, Emily strong as ever while Maria leaned all of her weight on her, she reminded Emily, 'I can't promise to walk as far as the paper shop.'

Emily knew how strong the old lady was, and she was not going to play her little game. 'All right,' she said, smiling to herself, 'if you don't make it, I'll leave you on one of the benches along the embankment, and pick you up on my way back.'

'Huh! You make it sound like I'm a dog or something!'

As it was, Maria not only made it to the shop, but she happily engaged the shopkeeper in a heated argument about the 'exorbitant' price of his chocolate peanuts. And no matter how hard he tried to explain that he wasn't responsible for setting the prices, the more she took him to task. Until, in the end, he gave her a packet with his blessing.

'That was very naughty, Maria,' Emily reprimanded as the two of them sat on the bench beneath the willow tree.

'Do you want one or not?' She held the sweets out, and Emily was obliged to take one. 'And don't look at me as though I'm a thief!' she protested with a wicked little smile. 'Anyway, I expect you'll pay him next time you go into his shop.'

'I certainly shall.' Emily wasn't really shocked. She knew Maria only too well. So she ate the sweet and enjoyed it. And the two of them sat in the sunshine and dreamed of things long gone.

When, some time later, a man and his dog strolled by, Maria was horrified when the dog was let off its lead and promptly squatted to foul the grass. 'You should be ashamed!' she yelled at the man, waving her stick threateningly. 'You deserve to have your nose rubbed in it.' At that point, Emily decided it was time to take her home.

Pausing at the kerb edge when a van came in sight, she suggested, 'We'd best let the van go by, Maria.' She didn't want to get half-way across the road and then have to hurry the old lady.

Bill Barrington was on his way to a solicitor in Castle Street. But he was not in such a hurry that he couldn't wait for the two ladies to cross the road. Slowing the van down, he made sure there was no traffic coming the other way before indicating for them to cross.

As they passed by, he smiled. Blushing fiercely, the younger woman with the limp returned his smile. It kept him warm all the way home, and he began to regret not having got out of the van to assist her with the old lady. Finally pushing the incident aside, he firmly chided, 'You've been on your own for so long, you've forgotten how to be a gentleman.'

Matt stood looking out of the window, his hands thrust deep into his trouser pockets, his shoulders slumped forward and all the anxiety of the past week written on his face. His thoughts were still tortured. How could it be that in one moment a man was blessed with everything that made life worth while, holding the world in the palm of his hand, then so swiftly had it all cruelly snatched away? Turning his head, he glanced at the mantelpiece clock for the umpteenth time. It was still not ten a.m. Already the day seemed neverending. He sighed, a long deep sigh that swelled his chest and lifted his shoulders. What in God's name was happening? *Why* was it happening? He cast his turbulent thoughts back, searching for an answer. He could see none.

Outside, the sun was brilliant in a cloudless sky. The sun's warmth shone in through the window and played on his face. The lawn was lush and green, smooth as velvet, and the flowering shrubs made a glorious display of vivid colours. Chattering starlings strutted about the garden, proud and beautiful, the cooling breeze ruffling their dark iridescent feathers. In such a magnificent world, how could everything be so wrong? In spite of what the doctor had said, and in spite of Cathy's own repeated assurances, deep down inside him Matt knew something awful was happening. Something frightening. Something . . . evil. Some wicked inexplicable thing that threatened to destroy him and Cathy. He felt it as surely as he could feel himself breathing. Worse, he felt helpless, shamefully utterly helpless. At first he had convinced himself that it was all in his imagination: that strange look in Cathy's eyes when she thought she was not being observed, the restlessness in her . . . the unpredictable swings of mood and the way she spoke to him sometimes, almost as though he was a stranger.

Then there was the night when he and Cathy had made love; when in the space of a single heartbeat he had seemed to hold *another* woman in his arms, a dark, hostile creature whose black eyes were alive with malice. And yet it could not have been. *It could not have been!* But now this? Every minute of every day during this past week, he carried the imprint of that awful scene in his mind. Even before Joanna had come running up the yard towards them, terrified and in tears, he and Joseph had heard Cathy's unearthly screams.

When he saw her there, cowering in the corner, her arms flailing the air as though fending off some attacking demon, his heart had almost stopped. But thank God his arrival had calmed her, and she had gone quietly, thankfully, into his open arms. Even now, the sight and sound of his lovely Cathy so distraught was too vivid in his heart.

Unchecked, the tears flowed down his face. God alone knew how he would turn the world upside down to help her, if only he knew how. *How could he help her?* He was lost. Now, it was *his* turn to ask – raising his face to the sky he murmured softly, forlornly,

'Don't turn your back on us, Lord. Don't desert us.' He closed his eyes, imagining some great and powerful being in his heaven, who only had to lift one finger and all would be well again. He knew instinctively that was not the way. But he prayed all the same. He did believe. It gave him hope in his deepest despair.

Hearing her move about upstairs, Matt went to her. 'I can stay with you if you want me to? We could go on a picnic, what do you think?'

'I'd rather stay here.'

Since the incident at the stables. Cathy seemed strangely subdued. This morning she looked pale and ill. 'Won't you talk to me about it?' Matt asked anxiously. But, like so many times of late, she turned away, and he was at a loss as to what to do next.

'There's nothing to talk about.' She smiled, but her smile was a sad expression that tore him in two.

Going to her then, he folded her in his arms. 'What's happening to us, sweetheart?'

'I don't know what you mean.' She knew what he meant, and she realised that something was horribly wrong with her. But, as yet, she didn't understand what was going on in her own head. One minute she was afraid, desperately needing him, and the next she couldn't bear him to even touch her. Now, when she looked up to see the anguish in his eyes, her heart was like a lead weight inside her.

'I want you to see a doctor.'

Startled, she pulled away. 'No.' At the back of her mind was the fear that he might think she was going mad, and have her put away.

'All right.' Matt sensed her fear. He took a step towards her, but the warmth between them had been broken. He cursed himself for that. 'If you won't spend the day with me, I'm going to the stables. Do you want to come along? Laura's longing to see you.' She shook her head. 'All right then. But I won't be long.'

'Is Edna here?'

'Not yet.'

Cathy wanted so much to talk to him, to explain how afraid she

161

was, and how she really believed she was losing her mind. But he wouldn't understand. And how could she blame him?

He would have kissed her then, but something in her manner warned him not to. 'I'll be back as soon as I can.'

Going to the window, she watched him stride down the lane towards the stables. 'Love you,' she whispered. And no sooner were the words out of her mouth than she was filled with a terrible hatred that shook her to the core, and not for the first time she feared for Matt's safety.

When she saw Edna coming towards the house, Cathy ran downstairs to meet her. The kindly soul was shocked by Cathy's request. But she was wise enough not to show it. 'If that's what you want, of course I'll help you,' she said.

It didn't take long to move Cathy's few things out of the main bedroom and into the one at the far end of the corridor. 'I'm having a few sleepless nights,' she told Edna. 'It's fairer on Matt if I move out for a while.' She didn't explain how she woke in the night with murder in her heart. She didn't explain, because she couldn't. In her whole life she had never felt so alone.

When Matt realised what had been done, his first reaction was one of anger. Then he wondered if this was the beginning of the end of his marriage. Finally, before he faced Cathy, he rationalised the situation, and decided not to make a fuss. 'I don't want you to do this,' he told her. 'If you have another nightmare, I want to be close on hand.'

'I'll be fine,' she assured him. 'A few days, that's all I need. A few days on my own.'

A week later, Cathy and Matt still slept apart. Every night, Matt waited for her to come to him. And every night he grew lonelier and more afraid for her. Even in the daytime there was a distance between them, a painful chasm which it seemed he could not cross; nor did she want him to. He had no answers, only the fervent belief that it must come right. It had to! For he loved Cathy more than life itself.

Matt and Edna came into the hallway from different directions, she from the kitchen, he from the front room. 'Are you sure you don't mind coming over each day, Edna?' he asked. 'Just until Cathy's fully recovered?' Edna's presence always made him feel more comfortable inside. In spite of her rough and ready appearance – the tousled greying hair and the bulky misshapen figure that looked untidy in whatever she wore – Edna was worth her weight in gold. Through the good times and the bad, she was always there. Nothing was ever too much trouble for her.

'Shame on you!' she retorted, with an impatient toss of her head. 'You shouldn't even ask such a thing.' Leaning towards him, she asked in a more intimate voice, 'Did she eat the breakfast I cooked?' When he frowned and shook his head, she flashed an angry look up the stairs. 'I *knew* I should have stayed and watched her finish off every mouthful.'

'It wouldn't have made any difference even if you had stayed,' Matt told her with disappointment. 'She can be painfully stubborn when she sets her mind to it.'

'Aw, look now, don't go driving yourself crazy.' Edna had seen the pain in his dark eyes, and her old heart went out to him. 'She'll be right as rain in no time, you mark my words.' The conviction in her statement belied her true fears. At one time or another in her life she had seen many things, but Cathy's ailment was beyond her. Joseph had described what happened down there at the stables. It had shaken him badly. It had shaken her also, but while Joseph had got over the shock, hers had only been strengthened by Cathy's perplexing behaviour ever since.

Edna had convinced herself that Cathy's malaise was not of the kind to be cured by pills and medicine; there was something about that young woman's suffering that came from the soul. If only Edna dared speak the truth, it would be to warn Matt that it was not a doctor Cathy required. Not a doctor, but a priest. But then she was just a foolish old woman who could be wrong, and who was loath to confess her thoughts. What did she know of these things anyway? Not enough to risk losing two valued friends and the respect of her old man, that was for sure. All the same, *there was something*. She felt it in her bones.

'I'll make a start on the housework,' she told Matt now, 'but

163

first I'll brew a fresh pot of tea, and perhaps persuade Cathy to have a piece of toast and marmalade. And don't look so worried. Like I said, we'll get her well if it's the last thing we do.' God willing, she thought. We'll get her well – if God's willing.

'What would we do without you?' Already, Matt's spirits were lifted. Edna had a way of doing that. It was the same when he was a boy. And ever since his parents died.

'Oh, you'd manage well enough, I dare say, Matt Slater.' He would have gone up the stairs then, but she laid a large coarse hand on his arm, saying, 'Joseph tells me you've hardly set foot in the yard this past week?'

Matt looked away, flooded with guilt. 'I haven't had the stomach for work,' he murmured. 'Cathy's all that matters to me. Nothing else . . . only my Cathy.' His voice tailed away, the heartbreak already betrayed.

'That's how it should be,' Edna told him quietly. 'You love her, and it's a joy to see. But don't turn your back on everything else, Matt.' After all these years, she looked on him like a son. It hurt her to see him so desperately worried. 'I can stay with Cathy most of the day. She'll come to no harm with me, and you can see for yourself how much better she is. What happened was a bad thing, but it's over, and she's mending well. If you don't work, you'll only brood. It's not good for either of you. Trust me, won't you? You get back to your work in the morning and let me keep a discreet eye on Cathy. Will you do that?'

Matt did not reply. Instead, he half-smiled at her and went slowly up the stairs. Some way up, he turned to look down on her. As he had suspected, Edna was watching him, her anxiety so obvious. 'You're a good woman,' he told her. 'I'll bear in mind what you've said.'

'That's all I'm asking, son,' she replied. 'Just think on it, and happen it won't be too long before Cathy herself comes back to the yard. Sometimes work can be the best medicine of all.' Satisfied, she swung away and went smartly into the kitchen. With Matt never far away this past week, she had not been able to have a proper talk with Cathy. And *somebody* had to! In spite of his deep

164

concern, Matt had been like a tower of strength to Cathy . . . talking to her and waiting patiently for her to confide in him, but – for some reason known only to herself – Cathy seemed more nervous and restless whenever Matt was near. Edna had seen with her own eyes how Cathy had looked at her husband when he was not aware of it. And it wasn't just resentment that Edna had seen in Cathy's eyes – it was a deeper, darker emotion, *a murderous thing*.

Edna was not a woman given to imagination. She knew what she had seen; she sensed the underlying confusion and terror in Cathy. Thankfully, Cathy looked on Edna as a friend. With luck she would confide in her, if there were only the two of them in the house, alone.

The following week, Matt persuaded Cathy to spend the day by the river. Her father was joining them. He, too, had been desperately concerned for Cathy's health.

Now, when he came into the bedroom, Matt was taken aback. Cathy was still in her dressing gown, her fair hair uncombed and a faraway look in her grey eyes as she sat by the window, her arms on the small chest of drawers, and her gaze intent on the sheet of paper she was holding. 'Cathy.' Matt called her name softly, as he came across the room towards her. She never stirred, nor did she look up. Stiff and unmoving, she seemed to him like a china doll. In the golden sunlight that streamed in at the window, bathing her in its glow, she had never looked more beautiful. Yet the picture tore at his heart, for nor had she ever looked more sad and lost.

'Cathy . . . why aren't you ready? Your father will be here any minute.'

She appeared not to have heard him. Tenderly, he stroked her hair, his gaze drawn to the paper in her hands. He froze with shock. 'Did *you* do this?' he asked. Reluctantly he reached down and slid the paper from her hands. She did not resist. 'Cathy, I asked . . . *did you do this*?' His voice was trembling as he deliberately suppressed his anger. Yet when she still did not answer, he thrust the paper in front of her face. 'It's hideous!' he told her, trembling.

In a cunning move that took him by surprise, she snatched the sheet of paper from him and sprang out of the chair. 'Go away!' she yelled, backing from him, her body arched forward and her eyes spitting fire. 'Why don't you leave me be? Why won't you *ever* leave me be!' She clutched the paper to her breast, cradling it like a mother might cradle a child. Suddenly she was sobbing, deep racking sobs that destroyed him.

Shocked, he moved cautiously towards her. 'All right . . . all right, sweetheart.' Holding his arms out, he sent her all the love he could. He was out of his depth. She *looked* like his Cathy, and, beneath the hostility, her voice was the same. But he was more afraid than ever that he was losing her.

Suddenly she jerked her head up. The sobbing stopped as abruptly as it had begun. She was laughing – a cruel grating sound that stopped him in his tracks. When she spoke, it was in a low, broken voice from deep, deep inside. 'Are you hurting . . . Matt Ryan? . . . *Tormented?*' The awful voice fell to a harsh whisper. 'Oh yes, *but not ready . . . to die.*'

If Matt had suspected his own sanity, if he had half-believed that something evil had come between them, he now believed it more than ever. Even as he stared at her, fighting the chaos within him and mortally afraid for both their souls, he saw Cathy's face soften and blossom. He saw the torture fall away from her lovely features and now, when she spoke again, there was no malice in her voice, nothing sinister – only the bright smiling tones that he knew and loved.

'Matt!' Surprise emanating from her face, she rushed towards him, planting a hurried kiss on his mouth. 'Leave me be, please, or I'll never be ready.' Glancing at the sheet of paper in her hand, she seemed momentarily confused, a frown cutting deep into her forehead. Then she screwed up the paper and threw it into the round wicker bin by the bed. 'Is Dad here yet?' she asked, turning her back on Matt and going to the wardrobe. Flinging open the wardrobe door, she pushed the clothes back and forth along the rail, searching for a suitable outfit.

'No.' Matt hardly recognised the small, distant voice as being his own. Surreptitiously he side-stepped to scoop the discarded sheet of paper from the waste bin. 'Cathy . . .' He was hesitant, unsure. She had called him by a strange name . . . Matt *Ryan*.

'Yes?' She withdrew a pair of white culottes from the wardrobe and turned to look at him, waiting for his answer and regarding him with concern. She saw how tired he looked, how anxious. Laying the culottes on the bed, she went to him, threading her arms round the thickness of his waist and putting her head to his chest. 'Please, Matt, don't worry about me.'

The nearness of her was heaven, the warm, pleasant smell like roses after rain. Like before, so long ago, she subdued the pain in him. He wrapped himself around her, drawing her into him. 'Oh, Cathy.' His soft murmur was a cry from the heart. Reaching down, he cupped her chin in his hand, tilting her face, all the furore alive in his eyes as he met her quiet grey gaze. 'How can I help but worry about you?' he said, simply. 'I love you.'

She smiled, but it was a sad, unconvincing expression. He knew the struggle beneath. It was too much like his own. 'I know you do,' she told him, 'and I love you.'

'We don't have to go to Bedford,' he said, a small hope kindled in him. 'We can make our excuses . . . stay here and talk.' When she gave no reply, but glanced towards the window, that faraway look returning to her eyes, he urged, 'You'd like that, wouldn't you, Cathy? You'd rather we stayed here.' Hesitantly now, careful not to alarm her, 'We do need to talk about what happened last week . . . about the way you are, Cathy – the way we were.' In her silence he grew bolder. 'I'm afraid, sweetheart. There are so many things I need to understand.'

'No.' She pulled away. 'I don't want to talk. We've talked enough, I think, and I promised my father we would go to the river with him today. It's the first time I've been out in a week.' She put her small hands flat on his chest and plucked absent-mindedly at the buttons on his shirt. 'It's difficult for me, Matt. Please don't make it any harder.'

Matt felt himself falling apart inside. With every word she was putting a wider wedge between them. All his hopes were dashed, all his fears unresolved. 'Just now, sweetheart . . .' he began, not sure how to say it, 'just now, you called me by another name.'

Anticipating what he was about to ask her, Cathy interrupted. 'Like I said, I don't want to talk about it.' And she didn't. Because she was too afraid. If only Matt knew the vivid nightmares that would not let her be . . . haunting, persistent nightmares that stayed even in the brilliance of a summer's day . . . terrifying images that had no recognisable form, no substance, creeping things that swam into every dark corner of her being. Sometimes the nightmares were too awful to bear; sometimes they brought terror, often they brought immense joy. Always they were with her. *But she must not tell!* The voices had warned her. They were warning her now. She must never tell. Matt did not know. He did not understand, how could he? A spiral of hatred wormed up inside her; his touch was repugnant to her. The desire to hurt him was overpowering . . . the need to see him suffer, to see him dead. Like before, she felt a lingering regret. Half-heartedly she fought against the sucking darkness that swept over her, burying her every normal instinct. Then, like a drowning soul, she stopped resisting. It was bitterly sweet.

'Don't want to talk.' Her voice was barely audible, her fingernails penetrating the thinness of his shirt pricking his skin like razor-sharp knives.

'We *will* talk!' Incensed by the terror she wrought in him, he clasped his large fists over her hands, flattening them, pinning them to his chest. 'I want you to see a doctor, Cathy. *For God's sake listen to me.*'

'I've *seen* the doctor!'

'No, you haven't. Not the kind I have in mind.' He lowered his voice, desperate, pleading. 'Let me arrange it, sweetheart.'

'You think I'm mad, don't you?'

Her remark took him by surprise. Guilt was written on his face. 'I don't think that.'

She laughed. 'I'm glad to hear it.' Reaching up she kissed him full on the mouth, awakening his passion, then cruelly suppressing it as she broke away. 'Give me five minutes,' she asked, going to the drawer and taking out a towel. Pausing on her way into the shower room, she turned her full, lovely smile on him. 'You know, Matt . . . I'm really looking forward to going out.'

'That's good, sweetheart,' he said warmly. And it was. When he saw Cathy like this, free of the shadows that haunted her face, and more like her old self, his fears and suspicions seemed unfounded. In fact, he was made to wonder whether it wasn't *himself* who was exacerbating the situation. More than that, and far more disturbing, he wondered again whether it wasn't him who was going mad. From now on, he would view Cathy's recent illness with proper sympathy. The doctor had attributed Cathy's panic attack to quite normal pressures, the excitement and hard work leading up to the wedding and the sad fact that Cathy had no mother to help her through it, the honeymoon itself which, though it had been a once-in-a-lifetime experience, was also arduous and uniquely demanding in terms of time and travel. And, more recently, there had been the sheer back-breaking work of preparing for the biggest equestrian event. On top of which, while he had quickly settled back into a much-loved and familiar routine, Cathy was still getting accustomed to a whole new way of life.

The more he thought on all these things, the more Matt convinced himself that he was not being fair to Cathy. No wonder she had grown cold towards him. It was no more than he deserved!

As he left the bedroom, Matt could hear her singing in the shower. His heart felt lighter. Only for one brief moment was his newfound hope depleted, and that was when he reached the kitchen and straightened the sheet of paper out, wanting to satisfy his curiosity about the drawing he had seen there. The first side was blank; he turned it over. *Both sides were blank.* There was no sketch, no mark at all. His curiosity heightened, he ran back up the stairs, convinced he had retrieved the wrong piece of paper from the waste bin. As he bent his head to look into the bin, he could hear Cathy preparing to emerge from the shower. Puzzled, he quickly left the room. *The waste bin had been empty.* So he *had* got the same sheet of paper that Cathy had drawn on. More than ever he was convinced it was not Cathy who needed to see a psychiatrist, but himself.

The sketch he imagined he had seen on that paper was still vivid in his mind. It was the picture of an old woman, burning on a pyre, her toothless mouth open, her eyes wide and terrified. In the background was a man, not unlike himself . . . a tall, dark-haired man. He was striding into the ocean, a strange and haunting look on his face as the waves reached out in the shape of many hands, caressing him, engulfing him. *That* was what Matt had seen. But then, he could not have seen such things, for the paper was blank. Like so many other things of late, he must have imagined it.

The old lady was determined. 'It won't be long before I'm buried six feet beneath the earth,' she said impatiently. 'I won't be going anywhere *then*, that's for certain. So, while I've got the use of my legs, I don't intend to be strapped in a push-chair like a helpless baby!' Having said her piece, she clasped her two gnarled hands together and pressed herself firmly into the armchair.

Emily remained silent for a moment, feeling utterly exasperated as she stared down on Maria. Lately, Maria had been unusually short tempered. Emily wondered whether she felt ill or in pain, but each time she broached the subject, she would emphatically deny any such thing. Yet there *was* something playing on Maria's mind. Emily was sure of it, and it was a source of great concern to her. 'What am I going to do with you?' she asked, shaking her head. 'You know how easily you tire, Maria, and it's such a hot day.'

'When I get tired, we'll walk back again,' Maria retorted.

'Would you rather not go?' Emily recalled the last time she let Maria talk her into going out without the wheelchair. Maria had insisted on walking too far before she admitted how exhausted she was. Then she had stubbornly resisted Emily's suggestion that they get a taxi home. The long walk back had been excruciatingly slow, and obviously painful for her. Emily was adamant that never again would she allow Maria to talk her into leaving the wheelchair behind. She was adamant now.

'I've set my heart on going along the riverbank today,' declared Maria, 'it's been too long since I ventured outside this house.'

'All right, then,' Emily conceded, with a little smile on her homely face, 'but we take the wheelchair.'

'No!' Maria's face had lit up on Emily's first words, but now she was both surprised and resolute. 'No wheelchair. Either you accompany me *without* that contraption, or I go on my own.' She gripped her bony hands round the chair arms and began struggling upright.

'I didn't say you had to *sit* in the wheelchair,' Emily told her, offering a helping hand. 'I said we'll take it with us.'

'Why?'

'Just as a precaution for when you get tired.' She smiled into Maria's bright blue eyes. 'And you *will* get tired. Admit it.'

The old lady was standing now, leaning lightly on the other woman's arm. Maria looked much younger than her great age, even pretty with her iron-grey hair rolled into a thick halo round her head. In spite of the labyrinth of lines across her face and neck, the hint of past beauty was always evident in the full-shaped mouth and sparkling blue eyes, and in the proud way she held herself. Normally she was content to leave her choice of dress to Emily – although every item in her wardrobe had been of her *own* choosing – but on this particular morning she had insisted on wearing the prettiest frock.

Maria had woken with a strange mood on her. It was almost as though she sensed her life might too soon be over. Always aware of her vast age, Maria had recently smelled the Angel of Death close by. It was not a pleasant thing, yet she was not afraid of death itself. In fact, there were times – when her mind gentled back over the years, and the loneliness became too unbearable – when she was almost impatient for that long, final peace. But she *was* afraid . . . of how quickly the days, weeks and years seemed to rush by. Time was the enemy! Time was fast running out, and she still had much to do. There were those, younger and more deserving than her, who were in mortal danger. These innocents were already under the influence of an awesome and terrifying evil. And only she, Maria Hinson, the one remaining blood kin to Matthew Slater, might hold the key to his salvation. Somehow, there were things let loose against that young man . . . ageless, vindictive things that were hell-bent on destruction.

Gradually, and with the help of a secret outside source, Maria had begun to fit the jigsaw together. A closer inspection of those artefacts which had once belonged to Ralph and Maria Ryan told her two very important things; one which had not occurred to her before, and another which she could not have been aware of until Matthew Slater took his bride to Australia.

Firstly, nowhere in Maria Ryan's diary was there any mention of a particular tallow doll – nor indeed were there any entries whatsoever that referred to a doll of any kind. This had intrigued the old lady. Day and night she had agonised over it. One thing she could tell right away from her grandmother's beautifully kept diary was that Maria Ryan never missed a single day without entering every detail, however trivial. Why then was there no mention of that doll?

Deeply puzzled, she had churned it over and over in her mind, irritated because she had not noticed the omission on the one occasion, long ago, when she had read her grandmother's diary. But then, it had been little more than a hurried glance. Peering into something so precious as a woman's private thoughts was somehow repugnant, and yet how else would history be passed down through generations, if it was not primarily through the written word? All the same, the old lady had long ago secreted the diary away, together with all of her grandparents' treasured things.

When she saw Matthew Slater's picture in the paper, though, and realised with a mingling of pride and horror that he just might be the last living male link to the past, curiosity and a sense of impending danger had obliged her to take out the diary. It was then she saw that there was no mention of the tallow doll . . . the same doll which Maria Ryan's dearest friend, Elizabeth Manners, had assumed was a gift to Maria from Ralph. Down the years, the assumption was never questioned. *Until now!* Could it be that the tallow doll had not been a gift? Or even that it had not belonged to Maria Ryan? And, if not, then where did it come from? And why did Elizabeth Manners tell Agatha she had 'found it lying on the floor of your mammy's parlour'? If it was not Agatha's and not Maria Ryan's, then where had it come from?

Maria had learned to her cost that the tallow image was evil; created by evil, and emanating evil. All these years it had lain dormant, quietly brooding beneath the earth. She had at times been tempted to make sure that it was still there. But she was too afraid. Instead, she watched from the window, keeping vigil, being at last convinced that what she had put deep in the ground remained trapped there all these years.

Yet, she had recently discovered, from the detective she hired, that Matthew Slater and his young wife were plagued with troubles. Maria suspected it to be the same dark merciless force which had plagued *her* ... used her to conduct its awful, murderous acts. Was there a link between that demon which was buried out there in that black earth, and the demon that stalked Matthew Slater? Maria had come to believe that the two *were* somehow connected. And that the answer lay in the second discovery she had made in her grandmother's diary.

Shortly before the drowning of Ralph Ryan, and the tragic death of Maria, there was an entry in Maria's diary which spoke of her fear 'that my dear husband is in the grip of a dark and relentless depression which appears to affect his mind. It seems to stem from his work. The pending execution of a woman convict is preying heavily on his mind.' Elizabeth Manners had described to Agatha how her mother, Maria, was greatly troubled by Ralph Ryan's work at the Fremantle lunatic asylum.

Maria absentmindedly agreed when Emily insisted that she wear the long blue cardigan over her lightweight dress. She was too preoccupied to argue. It was all becoming much clearer now.

According to her recent information, one of the places visited during Matthew and Cathy Slater's trip to Australia was none other than the Fremantle lunatic asylum, the very institution where Ralph Ryan worked. There was the link! As yet, the deeper significance of it all had eluded Maria. But she *would* root out the truth of it. She must! *For time was running out, and souls were in danger.*

'Will you be warm enough, Maria?' Emily manoeuvred the wheelchair along the path to the front gate; the old lady walked carefully behind.

'Of course I'll be warm enough,' Maria retorted, picking her way slowly along the crazy-paving. She kept her eyes down, afraid of falling, knowing how brittle were her bones. 'You've got me trussed up like an oven-ready turkey! If anything, I'll be *too* warm!' She glanced up, her blue eyes blinking in the bright sunlight. She could feel its warmth on her face, yet Emily was right to make her wrap up cosily, because her old body was slow to warm these days. 'My blood's running thin,' she mused sadly. 'Thinning to water.' Briefly, Maria's thoughts returned to her grandmother's diary. The more she thought on the entries there, the more anxious she became.

It was a glorious day, with the sun beating down and a gentle breeze tempering the humidity. The many large flower beds all along the embankment were a blaze of colour. Ice-cream vans were parked at every bend with queues of people spilling over the footpaths. Excited children could be seen and heard running and skipping in and out of the benches. Youths sped up and down the broad walkways, proudly displaying their skills on bicycles and skateboards. Dogs chased and yapped, meandering swans and geese searching for titbits fled away, wings wide, necks stretched in noisy protest. On the river itself, manned canoes sliced through the water, their muscular crews bent forward in tense delibera-tion, and occasionally the harsh commands of a coxswain would spur them on. It seemed as though every man, woman and child in Bedford was congregated here on this day of leisure.

Bill Barrington had finished his ice-cream and was leaning back on the bench, a look of contentment on his face as he tightened the rein on the two dogs, who were eager to be away. Now, as he turned to Cathy, his eyes squinted against the sun as she leaned forward to plant a kiss on his cheek.

'Thanks for inviting us out today, Dad,' she murmured.

'That's right, Bill,' Matt rejoined, his heart gladdened to see Cathy so obviously happy. 'I'd forgotten how relaxing the river is.'

'I love it here,' Bill confessed. At heart he was a lonely man, more so now that Cathy was no longer at home. He often came to the river, just to sit, and to remember a time when he was not so lonely. 'It's peaceful here.'

'Not so peaceful today, though,' Matt said, glancing up and down the embankment. 'Seems like everybody had the same idea,' he observed. 'But I know what you mean,' he admitted, 'there is still something uniquely peaceful about the river.' Sliding his arm round Cathy, he drew her into him. For a while they remained so, she with her fair head against his broad shoulder, and he with his arm crooked about her neck, his head bent to hers and his lips parted in her hair, his senses filled with her gentle fragrance. The way it should always be, he thought. Since he and Cathy had returned from their honeymoon, so many things had transpired to threaten their happiness . . . wicked, inexplicable things. It had been a bad time.

Now, with Cathy content in his arms, he felt at peace with the world. Life was good. While Cathy stirred against his body, exciting his deeper instincts, the urge to make love was strong in him. He had the irrepressible feeling that Cathy would come back to their own bed tonight. Suddenly, all was well with his world and the bad things seemed as though they had never happened.

'Shall we wander on?' Bill's arm was aching from restraining the two dogs. He was loath to let them loose before they crossed the footbridge which would take them away from the road and on to the broader playing fields.

'Yes. Let's make our way to the lock,' Cathy suggested. She sprang from the bench and began straightening the creases in her white culottes. Bill smiled to himself. Even as a child she was always fascinated by watching the small cruisers go through the lock.

At the bottom of the arched footbridge that spanned the river, Emily and Maria were finding difficulty in manoeuvring the wheelchair. Recognising the women as the ones he had seen crossing the road some time back, Bill, along with Matt, hurried forward to lend a helping hand, giving the dogs to Cathy and leaving Emily to support the old lady as she went slowly to the other side.

'Thank you so much.' Emily had one hand on the wheelchair and the other on Maria. 'She would insist on crossing the footbridge. She so much wants to see the bandstand,' Emily explained to Bill. 'I'm sure I couldn't have managed on my own.' She flicked her grateful glance to Matt and Cathy. 'Thank you. You're very kind.'

'It's no trouble,' Matt told her.

'None at all,' Bill rejoined. 'I'm just glad we were on hand.' He smiled down on Emily, entranced by her pretty brown eyes. He had noticed her slight limp, and the dark blemish on her face, and he thought how neither affliction detracted from her loveliness. He guessed her age to be somewhere between forty and fifty years, but there was an innocence about her that lent an air of youth. Now, as she smiled up at him, he wanted to know her better.

'Emily! Don't stand there daydreaming!' Startled, Maria had recognised Matt and Cathy from the newspaper picture. Confused and afraid, her first thought was to get away from them; get right away. She had to think. Her mind was in turmoil.

'All right, Maria,' Emily told her, but she kept her gaze on Bill's face. 'Thank you again,' she murmured, quickly turning away when his smile intimately deepened and she felt the rush of colour to her face. In a matter of minutes she had helped the anxious old lady into the wheelchair when, with only a brief, hesitant backward glance, she went on her way, following the path which would take them to the bandstand. Beyond that was the lock. Emily felt the small party following behind. The memory of Bill's tender gaze stayed with her, making her feel warm and pleasant. No man had ever looked at her in that way. She suspected no man ever would again.

Maria was remembering too, but hers was a different memory, and she was neither warmed nor pleased. Instead, she was greatly agitated. Seeing those two in the flesh had raised all kinds of fear in her. For so long, she had been forced to guard her most inner thoughts from that malign influence. *It was never far away.* Time and again it had tried to infiltrate her mind, to use her as a means by which it might escape the grave to which she had committed it. But, always, she resisted. It was a battle of wits, a constant struggle for supremacy.

Now, though, Maria had done the unforgivable. In that moment when she had recognised Matthew and Cathy Slater, she had been so riveted with shock that, for an instant, for the briefest instant, her guard was down. She wondered at the possible consequences, and was panicstricken. 'Take me home!' she insisted now. 'I want to go home.'

'But we've only been out a short while,' Emily protested, being cruelly forced from her contented reverie and now anxious to convince Maria that the weather was, after all, ideal. The sun was less intense now, and the breeze decidedly pleasant. Besides, up to a moment ago, Maria was enjoying her outing; she had said so herself. Maria, though, was adamant. Nothing Emily said could persuade her to stay out any longer. So, with one being reluctant and the other secretly frantic, they began their way home. The easiest and shortest route was back along the same path and on towards the footbridge. Maria's big old house was almost directly opposite.

The two women did not go unobserved. The man had parked his hatchback not too far away. Lounging on a bench which overlooked the river, he was feeding his half-eaten sandwich to the ducks, his attention seemingly taken by their noisy antics, but his shifty, watchful eyes were on the wheelchair, following its every movement. Neither Emily nor Maria had been out of his sight since the moment they emerged from the footbridge. Occasionally he would raise his head and look beyond, to another small group who had turned loose the two playful black Labradors and were now strolling in his direction, heading for the lock.

The man aroused no suspicion. He was merely a middle-aged fellow clad in dark trousers and white open-necked shirt, his face neither handsome nor unattractive, but altogether ordinary. One more hard-working 'ordinary' man, seeking a peaceful few hours by the river. And so he watched and waited, biding his time, pursuing a purpose.

There were others whose interest had also been aroused by Emily and Maria. Bill Barrington had been inexplicably drawn to Emily. Some deep, latent need in him was touched by her sincere brown eyes. After they parted company, he had watched her all the way along the path. He watched her now, as she returned, pushing the old lady in the wheelchair, her head occasionally turning to smile at the many laughing, excited children all around. As she came closer, he wondered how he might speak with her again. There was an irritating nervousness in the pit of his stomach. He silently laughed at his foolishness.

Cathy was another who watched, discreetly observing the approaching ensemble, a strange sensation taking hold of her . . . almost as though she was observing not through her own eyes but through someone else's. She was elevated above it all, observing everything around, yet not seeing . . . aware of the noise, but not hearing it. Suddenly there was a great calm in her, yet she was also restless and possessed of a tremendous, frenzied energy. She was strolling with Matt, holding his hand, yet whereas it had been warm, it was now shockingly cold, his fingers seeming not to touch her. Just ahead her father was playing with the two dogs. They were bounding after him, loudly barking when he dodged behind a tree. And all the while the wheelchair came nearer. Now Cathy could see the women's faces clearly; soon she would see the whites of their eyes. Already she could smell the fear – she could even taste it, bitter on her tongue, creating delight in her heart. Closer they came, closer and *closer*. She could hardly breathe. Now! *Now!* The wickedness surged through her. Be still, Cathy . . . *be still,*

Cathy! The dogs were silent now, ears pricked, wide eyes staring at Cathy.

Even before she looked up, Maria knew. In her heart she knew. It was just a feeling, unreal but all-consuming, a feeling like no other. So long . . . it had been so very long. Yet she knew the sensation of old. It was there when both her parents had died, when she had seen her own brother crushed to death, and on that day when her husband was thrown from his horse. It was there when the news came of her sister's horrific death. It was here now. Stronger than ever! She tried not to look up, willing herself to stare ahead, trying to concentrate on the noises around her, mentally grasping at anything that would create enough chaos and confusion in her mind to drive away all else. *But it was powerful.* Too powerful. She could hear it now, murmuring inside her, whispering, 'Look up, Maria, *look up.*' Tremulously she raised her sorry eyes, her reluctant gaze drawn to Cathy. Their eyes met. Long-ago witchcraft fled between them, sending a chill through her. She saw it then, darkly evil, malign, unbelievably exquisite. Like so many times before, she fought against it. Long ago she was no match for it, but that was *then*. Before she knew, before she had seen it.

'No, curse you!' The cry broke from her, shattering the spell. But it was too late! In an instant the dogs were on her, toppling the wheelchair, tearing at her flesh, bent on ripping out her heart; because she knew. *She knew!* All around the screams echoed, piercing, like the agony that speared through her, and still she fought like the very devil, but beneath the onslaught her strength was slipping away. Her hands reached out; warm red blood ran down her face into her mouth. It was oddly comforting.

'Jesus Christ! They're killing her!' Matt battled to drag the crazed dogs away. Bill was there . . . and the man – the 'ordinary' man – who had rushed to the scene and thrown himself into the furore, forcing himself between the savage beasts and the old lady.

Cheated and incensed, they turned on him, showing him no mercy. Maddened beyond all restraint they lunged at him time and again, incisive teeth splitting into him, his anguished screams spurring them on. For him, for the old lady pinned beneath his bloodied, writhing body, there seemed no escape from the killing space.

Amidst the uproar, the oar sliced through the air, smashing into bone, spattering the deranged brains beneath. There were no yelps, no lasting pain, only an eerie silence when the two beasts crumpled to the ground. The body of the man was soaked in its own blood, a twisted, grotesque thing not easily recognisable, insides out, hideous chunks of raw flesh torn out and still wedged between the dogs' teeth.

For the briefest instant after the attackers were felled, the silence was uncanny, shocked, disturbed only by the soft, horrified murmurs, and the sound of broken sobbing. Emily came forward on shaking legs.

'No.' Bill slid his arm round her shoulders, gently drawing her back. 'Don't . . . please.' She glanced down, looking beyond the man's remains. Just an 'ordinary' man; a brave and foolish man. Restrained by Bill's strong arm, she resisted, then something made them both jerk around. A small, whimpering sound, feeble, but alive.

'God Almighty, she's still alive!' the cry went up. They moved quickly. Soon the police were there, and the ambulance. The old lady was badly mauled, but still alive. Tenderly they placed her on the stretcher, the 'ordinary' man's blood dripping from her skin, staining her clothes. In pain, she half-opened her eyes, not so blue now, not so vivid, but haunted. First they looked down at the one who had lost his life to save her. The face was mangled, but she recognised it – the thick brown hair, the unusually green eyes, stiff with shock. She knew him and she mourned his loss. He had paid the price. Somehow she had survived.

Sadly, Maria shifted her gaze. Now, when she and Cathy exchanged glances, each sensed the bond between them. Its deed done, but not quite victorious, the malevolent force was gone, no doubt to hide in darker places, to secretly fester, to recover its energy. But it would be back, she knew that. *Relentless, insatiable, it would be back.* She saw the tears fall down Cathy's lovely face and her old heart went out to that unhappy soul.

180

Smiling in her pain, she held out her hand. Cathy gripped it tight. '*Fight it, child,*' Maria whispered, '*trust in God.*' She herself had long forsaken the Almighty. Now there was no place left to turn. Her eyes swivelled upwards to see Emily ever near, always loving. A sense of calm settled on her, then her eyes closed and the ambulance doors shut out the world, save for Emily, who went beside her dearest friend, quietly crying, and praying that she would not soon be mourning.

Through the back window of the speeding vehicle, Emily saw the curious, milling crowd. Her gaze was drawn to the young woman to whom Maria had spoken, and who was staring after the ambulance. There was the young woman's husband, his head bowed as he talked with the policeman. Beside him stood the older man. Both men were badly cut and bleeding; both had fought desperately to pull away the dogs. No man could have done more. The older man glanced up, his scarred eyes following the ambulance, searching for her. These people were good people, Emily knew. She knew, also, that she would see them again.

Cathy had been to the hospital twice before, and each time she had lost the courage actually to go in and see the old lady. Instead, she had got as far as the desk and then hurried away.

This time she spoke to the nurse behind the desk. 'The old lady who was involved in an attack down by the river. How is she?'

'Are you a relative?' The dark-haired nurse had not seen Cathy before. Her instructions were very clear. Only relatives to visit.

'No, but I was there. I just wondered if she was making a good recovery.' She felt somehow cornered, so nervous that the sweat was trickling down her back, sticking her blouse to her shoulder blades.

The nurse eyed her curiously. 'Are you ill?'

Seeming not to have heard, Cathy glanced nervously about, before asking in a whisper, 'The old lady . . . she will be all right, won't she?'

'We're doing all we can.'

'Can I talk to her?'

181

'I'm sorry. Unless you're a relative?'

'No.' Cathy felt ill. She had to get out, but she had desperately needed to talk with the old lady. Suddenly it was all important.

'I can let you see her through the window, if you like?'

'Yes, I'd like that.'

Cathy hadn't known quite what to expect, but when she looked into the room where Maria was fighting for her life, she was moved to tears. 'She looks so pale and still.'

'She *is* very old. But she's holding her own. I've never known anyone with such a strong will to live.'

Cathy's attention was taken by the woman seated at Maria's side, her hand entwined with the old lady's. She recognised her as being the same woman who was with her when the dogs attacked, and her heart went out to her. For one unthinking moment she was tempted to ask the nurse if she could speak with the younger woman. But before she could speak, the nurse addressed her.

'I'm sorry. I'll have to ask you to leave now.'

The nurse dropped the outer curtains, but the scene lived on in Cathy's mind. 'I'll pray for her,' she said simply. And she did.

Chapter Ten

'He's a vicious bastard.' Red faced and breathless, Joseph reined in the horse. 'I think that'll do for one day,' he told Matt, who had been watching Joseph take the animal through its paces.

'What d'you think? Should we agree to train him on?' Matt asked, a frown on his handsome face. 'Or d'you think he'll prove to be too much of a handful?' Joseph and Matt had conquered rebellious horses before, but this one had a deep-down nasty streak in him. Eighteen hands high and unusually broad in the chest, he was immensely strong and muscular. 'He's got all the qualities to make a top dressage horse, but he's lapsed into some dangerously bad habits, and I'm not sure whether we'll ever ride them out of him.' Matt watched as Joseph dismounted, in a surprisingly agile manner for someone who was no longer a young man. 'What d'you think, Joseph?'

Joseph sighed, regarding the horse with dismay before at length saying, 'You're right. He's got what it takes, but yes, he'll need a lot of work before he's ready to mix with civilised horses.'

'We refuse to take him, then?' Matt hated to turn any animal away, but this one was a rebel. Uppermost in his mind must be the safety of his grooms and the horses already in his care.

Joseph, also, hated to admit defeat. 'What say we give him another few days?' he suggested. 'Seems a shame to give up on him.'

Matt thought for a moment, his critical gaze roving over the magnificent lines of the animal. He was certainly a champion in the making, if only they could rectify the legacy of bad treatment as a colt, and a catalogue of shameful neglect right up until a few days ago when the new owners had bought him at a sale. They

183

were convinced that if anyone could train him, Matt Slater could. 'He's a beautiful creature, and no mistake,' Matt conceded now. The stallion was the darkest bay he had ever seen; almost black, with a proud bearing, and, surprisingly in view of his iniquitous character, his eyes were big and kind, though too often shifty and nervous. 'I don't know.' Matt was torn two ways. Suddenly he knew he could not readily commit the stallion to the knacker's yard. 'One week, then. If he's still unmanageable after that, we'll have no choice but to turn him away.'

Laura was consulted as the two men returned the stallion to its stable. She was in full agreement, though, 'Don't ask *me* to exercise him.' She knew her own limits.

'I think it's best if we leave Joseph to handle him, seeing as he's started with him. One man, one horse . . . that's a sensible rule,' Matt decided.

While Joseph settled the stallion for the night, Laura walked back to the tack-room with Matt. She knew how bad things had been between Matt and Cathy, and that awful business two weeks ago had seemed to worsen them. At least, Cathy still did not venture into the yard and, judging by Matt's quiet mood these days, all was still not well between him and his new bride. Laura hated to see how unhappy he was. There had been disappointment in her own life and she was no stranger to pain. She had learned to live with the loneliness. At one time she hoped that her friendship with Cathy might flourish, but, lately, Cathy seemed somehow hostile to her. Anxious to engage Matt in conversation, she said quietly, 'You miss the dogs, don't you?'

For a long agonising minute he gave no answer, walking on, his head down as though weighed with all the troubles in the world. Presently, he turned and looked at her, the horror of a certain memory betrayed in his dark eyes. 'I'll never understand it, Laura,' he murmured, looking away again, the thick rubber soles of his wellington boots striking the concrete with a muffled squashy sound as he quickened his step. 'What in God's name possessed them? I still can't believe it!' The dogs had been put down. He missed them like hell.

'What will happen, do you think?'

'I'm not sure. Banned from keeping dogs . . . a colossal fine, or both. Whatever the court decides, it won't bring that poor fellow back, and it won't help Maria Hinson.'

'They can't impose a jail sentence, surely?' There was fear in her voice. 'It wasn't your fault. You and Cathy's father did all you could to pull the dogs off.'

'I don't know, Laura. All we can do is wait.'

'When is the hearing?'

'The date hasn't been set yet.'

'The old lady – how is she?'

'Mending, but still very ill. Bill's been to the hospital several times. It's difficult for the old lady's companion to get there, so Bill picks her up and takes her in.' He smiled. 'I think he's really smitten with her.'

And I'm smitten with *you*, Laura thought shamefully. She had seen how these past weeks with Cathy had got to him, and now this latest tragedy. She wanted to tell him how sorry she was. She even started. 'Matt?'

'Yes?' They were at the gate now and he was looking down on her.

Her courage faltered. 'Nothing. It's all right.'

Smiling, he kissed her affectionately on the forehead. 'I can't tell you how much I appreciate the way you've taken up my work when I've been with Cathy.'

'Think nothing of it.' In truth she would rather be here at the yard than at home in her lonely bedsit.

'You know, Laura, I do wonder about you.'

'Oh, why's that?'

'Forgive me, but you're a very attractive woman, and yet there seems to be no man in your life. Don't you want marriage, babies, all that?' She was so good with the children here, it seemed only natural to him that she would want some of her own.

'I did, but not any more.' The silence between them was momentarily awkward.

He felt he had struck a bad chord with her. 'I've got a bloody cheek, prying into your private life,' he apologised. 'Look, when Cathy's well, I want you to come and have dinner with us, I know she'd like that. She's taken a shine to you.'

'And I've taken a shine to her.' Cathy was going through a bad time right now, but it would be good to make friends with her. 'An evening with you and Cathy sounds like a real treat. I don't have much of a social life.'

'What? No sweetheart?' He laughed. 'There I go again . . . prying.'

'There *was* someone, but we split up when I moved away from Liverpool.'

'I'm sorry.'

'Oh, it's all water under the bridge.'

'What about friends?'

She laughed nervously, gesturing towards the horses in the stables. They were her life now. 'What you see is what you get.'

'When she's able, you'll have a good friend in Cathy.'

Laura nodded. 'I know. And Matt . . . if there's anything I can do?'

'Thank you for that.'

Deliberately changing the subject, she asked, 'That man who was killed . . . it was merciful that he had no family.'

'None they could track anyway.' He opened the gate, keen to get back to the house. 'Goodnight, Laura.'

'Goodnight, Matt.'

As he went one way she went the other. 'Watch him, Cathy,' she murmured. 'There's many a woman who would beg and steal for a man like that.' Laura knew only too well how cruel and deceitful men could be. Matt, though, he was different. And he idolised Cathy.

Her thoughts returned to a letter she had received only that morning. Taking it from the pocket of her breeches, she read it again:

Dear Laura,

Please don't be angry with me. I know I've let you down badly, and I'm sorry. I would give anything for us to put all the regrets behind us and make a new life together.

The other woman was a mistake. I don't know how I could ever have imagined I loved her. I can't forgive myself for having caused you such heartache, especially when you have already known such tragedy in your life.

I can't bear to think of you now, alone, without any family. Please, Laura, find it in your heart to forgive me?

You must know I still want you. Please write.

All my love,

James.

With tears in her eyes, Laura crumpled the letter in her fist and threw it on the manure heap. 'It's too late,' she murmured bitterly. 'We could never be lovers again.' She remembered how it was, and she couldn't bring herself to forgive him. Yet she needed a friend. That was all. No commitments. 'Maybe we could be friends again . . . one day,' she wondered aloud. It was something for her to think about.

Pulling off his boots, Matt left them by the step and went into the house. 'Cathy, I'm home.' He shut the kitchen door behind him. There was no sign of Cathy, yet she couldn't be too far away, he thought, because the pan of vegetables was simmering on the hob, and through the glass in the oven door he could see that the pie was almost ready for taking out. The delicious aroma permeated the room. There were flowers and a vase on the draining board, where Cathy had obviously been in the process of making an arrangement for the table. Going into the dining room he saw that the table was set for two. Still no sign of Cathy. Returning to the hallway, Matt called up the stairs. 'Cathy, are you up there?' Still no answer. Thinking she might be out in the back garden, he went by way of the sitting room and out through the patio doors. A quick but thorough search told him she was not there either. Puzzled and irritated, he came back into the cottage and looked again in every room. Cathy was nowhere to be seen.

As he was coming out of the dining room, he was intrigued to hear a low and haunting melody issuing from upstairs. At first he thought someone had switched on a radio somewhere in the cottage, but then he realised it was someone close by. Cathy, perhaps? *Yet it did not sound like Cathy.* The voice was that of a stranger, and the melody, too, was unlike any he could remember.

As he climbed the stairs, following its source, Matt thought he had never heard anything so lovely. It was oddly hypnotic, floating into every corner of his being, filling him with deeply pleasant sensations. Entranced, he went on, up the stairs and along the landing. He was almost there. The soulful melody was coming from Cathy's room. Curious, he pushed open the door.

At first he didn't see her. The evening sunshine poured in through the dormer window in a thin, brilliant shard, blinding him for a second until his eyes grew accustomed. The room was small, sparsely furnished with only a narrow oak wardrobe, a small, matching chest of drawers, and a three-quarter size bed. The walls were emulsioned in a blue pastel shade, the cushions, curtains and bedspread were all in a quiet, pretty floral pattern. Beside the bed stood a barrel-backed rocking chair. Cathy was curled up there, her legs tucked beneath her and her head half-turned to the window. There was a faraway look in her eyes. The plaintive melody was softer now, more beautiful. Matt remembered. Of course! He *had* heard that melody before. In the car . . . when they were returning from the airport. His heart leapt as the memory became more vivid. It was when Cathy attacked him, tearing the doll from his grasp. The lilting tones were deeply affecting. Suddenly he did not find it so pleasant. 'Cathy, are you all right, sweetheart?' He wanted her to stop now. 'Cathy?' He came further into the room, sweeping his gaze over her. He loved her so much, so very much. So small and vulnerable; so lovely, like a doll. *Like a doll.* Instinctively, he peered closer.

Cradling the tallow doll, Cathy was slowly rocking back and forth, her fingers tracing its chiselled features, stroking its hair.

Suddenly, he froze. There was something different! But what? He was standing before Cathy now, and still she did not look up. The tune was no longer gentle on the ear; it was harsh, mournful. Stooping, he reached out to touch her. 'Cathy . . . Cathy.' He wanted to take her in his arms. But something held him back, some intangible thing that came between them. He had never been more afraid. Was it him? Was he insane? His gaze was drawn to the doll in Cathy's arms. The truth stabbed at him like the point of the blade. It was not the same doll . . . then it was! The features that Cathy traced so lovingly had not been the craggy features of an old woman, but those of a strikingly handsome creature, and the grey wisps of hair had become long thick shanks of deepest black. It was uncanny! Shocked, he drew himself up, burying his head in his hands, softly groaning.

Suddenly, the singing stopped and Cathy's voice punctured his frantic thoughts. 'Matt . . . oh, I'm sorry. I didn't realise you were home.' He opened his eyes; the palms of his hands were now flat against his ears, straining the facial skin, making his eyes seem bulbous. What the hell was wrong with him? His gaze dropped to the doll in her lap. It was old and ugly.

'You look tired,' Cathy remarked, carefully arranging the doll in its place on the window ledge before scrambling to her feet and sliding her arms round him. 'Bet you're starving.' She casually regarded his face, thinking how extraordinarily good looking he was.

It was then she noticed the strange expression, the alarming manner in which he was staring into the window. Curious, she half-turned, her eyes following Matt's gaze. He was staring at the doll. She reached out and held it up, the incoming sunlight creating a unique halo all around it. For an instant, one astonishing instant, the doll was incredibly beautiful. 'It's like nothing I've ever owned before,' Cathy said breathlessly. When Matt made no comment, but continued to stare grimly at the object, she reprimanded him quietly. 'You don't like it, do you? You've never really liked it.'

'It's a repulsive thing.' In spite of the tumult it caused in him,

189

he could not take his eyes off the gruesome image. Old, grey faced, with random isolated hair-stumps; not at all like the younger, beautiful creature he had seen. *Or thought he saw*. Trembling inside, he stretched out a hand to touch it. It felt hard, unyielding. On impulse he snatched his hand away.

Placing the doll back in its corner, Cathy moved away. 'We'd best go down,' she said, 'or the meal will be ruined. I felt suddenly tired, came up for a nap.' She massaged her temples, momentarily pausing, closing her eyes. 'I've still got a headache though,' she confessed. It had been creeping up on her all day. She thought a short sleep might be the best cure. But she hadn't slept, or, if she had, it was a bad sleep, disturbed by frightening dreams and weird gyrating shapes.

'Cathy . . .' Matt turned to look on her. All the old fears were coming back.

'Yes?'

'What were you singing just now?' Had he imagined that as well?

Cathy smiled. 'Was I singing?' The smile erupted in a small laugh. 'I don't *usually* sing in my sleep . . . do I?' The smile faded away. She felt his fear. Suddenly it was *her* fear too.

Crossing the room, Matt took her in his arms, sighing deeply as he pressed her to himself. He knew the tragic incident by the river had caused her so much anguish, caused them both so much anguish. Yet, it seemed they could find no comfort in each other. In the dark hours he would lie in the adjoining room in his own bed . . . *their* bed . . . thinking of her, so near, so far away, and the loneliness was almost unbearable. When would it end? Dear God above, when would the loneliness end? Dropping his head to hers, and growing intoxicated by her nearness, he asked in a whisper, 'What's happening to us, Cathy?' He felt her stiffen in his arms.

'What do you mean?'

'You know what I mean . . . why won't you come back to me?'

'I will.'

'When?'

'Soon.'

'Now? Please, sweetheart. Come back to me *now*. I miss you so much . . . love you so much. Yet I can't get close any more. We're losing each other.'

'I don't know what you mean!' Frantic, she wrenched herself from his embrace, meeting his agonised gaze with strong steely eyes.

'Yes, you do.' He nodded his head slowly, his gaze unflinching. 'Do you love me, Cathy?'

'I've always loved you,' she said. Her answer was immediate, the truth shining in her eyes. 'You know I always will.'

'Then what is it?' He was relieved but hurt; confused by her response. 'Is it because you don't want a family yet, is that it?'

'No,' she lied. If things were normal, she would want a family. But things were *not* normal. Some deep, persistent instinct warned her against going to him; warned her against bearing his children. There *was* something very wrong between them, though she would not openly admit it. She loved Matt more than life itself, but then he had the power to raise such loathing in her. She didn't understand. She was not sure what to do. That old lady . . . Maria Hinson – *she* knew. She understood. Cathy had felt that . . . seen it in her tragic eyes. When Maria was well enough, Cathy would tell her everything. Until then, she would not go back to Matt's bed. She dare not! Nor would she let him get too close. Too close was dangerous.

Throughout the meal, Cathy could feel Matt's eyes on her. All evening long she evaded his unspoken questions, going quietly about her work, seeming calm and untroubled on the outside, while on the inside she was in turmoil. A part of her longed to share the burden with him, but another part – more secret – cautioned her against it. She wondered why it was, that when people were in great pain and trouble, they could not bring themselves to discuss that trouble with a loved one? Like Matt, she felt there was some ineffable presence between them – a devilish thing that both frightened and fascinated her. She wanted to expose it, to destroy it, and yet, at the same time, she was terrified of the consequences. Certainly she could not tell Matt of her fears. He would not understand. Besides, he created too much conflict in her; too many malevolent thoughts. But then, didn't they say how love and hate were two sides of the same coin?

Maybe that was it? It was true that there were times when she had the strongest desire to see him dead, to kill him with her own two hands. He would never know how close she had come to taking his life . . . the other day when he was in the paddock, she had stolen into the tack-room and taken the shotgun from its safe place, even pointed it at his back, before relenting. Again, when they were in the kitchen and he was turned away, she wanted to plunge the boning knife through his heart. Only last night, when she suspected him to be asleep, the awful temptation was there, like a small persistent voice, urging her on.

Each time, when the compulsion to take his life was strong in her, Cathy had drawn on her own deep reserves of strength, and on the love she had for Matt. A love as persistent and alive as the voice that would deny it. Lately, though, she felt her strength ebbing away and her love for Matt being gradually swallowed up. Now, she could not help but cringe when he touched her. Matt knew that and it was breaking his heart, his spirit. It was breaking her also, beginning to erode at everything that made life worthwhile.

'Won't you talk to me, sweetheart?' Matt had seen how agitated she was, the way she fidgeted in the chair, pushing her food back and forth on the plate and keeping her sorry gaze downcast. It tore him apart to see her like this.

'Nothing to talk about,' she said with a smile, before beginning to clear away the plates. She noticed that Matt had hardly eaten anything. 'Have you finished?' she asked with disinterest.

When he merely nodded, she slid the plate away and went into the kitchen. He followed, coming up behind her and snaking his strong arms round her tiny waist. When, unexpectedly, she relaxed to him, his hopes soared. Putting his hands on her shoulders he drew her round, looking down on her uplifted face and sensing her great love for him. Without a word, he bent his head to hers, his lips playing against her mouth, delicious sensations flowing through him. Now, she was pressing into him, pulling him down, giving herself. Passion long denied fired his blood. He felt her pouring through him, exciting him, making him want her more and more. Moaning, he ran his mouth over her neck, her shoulders, his tongue teasing the soft velvet skin, his need of her growing like a fist inside him. He felt her peeling away his clothes, her need every bit as urgent as his. In that moment when he would have eased her to the floor, he saw how she smiled up at him, *through darkly taunting eyes*, eyes that were avaricious and menacing, black as night, smiling at him, devouring him.

Horrified, he snatched away, staring into those alien eyes, all manner of terror surging through him. And still she smiled, softly laughing. He could hear his own voice, just a whisper, a prayer . . . *'Dear God!'* And then another voice, Cathy's voice. No . . . *not Cathy's voice!* *'Love me.'* The voice was gossamer, without substance, a mournful sound. Above it he could hear the awful screams, *his* screams, silent, trapped inside his head. The screams stabbed his brain, splitting it asunder. Now the silence – eerie, more terrifying.

Through the blackness he heard a voice, Cathy's voice, familiar and gentle, echoing the fear inside him. 'I'm sorry,' she said. That was all . . . 'I'm sorry.' Anguish in her voice, sadness greying her face. *'I'm sorry.'* One last painful look and then she was gone. He did not follow. He was afraid, for her safety, for his own sanity.

Lying in her bed, Cathy heard him climb the stairs, slow, cumbersome footsteps more reminiscent of an old man than of Matt. The chasm between them had widened until there seemed no way across. Sad and exhausted, she drifted into sleep. The chasm was there in her shadowy world – she on one side with outstretched arms, he on the other, calling her name, moving further and further away. The dream was fitful now . . . snarling dogs, the stream turned red with blood. She was running, running in the dark, cold and wet, her nightgown clinging to her in the rain. *'Ralph!'* She called his name, but the wind carried her voice far away. In the distance she could see him – tall, dark, his lovingly familiar figure striding on, and on, into the ocean. Now the hands, so many hands, hidden in the waves, sucking him down, down . . . *down. He was drowning! Even as she watched.* She could not save him. Crumpling into the sand, her sobs were terrible to hear. The sobs carried over, waking her. 'Matt.' She whispered his name, silent now, listening.

She could hear his footsteps in the next room, soft muffled footsteps, slow and deliberate, backwards and forwards, backwards and forwards. He was tormented. She was more tormented. Stricken by all she had seen and heard . . . by the sound of those footsteps and the knowledge that he was suffering like no man should suffer. Cathy slid from the bed, tiptoeing to the door, meaning to go to him, *wanting* to go to him. But then the resentment was creeping in, tempering her compassion, and the voice . . . that sweet voice deep inside her – 'Now, Cathy, *kill him now.*'

For a fleeting moment the temptation was great, almost too great. She did not want to kill him. Not Matt. But there would be no peace until she did. The old lady's words infiltrated her mind. 'Fight it,' she had said. 'Trust in God.' Summoning every ounce of strength in her, Cathy struck home the bolt on the door and returned to her bed, not to sleep or to dream, but to remain vigilant all the night long. Soon she would do what must be done. There was evil in her. A badness that was killing her, killing Matt, mercilessly destroying them day by day. Tomorrow she would mark the old lady's words, and do what must be done.

Chapter Eleven

Emily almost ran down the passage. These days she hardly noticed her limp. When she saw Bill's burly outline through the door glass, she felt the flush of pleasure colour her face. 'Calm yourself, Emily,' she chided in the mirror as she tucked in a stray hair. 'unless you want to frighten him away.' The very thought of frightening Bill away made her shiver. He was her strength, and – dare she say it – she had grown to love him dearly.

When she opened the door, she was more at ease, although the bright smile on her face showed her excitement. 'Oh, Bill, how lovely to see you.' Ushering him into the kitchen, she followed behind. She felt so natural with him now, so contented when he was around.

'You've been out in that garden again, haven't you?' He noticed the earth on her fingers and the small trowel was still protruding from her apron pocket. She was flushed and slightly breathless, and from the stoop of her shoulders, he knew she was tired.

'It helps to keep my mind off things,' she confessed. 'But you're right. The soil is so hard and I'm not made for bending.'

'Sit yourself down, and I'll make us a brew.' He felt at home here, in Emily's delightful company.

Seating herself at the table, she asked, 'Did you come especially to see me, or were you delivering round here?'

'I hope you don't mind, but I came to see you.' He scooped the tea into the pot and poured the boiling water over it. Emily always had a kettle on the boil in case he should turn up unexpectedly, as lately he often did.

Placing the tray on the table, he laid out the cups and saucers, and sat on the chair opposite Emily's. 'It's the highlight of my day, coming to see you,' he revealed, 'but if you'd rather I didn't, you've only to say?' All the while he was speaking to her, his eyes were shining.

'Oh, Bill! How can you even *think* such a thing. You know how much I look forward to seeing you.'

Satisfied, he put out his hand, inwardly thrilled when she took hold of it. 'I'm an old fool, Emily,' he began, 'but . . . don't be surprised if I fall head over heels in love with you.'

She was speechless, blushing to the roots of her hair and shyly looking down at the patterned tablecloth. 'Really?' she stuttered. 'Oh, Bill!'

Realising that he had embarrassed her, he was quick to change the subject. 'How is Maria?'

'I phoned earlier and they said she was the same.' Emily was deeply disappointed that he should have changed the subject so abruptly. Still, she consoled herself with his wonderful confession that he might feel the same way towards her as she felt towards him. 'I wasn't going to see Maria until later, but it won't take me long to get ready if you're in a hurry.'

'I've done my work for the day, so whenever you want to go is fine by me.' He smiled back at her, then began slowly sipping his tea, his mind fleeting back to Cathy.

Emily had not missed the troubled look on his face. 'What is it, Bill?' she asked. 'What's bothering you?'

'You've got enough to worry about with Maria.' Emily had become very dear to him, and there were things he wanted to talk over with her. But he felt it unfair to impose at a time like this.

Emily would not be put off. 'Please. It's always best to talk your troubles over with someone.' Shame infused her thoughts. She too was guilty of having secrets. There were certain papers she had discovered in Maria's room, which had greatly troubled her. But, as they concerned Bill's family, she was still not sure what to do about it. For the moment she had decided to say nothing, until she had an opportunity to discuss it all with Maria.

An expression of relief flooded Bill's face. 'You're right, Emily,' he conceded. 'I've been longing to talk it over with you. There's no one else, you see . . . no one else I can turn to. Matt's eaten up with worry, and while I'm assuring him that everything will be all right, I can't sleep, I can't think clearly. To tell you the truth, I don't know how to cope with it.' Placing his cup on the table, he lowered his head and ran his hands through his hair, groaning like a man in pain. 'It's Cathy.' Raising his head he looked at her with stricken eyes. 'I'm out of my depth, Emily. Even the doctors can't say what's wrong with her.'

'If she's ill, it could be the shock of seeing those dogs attacking Maria. I'm sure it affected us all.'

'I've thought of that, and yes, I'm sure it all played a part in her illness. But she's *different*, Emily. Sometimes I look at her and she's nothing like my Cathy. Oh, I don't mean physically. But . . .' He was so driven by his fears that he stood up and began pacing the room. 'One minute she's the same old Cathy, thoughtful and concerned about me and Matt. Then the next minute she's morose and distant, like a stranger.' His voice fell almost to a whisper. 'There's something awful happening to her, Emily. Something devilish . . . destroying her, destroying Matt.' He was tempted to reveal how Cathy attacked Matt in the car on the way home from the airport. And that was *before* the awful incident with the dogs.

'I'm convinced it's the shock of what happened down the embankment,' Emily assured him. 'Be patient with her, Bill. She'll come through it.'

Sighing deeply, he smiled on her. 'I'm sure you're right.' He rebuked himself for having told her. 'I shouldn't be loading my troubles on to you. But thank you for listening and you're right, it has helped.' Though he felt better for having confided in someone else, he still couldn't rid himself of the feeling that Cathy would not 'come through it' so easily. God only knew, he'd prayed enough. But instead of regaining her health, Cathy seemed to be sinking into a world of her own. Forcing himself to speak with a lighter heart, he told her, 'Get yourself ready, then, and we'll go and see Maria.' He thanked the Good Lord for having brought him to Emily. She was an oasis in his troubles.

197

Upstairs in Maria's room, Emily stood looking down on the bedside drawer for what seemed an age. Her thoughts were in turmoil. 'Should I tell him?' she asked herself aloud. Going to the drawer, she opened it and peered inside. The wedding picture of Cathy and Matt stared back at her from the newspaper cutting. '*Why* would Maria cut out a picture of their wedding, when at that time they were complete strangers to us?' She fought with her conscience. 'I ought to take it down and show him . . . and the notebook too.' But she recalled how frantic Bill was about Cathy's state of health. 'No. He has enough on his mind. Maria will tell me. When she's well enough, all of this will be explained, I'm sure.'

Quickly now, she went to the bathroom where she washed and cleaned her teeth. Going into her own room, she brushed her pretty hair and changed into a blue two-piece, with a white blouse beneath. A few minutes later she came down the stairs, smiling and happy just to be in his company.

'You look lovely,' he said. And for the first time in her life she actually dared to think she was.

It was morning. Cathy propped the hastily written note on top of the kettle. She knew he would find it there. The first thing Matt always did on coming into the kitchen of a morning was to put the kettle on. Once he had had his early cup of strong black coffee, he was ready to face the day head on. The note was short and simple, telling Matt, 'I'm driving into Bedford. Expect me when you see me. Cathy.' She was tempted to assure him of her love, or at least to draw a kiss on the bottom of the note in the way she used to. But she was too mixed up inside, too unsure and afraid. Recently, she had begun to imagine someone looking over her shoulder. Watching everything she did. Silently assessing it.

Eager to leave before Matt came down, Cathy looked up at the clock. It was six a.m. Too early yet for her errand, but she must go now. Now or never, without telling *anyone* her purpose. In another hour she would not be able to sneak quietly away, because Matt would be here, and the yard would be full of busy, curious people.

Taking the pretty pink jacket from the chair-back, she glanced round the kitchen. This lovely kitchen had been her pride and joy, a wedding present from her father. She and Matt chose the units a week before their wedding. The kitchen was fitted while they were away on honeymoon, and, since their return, they had spent many contented hours here, lingering over breakfast, with Matt spelling out his plans for the yard, how he intended to build on it. 'Expand and prosper.' Enthralled, delighted in his company, happy just to be near him, to be a part of his life, Cathy knew she could never love anyone else in the same way she loved Matt. That love had not gone away. It was still alive in her. Only now, it was a painful thing, curled up inside her. Imprisoned.

'Oh, Matt . . . Matt.' She shook her head from side to side, her quiet grey eyes roving the room and being drawn to the wide window with its pretty frilled curtains. This was a lovely, sunny room, spacious, yet cosy. The floor to ceiling oak units were in a rich mellow shade, several of them were glass-fronted, displaying her collection of jugs and teapots. There was a round table with four ladder-back chairs, a Welsh dresser – again festooned with jugs of all shape and colour – and every labour-saving device available. Matt had even installed a dishwasher, but as yet it was unused. Cathy was an old-fashioned girl at heart, 'Still tied to the dishcloth and tea towel,' Matt had joked. And it was true. Cathy was content to stay that way. Besides, with only the two of them it seemed quicker to wash up in the traditional way.

Sighing, Cathy wondered whether things would ever be the same between her and Matt. Oh, how she prayed they would be. Yet, at this moment in time, she could not envisage it. Every day they grew further apart, every look, every word, was another nail in the coffin of the joy they had known together. 'Trust in God' the old lady had said. More than ever, Cathy was convinced she had come to the right decision. Heartened, she collected her bag, draped the pink jacket over her shoulders, took the car keys from the pocket and quietly left the house.

The day was perfect. Small isolated clouds lazed in the sky like fat white cats watching the world go by – no desire to move, no breeze to kiss them along. The stillness in the air was uncanny. Suddenly Cathy felt chilled, apprehensive. Quickly now, before she weakened, Cathy unlocked the car door, climbed in, started the engine and was soon on her way, into the lane, past the yard and out, on to Safford Lane. At the crossroads, she lingered awhile. A left turn would take her into Bedford – where she had told Matt she was going – the road to the right went through Appley and on to Roburn. She glanced at the dashboard clock . . . six fifteen. Still much too early. She began to grow agitated. What to do? How to spend the next hour? She was growing afraid now. The longer she waited, the more her confidence was eroded. That creeping sensation was rising in her. It was never far away, but there *were* times when her thoughts were lucid, when good suppressed evil. It was during one of those lulls that Cathy had decided what she must do. It was only murmuring now, slowly awakening, but already she felt it writhing, beginning to assert its malevolent influence. Sometimes it was hard – impossible – not to let her senses submit. There was something so incredibly beautiful there, so sweet and persuasive. A sudden thought occurred to her, and it made her blood run cold. This malign influence that played on her night and day . . . did it know what she was thinking? *Had it somehow learned of her intention?* Back came the answer from within herself. *It did know!* And it knew she was planning to betray it.

Growing increasingly agitated, Cathy swung the car to the right. She had to get to Roburn. There was no time to waste. Already, that strange devastating calm was settling on her. She had not understood. She did not understand now. Yet she was convinced of one thing; either she was losing her mind, or there was an agent of unspeakable evil at work on her. She had never been one to believe in such things . . . things of the dark, things that you could neither touch nor see, neither smell nor hear. And yet she could 'hear' this wickedness in her, because it had a voice, a whispering enchanting sound that was hard to resist. It was too strong, too intense.

There was little traffic on the road as yet. Normally, what with the new motorway junction and the many lorries that left and joined the motorway here, it would take a good half hour to travel from Holden to Roburn. Today, at such an early hour, it took only twenty minutes. When Cathy turned in off the main road and drove into the car park of All Saints' Church, the clock on the dashboard showed Cathy that there was still twenty-five minutes to go before seven a.m.

Switching off the engine, she made no move to get out of the car. Instead, she snapped loose the seat belt and leaned back in the chair. She felt nauseous, suddenly unable to breathe. It was as though two iron-like hands were pressing into her throat, squeezing the breath from her lungs. Through the windscreen she could see the red-bricked church with its thick stumpy spire, and the words in Latin over the door 'Ferme En Foy' . . . her father had once told her that the words meant 'Forever Open'. If so, it was a lie, because the tall, arched inner doors were tightly shut, and the iron outer gates were padlocked. A bubble of wickedness rose in her, bursting in a low, garbled laugh, then the voice, her voice, but not easily recognisable, whispering aloud. 'How can you trust a God who lies?' The smile slid from her face. Stronger, still afraid, she challenged, constantly reminding herself of what the old lady had told her. 'Fight it,' she had said with tears flowing down her aged face. 'Trust in God.'

Getting out of the car, Cathy leaned her arms on the roof, her anxious gaze flicking from the church to the priest's house close by, then beyond, to the churchyard. Above the low-rising wall could be seen line upon line of memorials, granite crosses and extravagant urns, open books and statues of angels. Always in the summer months the graveyard was a blaze of colour, each and every grave lovingly dressed with beautiful plants and flowers. In the far corner, beneath a magnificent cedar tree, the whole area was densely covered in a carpet of reds and golds, wreaths, sprays and floral crosses. The flowers were new. The loss was recent, the grief lingered in the air like incense.

'All right, are you, miss?' The old man's voice startled Cathy out of her dark meditation. 'Are you waiting to get into the churchyard?' he asked kindly. He paused beside the car. Taking off his neb-cap, he placed it on the car roof. Leaning his shovel against the wheel, he waited, his old face tipped upwards, mouth open to show a crooked yellow set of teeth. With the sun glistening on his shiny bald head and his shocking white whiskers jutting out from beneath each ear, he resembled a gargoyle.

'No. I've come to speak with the priest,' Cathy told him, at the same time reaching into the car and taking out her bag and jacket. Putting the jacket on, she locked the car door and dropped the keys into her pocket.

'Father Patrick, yer mean?' Cathy nodded. 'Well now, 'e ain't usually about at this time of a morning, unless o' course 'e's called out ter give the last rites or some such emergency.' He regarded Cathy with curiosity. He could see that she was under some sort of stress. 'Got a relative tekken bad, 'ave yer?'

'No, nothing like that.'

'Can't you come back later?'

'No. I have to see him now.'

The old man stared hard at her. He could see the sweat beginning to trickle down her temples. As the sun wasn't yet fierce and there was still a bit of a nip in the air, he thought the young woman must be ill. He scrutinised her for a moment longer before revealing, 'Like I said, 'e ain't usually about at this time of a morning, but there's a special service first thing today.' He jerked his thumb backwards over his shoulder. 'Ye'll find him in there.'

Cathy was surprised. 'You mean, in the church?'

'That's right, miss.'

'But . . . the doors are locked. How do I get in?'

'Down the side. There's a small door . . . ye'll see.' He quickened his step, widening the distance between them. He seemed a homely sight to Cathy, his aged figure shuffling along, the cap resting loosely to one side of his head and the shovel balancing on his shoulder after the habit of a lifetime.

When the old man had gone through the gate and into the churchyard, Cathy followed the narrow shingle path which led down the side of the church and on to a small paved area.

Presently she came to a small arched doorway, leading into the nave of the church. Uncertain and nervous, Cathy pushed open the door and ventured inside. It struck dark and cold. For a moment she could not see, could not distinguish one shadowy shape from another. And then, she saw him . . . Father Patrick. A middle-aged man of medium height, with a shock of brown hair and an aura of tranquillity about him. He was standing before the altar, his long black robe incredibly stark against the white altar cloth.

Coming nearer on quiet footsteps, Cathy kept herself half-hidden behind the broad granite column. Her mind was in chaos. Suddenly she was afraid, her hands damp with sweat, her heartbeat so loud she was sure the sound must soon echo from every wall. Her unhappy grey eyes were involuntarily raised to the magnificent crucifix on the wall above the altar; its size and radiance was overwhelming. All manner of emotion surged through her as she looked up, silently observing the man on the cross, a man so graceful, so beautiful, tragic yet victorious, his eyes looking down on her, eyes that seemed to search deep into her soul, to smile on her, *and to condemn her.* In her heart Cathy reached out to him. She felt his presence. She also feared it. This was *his* house, *his* domain. She had no place here. Yet she lingered, mesmerised by those dark all-seeing eyes, overcome by the peace and harmony that was here. The conflict in her grew stronger. That same strange conflict that mingled love and hate until she had no way of separating one from the other. Suddenly she was too ashamed to stay. Disillusioned, she turned to leave.

'Is it *me* you've come to see?' The voice was soft, reverent. Pausing, Cathy looked over her shoulder. She was crying. 'Ah.' He had seen her tears. He came forward. 'You've got this far, child, don't go.'

'I should never have come.' Cathy surreptitiously wiped the tears with the back of her hand. It was too late for tears. It was too late for her. She turned to face him. The eyes that searched his features were not so grey, not so gentle. Inside she was beginning to harden. Beginning to despise.

'Something brought you here,' he insisted quietly. 'You were troubled, you're troubled still. Won't you confide in me?'

Unable to look him in the eye, Cathy lowered her head. She was swamped with guilt, unsure and in pain. The struggle. Always the struggle. It was winning, she knew. That fiendish thing inside her was spreading, engulfing all that was good. Soon, she would be helpless against it. Now, Cathy. *Speak now, or it will be too late!* Suddenly, like a light in the darkness, the old lady's words came back to her. '*Trust in God.*' Cathy raised her head, meeting that kindly gaze with determination. 'Help me,' she whispered. The pain was intense. Crucifying.

'If it's in my power to help you, child, I'll do all I can.' In that moment the altar boy appeared from a partly concealed opening at the far end of the aisle. Cathy stiffened, preparing to leave. 'No, it's all right.' Father Patrick came to her side. He smiled. 'Mrs Jarvis will shortly have my breakfast ready,' he told her softly. 'You wouldn't say no to a cup of tea, I expect?'

A moment's hesitation, then, 'I'd like that.' There was an urgency in her now, a strong inexplicable urgency to get out of the church, out of *his* domain. He was looking down on her, watching her. *Judging her.* Something inside her resented that.

The priest's study was exactly as Cathy might have imagined it . . . sturdy dark furniture, a spacious desk strewn with papers and all kinds of literature; behind the desk were shelves of books from floor to ceiling, lovingly tended plants on almost every surface, and two deep brown leather armchairs, one each side of a lovely old fireplace. Now, when she was seated in one and Father Patrick in the other, the tray containing tea and toast on the low table between them and the tall willowy figure of Mrs Jarvis having left the room, Father Patrick poured the tea into the pretty china cups, afterwards handing one to Cathy and leaning back into the chair, at once enjoying great gulps of the hot refreshing liquid.

'Now then,' he started, replacing cup and saucer on the tray. 'We have a while yet, before I'm needed in the church.' He quietly regarded her. In his work he had seen much distress and all kinds of pain, but rarely had he seen such suffering in the eyes of one so young. 'I'm glad you found the courage,' he told her now, 'it's

204

never easy, I know. All too often, I'm afraid, people find it impossible to express in words what's troubling them.' He smiled into those desolate grey eyes. He prayed it was in his power to help her. Waiting a moment, he gave Cathy the opportunity to speak. When she deliberately averted her eyes, looking down and toying with her cup and saucer, he said softly, 'You're not one of my parishioners, are you?' She shook her head. He went on, eager to draw her into a conversation, wanting only to reassure her. 'Not that it matters whether you're my parishioner or not. I know you must have your reasons for not going to your own priest.' Still she did not look up. 'We're all men of God,' he said, 'but we can't help you . . . *I* can't help, unless you trust me.'

His words touched a chord. 'Trust me . . . trust in God.' When she spoke now, it was in a voice so low and tremulous that he could hardly hear her. 'I'm so afraid, Father.' Summoning all her strength to suppress the rising contempt, she looked up, meeting his quizzical gaze with renewed confidence. He had to know! She must tell him everything, or lose Matt. Matt was her love, her life. She would not want to live without him. 'I'm afraid, Father.' Her voice was stronger. *She* was stronger.

'What is it you're afraid of?'

Cathy considered his question. What *was* it that she was afraid of? How could she describe the turmoil inside her? . . . The way her love was slowly being eroded? The insane unpredictable urge to kill her own husband? The nightmares that spilled into her waking hours? The hatred? The wicked and terrifying moods that invaded her body and soul? How in God's name could she begin to explain? Suddenly she wanted to laugh in his face. The fool! How could he ever hope to understand? A cold hand squeezed her heart. Chilling merciless fingers. She shivered. Already her mood was darkening. Now, when she stared at Father Patrick, the stricken grey eyes were streaked with black. '*Fight it!*' The old lady knew. Cathy had sensed it, seen it in that aged face. *Fight it or die!*

'Let me help you, child.'

'Is there such a thing as . . . being possessed?' The question startled even her.

Father Patrick made a small discreet sign of the cross on himself. 'What do you mean? What makes you ask such a thing?'

'I love him, Father and – God help me – I don't want to hurt him . . . Matt, my husband.' Fear was coursing through her now, fear . . . and an overwhelming sensation of excitement. Quickly! Hurry, Cathy! 'Sometimes I want to kill him with my bare hands. I hate him so much.' She could feel that hatred now, boiling inside her. 'The voices are never far away.' She was agitated, the words tripping one over the other in her haste to tell. Restless beneath his shocked stare, drawn to the quiet beauty of his sapphire blue eyes, she went on. 'The nightmares are worse,' she confessed, springing to her feet and going to the window. She stared out. The storm clouds were gathering, the morning was dark as night. There was a fury in her.

'What *kind* of nightmares?'

'*Frightening* . . . full of evil things. They won't let me be.' Her voice was quivering. She was breathless, her emotions in turmoil. *Tell him everything. EVERYTHING!* 'There's a terrible compulsion to destroy . . . destroy my husband . . . *us*. Everything that's good.'

He looked at her, then looked away when his gaze seemed to disturb her. 'Have you told your husband these things?'

'No.' She resented his question. Irritated, she came away from the window, pacing up and down behind him. 'I've told no one. They wouldn't understand. *You* don't understand!' She laughed, a soft unlovely sound. When he looked round in surprise, she was standing with her back to the wall, her head bent forward. She was softly crying.

Deeply moved, he went to her, his long fine fingers stroking her hair, his manner quietly persuasive, coaxing, in the way a father might coax his child. 'You mustn't punish yourself,' he told her gently. She kept her head down, but lifted her gaze. He gasped, shocked by the animosity in her coal-black eyes. He would have slid his fingers from her hair, but she reached up to entwine them in her own. It was *then* that he sensed the primeval badness in her. *An evil so powerful it shook him to the core.* She smiled, raising her face to his. He had never seen such dark wicked beauty. It was strange to him, uniquely fascinating. Her black limpid eyes never flinched, smiling into his, reaching down, touching not the priest . . . but the man, for he had been first the man and then the priest.

He was galvanised, fascinated, all his primordial senses quickened to agonising delight. So often when he was barely a man, temptation had come to him, and like any young reckless youth he had succumbed, tasting the wine, bedding the women, living each day as though it was his last. Tearing at life like a starving man, his appetite had been insatiable. But that was another day, another time. Ashamed and repentant, he had found his true vocation. And yet, the youth was still himself. He could never change that. The memories were always there and the shame. Sometimes the longing, too, was never far away. But that was his penance. In his every prayer, and through his every waking hour, he had long sought to exorcise the wasteful sins of his youth; to purge his soul of all that would have destroyed it.

He had not succeeded. He never would, for a man's soul was many things, each being an integral part of that man. He was a priest, a man of God. He wore the long black robe and he led the congregation in prayer. He buried the old and baptised the new, he married the lovers, and was confessor to the sinners. Yet, through all of that, he was still a man, the same man, weak and alive with passion. For so long, he had channelled that 'passion' into his work, into his beliefs and towards his salvation. Now, though, when he looked into those burning dark eyes, passion was the master. She knew. *She had seen the weakness in his armour.* She was calling him, murmuring, awakening the deepest longing in him. He tried so hard, so very hard to resist the temptation, but then the Devil was cunning and pleasures of the flesh so sweet.

Her fingers moved deftly until, now, he could feel her nakedness against his lower body. He was drowning. *Drowning.* Many hands embraced him, pulling him down, lapping over him, gently rocking him back and forth. Such pleasure. Now, the ocean was stormy, frenzied, finally exploding through him. *Taking his soul.* Exhausted, shamed, he softly moaned, his mouth against hers.

Exquisite. Destructive. It was over. Too late. Laughing, she pulled away, her black eyes victorious. Her footsteps across the room were like the pad of a cat. He heard the door close. The ensuing bitter moments seemed endless. After a while he went to the window, looking out, bitterly remorseful. When his stricken eyes met with those of the old man coming from the churchyard, his shame was overwhelming.

Cathy had lost track of time. Now, her senses quickened and she realised she was on the embankment. She could not recall driving into Bedford, nor parking her car opposite the footbridge. Groaning, she straightened herself in the seat and released her safety belt. Glancing at the dashboard clock, she was taken aback to see that it was midday and the whole morning was gone. But where? *Where had the hours gone?* A strange quintessence enveloped her, a lingering exhilaration. And yet it was tinged with dread. In that first rush of awareness when she had emerged from sleep, there was only a quiet, comforting void. Now, the fear was creeping up, infiltrating every corner of her mind. The pain was physical, yet not excruciating like before . . . like before . . . *like before!*

She unwound the window, gulping at the incoming rush of air. Oddly familiar sounds invaded the car – ducks and geese loudly squabbling amongst themselves; people strolling by and laughing, or quietly talking, the distant hooting of car horns and the unmistakable drone of traffic. Normal, yet not normal.

Collecting together her handbag and jacket, Cathy wound up the window and got out of the car. She was hungry, and her throat was dry. Locking the car door, she glanced about. On the other side of the river two dogs splashed in and out of the water. Two dogs . . . not Labradors . . . not like Matt's dogs. The awful memory was too stark. Matt! Where was Matt? Her heart sank. Now, the picture was clearing. She was losing him. But, there was something else. What? What else?

'Lovely day.' The woman smiled as Cathy swung round, almost colliding with her. A small prim figure with sharp features and wearing a pert little hat, she bore an uncanny resemblance to the terrier at her heels. Cathy returned the greeting and hurried towards the footbridge.

There was a small café on the other side of the river. She had to think, to get some sort of order in her mind. It was only a short distance, over the footbridge, then along the embankment to the old boathouse. The café was next door. The sun was blazing down. Pausing awhile to watch a group of small children at play, Cathy's heart lightened. Normality was all around her. Curiously, though, she did not feel part of it. She was outside, merely an observer. Her life was back there, with Matt. *Matt!* Where was he? The warmth of the sun was pleasant, tingling on her arms and face. Inside, she was cold. Fear was a cold relentless thing.

The cool interior of the café provided welcome relief from the hot sun. 'Thank you.' Cathy smiled up at the waitress, a pretty young thing with wide-awake eyes and a shocking-yellow ribbon in her hair. She put the tea and toast in front of Cathy and walked back to the counter.

Sipping the refreshing tea and gazing thoughtfully out towards the river, Cathy felt more relaxed. Of course! She had left the house before Matt that morning. She recalled her reasons – the note she had propped against the kettle . . . 'I'm driving into Bedford', it had said. But the note was a lie. She had never intended to come into Bedford today. Then why was she here? Because she was ashamed? Yes! That was it. This morning she had gone to see the priest. She had wanted to confide in him, to confess her fears and to ask his advice. She recalled how he had taken her into the house. She had started to tell him, she remembered that, and she was desperate that he should know the whole truth. But then, she had grown agitated, her courage had left her and all hope went with it. She could see herself running from the priest's house, ashamed, disquieted, still haunted. She racked her brains. There was no peace of mind. Nothing to give her hope. The priest had been a glimmer of hope. Now, there was none.

'Will there be anything else?' The waitress collected the crockery.

'Just the bill, please.' Impatient, Cathy followed the girl to the counter where she paid the bill and left a generous tip. On the way out, she stepped aside to let an old lady pass. Emerging into the sunshine, Cathy hurried on towards the footbridge. *The old lady!* That was it. That was why she had come to Bedford. Maria Hinson was still in hospital, Cathy knew that because while she and Matt had visited her only twice since the accident, Cathy's father, together with Emily, had been a frequent visitor to the old lady. His growing friendship with Emily was one of the good things to come out of that dreadful tragedy.

Suddenly, the urge to see Emily and to talk with her was strong in Cathy. Determined, she crossed the footbridge, and ran to the other side of the road. Here, she paused on the pavement, scrutinising the impressive row of grand old Victorian dwellings. According to her father, the house was a 'splendid place with bay windows and its original lattice arch'. Another time he had also mentioned how the house was 'almost opposite the footbridge'. At first, Cathy went in the wrong direction, which took her half a mile along the embankment to a relatively new block of flats. Retracing her steps, she soon found the house. Her father was right. Belonging to a bygone age, detached from its neighbours and standing well back, Maria Hinson's house still had an air of grandeur about it. Surprisingly large, and double-fronted, with wide bay windows and a deep imposing archway over the door, it was exactly as her father had described. Straight away Cathy could understand why he had enthused about it.

Standing outside the door, Cathy was assailed with doubts. How would Emily receive her? After all, they were virtual strangers. In truth, Cathy was not sure *why* she wanted to talk with Emily. Maybe she had wrongfully drawn the conclusion that whatever the old lady knew, Emily might also know. With renewed determination, she tugged on the ancient bell cord. Somewhere in the depths of the house a deep-throated peal rang out. Footsteps quickly approaching, then a pause, before the heavy panelled door swung back to reveal a woman with a surprisingly youthful figure. Cathy's grey eyes appraised the face, the smooth taut skin, marred only by the splash of darker colour, and the brown eyes, pretty, quizzical.

'Why, it's *Cathy*, isn't it?' Emily came into the daylight, one arm thrusting wide the door, the other arm extended in greeting. 'Come in, please . . . come in.' Her smile was quietly lovely, the eyes sparkling with pleasure.

'You don't mind?' Cathy had not known what to expect, and yet she was not altogether surprised by Emily's genuine welcome. Bill Barrington was a good judge of character. His praise for Emily was without reservation. In fact, his enthusiasm had prompted Matt to remark, in Cathy's presence, 'I've never seen your dad so happy. This Emily is good for him.' Cathy thought so too. She had long suspected how lonely he was.

Fussing with pleasure, Emily installed Cathy in the little-used room whose casement doors opened out on to the back lawn. 'I love this room,' she explained, waiting until Cathy was seated in one of the floral patterned armchairs facing the terrace. 'Maria hates it.' She sat in the adjacent chair; from here she could easily address herself to both Cathy and the colourful delights of the garden. 'She's a darling, but when she takes a dislike to something . . . or someone . . . there's no changing her mind.' She smiled, a wide, honest smile. 'Stubborn as a mule, she is!'

'Maybe that's what pulled her through,' observed Cathy. 'She *was* badly mauled. A lesser person might not have survived.'

Her face now serious, Emily nodded. 'You're right, of course,' she said quietly, 'Maria is a marvellous old lady.' She glanced at Cathy, her eyes suspiciously bright. 'She's like a mother to me. After my parents died, I don't know how I could have managed without her.' Suddenly her smile was back. 'But, thank God, she's recovering well.' She edged herself forward on the chair. 'Are you sure you won't have a cup of tea? . . . coffee? . . . a cold drink?'

Cathy shook her head. 'I've only just come from the café, but thank you all the same.' Such pleasantries, idle chit-chat, were taking her away from the point of her visit. No, she did not want tea or coffee or a cold drink. What she wanted . . . *needed*, were answers. What she would rather talk about was the way the old lady had looked at her when they carried her into the ambulance! *Why*, when she must have been in considerable agony, did Maria Hinson deliberately seek Cathy out? Why the strange look in her stricken eyes when she mingled her gaze with Cathy's? What was she so desperately trying to convey? What did she mean when she whispered for Cathy's ears only . . . 'Fight it' . . . 'Trust in God.' Because she knew. *That was why!* Somehow, she knew what Cathy had been suffering. In some disturbing unaccountable way, she was able to identify with Cathy . . . a stranger, and to send her a message that was both comforting and intriguing. Why? How could that be possible? Twice, Cathy had gone to the hospital, where she hoped to find the answers. Each time, she had found her to be heavily sedated. At that time, so soon after the accident, Maria Hinson was not expected to recover. Outwardly calm, Cathy said, 'You must be wondering what brought me here today?'

Emily smiled. 'I thought there might be a special reason.' Cathy would have gone on, discreetly edging towards her reason for coming here, but Emily put out her hand, interrupting. 'I think I knew as soon as I saw you standing outside,' she said a little sadly, 'and I can't blame you. After all, your father is a successful businessman, and you must know how lonely he is . . . how vulnerable.' She was anxious now, her voice hesitant. 'But I wouldn't want you to think I was a gold-digger, or that I would take advantage of our friendship. Your father is a wonderful man, kind and considerate, but I would never hurt him. I know what it's like to be hurt and lonely.'

'No, oh no!' Cathy was shocked to see how upset the other woman was. 'You couldn't be more wrong about my reason for coming here,' she assured Emily, smiling when that dear soul raised her eyes in relief and surprise. 'I'm delighted that he's found a good friend in you. He *has* been lonely, yes.' She laughed aloud. 'But he's not a wealthy man, so it would take more than a stretch of the imagination to think he might be pursued by a gold-digger. Although, of course, he is "well breeched", as Matt might say.' Now, when she thought of Matt, the small bubble of laughter burst inside her. In her mind's eye she could see him, his tall handsome figure, sincere dark eyes. Her heart ached with love. Her mood darkened.

'You *didn't* come here to voice any fears, then? About me and your father?' Emily was now curious.

'No. Believe me when I say that you have been a real tonic for my father.' In fact, Cathy believed her father to be falling in love with Emily. Now she hoped her father's love for this gentle soul might be returned. Some deep instinct told her it was. She welcomed it. 'I came to enquire about Maria.'

'That's very kind of you. No doubt your father has told you of the doctors' hopes for her full recovery? Although, of course, she has a long way to go. Her wounds are healing and she is responding well to treatment, but she's still very ill. Being of such a great age, there is always the danger of pneumonia.' Emily's love and concern for the old lady shone through. She would have gone on in greater detail, but she was suddenly aware that Cathy was waiting to say something. 'Forgive me,' she said, with an embarrassed laugh, 'but I do tend to go on a bit where Maria's concerned. Like I said, she has always been like a mother to me.'

'I understand,' Cathy told her, reaching out to touch her fingers against the nervously clenched fist, 'and we're all so very relieved that she's recovering well, but I hope you don't mind, only it was something else that brought me here today . . . something that Maria said to me. It's played on my mind ever since.' The brown eyes were searching her face. Cathy had the uncanny feeling that Emily knew exactly what she meant.

'Something she said?'

'Yes. On the day of the accident.' Cathy began fidgeting, not certain how to explain. 'Her eyes sought me out. She said something . . . strange . . . "Fight it," she said.'

'And to "trust in God"?'

Cathy was shocked. 'You heard? You heard her say that?'

When Emily nodded, a deep frown on her face, Cathy persisted. 'What did she mean?'

Emily rose to her feet and went to the casement window. There was a sadness in her features. For what seemed an endless moment she gazed out across the lawns, a distant look in her eyes. Presently she turned to ask Cathy, 'Don't *you* know what she meant?'

'No.'

'Oh.' Disappointment. 'I was hoping you might have the answer.' Her kind brown eyes roved Cathy's lovely features. 'It was a strange thing for her to say, I agree.' Her gaze was intense. Behind her the garden was a myriad of blooms, the vivid colours almost blinding. Silhouetted in the hazy sunshine, Emily's small frame was a black looming shape, her features indistinguishable against the brilliant backdrop. Only the voice was easily recognisable. 'I've thought about it a lot . . . what she said to you. It would be like Maria to want you to "trust in God". Maybe because she knew how close to death she was, and how devastated we all were. But I can't know what she wanted you to fight. And the way she addressed herself only to you, Cathy . . . intimately . . . not wishing anyone else to hear. Almost like a secret. That was very strange, I thought.'

'And you've no idea what she meant?' Cathy's instincts told her that Emily knew more than she was revealing. Suddenly, there was a kinship between them. It made Cathy bolder, gave her hope. 'You do know something, don't you?' she insisted. 'Something you're not telling me.' When Emily remained silent, her head bending to the carpet and a strange awkward silence descending between them, Cathy stood up, her two fists clenched together, desperation betrayed in her voice. '*Please!*'

Emily raised her head. She was deeply hurt to see how distraught Cathy was. 'Yes, there *is* something puzzling me. I would ask Maria, but she's still very ill, and besides, it may be nothing. I can't understand it, though. In fact, I had almost made up my mind to talk with your father about it.' She made a small nervous laugh. 'To be honest, though, it's none of my business, but it does seem so odd.' She studied Cathy through frowning eyes. 'Have you been to this house before?'

'Never.' Cathy was intrigued by her question.

'And Maria . . . had you ever met her before the day of the accident?'

'No.'

'Your husband, Matt, or your father, did either of them know Maria before that day?'

Disturbed by the questions, Cathy shook her head. 'I don't think so. *No!* I'm sure of it.' On impulse she put out her hands, gripping the other woman's small shoulders. 'What is it you're trying to say, Emily? Why are you asking these questions? Is it because you know why Maria said these things to me . . . *to me and no one else?*'

For a long time, Emily quietly scrutinised Cathy's anxious face, as though searching for answers of her own. Then, in a voice that was both soothing and penetrating, she made a remark that took Cathy unawares. 'I don't know why Maria said those things to you, but I suspect that you know!'

More afraid than ever, Cathy took her hands from the woman's shoulders and turned away, deliberately playing her gaze on the garden . . . on the wizened misshapen tree in the shaded area by the wall. 'I've been troubled lately,' she confessed in a low murmur. Emily came to her side. Cathy was comforted by her nearness. 'Things aren't too good between me and Matt.' She laughed, a painful sound. 'Oh, it's not that we don't love each other,' she said, 'because it's still there, the love, the need, the way it was. But there is something else, hard to explain, a kind of . . .' She paused, not knowing how to describe the black moods that kept her from him. How could Emily understand? She turned and shook her head in despair. 'I'm sorry,' she said softly. 'I didn't mean to burden you, especially at a time like this.'

'I want to help, if I can. If you'll let me?'

'Maria . . . that day. I didn't understand. It was as though she felt the turmoil in me. As though she *knew*.'

'I'm sorry, Cathy.' Emily's face was filled with kindness, and regret. 'I can't help you.'

215

Disillusioned, Cathy collected her bag and prepared to leave. 'Would you mind if I went to the hospital? I would dearly like to sit with Maria for a while.' She was in no hurry to get home. There was only more pain for her there.

'That is kind of you, but when I went earlier today, there was little change. She won't know you. Sleep is her quickest route to recovery, they say, and she is heavily sedated.'

'I understand.' Cathy waited for Emily to lead the way across the room and into the hallway. At the foot of the stairs, the two women paused, Cathy saying, 'I would like to sit with her awhile, if that's all right.'

Emily nodded. 'She would like that, I think.' Emily had taken an instinctive liking to Cathy. She recalled how Bill had feared for his daughter's health and it pleased her to see how well Cathy seemed. Now, going against her instincts to wait until Maria was well enough to discuss it, she felt the urge to confide in Cathy. Cupping her hand beneath Cathy's elbow she said, 'You remember I said something had been puzzling me?' When Cathy affirmed that yes, she had been made curious about the other woman's remark, Emily told her, 'There's something of Maria's I think you should see.' From the top of the stairs she led the way along the spacious landing to the old lady's bedroom, her steps quickening the closer she came, and a look of determination shaping her features. 'When you see what I found, you'll no doubt understand why I asked you all those questions.' Enthused now, and convinced she was doing the right thing, Emily swept into the bedroom. 'This is Maria's room,' she explained, 'the place in this house which she loves the most.'

Coming into the room, Cathy immediately felt Maria's presence. It was overwhelming, enveloping like the cold clammy air of a dark foggy night. Once before in Maria Hinson's presence she had felt a kindred spirit. She felt it now, and she could hardly breathe. There was a timelessness here, enveloped in the dark wooden furniture, the lightshade with its long creamy fringe, the brown patterned carpet and the thick patchwork bedspread. The air was clinging, but uniquely pleasant, all kinds of aromas mingling into one . . . the dry musty smell of many flowering plants, rose polish from the furniture and linoleum, the clean sharp smell of freshly laundered bed linen and the stinging odour of camphor oil. Little brass plant pots bright with blooms bedecked the windowsill, and all around on every wall hung various small pictures and pretty cameos.

The crucifix over the bed sent a shock through Cathy, bringing another into mind, with the church, and the priest whose sapphire-blue eyes had seemed to devour her. *There had been danger there, with him.* He evoked a certain kind of terror in her; she had gone there seeking help and he had sent her away disillusioned. And yet there *had* been a certain degree of amity in the church, in *his* domain. But it was cruelly short lived, like every hope she ever had. This house was Maria Hinson's 'church'. This room was *her* domain. It awakened those fiendish murmurings inside Cathy, that same deep-down horror which had seen the carnage in the stable and had watched impassive when the dogs tore into human flesh as though it was paper. The same horror that stalked her dreams and lingered into the waking hours – the very same horror that came between her and Matt . . . vague, insubstantial, yet implacable and real, a presence so intensely overpowering that she was driven to a priest's house . . . to God's house, only to find in the last desperate moments that it was stronger than she, its appetite insatiable.

The horror was always there, festering and growing, creeping into every corner of her being, invading her heart, her very soul. That same horror was here, *here*, in this room, in Maria Hinson's domain. Hidden away in everyday things, it was a horror too much like her own, yet nothing like it. Two sides of the moon, dark and light, black and white, right and wrong . . . a perfect opposite, the same. *The same!*

Coming deeper into the room, Cathy visible shuddered. Yes, it was here. *It was here.* And the essence of evil was so strong she could taste it. She was trembling now, wanting to run, desperate to stay. She was in a state of terror. Conversely, she was comforted by the instinctive knowledge that she was no longer alone. The old

lady was here. Giving her strength – 'Fight it' . . . 'Trust in God.'
She understood now. Yet that understanding only created more
questions, a deeper intrigue.

'Surely you're not cold?' Emily had gone to the bedside cabinet,
where she opened a drawer and withdrew what looked to be a
piece of newspaper. When she glanced up to see Cathy shivering,
hugging herself, she went to the window and dropped it shut. 'The
sun doesn't get round here until later in the day,' she explained.
'I'm one of those lucky people who don't easily feel the cold.'
Casting a puzzled look in Cathy's direction, she said, 'I found this
when I was turning Maria's mattress. She wouldn't let me do it
before. In all the years we've been together, ever since my parents
died and she took me in, I've never known her to be so secretive.
We've never deliberately kept things from each other. Until now.'
There was a sadness in her voice, and disbelief.

After handing the piece of paper to Cathy, she went on talking,
describing in detail the recent uncharacteristic behaviour of
Maria. Carefully observing Cathy's reaction to the item she had
found, Emily went on. 'I knew she was hiding something . . .
keeping things to herself. And I've had the feeling for some time
that she was desperately worried, but she wouldn't confide in me.
These past few weeks she's been sleeping badly, crying out,
suffering terrible nightmares. Oh, I know she's very old, and I
know I tend to be over-protective towards her, but she wasn't *ill*.
Not physically ill. She had these moods, you see, awful bouts of
depression, like there was something quietly gnawing away at her,
but she wouldn't say. She only told me to stop fussing!' Now Emily
saw how shocked Cathy was, how stunned by what Maria had
secreted away and guarded so closely. She went on, 'Do you see
now why I was puzzled when you said you had never known
Maria before?' she asked quietly.

Cathy stared at the item in her hand. It was the newspaper
cutting which showed her and Matt on their wedding day.
Clutching it tight in her fist, Cathy turned towards Emily, sinking
on to the bed, her face uplifted, curious, perplexed. 'I don't
understand,' she murmured. 'Why would Maria Hinson cut out a

picture of me and Matt? What could she want with it? And why would she hide it away? . . . Keep it secret from you?' Cathy slowly shook her head. 'I just don't understand!'

'You still say you met her for the very first time that day on the embankment? The day the dogs attacked?'

'Yes! Until that day I had never seen her, never even heard of her.'

Into her mind's eye came the look on the old lady's face, the eerie sensation that had passed between them. *She* had never seen Maria Hinson before, but Maria had seen her, had gone to the trouble of cutting the wedding picture of Matt and her out of the paper. More than that, she had hidden it away, not even told Emily. What did it mean? Why would Maria Hinson do such a thing?

'I did wonder.' Emily's quiet voice permeated Cathy's deeper thoughts. 'You see, Maria was widowed. Oh, she never talks about the circumstances of it, although from the bad dreams, when I've had occasion to comfort her in the dark hours, I believe she lost her husband in a cruel accident. That was almost a lifetime ago. There were no children. That much she did tell me. And I do know she loved him deeply. It made me wonder about the newspaper cutting of you and your husband on your wedding day, so romantic, the both of you so obviously in love. It might have reminded Maria of what she had lost.'

'And you think *that* was why she cut the picture out?' Cathy was not convinced. In her deepest heart she knew also that Emily was not convinced either. Then, there was the way Maria had looked at her. 'Fight it,' she had said. It was as though Maria Hinson had seen the unhappiness in her, knew its cause even!

Cathy sensed the deeper truth here, a mystery which only the old lady could solve. 'She *hid* the picture, Emily,' Cathy reminded the other woman. 'She hid it from you. Why would she do that?'

Emily shook her head, the frown cutting deeper into her features. 'I don't know,' she confessed, 'and we can't ask her. I'm not even sure that we have the right.'

'*I must know!*' It wasn't just the picture. Cathy saw that as being only part of a greater mystery.

219

'Yes, I understand, of course,' Emily conceded, 'but not yet. Not until she is well again.' Her purpose clear, she took the cutting from Cathy, replaced it in the drawer and went to the door, where she waited. 'I'm sure she didn't mean anything by it. Like I said, she's very old, and she lost her own romance a long, long time ago.'

Cathy made no reply. She did not believe it was as simple as Emily imagined. Besides which, she had a lingering suspicion that Emily knew more than she was prepared to reveal. Now, when she followed Emily out of the room and down the stairs, Cathy felt inexplicably drawn back to the old lady's room, to a certain essence there, a kind of fear. Some strange awareness made her feel as though she belonged, as though she and Maria were part of a greater conspiracy.

'I'm glad you came to see me, Cathy.' The two of them were at the front door now, Cathy outside, Emily inside. There was a sense of friendship between them. 'And you really don't mind about your father and me?'

'Of course not,' Cathy smiled, taking the other woman's hand in her own. 'You've brought a new purpose back into his life. He really is so much happier for knowing you.'

'I'm glad.' Emily's face blushed pink. 'I *am* very fond of him. And he's so good, helping me about the house, taking me to the hospital and all. He's even volunteered to be here when I interview the new gardener. The present one is due to retire soon, and I doubt whether we'll ever get anyone as good. Normally, anything to do with the garden is Maria's responsibility. She won't have it any other way. But, I'm afraid it's up to me now. All I want Maria to do is to concentrate on getting well again, and coming home.' Her brown eyes were suddenly bright. 'I do miss her so.'

Lost for words, Cathy mumbled reassuring sentiments and said goodbye. When the door was closed, Emily went quickly back up the stairs and into Maria's room. Here, she opened the drawer into which she had replaced the newspaper cutting. Dipping her two hands deeper into the recess, she brought out a small red notebook. Sinking on to the bed, she flicked through it, pausing occasionally to read a particular entry, the look of consternation on her face deepening by the minute. 'I couldn't show her *this*. What are you up to, Maria?' she whispered to the empty room. 'You're up to something, Maria. What is it?'

The red notebook was much more disturbing than the wedding picture, for it was like a diary, a detailed and meticulous report on the movements of Matt and Cathy Slater, from the moment they boarded the plane for Australia. The whole of their stay there was recorded, and every day since their homecoming, right up to the day before the horrifying attack on Maria and that poor man. Recounting every move that Matt and Cathy had made, together with a resumé of everyone they had been seen to converse with, and every place they visited, the detailed accounts were the worst invasion of privacy. Emily was shocked. There were details of how Cathy's mother had deserted her husband and child all those years ago. And it revealed the tragic manner in which both of Matt's parents had lost their lives. The last piece of information was underlined in red.

For what seemed hours, yet was no more than moments, Emily sat on the edge of the bed, head down, eyes staring at the book pressed between her hands. The image of Maria rose before her, and it was almost as though she was seeing a stranger. The writing in the book was not of Maria's hand; Emily was certain of that. It followed, then, that the account of Matt and Cathy's movements was entered by another. Emily hated herself for thinking it, but she could only conclude that Maria had appointed a private investigator. The idea was preposterous! And yet, what other explanation was there? 'When? *How* could you have done this?' Maria never left the house without Emily, and Emily never left her alone, except for a few hours on a Friday. *Friday*. But no, it wasn't possible. If there had been anyone calling in her absence – a man, a private investigator – *Sally* would have told her. Emily's first instinct was to go to Sally and question her, but then she remembered. Sally had left her job here, left the area, the very day after Maria and the man were attacked.

There was nothing else for it but to wait until Maria herself was able to explain. And she must explain, for the sake of her long and intimate relationship with the woman she had raised from a child, and who was now so shattered by the discovery she had made that she wondered whether she and Maria would ever be the same again. Oh, she loved the old lady, adored her like the mother she had been, but Emily had always trusted Maria implicitly, without question. She was disillusioned. *And afraid.* For there were three other entries in the back of the book, all in Maria's own hand. One related directly to Emily herself. She read it aloud now: ' "I long to tell Emily the truth but I dare not. For her own sake, she must never know." ' Beneath that was an entry in such frantic scrawl that Emily could hardly read it. What she could decipher was as follows:

> Through the flames
> Eye to eye
> Only then . . .
> . . . will die.

and in brackets beside it: 'If only I knew what it meant, it might be in my power to ward off all evil.'

On the next page, in large black scrawl were the words, 'I believed it might be over at long last, but I was wrong. *God help him!*'

Thankful that she had not disclosed the notebook to Cathy, Emily hid it deep in the drawer. Afterwards, still lost in thought and made uneasy by the things she had read, Emily crossed to the window, where she looked out towards the river. She was astonished to see Cathy on the opposite side of the road, standing beside her car and staring back at the house. Then, while Emily tried unsuccessfully to attact her attention, intending to wave goodbye, Cathy got into the car and drove slowly away.

Some short way along the road, Cathy eased the car to a crawl. In the mirror she could still see the house. She smiled, a secret, murderous smile. There was danger in that house, and there was a part of *her*! Out there, in the garden. A part of her that was the heart itself, dormant, impatient. 'Soon,' she murmured through her smile. 'Soon now.' The time was close. She was not altogether free, not yet whole. But it would not be long now. *Then her power would be formidable!*

'Where in God's name have you been?' Bill Barrington swung round as Cathy came into the kitchen. 'Matt's been going crazy!' He had been making himself a cup of strong coffee, but now he strode across the kitchen to confront her, momentarily shocked by her unhappy, haggard face. 'For Christ's sake, Cathy!' He lowered his voice when she raised her sombre grey eyes to his. 'What's going on? What is it between you and Matt?'

'Where is he?' she asked in an odd flat voice. Since leaving Maria Hinson's house earlier, Cathy had driven for many miles, not knowing where she was going, not caring. Eventually she had found her way back to Milton Keynes, where she parked the car outside the vast enclosed shopping centre and wandered round, going from shop to shop, sitting in the tea-room over Boots the chemist's for almost an hour, until the waitress told her, 'We're closing now. You'll have to leave, I'm afraid.'

From there, Cathy had gone to Willen Lake and walked its perimeter until the day grew cold and thoughts of Matt urged her home. All day long she had pent up her feelings – withering, compelling feelings that made no sense, yet made every sense. Now, the feelings had subsided, leaving her physically and emotionally exhausted. At this moment in time, it would not have mattered to her whether she lived or died; sometimes death was preferable to life. She needed Matt so badly, and yet she could not bear the thought of him near her. She was plagued with guilt, haunted by fear, and always deeply, inexorably suspicious of his every move, his every word.

'Matt's out looking for you,' her father replied, following her across the kitchen. When she sat in the chair, her arms spread out over the table, her eyes looking up at him, childlike and imploring, he seated himself opposite, his thick worn fingers closing over her

223

dainty hands. 'He rang me just after five . . . begged me to come over and stay by the phone while he went in search of you. Oh, Cathy, he was almost out of his mind with worry. Where have you been? *Twelve hours* you've been gone! Couldn't you have gone into a phone booth and told him when you'd be home?'

Before Cathy could reply, the intermittent buzz of the telephone interrupted. Scrambling from the chair, Bill hurried to the dresser and grabbed up the receiver. 'Slater's Farm.' There was a brief pause, when he listened intently, then, 'It's all right, Matt. Cathy's here.' Another pause, before he replied in a reassuring voice, 'No, no, she's fine. She walked in about five minutes ago . . no, she didn't tell me.' A longer interlude, when Cathy's father turned to look on her, his attention on what Matt was saying, but his eyes telling him how desperately tired Cathy looked. 'Okay, Matt. Yes, of course I'll wait with her. Don't worry. Just make your way back.' He put the receiver down, wondering why Matt had not asked to speak to Cathy, nor she to him. He had recently suspected that all was not well between his daughter and Matt. It hurt him to realise now just how serious were their problems. 'I expect you'd murder for a cuppa?' he said. When she smiled at him and nodded, he returned to the cupboard and took out a small mug, into which he put a heaped spoonful of coffee granules. Boiling the kettle again, he poured the hot water into both mugs, added milk and sugar, and brought them to the table, where he put one down before her. Easing into the chair, he began sipping the warming liquid, quietly regarding her awhile. 'Cathy . . .' he began.

'I know what you're going to say,' she interrupted, 'and you're wrong. Oh, it's true we're going through a bad patch right now, Dad, but,' she gently tapped his hand and smiled, 'we'll work it out, I promise.' She bitterly regretted her father being aware that all was not well between her and Matt.

Bill slowly nodded his head, his eyes appraising her face, his fears not calmed by her assurances. There was something horribly wrong here, and nothing Cathy said would convince him otherwise. He knew his daughter better than most fathers could know their children. Since Cathy's mother had deserted them, he had been everything to her . . . father, mother, friend and confidante. They had always talked things through, shared their troubles, their joys and their ambitions. Suddenly, there was a barrier between them. Cathy's bright, outgoing personality was markedly changed. These days she was unnaturally quiet, morose and secretive; there was a hardness about her, an unattractive trait that had never been part of her character. In all the years when he had watched her grow from infancy to girlhood, and then into womanhood, he had never seen her look so unhappy, so deeply sad that even now, after she had caused him and Matt such anxiety, he could not be angry with her. 'Do you believe that, sweetheart . . . you and Matt can work it out?'

'I'm sure we can,' she replied thoughtfully. In her sorry heart she prayed there was a way. Yet she was afraid, sensing that already it was too late. She had lost him. Now there was little purpose in going on. Oh, but yes! There *was* a purpose. The pain rose in her, suffocating every other sensation. She had nearly forgotten. She must *never* forget again. However instinctively abhorrent the purpose was, she must not lose sight of it.

'Are you all right, Cathy?' Even as he observed her, he saw the change overcome her features, and he was shocked.

'Yes. Of course.' She pushed the mug of coffee away and rose to her feet. Rounding the table, she bent to kiss the top of his head, leaning on him, her arms about his neck and her face pressed to his temple. 'Thank you for being here when Matt needed you,' she remarked softly, 'but you don't have to stay.' She playfully rocked him back and forth. 'I'm sure you'd rather be with Emily.'

Surprised, he looked up, at once amazed to see how quickly she seemed recovered . . . the same Cathy he knew and adored, the same bright twinkling eyes and teasing manner. Relief flooded his heart. 'Why, you scamp! What do *you* know about Emily, eh?' he demanded.

'Aha! What would you say if I told you that this very day I paid a long and interesting visit to your darling woman?'

'You did?' He struggled to free himself, but her arms were

225

locked tight round his throat. 'Why would you do that?' He laughed, a quietly embarrassed laugh. 'And what do you mean . . . my "darling woman"?'

'I mean you've set your cap at her, and I'm glad.'

'Really?' His delight was obvious.

'Yes, really. She's a lovely woman, Dad, warm and sincere.' Memories came flooding back, bad memories of the night when her mother deserted them. 'She won't hurt you, I'm sure.' Suddenly she withdrew her arms from his neck and wandered to the dresser, where she absentmindedly tapped her fingers against the telephone. 'Where's Matt?' she asked again, her grey gaze drawn to the window, the image of Matt strong in her mind. She was aware that her father had turned in his chair and was closely regarding her. She did not look at him.

'He searched the whole of Bedford for you . . . scoured the embankment. Then he thought you might have gone on to Cambridge. He knows how you like to rummage about in the old bookshops. He couldn't find you, though. That was when he decided to check whether you'd returned home.'

'Was he pleased when you told him I was here?'

'*Pleased!*' He was out of his chair now, hurrying towards her. 'For heaven's sake, Cathy, what do *you* think? Of course he was pleased! And relieved, and wanting to get back to you as quickly as possible.'

'How long will he be?'

'Can't say for sure . . . depends on the traffic.' He glanced up at the wall clock. 'Ten past seven . . . shouldn't be too busy at this time of night. Three quarters of an hour, maybe.'

'Did he ask you to stay with me?'

'Yes.'

Cathy swung round, looking directly at him. 'Do you want to?'

He stared back at her, curious, hurt. 'Well, of course I want to. Unless you'd rather I didn't?' It had not occurred to him that Cathy might think his presence here an intrusion. It occurred to him now. And though he did understand, it was still a painful realisation. 'Is that it, Cathy? Would you rather me not be here when Matt gets back?'

Cathy saw the fleeting hurt in his eyes, and she was filled with remorse. 'You're a good friend,' she told him, reaching out and touching his face, 'and I could not have wished for a better father.'

'But?' He was smiling now. The hurt had passed.

'You're right. Matt and I do have a great deal to talk over. Some of it might get a little heated. It would be best if you weren't here when he got back.'

'I understand.' He returned to the table and drank the remains of his coffee. Bringing the mug to the sink, he rinsed it out under the tap and placed it upside down on the draining board. 'Maybe I will go and see Emily after all . . . take her to the hospital.' He came to Cathy and kissed her on the forehead. 'You and Matt are so right for each other,' he said anxiously, 'don't throw it away, sweetheart. It can't be so bad that you're not able to put it right between the two of you.'

'Don't worry.'

He looked at her now, so calm and confident, and he remembered that desperate, haunting look he had seen in her only a short while ago. 'If there was anything else troubling you, anything you couldn't discuss with Matt . . . you would turn to me, wouldn't you?'

'Haven't I always?' she told him firmly. 'But there is nothing, Dad. Matt and I will sort it out.'

'Promise?'

'Like I said. Don't worry.' One way or the other, she thought bitterly, she and Matt would 'sort it out'.

'Then I'll leave you to it. Tell Matt I've gone with Emily to the hospital.' Suddenly he remembered. 'You didn't tell me . . . why did you go to see Emily?'

'I was down by the river, it seemed the natural thing to do.'

'I'm glad you like her, Cathy, because I've grown very fond of her, and I think she feels the same way.' He did not tell Cathy of his intention to ask Emily if she would consider marriage. It was still too soon. Cathy might not understand. But she was young, while he and Emily had seen life slipping by too fast.

'Don't keep her waiting, then,' Cathy teased, seeing him to the

227

door and remaining there to watch him stride away. How she wished she could have confided in him, but there was no way to begin, nothing he could do. After years of real loneliness, her father had found someone to share his life. She was glad of that. Let him enjoy his newfound happiness. She would not over-shadow it by revealing the pain and horror that stalked her every moment. But what of Matt? Could she tell him? *Dare* she tell him? How could she start? How would he understand? Half of her cried out to tell him, to seek his help. But then there came the fear, the resentment, part of her craving his love, part of her craving his blood.

Suddenly she was afraid to tell him, terrified that he might guess. They had been so very happy, so much in love. Was it *Matt* who had changed? Was it *her*? Or both of them? So often of late she had toyed with the idea of leaving Slater's Farm to begin a new life of her own many miles away from here. Each time she had let the thought enter her mind, another, more powerful, had told her that she must stay. Here, she had a role to play out, a certain need to satisfy. Matt was to be punished. He could not escape. Soon, he would know, but it would be too late then, too late for him. Matt was a sinner, condemned. She was the executioner. There could be no pardon. Not now. Not ever.

Twenty minutes elasped, then it was half an hour, now forty minutes, and still Matt was not home. Cathy had wandered the house, looking out of every window in every room, nervous, anxious to talk with him, wanting him to understand, to forgive. She prayed they could find each other again, go right back to where it all started to go wrong. She loved him so much. Why couldn't she tell him? What was it that kept them apart? How could their happiness have been so eroded? Why? *Why? WHY?* Suddenly, her mind was clear, her heart brimming with love for him. Things would be all right between them now. *They would.* She would *make* them all right!

Glancing at the clock, she saw that it was ten minutes past eight. Where was he? Eager now for him to walk in through the door and take her in his arms, Cathy grew excited. She *would* talk to him . . . tell him of her deeper fears, and trust his guidance. He would know what to do. Matt was always the strong one. 'Matt will know what to do,' she said aloud, the conviction growing in her.

Coming into the hallway, she paused to examine her reflection in the long mirror. All was familiar . . . the small trim figure and the corn-coloured shoulder-length hair, the wide-awake grey eyes, the bright lovely face, all the same. Leaning forward, Cathy spoke into the mirror. 'Matt will know what to do.' Dark eyes smiled back, the full lips parted, softly laughing, the voice was mocking. *'Matt will know what to do.'* The eerie calm infiltrated every corner of her being, an echo; in the mirror she saw herself, saw a stranger, saw what she must do. Slowly, she moved away, her black heart soaring, purposeful. There was no fear, no pain or regret. Only a unique and sinister dedication that was ageless, relentless. At last, at long last, the time was near, so near. And she had waited so very long.

In the bedroom, Cathy watched from the window, cradling the doll, softly singing, waiting for Matt to come home. It was growing darker now, the daylight fading fast, black scurrying fingers scraping away the last remaining rays of the sun. Soon the blackness would be supreme. She laughed. That was how it should be. 'Where is he?' she asked the doll, tracing the tip of her finger over every feature. 'Matt must know we're waiting for him. Why isn't he here?' The doll stared back, deep empty eye-sockets, silent, compelling. Cathy nodded. She understood.

Replacing the doll on the windowsill, Cathy slipped off her shoes and went on bare feet to the bedside cabinet. Here, she picked up the small marble clock. It had stopped. She switched on the transistor radio, the ensuing music enchanting her. She began bending and swirling to the rhythm, deeply satisfied, a wonderful sense of power gripping her. The music accelerated, her dancing became frenzied. Faster, faster. Excitement coursed through her veins. Oh, such a longing. Wanting. A devilish mood took hold of her.

Suddenly, the music stopped. A voice came on the air,

introducing the next record. Laughing, exhausted but exhilarated, she switched off the radio and threw herself on to the bed, her heart beating furiously. Turning sideways, she looked at the bedside clock .. eight thirty-five. *Where was he?* Already the evening shadows were darkening the room. Had he left her? Was he even now travelling further and further away from her, leaving for good? No. *No!* He was on his way home; he had to be. But where was he? Why was he so late?

The questions tumbled over and over in her mind. She was agitated, then afraid, lonely. And tired, oh so tired. She ached like an old woman, her bones feeling like lead weights pressing against the bed-cover, her eyes burning, hurting inside her head. With a sigh she closed her eyelids against them. She had no strength, no resistance, it was ebbing away, her life was ebbing away. Sleep swayed her in its soothing arms, hypnotic, paralysing. Soon the darkness descended and she went willingly, longingly, into its embrace.

It was his presence that woke her. In the blackness of the room she sensed he was there. It made her warm, and wanted, and she knew she had won. Secretly smiling, she raised herself on one elbow, her grey eyes penetrating the darkness, exquisite grey eyes, marbled with shadows, avaricious and compelling, feeding on the tall, masculine figure now straddling the open doorway and silhouetted against the light from the landing. Slowly, he came forward, his breathing harsh and rhythmic, his steps determined. He wanted her as never before. He would not let her leave him, ever again. They would live together, or they would die together. He heard her voice, softly calling. Enchanted, he gazed down on her waiting, watching while she undressed, her clothes slithering to the carpet, making a curious misshapen pile there. One by one he dropped his own discarded garments on top, smiling when he saw how they mingled with hers, entwining one about the other. He heard her call his name – it sounded like the soft swish of silk.

For a moment he imagined she called him by another name, a name he thought he had heard before, a name that was in his head, in long-ago memories, stirring something in him, making him uneasy . . . 'Matt . . . Ralph' . . . which one? Somehow it was not important. *They were the same.* He lingered awhile, his dark eyes roving her nakedness. She saw his need, and her smile enticed him, the low guttural sounds she made only heightened his agony. Yet he was loath to touch her, reluctant to break the spell. Instead, he continued to gaze on her nakedness. In the half-light she was more magnificent than ever before, desirable in a way he could not remember. She was softly moaning now, arms held out to him, her long shapely legs opening to reveal a darker enticement, her body arched and writhing in anticipation.

When she saw him make no move towards her, she lowered her arms, touching herself, stroking her hands over the contours of her body, long velvet fingers probing that dark inviting triangle, showing him, teasing him, her moans growing feverish and impatient. In the shifting shadows she could hear his breathing, erratic now, greatly excited. She laughed softly. *'Love me,'* she whispered. He came forward slowly, agonising slowly. Then the slight dip of the bed as he brought his weight to bear. His whole body was taut, hard against her. She reached up to wrap her arms round his neck, winding her fingers in the tousled strands of his hair, wrenching him forward with a sudden viciousness, her face touching the sweat of his skin, the tip of her tongue snaking deep into his mouth, probing its softness, tasting his essence, pleasantly aware of the stiffness that probed her lower body. Between his anguished cries she heard him murmur her name. 'Cathy . . . Cathy.'

The name aroused a greater need in her. The need to cause pain, to wreak havoc and destruction. With a sudden twist of her body she was above him, her legs astride his narrow muscular thighs, thrusting herself on to him, again and again, reeling back when his hands came up to fondle her breasts. He raised his head from the pillow, mouth half-open, searching, wanting her lips on his, his green eyes half-closed, heavy with passion, jerking open with every deep penetration.

Now she was teasing again, holding away, softly laughing.

Groaning, he clutched his strong hands about her shoulders, throwing her off and laughing when she spread herself beneath him. His hands slid down, caressing the firm roundness of her buttocks, raising them to him and crying aloud when he eased forward, pushing deep into her. Instantly they were locked, frantic, passion exploding in sensuous savagery. Release, pleasure. But still he held her, strong possessive arms pinning her to him, the fluid of her body warm on his skin. Loving her still, he raised his head to kiss her. She turned away. He gently laughed, easing off, sitting on the edge of the bed, hunched over, his head leaning forward in his hands. 'You frightened me today, when you didn't come home.' His voice was breathless, muffled, his face hidden in the palms of his hands. 'Don't ever do that to me again, Cathy.'

When she made no reply, but he felt the touch of her fingers on his bare back, he half-turned. Then her whisper. 'Go and shower . . . later we'll talk.'

Depleted and sticky with sweat he reached out behind him, squeezed her hand in his and nodded. 'Love you,' he said. In a moment he was gone, the sound of spraying water filtering into the bedroom. In the gloom, the black eyes were brilliant as diamonds, deep and opaque, cavernous like pockets of a night sky. A small laugh, a murmuring of words that were unintelligible. Wickedness, such wickedness.

'I've left the shower running for you.' Matt emerged in the shard of light from the bathroom, his arms bent upwards, vigorously rubbing the towel over his thick earth-coloured hair, his naked limbs glistening. Coming towards the bed he said, 'You know I couldn't live without you.' He felt dizzy, light headed. He thought it must be the booze. When he couldn't find Cathy he had been worried sick, half-crazy that he would never see her again. Afterwards, when Bill had told him she was safely home, his anxiety turned to bitterness. He wanted to lash out, to hurt her like she had hurt him. The boozer was warm, friendly; the company took his mind off his troubles, stilled that murmuring voice inside him . . . the persistent voice that warned him his life

232

with Cathy was over. *He would rather that life itself was over!* He felt the urge to punish her . . . had even contemplated staying away all night. He almost had. But his love for Cathy was too strong. 'I'm sorry I didn't come straight home, sweetheart,' he told her, rubbing the towel to the back of his head, and staring towards the bed. In the half-light he could not see her eyes. He wondered if they were smiling, whether she had really forgiven him, hoping that – at long last – all would be the way it was. He peered at her; she recoiled into the shadows. 'Why don't you put the light on?' he suggested.

'No.'

'Okay.' He had been startled by the harshness of her voice, but then he laughed. 'You're surely not shy all of a sudden?' He remembered with a tingling shock . . . Cathy *was* shy. She had always been shy when he saw her nakedness. He recalled how she had been just now . . . boldly taunting him, unashamed, savage in her love-making. He also had been savage, wild like an animal. He grew excited at the memory, but then it was a strange, empty excitement, devoid of love, robbed of the wholesome and satisfying emotions that had first drawn him to Cathy and afterwards had kept them together, brought them ever closer.

Suddenly, he knew how she was feeling . . . why she would not put the light on. Shame washed over him. And regret. A strong feeling of regret, that when he had joined with Cathy just now, it was like joining with a stranger. An awful awareness grew in him, a small memory of strange dark eyes. Horror rippled through him. Dropping the towel to the carpet he snatched up his trousers and pulled them on. *'Put the light on, Cathy,'* he said in a trembling voice.

In the half-dark he saw her arm flick out, heard her chuckle, an ugly sinister sound. The sudden rush of light was blinding, disorientating. He blinked, *and opened his eyes to a nightmare.* He was staring at a stranger! The face was old, repulsive, lines of time deeply etched into the yellowed skin, leering at him, chuckling. Wisps of grey hair made a spidery pattern against the pillow, gnarled and twisted hands beckoned to him, curved nails bent

233

over the fingertips. Her body was withered, loose folds of flesh making her horribly misshapen. Naked, she was laughing now, chortling, a fiendish expression on her ancient face.

Above her laughter he heard the screams, *his* screams. His mind was fragmented, in chaos. *'Cathy!'* He closed his eyes and rolled his head from side to side, his whole being churning in horror . . . one last hope that he would open his eyes and the nightmare would be gone . . . Cathy would be lying there as before. In the eerie blackness of his mind he could not shut the wizened image out – she was there, burning like a twisting flame, staring, beckoning, laughing.

When he opened his eyes the nightmare had not gone away. His cries mingled with her laughter as she lunged at him, the blade slicing the air, stabbing his neck, cutting his hands when he grappled desperately to save himself from the savage onslaught. Pictures sped through his mind – of Cathy, of himself, together . . . here. But it was not Cathy . . . *not Cathy! It was not Cathy who had lain in his arms!* With a scream that was terrible to hear he thrust the knife from her hand, madness in his eyes, murder in his heart. His fingers felt her scrawny neck. The touch repulsed him, filling him with unbearable disgust. He could hear her chuckling, a low gurgling noise as his fingers locked tight, pressing into the reptilian skin, cutting deep, killing, *killing*. He was crying now, his fingers an iron collar round her neck, squeezing mercilessly.

When at last she was silent, limp in his grip, he pulled away, letting her slump to the floor, her saliva mingled with his blood, trickling down his hand. He shuddered uncontrollably when the witch-like face rolled sideways, the black eyes staring at him from horrifying depths, mocking him. Backing away, he went into the bathroom to cleanse himself. In his mind her laughter followed, evil, touching every nerve. He leaned over the toilet basin to spew out the churning contents of his stomach. Still the laughter – everywhere – all around.

Like a man waking from a trance he came back slowly into the bedroom. The laughter was gone. His shocked eyes looked down on the limp, still body there. *It was Cathy.* CATHY! Horrified, he froze, staring. Unbelieving. He fell to his knees, tears rolling down his stricken face. With a cry he grabbed her into his arms, rocking her, talking to her, asking her forgiveness, asking God's forgiveness. In his arms she was lifeless, like a doll. Like a doll! Suddenly he snapped inside, the awful impact of what he had done bringing its own madness. *'No!* . . . *Dear God* . . . *No!'* He looked again at her face, lovely, innocent, his Cathy. Through his tears her face was a blur. The grief, the guilt, and horror, it was too much. With a cry he pushed her away and fled the room, fled the house, running, into the coming dawn. Into oblivion.

Behind him, the lights went on in Joseph's cottage. They had been woken by the screams, screams of terror that chilled their hearts. They too were running, towards the house, towards the carnage there. But he did not see them. Like a man possessed, he sped away, the blood from his bare feet spraying the hard uneven road, and all kinds of devils at his heels. He was a man lost, a man whose only sin was his link with the past, with an unforgiving, unrelenting evil.

On and on he went, across the fields, through the woods, not knowing where he was heading, not caring. When he came to the canal, he paused a moment, his scarred eyes searching the fathoms, anticipating the cool waters lapping over his head. The experience would not be new, for he had endured it many times in his worst nightmares. No . . . *this* was his worst nightmare. He looked at the sky. The stars were twinkling. Like Cathy's eyes, he thought with a spear of pain. *Like Cathy's eyes!* He swayed forward, a strange elation as he fell through emptiness, tearing his body on the hard branches that lay like knotted boulders beneath the cold aqueous surface. He closed his eyes in the spearing pain and gave himself to the depths. When the waters closed over his dark head *she* was beside him, her black impenitent heart urging him on.

In the eerie silence of the depths he had not heard the shout, nor the running feet. When they dragged him on to the towpath, he did not know how desperately they fought to save him. Without Cathy, he would prefer not to live.

*

235

Barely conscious, aware of a peculiar floating sensation, Matt knew he was not drowned. There were voices all around. Instinctively he moved. The pain burned inside him, firing his lungs, splitting his head.

'Easy there, matey.' A roughened hand reached out to steady him. Smells assailed his nostrils . . . human smells, of sweat and hair, and stale tobacco. He struggled to sit up, but it was like holding back an avalanche; exhausted he fell back against the coarse blankets. 'Yer a lucky man.' The voice was rich, vibrant. It had a smile in it. 'I only just caught a glimpse of yer in the coming light. Good God, man! Life can't be so bad that yer want to end it.' The smile had gone. Only shock remained.

'Leave him be, Josh.' Another voice intervened, feminine, kind. 'Let him rest.'

'Aye, yer right. There'll be time enough fer talk. Time enough to persuade him that things can't be so bad.'

'We mustn't wait too long, though. The authorities are already impatient to see us on our way.'

'True! It might be dangerous to linger in these parts.'

'What's the plan?'

A long pause, then, 'We can't just leave him here. By rights, the feller needs to be in hospital.'

'No need for that, Josh. We can look after him. We should move on, though, before daylight.'

'Happen we oughta take him to a hospital . . . leave him in more capable hands.'

In the dark confusion of Matt's scattered thoughts, the voices droned on. His senses were failing fast. There was a dulling sensation of horror in him, such abject horror that he wanted only to die. The voices spoke of taking him to 'a hospital' . . . of 'danger' and 'authorities'. The words swam in his head; meaning-less words. Only one word stood bold and consistent . . . Cathy. His heart was broken. He had done something that made life unlivable. What had he done? Dear God above, *what had he done!*

'He's trying to say something, Josh.' The feminine voice was very near; the smells were different now . . . heather, and the dry musty tang of newly plaited wicker. 'What's that?' The smells enveloped him, the long strands of her hair brushing his bruised skin. When he murmured now, it was not in a voice he recognised, though he knew it must be his voice, harsh and croaked, issuing through stiff sore lips.

'What's he saying?'

'I'm not sure . . . Cathy, that's what it sounds like . . . Cathy.' The voice turned away. 'There'll be questions if we take him to a hospital . . . forms, and time-wasting . . . mebbe even the authorities. After all, we did fish him out o' the canal. I don't want no more trouble with the authorities, Josh!'

'What are you saying?'

'Put a distance between ourselves and this place. We'll take him with us. God knows we've been glad of a helping hand ourselves, many a time.'

'Fair enough. That's what we'll do.' A pause, then, 'D'yer reckon he's running from the law?'

'Who knows? Strange, though, Josh . . . what was he doing in the early hours, wandering about with hardly any clothes and no shoes to his feet?'

There was a small gruff laugh. 'Happen he weren't running from the *law*. Happen he were getting clear of an incensed husband!'

'No.' The woman turned to regard the broken figure of the man whose life they had saved. 'No. I don't think so, Josh. Look at him. The gashes on his neck and hands. Think of the awful expression in his eyes when he first opened them. There was something tragic there, Josh. Something that don't bear dwelling on. I'm thinking that when he's fully recovered . . .'

'*If* he's fully recovered!'

'All the same, I don't believe he'll thank us for fishing him out of the river. Whatever he was running from, it must be a devilish thing . . . when a man chooses to die because of it!'

Matt felt the warm broth being forced between his lips, into his throat. He couldn't swallow. Turning his head away, he was beset by all manner of emotion. Quick tears fell down his face, salty on his mouth. *'Cathy . . . Cathy'*. The coarse blanket was gently pushed beneath his chin, the hand stroked his forehead and the fever raged in him. Her voice filtered through the bedlam. 'A devilish thing' . . . 'a devilish thing.' He was swaying, floating from side to side. The low rhythmic vibrations were oddly soothing. A sense of movement – gliding – and soon all was dark again; he was at peace. But peace was not a lasting thing. It was only the lull before the storm.

'I weren't sure whether to call you or not, Mr Barrington.' Joseph's face revealed the depth of his anxiety as he stared at Cathy's father, his eyes big and round, flicking nervously from the other man's face to the bedroom and back again. 'Me and Edna, well, we didn't know what else to do. I was all for calling the police, but Edna said no . . . "Get Cathy's father here," she said, "he'll know what to do." '

'You did right, Joseph.' Bill Barrington had been stunned by the night's events. He was stunned now. 'And there's been no sign of Matt? You didn't see him when you came to the cottage?'

Joseph shook his head. 'No, we didn't see nobody. The door was swinging open, but there was no one in sight, not outside, nor inside . . . only Cathy writhing in agony, but, well, there weren't no harm come to her, nor were there any signs of a fight or anything like that.' He closed his eyes and dropped his head to his chest, shaking it from side to side, as though to wrestle out the memory. 'I'll never forget them screams, Mr Barrington. Awful, unearthly, they were, I don't mind telling you, they put the fear of God into me and Edna!'

At first, when he heard them, the screams put him in mind of somebody being tortured . . . the same terrifying noises that filled the air in the prisoner-of-war camp where he himself was incarcerated during the Second World War. That had been one nightmare. This was another. Such unspeakable things happened these days; murder, rape, all manner of violence. A body was never safe, not day or night. He recalled with a shudder the news of a local priest being found dead in his own house . . . hanged, they said. Such terrible, wicked things! He peeped at the other man from beneath frowning eyebrows.

'Like I said, it was hard to tell whether the screams were those of a man, or of a woman.' *Or neither*, he thought.

'You're a good man, Joseph,' Bill Barrington told him, 'a good neighbour.' When the footsteps were heard descending the stairs, both men looked towards the door. Almost immediately the doctor entered the room. 'Thank you for coming out so quickly,' Cathy's father told him. 'How is she now?' The doctor had been with Cathy for what seemed an age. 'She *will* be all right, won't she?' His voice betrayed the deep anxiety in him.

The doctor nodded, his bland expression giving nothing away. He glanced at Joseph. 'Would you mind leaving us?' he asked with a small stiff smile.

At once Joseph hurried from the room. The doctor's attitude worried him. He knew Edna had not been far away from Cathy. *She* would know. Edna would know. He meant to find her and reassure himself that Cathy would be all right.

'I've seen it coming a long while,' Edna told him. He had found her sitting forlornly by Cathy's bedside, holding her hand and talking to her as though she was a small child. 'You mustn't worry, darling,' she was murmuring, the tears bright in her friendly eyes. 'You'll be all right, I promise. Trust me . . . trust your Edna.' Gently, he had persuaded her away. Downstairs in the kitchen her emotions broke and she sobbed pitifully. He let her cry, busying himself with making a pot of tea that might refresh them all.

From beyond the hallway, Edna could hear the soft murmur of voices, then that of Cathy's father, raised in disbelief and anger. A sound like the slamming of a fist against the table, then a brief spell of silence before the urgent murmuring took up again. She knew what was transpiring there, in that room where Cathy and Matt had chatted and dreamed, laughed and loved, delighting in each other's company, young and carefree, and filled with hope for the future. She knew, and her old heart went out to that innocent pair. Yet there was nothing she could do. Nothing *anyone* could do. Except maybe God almighty!

Night was driven away, the dawn rose like a sceptre. Dancing shafts of iridescent hues marbled the sky as the day silently spread into the darkest corners. The sun was already warm on Cathy's pale stricken face when they brought her from the cottage. Gentle hands helped her into the waiting vehicle, and when her father sat beside her, his arm around her, his tearful face buried in her hair, she clung to him, drawing on his strength. So many voices pounded her head that they became one. 'What happened?' they wanted to know, and she could not tell them. 'Was it a nightmare? Was it *you* who screamed?' She had no answers, but still they asked, 'Was Matt here? Do you know where he is?'

Why didn't they leave her alone? *She told them about the badness, though!* But they didn't believe her, didn't *want* to believe her! Because it was too awful. She was not *Cathy* any more. The badness was in her. It was there again, another wicked nightmare, evil, predatory, killing her, killing Matt. *Matt!* Where are you? Help me, please help me! The hands were tight around her throat, squeezing the badness, but not hurting it. Never hurting it. Not killing it, because it could not die. She told them everything – how the badness lived inside her. How it loathed her . . . loathed Matt . . . wanted her to kill him! Oh no, *no*. How could she kill him? Stay away, Matt. 'I don't want to hurt him.' Her voice trembled with fear. She clung to her father now, digging her nails into his skin. It was there, always there, burning with fury, blaming her. *'I don't want to hurt him!'* She was frantic, struggling, long shivering sobs raking through her.

'All right, sweetheart . . . you won't hurt him. It's all right.' Bill spoke calmly, soothingly, though inside he was breaking up. He held her close, oblivious to the angry red scars on his neck where she had fought so desperately to free herself. He couldn't cope. He *had* to cope! For Cathy's sake, he had to cope.

He also had fought, resisted the doctor's diagnosis, that, in his opinion, Cathy was 'psychotic . . . a danger to herself'. It would tear him in two, to see her shut away, but he could see now that the doctor was right. There *was* something very wrong with his Cathy, his lovely gentle Cathy, who seemed to have lost all touch with reality. She spoke of being choked to death, yet there had been no mark on her. She talked about the 'badness' in her. Then, when she saw they could not believe her, she grew frantic, wild and aggressive. And the laughter! It haunted him still.

He would see that Cathy had the very best of care. But where was Matt? He *had* been home, because the four-track was there and the car beside it. Yet Cathy denied seeing him! But then, she was not lucid, not making any sense at all. Had he been home and gone straight out again? If so, where? And how? Had he gone away on foot? Did he call a taxi? Did someone give him a lift? Where in God's name was he?

Bill Barrington knew that Cathy had the answer somewhere in that tortured closed mind. He prayed for Matt to return soon. Maybe then the truth would emerge. *The truth!* What was the truth?

Chapter Twelve

Emily had been watching from the window. Bill had phoned earlier to say he was delivering in Bedford that Saturday morning. He had sounded incredibly weary. Already she had the kettle on and a freshly baked apple cake cooling on the side. He had brought new meaning to her life and now it was as though she had known him for ever.

When, suddenly, the knock came on the door she slewed round, astonished. She had relaxed her vigil only once, and that was when she went to put the kettle on. Surely he couldn't have parked his car and crossed to the house in so few minutes? Rushing to answer the door, she paused to peruse herself in the hallway mirror. Her face was flushed with excitement. 'You silly old fool. Emily!' she chided with a twinkling smile, astonished all the same at how much she had changed since meeting Bill. There was a new confidence about the way she dressed, more attractive somehow, like now, in the straight dark skirt and soft blue open-necked blouse; no more the flat uninteresting shoes, but stylish, and with a small heel. There was a glow of happiness about her, and the short smartly bobbed brown hair made a perfect cameo for her small, pretty face; her ready smile and bright sparkling eyes that drew attention from the long misshappen facial blemish which, over these past weeks seemed to have faded into insignificance beneath her blossoming love for Cathy's father.

Quickly now, with that oddly dipping motion characterised by her slight limp, Emily hurried along the hallway. On opening the door, however, her face fell in disappointment. It was not Bill. The short wiry-framed man took off his neb-cap, and looking at her through beady blue eyes, he explained, 'You did say Saturday morning, didn't you? . . . On account of how I wasn't able to make it in the week.' He had seen her disappointment and was taken aback.

'Oh, yes! The gardener.' At once Emily recalled the arrangement. 'Come through, Mr Wilson.' She opened the door wider, gesturing for him to enter the hallway. Nodding, he wiped his feet on the coconut matting and brushed past her, waiting patiently until she had closed the door and was leading the way towards the back sitting room and beyond, out on to the terrace. 'You haven't chosen an ideal day,' she told him, glancing up at the overcast sky. 'It looks like rain.'

Mr Wilson chuckled, fitting his neb-cap over his pale thinning hair and taking out a small sketchbook and pencil from his jacket pocket. 'Can't pick and choose the weather, I'm afraid,' he said, 'but you're right, it *does* look like rain, so the sooner I get started, the better.' When he stepped on to the lawn, Emily followed. There was a brief span of silence during which they each made mental calculations of how the redesigned garden might look. Emily was the first to speak. 'As I explained before, Mr Wilson, my companion is due to come out of hospital shortly. Certainly within the next two weeks. After that she'll spend another two weeks in the convalescence home. The work must be finished by the first week in October. It's to be a welcome-home surprise for her.'

'Hmm . . . early October, you say?' He scratched his chin. 'Short notice isn't it?'

'Do you think you can do it in the time?'

Without giving an answer, he scrutinised the old spacious gardens. He knew they had been well tended and much loved by his predecessor; he knew also that the old lady had kept a strict rein on the gardener, never allowing him full licence. The gardener himself had confided that much. 'Oh, I'm sure we can have it finished in time,' he assured Emily, 'providing, of course, you agree with my initial landscape designs.' He scribbled a few notes into his book, together with a sketch of the three lawns, the

243

corner where the shed and greenhouse were sited, and the position of shrubs and trees. 'That will have to go,' he remarked, pointing at the wizened apple tree. 'I can't imagine why it hasn't been dug up before now.' He stared hard at Emily. 'Am I to be given a free hand?' he asked pointedly.

For the first time during discussions with regard to the replanning of the garden, Emily hesitated. She knew how obstinate Maria had been where that tree was concerned. Emily had always believed it was because the old lady had planted the apple tree herself, and was stubbornly willing it to flourish. Over the years, though, it had been slowly dying, until now it was an ugly thing. 'I don't want you to make too much change. Maria wouldn't like that. But you're right. The tree is long dead and an eyesore. I'm sure she wouldn't mind if you dug it up. Then, if you could put a couple of benches at strategic points in the garden . . . and broader paths for the wheelchair.'

When Mr Wilson suggested he could replant the whole area she was horrified. 'Maria is too old for drastic change,' she said.

'Very well . . . take the tree up . . . two benches, and broader paths.'

'I'll leave you to it, then, Mr Wilson,' she told him before returning to her vigil at the front window.

'Don't you worry, m'dear. Day after tomorrow I'll be back to make a start. How does that suit you?'

'Fine.'

'Good. Then, if you'll excuse me, I'd best get started before the skies open!' He inclined his head, touched the neb of his cap in a polite gesture, and ambled down the garden, pausing now and then to make a careful entry in his book.

Content that he would do a good job – yet still disturbed by what Maria might say when she saw the apple tree uprooted – Emily returned to the front room, from where she kept watch for Bill. It was an hour since he telephoned, she reminded herself. He should have been here by now.

Twenty minutes later, at eight thirty a.m., Mr Wilson left. At five minutes to nine, just as Emily was beginning to wonder whether she had misunderstood Bill's earlier message, she was delighted to see the van draw up opposite the house. The van was instantly recognisable, a large red box-van, with written on the sides the promise to 'DELIVER NEXT DAY', and signed beneath in the title of 'BARRINGTON'S SMALL PARCELS SERVICE'.

Normally when Cathy's father was working he wore a navy linen jacket and the same coloured over-trousers – 'more presentable than an overall', he explained. Today, though, he was dressed in brown neatly pressed trousers and loose-fitting light-grey polo-necked jumper. He shivered as he came into the hallway. 'Feels like November,' he said, 'instead of early September.'

'I thought you weren't coming. In fact, I began to wonder whether I'd heard right.' Emily smiled when he put his two hands on her shoulders. 'It's good to see you, Bill,' she said, her brown eyes shyly observing him.

'Sorry . . . I got delayed on the last delivery.' He bent to kiss her, not a fiery passionate kiss, but a warm, loving gesture that bound their growing feelings for each other. They made their way into the kitchen, she glowing with happiness, yet still riddled by doubts as to the uprooting of the apple tree, and he proud in love, but deeply plagued by Cathy's fragile state of mind and Matt's mysterious disappearance.

'Is there no word yet?' Emily put the steaming cup of tea before him, afterwards sitting opposite him at the table. When he shook his head, his dog-brown eyes heavy with worry, she reached out to put her hand over his. 'You mean the police still have no idea where he might be?'

'I don't think they even *care* any more!' His voice was cutting, his expression condemning. 'If you ask me, they're not even looking for him now.'

'What makes you say that?' Emily was appalled.

'Something the inspector told me when I went in to see him yesterday.' He pushed his cup away and leaned back in the chair. 'He said I should consider how Matt had gone off in a temper after he and Cathy quarrelled. And that, in his experience, these "domestic upheavals" were little more than a storm in a tea cup. Sooner or later the man, or the woman, always turned up, that's what he said.'

'But it's been over a fortnight!'

'He knows that.'

'And there's no evidence that Cathy and Matt *did* have a quarrel.'

'He knows that too.'

'And Cathy . . . how is she, Bill?'

Unnerved by her question, he stood up. Thrusting the chair away he crossed to the other side of the room, on his face a thoughtful, troubled look. Presently, his sorry gaze resting on this woman who had come to be his rock, the only constant reassurance in his life at the moment, he murmured, 'What's happening to them?' – almost a question to himself, a question, yet not a question. 'How is it possible that in the space of three months the lives of two young people could be so tragically turned upside down? One minute they're deliriously happy, newly wed, going on the holiday of a lifetime, and in the twinkling of an eye, it's all changing.' Groaning, he covered his face in his hands and slumped forward. 'I can't help them,' he whispered. 'Dear God . . . if only there was a way to help them.' Now, when he felt the touch of her hand in his hair, he made a rough choking sound and grabbed her to him. 'Where is he, Emily? *Where in God's name is he?*'

'You think something bad has happened to him, don't you?' Her voice was gentle, reassuring.

'I don't know *what* to think! Cathy and Matt were always so in love. He idolised her. I can't bring myself to believe that he would just walk out on her. I *won't* believe it!'

'You told the inspector that?'

He nodded, lifting his face and easing her from him. 'Of course I told him. I told him he was crazy to think that Matt would just desert her like that! I told him how I spoke to Matt on the phone that night . . . when Matt told me how he was on his way home. He wasn't *angry*, Emily. Matt wasn't angry, I swear it. Oh, he was worried at Cathy going off for so long without letting him know where she was, and I dare say he might have been angry at first. But when I told him she was safely home, he was only relieved, concerned for Cathy. He even asked me to stay with her until he got back.' He dropped his arms, then raised them again to punch one fist into the other. 'I should have stayed! *Why didn't I stay!*'

'You're too hard on yourself. Time and again you've asked that question, and time and again I've told you, it was *Cathy* who begged you to leave, wasn't it? *Cathy* who insisted she and Matt had things to talk over, better discussed with only the two of them there? Isn't that right? Isn't that the way it was?'

When he looked at her now, it was with a determined expression. 'I really think the police have given up on him, Emily. It's up to me now. I have to find him.' He suddenly laughed, a harsh grating sound. 'I should be ashamed, spilling my troubles on you, when you've been so concerned over Maria.'

'Your troubles are mine,' she chided softly, 'and Maria's mending, thank God. It's only natural that your daughter plays heavily on your mind, and Matt too.' She paused, frowning deeply. 'You're right though – it is frightening, the way their lives have been devastated. I want to help, Bill. If there is anything I can do, please let me help.'

'You really are a good woman, Emily, and I know you're just as concerned as I am, but where do I start?' He was frantic. Cathy was responding well to treatment, but he had been shocked to see her yesterday. She was so withdrawn and morose, like a different person. And when she cried, it tore him apart. There had been real terror in her that day when they took her to the hospital. It was in her now, eating her away, destroying what was left of the gentle laughing girl he knew and loved. And when she asked for Matt – that was the worst thing. He had to lie and pretend, make all kinds of excuses. She never argued with him, or questioned what he told her. 'Matt . . . where's Matt?' she would ask, her tragic grey eyes imploring, then – when he tenderly explained how 'Matt will be along soon, sweetheart' – she would merely nod and turn away, her sad eyes brimmed with tears. He wondered whether she knew that he was lying, that Matt had gone missing

247

and every attempt to trace him had proved futile. He had no way of knowing what Cathy was thinking. She hardly ever spoke, and when she did, it was either to ask for Matt, or to repeat over and over how 'Cathy's been bad . . . bad. I don't want to hurt him . . . don't want to hurt him.' Then she would grow agitated, even violent, when she was physically restrained and sedated.

Those times were the worst. The very worst. Far worse than when she smiled that secret smile and sang the haunting melody that no one knew. On his last visit she had begged him to bring the tallow doll to her. And though he had never liked the thing, he was obliged to promise that he would take it the next time he came to see her. His assurance had appeased and greatly calmed Cathy. Now he wondered why he had not thought to bring the doll before.

'Advertise!' Emily's cry jolted Bill out of his train of thought. '*Somebody* must have seen Matt. It's worth a try,' she urged with growing excitement.

'But the police put posters of Matt up everywhere. Nobody came forward then, Emily. What makes you think they'll respond to advertisements?'

'Offer a reward!'

'Of course!' The idea intrigued him. 'Money talks, or so they say.' No doubt such an advertisement would draw tiresome cranks and opportunists, but, like Emily said, it was worth a try. Everything else had failed. Enthused, he grabbed Emily by the shoulders. 'You're right! It just might work, and God knows, I'd pauper myself to see Matt safely home, with him and Cathy back together again.' He laughed out loud. 'We'll do it,' he told her. 'First thing Monday morning, I'll go to the *Milton Keynes Citizen*, and the *Bedforshire Times*. Hopefully, I won't be too late for this coming week's editions.'

'All we can do then is hope,' Emily murmured.

'And pray,' he told her. 'All we can do is hope . . . and pray.'

The next day was Sunday, the day when Bill spent the longest time with Cathy. Emily had wanted to come along, but Bill had said no. 'Not yet, Emily.' He might have added. 'Not while she's

248

so unsociable and likely to fly into unpredictable nasty moods.'
But he spared Emily that much. She understood and did not press
him.

Slater's Farm was situated midway between his own modest
home and the town of Bedford. Recalling his promise to Cathy, he
turned off the main road and continued at a steady speed down
the narrow meandering lane that would take him to the cottage. It
was a few minutes past one; visiting time began at two p.m., so
there was just time enough for him to collect the tallow doll.

It had been a shocking morning, grey and overcast from the
outset, with a bitter winter's chill in the light easterly breeze. He
hoped it did not herald the end of summer; after all, it was only
early September. He bent forward, peering upwards through the
windscreen. He smiled wryly. At least it had stayed dry, and now
the clouds were beginning to shift away, revealing tiny blue
patches in an otherwise angry sky. 'Perhaps we'll have a sunny
afternoon yet,' he muttered, feeding the steering wheel through
his fingers and swinging the car into the cottage driveway.

He wondered whether Edna would be inside. According to
their mutual arrangements she would be, because what they had
agreed was that she would look after the cottage as before, being
always there between the hours of ten a.m. and two p.m., in case
Matt telephoned. After that, if Matt needed to reach either Bill or
Joseph, then he knew where to contact them. Bill himself would
have stayed over at the farm, in case Matt were to phone or return
unexpectedly, but, like it or not, he had a business to run and,
though he would not admit it even to himself, mingled with his
fears for Matt there was also an element of anger towards him. He
loved Matt as though he was his own son, but he could not
understand why Matt had made no contact. Surely he must know
that Cathy was desperate to see him? And why had it not been
obvious to Matt that Cathy was ill, that she must have been
heading for a breakdown, as far back as when they were returning
in the car from the airport?

With the awful memory of Cathy's vicious attack on Matt,
there came a rash of guilt. How could he expect Matt to have seen

249

that particular incident as the onset of a mental illness, when he himself had treated it only with passing concern. All the same, there were other things now. What in God's name had happened between Matt and Cathy the night he disappeared? And why hadn't Matt been in touch . . . if not with Cathy, then with *him?* Was he so bitter? Had he really turned his back on the life he had worked so hard to build here? And was his love for Cathy over? No! To each and every question, the answer was a resounding no. What then?

Frantically he searched his mind, going over even the smallest detail that might somehow be relevant. But there was nothing. No indication of the terrible sequence of events that had taken place, no dawning realisation, no easy answers. Only this awful, sinister silence. Feeling as grey and brooding as the day, he got out of the car and followed the path to the kitchen.

His spirits lifted when the door was flung open and there stood the homely figure of Edna. Normally, she would welcome him with a smile. Instead, there was a look of apprehension on her face, and she was biting her bottom lip in that characteristic way she had when something was worrying her. As she ushered him in, his heart sank. 'I'm sorry, Mr Barrington,' she muttered, 'The minute you rang I did what you asked . . . went straight up to Cathy's room to fetch the doll . . .' She paused, obviously upset.

'What is it, Edna? What's wrong?'

'It's *broke*, that's what!' She levelled her anxious eyes at him. 'Clumsy fool that I am, I tripped at the top of the stairs. It frightened me, I can tell you. Well, I grabbed at the banister to steady myself, but the doll fell out of my hands and tumbled down the stairs. Whatever will Cathy say of me, Mr Barrington, oh, and she thought so much of that doll.'

Thankful to have confessed, she eased herself into the chair, her fingers nervously tapping the table while she looked up at him, waiting for the tirade that must follow, and thinking how neither this man nor his daughter would ever forgive her if they knew the truth. *She had not tripped over the carpet!* Nor had the doll been broken accidentally, because she had smashed it *deliberately*. When

Cathy's father phoned that morning, to say how she had asked for the tallow doll, and that he was taking it to her, Edna had recalled the times when she had seen Cathy with that wretched doll . . . singing to it and holding it like it was a child in her arms. Well, there was something offensive about it, something disturbing. Cathy was ill. She must have been ill for a long time, and none of them had realised.

Edna had known, though, that all was not well with Cathy, yet it was not something she could have told Matt, or even Joseph. It was just a feeling, a deep-down feeling that even she herself did not fully understand. But that doll! There was something unhealthy about the way Cathy cherished it. The thought of Cathy keeping it with her in the nursing home . . . looking at it in that particular way she did . . . no. No! Edna was glad she had broken it.

'Can it be mended, Edna?' Bill had been flustered, worried about how Cathy would feel when he told her. Now, though, he could see how agitated Edna had become. There would be nothing gained by making the poor woman feel even worse.

She shook her head. 'No, it can't be mended. It shattered into countless pieces.' She jerked her head sideways, telling him, 'It's in the dining room. See for yourself. I put the fragments in a shoe box.' When he brushed past her on his way out of the kitchen, she told him, 'You'll find it in the sideboard cupboard.'

A few moments later he came back into the room, his face solemn as he stood before her, the shoe box in his hands. 'Is this the one?' he asked. When she nodded, he frowned. 'That's curious,' he murmured. She didn't hear and his expression softened. The mere suggestion of a smile played on the corners of his mouth. 'Don't blame yourself, Edna,' he told her with a rush of compassion, 'accidents will happen. The main thing is that you were not hurt.'

Relief spread over her kindly face. 'That's right, Mr Barrington. I could easily have tumbled down the stairs myself.' She visibly shivered. 'It don't bear thinking about.'

Replacing the lid on the shoe box, he lied, 'I'll have to try and get it mended. Cathy would want me to. You know how much comfort she gets out of the doll.' He laughed. 'Though I can't think why. Maybe it's to do with wanting children; I just don't know.'

'Maybe. But that doll . . . that awful thing, it would be more likely to give me nightmares than comfort.'

'Oh, I agree, Edna. To be honest, I've never liked it either, but,' his voice fell away, and she thought he seemed to be accusing her, 'we ought not to question Cathy's liking for the doll. It's none of our business, after all, don't you agree, Edna?'

'I suppose so, Mr Barrington.' *He had guessed.* She was sure of it; he suspected her of breaking the doll on purpose. 'It was an accident,' she assured him.

'Did you have a dizzy spell, Edna?'

'Quite likely,' she lied, 'I really haven't been all that well lately.' That was partly true. Since Cathy had been taken away and Matt was still missing, she had forgotten what it was to sleep the whole night long. These two were like her own, and it was a traumatic experience to see them torn apart in this way.

'Would you rather *not* oversee the cottage, Edna?' he asked now. 'I could get someone else, I'm sure, if it's all too much for you.'

'*Never!*' She was on her feet now, her eyes blazing into his. 'How could you even say such a thing? Get someone else indeed! I knew you'd be angry with me for breaking the doll!'

'You're sure you feel well enough to carry on here?' He deliberately ignored her comment.

'Of course I am.'

'All right, Edna, but if it becomes too much for you, you will say?' She did not speak, but nodded. He was sorry he had upset her. 'I'd better get off to the hospital,' he said, tucking the shoe box under his arm and turning away. 'Cathy watches for me.' Suddenly he was glad that Edna had so far refused his offers to take her to see Cathy. He would not offer again. Not after today.

He was just getting into his car when Edna came after him. 'I said I was sorry that I broke the doll,' she said, her voice low and strange sounding. 'I was lying, Mr Barrington.'

'Oh?'

'I was sorry at first, but now I think it's a blessing in disguise.' She still couldn't bring herself to confess the truth – that she had deliberately smashed it.

'What do you mean?'

'You think about it,' she urged. 'Just think about it . . . *how all the bad things only started when that thing was brought into the house.*' She pointed at the shoe box lying beside him on the passenger seat. Her hands were quivering; she began trembling.

'Go inside, Edna. It's too chilly for you to be out here without a coat on.' He wanted to laugh at her suggestion, but suddenly it was as though a dark blanket had settled over him. He felt angry, impatient, his mood darkening by the minute. As she hurried away, he thought about what she had said . . . 'All the bad things only started when that . . . thing . . . was brought into the house.'

For one startling, unnerving moment, he was half-inclined to believe her. But then he remembered how that poor woman must herself be ill. It was not surprising, of course, because she was no longer young, and she had been dreadfully upset when Cathy was put in a psychiatric unit. On the way back, he just might stop off and have a quiet word with Joseph. Maybe Edna *was* doing far too much. She was probably in need of a short holiday. Unless, of course, she knocked her head when she tripped and dropped the doll. Yes, that might explain it.

Leaning sideways, he took the lid off the shoe box and peeped inside. Why else would she have told him that the doll was in fragments when he could see with his own eyes that it was perfect – *not a crack or a mark anywhere on its unbecoming form.*

Wondering how Cathy could ever want such a thing, he thrust the lid back on. Just looking at the doll made his flesh creep. He had half a mind to throw it into the ditch. Only the thought of Cathy's distress stopped him from doing so.

As he pulled away, the skies opened and the rain spewed down with a vengeance. Switching the windscreen wipers on full speed, he was astonished when the raindrops hardened and a furious hailstorm was unleashed, the large white crystals lashing the windscreen and bouncing off the road like miniature golf balls. His visibility was dangerously impaired as the skies blackened, and day became night. Slowing to a crawl, he was deafened by the relentless impact of hail against metal. Then, as he was about to pull over and park by the side of the road until the storm passed, it stopped as instantly as it had started. In a moment, the sun broke through and the day was bathed in brilliance, the hail melted away, and it was as though the blizzard had never been.

Relieved, Bill glanced at the dashboard clock. It was almost one thirty. He would need to put his toe down if he was to make the hospital by two o'clock. Pulling out on to the main road, he activated the radio-cassette. Suddenly he needed to hear the reassuring songs on his favourite tape . . . the Beatles . . . Gerry and the Pacemakers – a bevy of 60s classics that never failed to cheer him. In the back of his mind he deliberated on the advert that would go into the local newspapers. He wasn't sure yet as to how he might word it. Strange, he thought, how he was convinced that Matt was not too far away. He believed also that Matt loved Cathy as much as he had ever loved her. Paramount in his thoughts was always the prospect of bringing Matt home. The advert was his best chance. He prayed Matt would see it, and respond.

Chapter Thirteen

It was midnight. Through the porthole, Matt could see the stars high in the heavens, tiny scintillating jewels against a black velvet scarf. Like every night for as far back as he could remember, sleep eluded him. Restless, he shifted in the hard unyielding bed, turning this way and that, his senses ebbing in and out, and the ever-wearing pain persistent and wicked, playing on his nerve-endings, sapping his ability to think, draining his energy, sucking at his very existence. He felt like a man drugged, his head too heavy to raise from the pillow, too tired, it was all too much; the effort was crucifying. Now, as he rolled on to his side, he could hear the voices – the same faceless whispering voices – a man and a woman. They were close, only an arm's reach away. 'Who are you?' he murmured, his own voice seeming stranger to him than did the other two. He waited in the darkness. No answer. Silence was oddly comforting. Rocked by the gentle roll of the barge and the muffled echo of the water slapping its hulk, he turned again, burying his face in the pillow. Then, as always, she came to him. 'Cathy . . . Cathy.' Smiling, bright like a child, her arms open, waiting, wanting him, in the sunlight her grey eyes sparkling, the breeze teasing her golden hair. Suddenly her smile faded and she was crying out, struggling in his hands, *his hands*, tight round her throat. *'Cathy!'* She oozed through his fingers, dark, ugly, and laughing, then crying.

'Shh, go to sleep. It's all right.' The voice bathed his mind, her touch was soft, and cool against his burning temples. Soon he was resting, a shallow troubled interlude before they invaded his thoughts again, the nightmares, the screams, the unearthly

255

laughter, the terror, the guilt and the helplessness, the awful, awful helplessness. He felt her move away, heard the voices far off, too distant, too vague. Weariness crept into every fibre of his being, such weariness; death would be a welcome release.

'Two thousand pounds' reward!' The man's voice was low, incredulous, trembling with greed. He thrust the newspaper before her eyes. 'We can't afford to ignore that kind of money. Think what we could do with it. And anyway, if you ask me, he's dying.'

'And you said *I* was hard hearted.' Her laugh sounded like the rush of water in the wake of a gently moving barge, soft, almost purring. 'He won't die. The wound has become infected, probably from the filthy canal water, but he won't die. I won't let him, you know that.' In her mind's eye she saw his handsome chiselled features, the thick mop of earth-coloured hair and oh, the dark frantic eyes, the way they looked up at her, tragic, beseeching. He was in her power. *She liked that.* Somehow he had created a hunger in her; a hunger that only he could satisfy.

'If I thought . . .' The man's voice was menacing. 'If I found out that you were keeping him drugged,' she winced with pain as he snapped his fist round a hank of her long, flowing hair, 'I swear I'd kill you!'

'Fool!' She spat the word out, wrenching herself from him. 'Why would I do such a thing?'

'Because there hasn't yet been a man that you can keep your hands off, because you're too beautiful for your own good and—' he paused, moving away. There was a brief span of quiet. When he spoke again his voice was filled with pain. 'Because you still haven't forgiven me; won't *ever* forgive me.'

'You're wrong,' she lied. 'That was a long time ago. Your one indiscretion. Do you think I would punish you for ever?'

'Would you?'

'Don't be foolish.'

'*Are* you keeping him drugged?'

'A small amount, yes, but only enough to dull the pain and give him time to recover.'

'That's all?'

'That's all,' she lied brazenly.

'And you have no designs on him?'

'I've told you.'

'Then why can't we turn him in? We could go a long way on two thousand pounds.'

'I dare say, but could you *really* turn him in?' Disbelief, then, 'It was *you* who saved him from drowning. And have you forgotten what it's like to suffer? To be hounded from place to place, treated like so much dirt?'

'No, I haven't forgotten. But what if he dies, what then? Have you thought of *that*?'

'He won't die.'

'Then how long do you intend to keep him on the barge?'

'For as long as it takes. I won't let you turn him in.'

'How can you stop me?' He laughed softly, caressing her hair. He knew she had lied. His instincts told him so. 'Two thousand pounds,' he reminded her.

'Judas money!'

'Let's not quarrel.' His hand slid over her sunkissed shoulders, plucking at the thin straps of her nightgown. 'It's such a glorious night, a night for making love.' He heard her sigh as the garment slithered to the floor. She was all woman, all his, but only for as long as he remained alert and cunning. At first he had felt compassion for the man. Now, though, he was bitterly jealous. And, for two thousand pounds, what did he care whether the man lived or died. This was *his* barge, *his* woman! And she was using *his* supply of drugs. The stranger was no longer welcome.

The officers had followed for many hours, waiting for the right moment. When the moon was dipping low and all was deathly quiet; that moment was now. Like slinky black rats they closed in, incredibly silent, frighteningly swift, swarming the vessel and overwhelming the unsuspecting occupants. In a matter of minutes it was all over. Nothing was left unturned, no one was spared. Not the couple who were locked in the last deliciously agonising throes of passion; not even the man who slept a fitful fearful sleep, a man gripped by a fever that would be the death of him, a man without purpose, without hope, riddled with guilt yet not really understanding why.

The intruders swept in under cover of night. They left when the dawn was beginning to herald a new day. Only one remained, to watch, to keep vigil over the now silent barge. Nothing stirred, no sound was heard to disturb the eerie solitude, only the morning song of awakening birds, and the soft swish of creatures moving beneath the rushes.

'Matt's dead, isn't he? *Isn't he?*' Cathy's grey eyes were hard and shiny as she confronted he father. 'You think I don't know. You keep things from me, but I *do* know!' She swung away from him. '*I know, because I killed him!*'

'No, no, Cathy, you did not kill Matt, please believe me.' He would have taken her in his arms, but Cathy backed away, her face clouded with suspicion, her eyes drilling into him, accusing, defiant.

'Where is he, then?'

Dropping his arms to his sides, he drew his gaze from her face. He couldn't bear to have her look at him in that way. He should never have told her that Matt was missing, but the doctor had persuaded him that 'She should know. She feels instinctively that you're lying to her, that Matt would have been to see her before now, if he was able. You must tell her, Mr Barrington. She's strong enough to accept the truth. Not knowing is far worse, when she imagines all kinds of horrors.' And so today, when she asked for Matt, he told her in as gentle a way as he knew how.

'Matt went away,' he explained. 'We're doing everything we can to find him.' At first she had not believed him, then, when she realised he was telling the truth, she had cried. Now her mood was more disturbing, for she was convinced that he was dead – that *she* had murdered him. The doctors had warned that she would suffer a whole gamut of emotions. That was why the nurse was present in the room, keeping a discreet distance but closely monitoring the

258

situation. He turned to look at the nurse now, to draw strength from her and maybe to find an answer. She only smiled and nodded. He looked away, returning his attention to his daughter. 'Cathy . . .' He took her by the hands, persuading her to come and sit down.

She snatched herself away; her look was contemptuous and she told him in a shrivelling voice, 'You liar! I don't ever want you to come near me again.'

'Don't say that, sweetheart,' he implored. He knew in his heart that this young woman was Cathy, his own daughter whom he loved more than ever, but now, when she stared at him through those glittering dark eyes, her face twisted with such loathing, he knew that he was fast losing her. In all of his life he had never been more afraid, never been more desperate. 'Try and remember,' he quietly urged. 'Try hard, Cathy. What happened the last time you saw Matt?'

'I have to go now,' she answered, positioning herself beside the nurse. 'Tomorrow they will hang me. I killed him, you see.' She smiled. 'I *meant* to kill him . . . *had* to!' In the sunlit room her eyes were markedly black. She seemed to grow in stature and he was shocked by her arrogance. 'They must be punished, every one.' She laughed softly. 'Let them hang me. *There are worse things than death.*'

Her laughter was frightening to him. For the first time he wondered whether she really was mad. He wondered also whether there was any way back for her. He moved towards her, to console and reassure her.

'No! Don't touch me.' She spread both her hands in the air, erecting a barrier between them. Shattered, he saw the nurse shake her head, warning him, leading Cathy away. In that moment before the door closed on them, Cathy looked back, her wide eyes regarding him with childlike curiosity. He was softly crying now, bitterly, unashamedly. Suddenly her lovely features softened and there was real sadness in her gaze. 'I love you, Dad,' she said, remorsefully. 'Don't cry. Please, don't cry. It won't be long before they let me come home. Tell Matt I miss him so, and I

259

love him with all my heart. Tell him that, will you? And tell him I'm sorry if I hurt him. Oh, please, tell him.' The tears fell softly down her face. *'I never wanted to hurt him.'* The nurse drew her away. The door closed with a soft thud.

'I'll tell him, sweetheart,' he called, brokenly. 'I'll tell him.' He heard their footsteps echoing down the long stark corridor. An unbearable silence descended. And still he did not move. It was all too much for him, more than any man should be asked to bear. He cast his mind back, to a few days previously, when routine police enquiries had led to Cathy being questioned about a certain priest who had been found dead in his own study . . . 'Suicide,' they said '. . . satisfied that no one else was involved'.

All the same, it was a sad mysterious incident and the police were obliged to question anyone he might have interviewed in the week leading up to his death. According to the housekeeper's information, and the old gravedigger, a particular description had led them to Cathy.

Cathy's answers to their questions were given in childlike innocence . . . yes, she had gone to see the priest and to seek his advice on her failing relationship with Matt, 'But he couldn't help me,' she told them tearfully. 'No one can help.' She described how, when she left, 'He was looking out of the window towards the churchyard . . . sadder even than me, I think.' The old grave-digger had substantiated Cathy's account.

The police were satisfied. The case was closed.

Bill was greatly relieved, though he wasn't sure why. As a child, he believed in God, in that all-powerful majestic being who answered his prayers and kept him safe. He still believed, even now. He had nothing else to cling to.

Chapter Fourteen

When the last of his equipment was loaded into the van, and the men were ready to move out, Mr Wilson reported to Emily. 'Finished,' he said proudly, the two of them looking round the garden. 'Exactly as you wanted it, and all done in time for Mrs Hinson's homecoming.'

'You have been as good as your word, Mr Wilson,' she agreed. 'Thank you.'

'Tomorrow, isn't it, when Mrs Hinson comes home?'

Emily nodded. She did not trust herself to speak. It would serve no purpose to tell him how desperately ill Maria was; 'Nothing more we can do,' they said. It was only natural that the old lady be brought home, to end her days in this grand old house which had been her home for over fifty years. That Maria would soon leave her was incomprehensible to Emily. Choking back the tears, she bade Mr Wilson go with her into the kitchen. Here, she paid her debts and he signed a receipt. Everything was too normal, too pleasant, too unbearably painful.

'If there's ever anything else you want done, a barbecue, or pergola, well, you won't forget to give me a ring, will you?' When Emily assured him that she would keep his card safe by the telephone, he was suitably gratified. 'You'll not find no better landscaper than me,' he remarked. He sauntered on to the terrace, hawkish eyes surveying his handiwork, his small pointed head nodding in satisfaction. 'A grand job, though I say so myself!' he decided.

'It is,' Emily agreed. It was exactly the the way she wanted it . . . wider walkways, and two lovely rustic benches, one half-way

261

down the garden, and one where the apple tree used to be. There was even a bird bath in the shape of two dolphins playing with a large round dish. Mr Wilson had been right to persuade her on that new addition.

'I've put some bulbs in the soil round the benches. You'll get a marvellous show next spring and summer,' he promised.

'I'm sure we will,' Emily remarked. It occurred to her that Maria may never see another spring and summer. She couldn't bear to think on it. 'Goodbye, then,' she told him, 'and thank you.'

'Wait a minute, miss!' He dug a grimy hand into the pocket of his overalls. 'One o' my men found this.' He held out his fist. 'It were nestled in the roots o' that old apple tree.' He unfolded the palm of his hand to reveal an odd-looking object with ugly dark particles of earth still clinging to it.

'What is it?' Emily was reluctant to touch it.

'Not sure, miss.' He picked at the object, flicking off tiny specks of mud. 'I reckon it could be a *doll* of sorts. You'd need to clean it up, but look . . .' He wet his finger and rubbed it over the smoother, upper part. 'That's a face, ain't it? Grimy though, but not rotted, d'you see?' He held it out again. 'That there apple tree must have been nigh on forty . . . maybe even fifty year old, and this 'ere artefact, well, it were right down deep, enmeshed in the roots.' He paused to examine it, a frown deepening the lines between his eyebrows. 'Funny thing though,' he said quietly. 'The roots hadn't speared it, like you'd think they would after all this time. No. In fact, they were all entwined round and round . . . like a cradle, you might say.' He thrust it forward. 'You take it, miss. I dare say when you've cleaned it up, the thing would make an interesting ornament.' He chuckled. 'It could even be valuable. After all, it's been buried in the ground so long you could say it were an antique!'

Now, when Emily took it from him, he discreetly wiped his hand down the leg of his overalls. Antique or not, he wouldn't like that thing sitting on *his* sideboard; it had a sickly, slithery feel about it. Strange that, because, as a rule, when a thing had been buried in the ground for so long it either fossilised or rotted away, and that object had done neither. Even the garment it wore was

262

intact, though to him it looked no better than a bit of sacking. 'I'll be on my way, then,' he said cheerfully, 'and don't you forget, miss, should you need anything else doing . . .' In a moment he was disappearing round the side of the house; the merry tune he was whistling echoed in the air long after he had gone.

Inside the kitchen, Emily took great pains to clean the object with the corner of a wet flannel, gently washing the hessian dress, the bare creamy-textured limbs and the long silken strands that shone coal-black in the incoming sunlight. Little by little the doll came to life. Now, as she carefully gouged the earth from every exquisite feature she was made to gasp aloud. 'Why, it's beautiful, so beautiful!' At first the doll had been cold and clammy to the touch, like a corpse must feel, she had mused with regret, but now, shining and vibrant, there was a warmth about it, a living vitality.

It occurred to Emily that the doll may well have belonged to Maria. After all, she herself had planted the tree and, if the doll was entangled in its roots as Mr Wilson had described, then it must have been unintentionally committed to an early grave at the very time the tree was planted. Emily wondered now whether the old lady had ever kept a dog – certainly she had never mentioned it, but it was the sort of thing a pet might well do – playfully take such an object from the house and drop it into the ground. Emily had no way of knowing *how* it had occurred, but she was convinced that this exquisite object did belong to Maria, and that somehow it had been lost all those years ago.

With the supposition came a rush of pleasure. She would keep it as a surprise for Maria's homecoming tomorrow. With that in mind, she put the doll carefully away in the china cupboard. Gazing at it awhile before committing it to the dark interior, Emily was fascinated by its ageless beauty. She thought it uniquely proud, curiously magnificent. She wondered about the hand that had so lovingly fashioned it. Was it made in the image of its maker? Could there really be anyone so stunningly handsome? She recalled Mr Wilson's words . . . 'enmeshed in the tree-roots . . . maybe fifty years'. So long. Almost a lifetime. Could it be that the roots had protected the doll from the ravage of time? 'Like a cradle', was how Mr Wilson had described its resting place. So many years! And yet, beneath the grimy deposits and the coating of blackened earth, the doll had remained untouched, unharmed. Each feature was elegant, the face compelling.

While she gazed on it, Emily was reminded of something she had read . . . 'The eyes are the mirror of the soul.' If that were the case, then the doll must have a dark, mysterious soul, for the eyes were black and scintillating, uniquely compelling in their sooty depths.

She closed the cupboard door. In her mind's eye she could still see the doll. Her thoughts wandered back to Maria, to the reason she was coming home. To die. *Maria was coming home to die.* Emily sat in the garden, a small forlorn figure, thinking how Fate could be cruel and kind at the same time, cruel in the way it had robbed her of her parents when she was only a girl, and now she was losing Maria. Yet kind in the way it had brought Bill into her lonely life. Bill. A warm, caring man whom she loved with all her heart.

As his image flooded her mind, Emily's spirits fell. He too had suffered, was still suffering, and there was nothing she could do to help him. It was a painful thing. Suddenly, the clouds obscured the sun and there was a chill in the air. Emily glanced at her watch. It was almost midday. A moment ago the sun was warm and brilliant, now it was dark and cold. Strange, she thought, how the weather can change in the blink of an eye. Shivering, she hurried towards the house. At two p.m. the consultant would be making his final decision on whether Maria Hinson was strong enough for her homeward journey. Right from the start, he had been against the old lady's request, but in her waking hours she was insistent, the lovable tyrant used to getting her own way. He relented only when it was promised that a nurse would be appointed to watch over her.

It was twelve thirty when the shrill tone of the telephone interrupted Emily; she was painstakingly arranging the blooms in Maria's room. She had bought the yellow and white chrysanthemums yesterday, and they made a lovely sight on the windowsill. One vase was enough, though, she had reasoned, because she didn't want Maria to feel as though she was exchanging one hospital for another.

Emily was surprised when the caller turned out to be Bill. Yesterday evening, they had sat here in the front room talking of so many things: Cathy and Matt, Maria, their own future. They did not make longterm plans. There was too much turmoil in their lives for that. Today was Monday, and Bill intended to start work at five a.m., delivering an urgent consignment of packages to Liverpool. He calculated it would take him at least five hours. So he expected to be home by ten a.m., showered and ready an hour later, after which he would spend a few hours with Cathy, who lately was growing more and more agitated with regard to Matt. At quarter to two he would collect Emily and drive her to the hospital to arrange for Maria's release.

Emily's voice betrayed her surprise. She had wrongly believed he was with Cathy. 'Is there anything wrong?' she wanted to know. He sounded excited, worried. When he replied, breathless and in a frantic voice, his words tumbling one over the other, her eyes grew wide. She put her hand to her mouth, stifling the cry there, sucking in her breath and her heart leaping at what he told her. 'Of course! I'll ring straight away,' she assured him. 'I'll tell them to let Cathy know you'll be late.' She grew quiet. He was talking again, his voice close to breaking. She sensed the trauma he was suffering. 'No, no, it's all right, you mustn't concern yourself about me. I'll get a taxi.' Now she was listening intently to his fragmented version of the sequence of events that had taken place that morning. 'Yes. Don't worry,' she told him firmly. 'Is there anything else you want me to do? Shall I come there when I've seen Maria?' A pause, then, 'All right, I'll wait for your call. And Bill . . . God bless.' Her eyes were bright with tears when she replaced the receiver. It was so cruel the way his hopes had been raised, and then shattered. On Bill's return from Liverpool the police had called at his house. *Matt had been found!* Bill's joy was short lived when they told him that Matt was seriously ill. Bill was with him now, and he was devastated.

'Stop fussing!' Maria Hinson's blue button eyes flashed a warning
to the two beleaguered ambulance men whose unenviable task it
was to convey her home and to install her in the bosom of her
family. As they negotiated the stretcher up the stairs behind
Emily's careful steps, they were incredibly gentle, handling her
patiently and with a degree of love. They marvelled at her spirit,
and were secretly amused by the manner in which she mercilessly
lashed them with her tongue. The pneumonia had taken its toll:
age and a weakened heart were killing her. Sheer stubbornness,
and a secret purpose, was keeping her alive.

'Don't be so ungrateful,' Emily chided, as Maria continued to
protest even while they lifted her into bed. She wanted so much to
put her arms round that frail old figure, but she knew how such
demonstrative affection would incur Maria's wrath. Emily had
prayed for her recovery and, for a time, it had seemed as though
her prayers were answered. Now, though, she saw the presence of
death in the old withered face, like a grey shadow, lingering,
waiting.

'We'll leave you to it, then.' The older of the two men smiled at
Emily, secretly relieved to be released of his burden. 'Unless, of
course, there's anything else you think we could do for your
mother?'

'I am *not* her mother,' Maria's feeble voice corrected the hapless
fellow, 'and no, there's nothing else you can do for me,' she added.

'All right, Ma,' he said, folding the stretcher and handing it to
his colleague. Turning to Emily he murmured, 'Take care of her.
She's a grand old sort. They must have broken the mould when
they made her.' Coming to the bed he looked down on Maria,
memories of his own late mother spiralling up in him. Death was a
sorry visitor, but not always unwelcome. All the same, he sensed
that this old lady was not yet ready to meet her maker. 'Cheerio,
then,' he told her, and with a broad smile, 'Now don't you go
doing anything foolhardy, will you?'

'Like what?' she asked, with a defiant twinkle in her eye.

He wondered what she had been like as a young woman; a

266

pretty little thing, he didn't doubt. 'We'll be off, then,' he said. Nodding to the other man, he went straight from the room. His colleague followed. A strange peace settled in the wake of their departure.

'You're a wicked woman,' Emily laughed, coming to sit on the edge of the bed, 'they won't forget you in a hurry.'

'Oh, I didn't mean to be difficult,' Maria admitted, 'but I was impatient to get home.' She closed her eyes, her whole body visibly relaxing.

Emily took a moment to gaze on her friend, so grand, so impossible. In that moment Maria looked incredibly old, yet young as an infant, small and helpless. Her iron-grey hair had always been thick and meticulously rolled into a fat halo about her face: now, though, the strands were baby-fine, trailing down her neck and shoulders. The paper-thin skin was loose and patterned with a thousand lines, all criss-crossing in a haphazard network, going in no particular direction, having no beginning and no end. Beneath the eyelids, tiny flickering movements indicated that she was not sleeping, or, if she was, then her dreams were haunted. Suddenly the thin frail body shuddered and the eyes popped open – shocking-blue eyes, vital and shining, but already touched by the creeping fingers of death. 'Don't leave me,' Maria pleaded, jutting out her arm and closing her fingers over Emily's hand. There was torment in her voice.

'I won't leave you,' Emily promised, 'you won't be left alone . . . ever.'

'Is that damned nurse here yet?'

'Soon. She'll be here within the hour.'

'I didn't want her. I only want you.'

'I know that, but she's kind and experienced.'

'Experienced in caring for the dying. Say what you mean, Emily. I've always taught you that.'

'Yes.' Emily choked back the sorrow and braced herself. 'She is experienced in caring for the dying.' Maria would never know the effort it took for Emily to say that.

The blue eyes stared out, a hint of anger making them brilliant.

267

Then a smile shone through as she told Emily, 'I'm not afraid to die. *Living* can be more frightening. It's so hard, pretending. Hiding.'

'That's a strange thing to say.'

The old lady smiled; it was a hauntingly beautiful smile. 'I worried for you, so afraid you would be left all alone. Now you have the love of a good man. You *do* love him, don't you?'

'Oh yes, Maria. I *do* love him, very much.'

'Thank God . . . he answered that prayer for me. Perhaps he will answer another.'

'I'm sure he will.' Emily was concerned. 'What is it? What's troubling you?'

Maria remained silent, her blue eyes regarding Emily; blue eyes soft with affection, hiding so many secrets. 'You will have to know,' she replied presently, 'but not yet. There is so much to tell. And too much on my mind.'

'You're tired. Why don't you rest?'

Maria squeezed Emily's fingers. 'I *am* tired, yes, but there will be time enough for me to rest. There are things to do, wrongs to put right. Afterwards I can rest for all eternity.' She saw how Emily meant to protest. 'What of Bill?' she said hurriedly, catching Emily unawares. 'Tell me about his troubles.'

Emily stiffened. Both she and Bill had taken great pains to keep his troubles from Maria. Deliberately ignoring her questions, she suggested, 'I think you should sleep a while now.' She made as if to rise from the bed, but the old gnarled fingers kept her there. Emily chose her answer carefully. 'I don't know what troubles you mean.'

'Don't lie to me,' Maria scolded. Her face was serious, her expression grim. 'He is a man haunted.' The thin, aged lips twisted in a half-smile. 'Don't think I don't know, Emily! I *do*! I know only too well what it is to be haunted. *Tell me!*' she insisted. 'For I won't rest until you do.' Her sharp blue gaze remained firm on Emily's face. She saw how Emily was inwardly struggling, wondering how she might reveal just enough to placate, and no more. *'I want to know everything!'* she demanded. When Emily hesitated, she struggled to raise herself up in the bed, an odd disturbing expression on her face. 'For God's sake, Emily, I have to know. Do as I ask. Tell me everything!'

Unable to comprehend Maria's desperate anxiety, but realising with a shock that suppressing the reason for Bill's 'troubles' would do more harm to Maria than revealing the truth, Emily reluctantly conceded. She explained how Cathy and Matt had greatly suffered in their marriage, and how it had slowly deteriorated, until now it seemed irretrievable. She described how Cathy had become mentally unstable and was assigned to an institution. 'Some weeks ago, something awful happened. Cathy was found in a state of terror . . . claiming someone had tried to strangle her. She was convinced that *she* had murdered Matt. She was found alone in the cottage. There was no sign of Matt, although the kitchen door was left open. The police were satisfied that Cathy's story was the product of an unstable mind. This was confirmed by the doctor, and Cathy was committed. Bill was shattered by it all.'

'When they found Bill's daughter, were there any marks on her neck to substantiate her belief that someone had tried to strangle her?'

'No.'

'Was there any evidence of a struggle there?'

'No.'

Maria was shocked into silence. All the old horrors were raised in her. It was as she feared. 'Before that night . . . were there any other incidents?' she persisted.

Emily searched her mind. 'Yes,' she said, amazed at Maria's determination, and far from distressing the old lady, the revelations appeared to stimulate her. 'I remember Bill telling me about Cathy having some sort of fit in the stables, when Matt had to take her home. She was strange for days . . . refused to leave the house. But then the arguments began to destroy their marriage. Bill said Cathy had changed almost beyond recognition.'

'And what of Matt?'

'The night they took Cathy away, he went missing. The police

269

failed to trace him. Even Bill's efforts came to nothing. He's been found now, though.' She hesitated.

Maria sensed there was something very wrong. *'He's dead, isn't he?'* she asked tremulously.

'Oh no!' Emily could at least assure Maria of that. 'He is not dead.'

'But . . . ?'

'He is very ill.'

'Tell me, Emily. When did it all begin . . . Cathy, Matt, when did it all go wrong?' Maria asked softly. But she did not need to hear, because she already knew. In that wedding picture they had been so much in love, deliriously happy as only the young can be. When they went on their honeymoon to Australia, they seemed not to have a care in the world. She knew that because, unbeknown to anyone but the poor detective who had met with such a sorry savage end on the river that day, *she had sent a shadow to follow them.* Yes, they had been happy. But all too soon, the evil had begun to manifest itself. How though? How could it happen? That was something she had not been able to fathom. She had agonised over and over. How could it happen?

She took a moment to quietly observe Emily, that kind and lovely woman whom she had so long deceived. Her fears that Emily would be left alone when she herself was gone from this world had thankfully melted in the warmth that flowed between Emily and Bill. They, too, were so obviously in love. Oh, not in a silly romantic way, for they were no longer young, but their pleasure in each other was a joy to see. Emily had never looked more radiant. Happiness shone from her pretty brown eyes, and her whole countenance was marked by a beauty that Maria had never seen in her before. For the briefest moment, her resolve faltered. *Was she right in revealing the awful truth to Emily?* Would there be anything gained by delving into the past? Raising the ghosts of those gone before?

These past days, she had searched her old heart for the truth, for guidance, for a glimmer of hope that the secrets – all the bad things which she had carefully recorded over the years – might die with her. She was old, no longer useful, and during those dark fearful days when she was close to death, there had been times when she wondered whether she was interfering in things best left alone, wicked evil things that may well end when her own life was ended! *Oh, if that were true, then she would have taken her own life without a second thought!* But a deeper instinct warned her that even when she herself was gone, the destructive force would grow even more powerful.

When, in desperation and terror, she had buried the tallow image, it had been with the fervent prayer that never again could it weave its awful carnage. But she had been wrong! Maria knew now that the enmity was relentless. Somehow it had found a way to outwit her, to wreak a terrible vengeance on two young innocents. Yet, even now, there had to be a way. There had to be. It was up to her. She had known that all along.

She waited for Emily's reply. When it came, she was not surprised, for Emily repeated what Bill had told her, that Cathy was taken ill in Australia and both he and Matt were deeply concerned for Cathy's health when, during the journey home from the airport, she made a particularly vicious attack on Matt. From then on things got progressively worse.

In order to learn all she could from Emily, Maria had resisted the weariness that threatened to rob her of her senses. Now it overwhelmed her. 'Please leave me,' she murmured, 'I want to sleep now,' and keep what little strength I have, she thought, and pray it will be enough.

Emily rose from the bed. She gazed down on that dear familiar face, quiet now, gently resting. In a soft voice she whispered to herself, 'You're a strange one, Maria, so very ill, and yet deeply concerned about someone else's troubles. You're a good woman, Maria Hinson. A good woman.'

Eyes tightly closed, the old lady whispered also. 'There are things you don't know, but soon you will. Things from an old woman's conscience. Unpleasant things that are not of this world.' When Emily leaned forward to hear what she was saying, Maria turned away. There would be time enough. Time enough.

It was all so painfully clear to her now . . . Cathy . . . the hideous hallucinations . . . just like the one she had as a child when she saw her small brother crushed to death only minutes *before* it actually happened. Poor Cathy. Poor tortured soul, crippled by a guilt complex, cruelly torn between love and hate. It was all as Maria had feared. 'There is badness in me,' Cathy had told her father, and Bill had confessed his worst nightmares to Emily . . . 'There's something happening to my lovely Cathy,' he had said, 'something devilish . . . destroying her, destroying Matt.'

Reluctantly, Emily had described it all. Maria was glad. But she was so tired, so very tired now. She heard Emily tiptoe from the room. Soon after, she fell into a deep troubled sleep, when all the awful memories came like long-ago phantoms to make her suffer. Weird and terrifying images quickened her senses. The dark silhouette gyrated in her frantic mind, elusive, warm from its grave, its long black hair flowing like a mantle about the slim shapely form. *It was alive.* The tallow doll knew her every thought. She must be careful. So very careful.

'No! Don't put the light on.' Cathy had seen her father enter the room, his bulky frame silhouetted in the light from the outer passage. She heard him call her name, then realised, with a rush of panic, that he was reaching for the light switch. Her frantic call caused him to lower his arm and peer into the semi-darkness. When he could not see her she laughed, but it was a strange, mirthless sound. 'I'm here,' she said softly, 'waiting for you.'

'Where?' He came forward. She had played these games before, and he did not like them. 'Where are you, sweetheart?' There was a strange smell in the room, heady, not unpleasant, but it churned his stomach. Unlike the usual clinical smell of any institution, it intrigued him. He had noticed it here for the first time, on the day they found Matt. It was stronger in the evening, lingering about Cathy like a perfume, and yet like no perfume he had ever encountered before . . . earthy, it was, and musty, *like there was something damp and old hiding in the room.* It had an intoxicating effect on him.

272

'Down here. By the window.'

Drawn by the sound of her soft laughter, he came towards the bed, to where the moonlight trickled in through the window. He glanced down. She was there, curled into the corner. The bars on the window had split the moonlight, making a weird pattern on her face and body. She was silent now, small and still, the doll cradled in her arms, her grey eyes looking up. In the half-light he could still see the torment in her lovely face. 'I know why you're here,' she whispered, a dark mysterious smile transforming her from within.

'I'm here to see *you*, sweetheart,' he said in a choking voice. To witness her like this was more than he could bear. But she was right. He *had* called at this late hour to explain as gently as he could how Matt had been found. He would not have told her of the circumstances – that it was during a raid by the drugs squad. Matt was barely alive when they took him away, 'pumped full of barbiturates', they said, but the others had confessed. Matt was innocent. His original trauma and their subsequent neglect of him was taking his life.

'I know why you're here,' she said again, mocking.

'I'm only here to see how you are,' he lied. He could not talk to her of other things, not yet. 'Don't stay there,' he coaxed, bending down and stretching out his arms to hold her, to raise her. She made a movement, so swift and sudden that he was caught unawares. The pain shot through his fingers. He reeled back, not realising first that the warm sticky wetness oozing over his skin was his own blood.

'*Go away!*' The words hissed into the gloom. Grey eyes peered out, dark with pain. Dark, almost black in the moon's iridescent glow. He had seen her like this before, and it terrified him. She was laughing now, shrieking with delight, *or untold agony.*

Suddenly the door burst open to admit two white-coated nurses. One of them flicked the switch. There was a crackling sound, a blue light zig-zagged down the nurse's arm, causing her to stagger in pain. The moon hid behind the clouds and the blackness was impenetrable. Only the tiny square of light through the upper door panel showed the fear on their faces. He was shocked. He never realised they were so vulnerable.

Groping his way towards the door, he threw it open, letting the light from the outer hall flood in. When they wrenched her from the corner she screamed, spitting and fighting like a tigress – like someone possessed, he thought, his sadness like a hard clenched fist inside him. Unable to watch, he went outside, leaning face front to the wall, ashamed, as though in being her father he had created her anguish. He could still hear her screams, awful, unearthly sounds.

Then, without warning, the screams were ended. In the deathly, ensuing silence he heard the sound of his own blood dripping to the ground . . . splish . . . splash . . . splish . . . splash. The hand on his shoulder startled him. He slewed round. When he recognised Cathy's doctor, relief surged through him, and with it came the sobs, heart-rending uncontrollable sobs too long suppressed. Understanding, the doctor led him away. 'She's been sedated,' he said. He spoke in that casual manner of all doctors – kindly, compassionate, yet irritatingly aloof.

It was almost ten p.m. by the time he returned from Casualty. 'Lucky not to have lost your finger,' they said . . . 'almost bitten through to the bone.' While he waited for the injection to numb the tissue, he had phoned Emily. He had never needed her more than he did in that moment. She promised to wait up for him, insisting that he stay the night. He spared her the awful details of what had taken place, but he could not hide his broken spirit.

'She'll rest now, Mr Barrington.' The doctor sat at one side of the desk, Bill sat at the other. 'I'm sorry. I misjudged the situation. I thought she should know about her husband. I did not expect that she would react with such violence.'

'*But I didn't tell her.* She looked so frail, so pathetic.' He stood up, wanting to leave, needing to see Emily. 'I'm a coward. I couldn't tell her.'

'Oh?' He shook his head, intrigued as to what could have triggered off such a violent fit. 'All the same, she *will* have to be told, I'm afraid.'

274

'I know! For God's sake, don't you think I know!' Sometimes he believed all of this wasn't really happening . . . that he was caught up in a nightmare. 'How can I tell my own daughter that her husband is at death's door? How can I put that burden on her, when her mind is so fragile?'

'Do you want *me* to tell her?'

'No! I don't want that.' He swung round, looking away for a moment, hiding the fear, the pain. Now he was staring at the doctor, slamming his good fist into the desk, venting the feelings that were crippling him. 'I'll *tell* you what I want! *I want Cathy back*. The lovely, gentle, carefree girl she was. That's what I want! And Matt . . . to bring him home, whole and well. Do you know what it's like to see him lying there in St Andrew's Hospital, a shell, just an empty shell? Alive but not alive! He doesn't even know when I'm there.' He covered his face with his hand and groaned. The next time he looked at the doctor, his sorry eyes told all. 'I would give all I own to turn back the clock, to see Cathy and Matt the way they were, so young, so much in love, with their whole lives before them.' He shook his head, his lips twisted in a sneer. 'Life is a cruel bastard.'

'There is nothing I can say to ease your grief,' the doctor confessed. 'All I can promise is that your daughter is being well looked after.'

'But can you cure her? Tell me that.' He still hoped.

'We can only do our best. The rest is up to Cathy.'

'And the devil!' Bill added cynically.

'No, Mr Barrington. It's up to Cathy, and the Good Lord,' the doctor corrected. Rising from his seat he went across the room. Standing with his hand on the door knob, his expression unyielding, he said, 'Go home, Mr Barrington.'

'Can I see her before I go?'

The doctor shook his head. 'Better not. She's been heavily sedated.'

'Tomorrow, then?'

'Tomorrow. She'll be much calmer, I promise.' He turned the door knob, a benign smile on his face.

Outside the door, the small figure crept stealthily away, on its face a devious and sinister expression. The voices spoke to her now, stronger than ever, darkly persuasive. 'You wanted Matt, didn't you, Cathy? Haven't you been searching for him? . . . longing for him? He's waiting for you, Cathy. You know you can't live without him. But you can be with him now, Cathy . . . *be with him for all time.* Don't be afraid. Go to him, Cathy, to your Matt, your love. *Go now, Cathy! NOW.*' The voice was unbelievably persuasive, powerful; too powerful to resist. As she fled headlong into the night, it went with her, murmuring deep in her mind, '*Matt . . . your love. Be with him for all time.*'

In her deepest heart Cathy knew that nothing else mattered. Only Matt. *Only that they should be together at last.* She had been uneasy in sleep, yet so exhausted, drained of all that made life worth living. She felt the doll warm and comforting in her hand. It gave her the will to go on. It made her strength formidable.

'Cathy did *that?*' Emily's brown eyes widened in disbelief. 'But why? Why would she do such a thing?' She stared up at him. He was a saddened figure, shocked, but not broken, not yet broken. He stood with his back to the empty fireplace, his thoughtful gaze reaching down to her. He made no reply, gave no indication that he had heard her. Instead he continued to gaze in a fixed dreamlike expression, as though drawing comfort from her presence but not yet able to wrench his mind from what he had seen in that small unfriendly room where Cathy had torn into him with such malice. He could not come to terms with it. The throbbing pain in his hand was nothing compared to the chaos inside him. Through his deeper thoughts he heard Emily's voice. 'Bill, why would Cathy do such a thing?' She was on her feet now, her loving fingers touching his bandaged hand.

Snapping the images from his mind, he slid his arm round her shoulders and forced a nervous smile. 'She didn't mean it,' he said, his voice belying the deep-rooted fear for Cathy's fragile sanity. 'It was my own fault. I should never have insisted on going to her at such a late hour. I'm sure she sensed that I was there with bad news.' He paused, recalling the disturbing atmosphere in Cathy's room. It was menacing, from the moment he came into it.

'You mustn't blame yourself. If the doctor agreed that she should be told about Matt, then how are you to know any better?'

He shook his head, and drew her into him. 'You're right, I know you are,' he murmured, burying his head in her hair.

'You'll stop punishing yourself, then?'

'Yes,' he lied, 'I'll stop punishing myself.' He kissed the top of her head and held her at arm's length. 'Maria? Is she sleeping?' When Emily nodded, he asked, 'And the nurse, is she here?'

'I've put her in the small room next to Maria's.' She smiled, rolling her eyes up to the ceiling. 'I heard her in Maria's room a short while ago. It's quiet up there now, so I imagine they're both sleeping. Between the two of us, we will be on hand whenever Maria needs us.' She looked directly into his face now, knowing somehow what his answer would be, even before she voiced the question. 'Will you stay the night? I've prepared the room across from mine.'

'I want to, Emily, oh, I want to,' he groaned, 'but I can't. You know that, don't you? I must be with Matt.'

'I know.'

'He doesn't realise I'm there. He's so quiet and still, he doesn't realise anything.' He visibly shook himself, gripping her by the shoulders and smiling widely. 'If you'll have me, I'll stay with you a while longer.'

'I would like that.'

'Good! Then what say I make you a cup of cocoa and we sit here together, talking and reminiscing like an old married couple?'

She laughed, but it was a small hollow sound. 'Yes, I would like that too,' she agreed. When, with a fleeting kiss on her lips he pushed her gently into the chair and went from the room, Emily leaned back against the soft plump cushions, events of the day pressing on her mind . . . her own darling Maria upstairs, beyond all help. And Matt, so tragic, so heartbreaking; for him, too, it seemed there was no hope. And Bill's daughter Cathy, what of her? Maybe she would be saved in the course of time, and with specialist help. Maybe, only maybe. She closed her eyes. There was no sound coming from above, only the distant muffled noises from the kitchen where Bill was preparing a tray for them. A rush of pleasure tempered her grief. 'Bill . . . Bill.' The touch of his name on her lips was warming, comforting, like a flicker of light at the end of a long dark tunnel. If the Lord was taking everything else from her, he was not leaving her destitute. He was taking with one hand and giving with the other. Scales of justice, she thought curiously, but where was the justice in destroying the lives of Cathy and Matt? Hard though it was for her to deal with, Emily had long realised Maria's great age, yet Cathy and Matt had hardly lived. It was so cruel, so very wicked!

Deeply stirred, Emily got out of the chair and began pacing the room. She felt unusually agitated, a sense of anger coursing through her. In a moment, and almost without realising it, she had crossed the room and retrieved the tallow doll from the dark interior of the drawer where she had earlier secreted it. When, a short time later, Bill entered the room carrying a tray, he was astonished to see Emily standing in the halo of light beneath the ceiling lamp, her eyes glazed in admiration as she turned the doll over and over in her fingers. At first, he couldn't tell what Emily was gazing at, although he saw how it fascinated her. Setting the tray on the coffee table, he came and stood beside her.

'What's that?' he asked, his sharp eyes picking out the obvious details in the artefact . . . the long flowing hair black as night, the magnificently etched features, and the stunning hypnotic eyes.

'The gardener dug it up with the old apple tree,' Emily explained, holding it out to him. 'It's very old. I believe it must have belonged to Maria.' She smiled at him and for a fleeting moment he did not recognise her. 'It's lovely, don't you think?'

'It's very beautiful,' he agreed, his eyes roving its perfect slender form and noting the details there . . . the bare feet, the eyes that seemed hollow, yet were not, and the dress, a curiously humble garment for such a proud and captivating creature. For a moment he was puzzled, intrigued but not knowing why.

Suddenly he knew. '*Good God* . . . how strange, Emily!' he

whispered. 'It could almost be a partner to the doll that Cathy brought back from Australia, except the other one is as hideous as this one is beautiful.' He laughed. 'Beats me how she could cherish something so downright ugly! It's the kind of monster that creates nightmares, I reckon.' A chill foreboding turned his stomach . . . *creates nightmares* . . . *monster*. No! He was being fanciful, grasping at straws, letting his imagination run riot. Those kind of fantasies belonged in the realms of childhood, when the bogeyman hid round every corner, and the slightest sound from beneath the bed was a long bony hand reaching up to drag you into some black pit seething with every kind of unmentionable creature.

Wrenching his thoughts back, he found *reality* far more terrifying. Only one thing applied to both now and the nightmares of childhood, and that was the awful helplessness he felt.

'I was going to surprise her with it, and show her how lovely the garden is now.' Emily was still hoping that Maria might see the garden, maybe even sit in it awhile, warmly wrapped in a blanket in her wheelchair. It seemed such a simple thing to ask, and yet she felt instinctively that it would never be.

It was nearing midnight when Bill got ready to leave. Coming into the hallway with Emily, he paused at the foot of the stairs and looked up. 'Do you think she's sleeping?'

Emily nodded, slipping her hands in his. 'I imagine so,' she replied, her concerned gaze looking up also. 'I'll stay with her tonight. The chair is comfortable enough.' As the two of them made their way towards the door, Emily glanced at his face. He looked incredibly weary. At the door he clung to her.

'I don't know how I could have ever come through all of this without you,' he murmured. She would have reassured him of her love and support, but in that moment the telephone rang out. Visibly startled and afraid that Maria might waken, she grabbed the receiver and gave out her number.

Curious as to who could be calling at this ungodly hour, Bill waited, silently watching her. When her expression turned from

279

puzzlement to alarm, he stepped closer; already the pit of his stomach was bubbling. When she held out the receiver, saying in a trembling voice, 'It's you they want, Bill,' his mind flew to Matt.

Taking the receiver he pressed it close to his ear, his heart thumping, his every sense in turmoil. 'Yes?' A slight pause, then, 'This is he.' His voice was stern, unnaturally calm. As he listened to the man at the other end of the line, he felt the colour drain from his face. *'Good God!'* He bent forward, huddling over the phone, his shoulders sagging as though a sudden unbearable weight was laid across them. 'Yes! Yes, right away.' He listened intently, before saying in a shocked, hushed voice, 'I understand.'

After the conversation was ended, he made no immediate attempt to replace the receiver. Instead, for what seemed an age to Emily, he held it over the cradle, his gaze downcast and his head slowly shaking from side to side as though he could not, or would not, believe what he had just been told.

Emily knew who had called, because the doctor gave his name to her. She came to Bill's side now, her anxious eyes seeking his. 'What did he want?' she asked quietly, knowing that the caller would never have contacted Bill here, at this time of night especially, unless it was an emergency; the gist of the conversation had only confirmed her suspicions.

When he swung round now, it was as though he had been momentarily stunned and Emily's voice had shocked him back. Dropping the receiver into its cradle he gripped his good hand round her upper arm, his voice incredulous as he gasped, 'It's Cathy. She's run away!' Before Emily could question him further he tore from her and yanked open the door, his face ashen in the overlight from the porch. 'I've got to hurry,' he said, rushing down the path, 'I think I know where she might be heading.' He hurried into the night, an intermittent streetlamp and the moonlight making him seem insubstantial, only a shadow flitting through the darkness.

'Where?' Emily called. 'Where will you find her?' She prayed with all her heart that Cathy had not harmed herself.

Back through the night came her answer. 'With Matt. I think

she may have gone to find Matt.' 'He had not forgotten his last devastating visit to Cathy, nor would he ever forget that demented look in her eyes when she hissed, *'I know why you're here!'* Somehow she already knew about Matt. Maybe she had overheard the conversation between the doctor and himself, when they had talked of Matt being close to death. Nothing was omitted from the conversation – not the dire state of his illness, nor the hospital where he was kept. Cathy had gone to Matt, he was sure of it, yet he hadn't said anything to the doctor just now, because the police had been informed and he could not take a chance. The last thing he wanted was that Cathy should be frightened, or torn away from Matt.

As he drove at speed to cover the twenty or so miles that lay between him and Matt – and maybe Cathy – he found himself softly praying that Cathy was safe. He recalled with a murmuring shock how she had leapt at him, like a savage thing; for as long as he lived he would not forget that. It would be ingrained in his mind for all time. Without warning a thought popped into his consciousness; it made him shudder. But that could not be! It *was* Cathy! *Who else could it have been?* Dear God, was he losing his mind? All the same, he had a feeling, a strange unsettling feeling. Somewhere in the depths of his mind all was not well. Not normal. Real and intimate, the voice was whispering, tormenting, murmuring beneath the surface, not recognisable, not something he had ever experienced in his whole life before. Made uneasy by his own thoughts, he pressed his foot down on the pedal . . . eighty-five . . . ninety.

Concentrating on the road ahead, he thrust all else from his mind. Nervous at the speed he was doing, he glanced into the mirror, his sharp eyes on the look-out for police cars. The motorway was curiously deserted. He swung his attention back to the road, after a moment peering into the rear-view mirror once more. *Something was troubling him.* Yet he saw nothing alarming. Hot and uncomfortable, he ran his finger along the edge where the collar of his shirt met his skin. He could hardly breathe. Convinced that the police must be following, clocking his speed, he glanced furtively into the mirror again. No. There was nothing. No one. *Yet he was not alone.*

Close enough to reach out and touch him, she bided her time, a black menacing form curled in the deeper recesses of the rear seat, her dark, sinister eyes watching his every move, her presence permeating the air with evil, reaching inside him. Merciless, she watched his discomfort with pleasure. Her power was tenfold now. *She was relentless.*

Emily had stood at the door until the bright red lights had gone into the distance. When she could no longer see the vehicle, she went back into the house; at the foot of the stairs she listened awhile. All was quiet. Satisfied, she returned to the sitting room, collected the tray and took it into the kitchen, where she placed it on the draining board. Checking that the house was secure, she then took a moment to tuck the tallow doll into her skirt pocket. As she did so, Bill's words came back to her . . . 'It could be the partner to a doll that Cathy brought back from Australia, except . . . hideous . . . creates nightmares.' It occurred to her in that moment, how Maria herself had lived in Australia for many years. Maybe Bill had not been far wrong, then? Perhaps the dolls were sold in the craft shops there? Certainly, *Cathy's* artefact had originated in Australia and if, as Emily suspected, this more attractive one *did* belong to Maria, then it was more than likely that it too was born in that country, being brought to England when Maria herself came here.

When a few moments later, Emily tiptoed into Maria's bedroom, it was to find her wide awake, and the nurse fast asleep, her ample form oozing over the armchair and her head lolling to one side, the small white cap askew on her neat dark hair. 'Shh!' Maria warned softly, putting a thin scabrous finger to her lips. 'She tried so hard to keep awake, poor thing.' As Emily drew nearer, the old face spread into a pixilated smile; in the yellowish glow from the nearby night-light the old lady's face looked shockingly aged, even the eyes that were once so vividly blue were painfully blanched and bulbous. *Death was an ugly predator.*

'Oh, Maria, I thought you were asleep!' Emily gently chastised. Coming to the bed and seating herself on its edge, she stretched out her arm to stroke the lank grey hairs from Maria's forehead.

Emily thought the small unintelligible sound to be a chuckle. 'You thought wrong, then, didn't you?' Maria teased, her voice croaked and hollow. The bloated eyes swivelled upwards, exaggerating the plicature of dry skin in the hollows beneath. In the gloom they searched out Emily's face, fixing themselves there with unnerving directness. *'Tell him,'* she whispered, 'it wasn't his fault, nor the dogs'. My time was running out long before.'

Understanding, Emily nodded. 'Rest now,' she said, 'you mustn't tire yourself.' She bent forward to kiss the high pale forehead. 'I won't be far away,' she promised. A sudden movement behind made Emily turn.

The nurse woke with a start, an expression of horror on her puffed, sleepy features. Scrambling out of the chair, she quickly offered her apologies, frantic fingers straightening the cap on her head, smoothing the crumpled skirt, then plucking nervously at the cuff of her blouse. 'Oh dear,' she kept saying, 'oh dear.'

'It's all right,' Emily assured her, taking her to one side. 'You mustn't worry. I don't expect you to sit with her *every* night. Remember our arrangements? We will *share* the night duty. You get some proper sleep now.' When the nurse began to protest, Emily insisted, *'Go on.'* Reluctantly, the nurse withdrew, but not before first checking her patient, then extracting Emily's promise to call her at any time should she be needed.

'Huh! I said all along I didn't need no nurse,' Maria retorted when Emily came back to stand by the bed. Shifting her eyes to stare at the door, she asked in a furtive whisper, *'Has she gone?'* When, quietly amused by Maria's intolerance, Emily glanced to the closed door before affirming that yes, 'she's gone to her bed', a slow devious look crept over the old one's face, her eyes narrowed to dark slits as they searched the four corners of the room. 'Are we alone?' she asked hoarsely.

'Just you and me, Maria,' Emily told her.

Maria made a small noise, moving her head slowly from side to side, looking about the room, searching. *For one awful moment she imagined there was someone hiding in the corner.* Now, when she shuddered, Emily drew the quilt over her small frail arms. 'No! Don't go, Emily. Don't leave me,' she pleaded.

'I won't,' Emily promised, thinking how Maria was like a child again, with a child's fears.

'Come closer,' she urged softly, withdrawing her arms from beneath the bedclothes and holding them out as though to cradle Emily to her heart. When Emily seated herself close to Maria, her face only inches away from that familiar aged face, the anxious voice went on in a whisper, 'I have a confession to make.' Thinking on all the awful things she must now confess, a chill rippled through her old bones. She had never been so afraid, but time was short. There was too much hidden away inside. She could feel her life ebbing away, but she must not give in. Not yet. How could she rest in peace when there was evil all around? It rose in her now, stifling her.

'A confession?' Emily was intrigued, her deeper instincts telling her that the old lady's mind was beginning to wander. 'Please, Maria,' she said softly, 'rest now. We'll talk in the morning.' She could see how desperately tired Maria was.

'No!' Maria tugged at Emily's sleeve. 'Mr Barrington . . . all of them. *I know.*' She was growing frantic now. 'It's all there. Oh, Emily, Emily, you must warn them!' In her excitement she had raised her head from the pillow. Now she sank back, exhausted, her breathing erratic.

'I won't listen any more,' Emily warned, 'not tonight.' She suspected that Maria was about to reveal how she had kept Cathy and Matt's wedding photograph and all the other snippets of information. Emily had been made curious about that strange discovery, particularly about the notebook. She was curious now, but she would not let Maria distress herself any further. 'I want you to sleep now,' she told her, thankful at least that Maria had closed her eyes. The abject terror in them was too unnerving. The old, the dying, their fears were so different, so intense.

'NO!' The voice was a small scream. The eyes popped open.

'Please, Maria, you mustn't be afraid.'

'You don't understand. I'm not afraid. *I am terrified!*'

Alarmed, Emily leaned forward to soothe her. She hoped such terror would not be *her* companion when it was time to leave this world. She saw it in Maria's face and it was an awesome thing. 'I'm here,' she said. 'I won't leave you, I promise. There is no need for you to be terrified. It's been such a long wearying day for you, Maria. Won't you rest now?' She forced a lightheartedness into her voice. 'And then in the morning, who knows, you might feel strong enough for me to wheel you into the back bedroom where you can look out of the window and see the garden. Oh, Maria, it's a delight!' She remembered the tallow doll. 'Oh, and I have something to show you.'

She took the doll from her pocket and stood it in the palm of her hand, sensitive fingers tightly supporting it. 'The gardener found this doll, Maria. It was tangled in the roots of that old apple tree. I think you must have lost it long ago. It's a delightful thing.' She smiled when the blue eyes sprang open to stare at the doll, the flickering glow from the night-light bringing its face alive. 'Bill said Cathy has one that's very similar, only hers is old, ugly. She brought it back from Australia . . .' She stopped when the withered fingers clutched at her, the blue eyes big and dark, the wrinkled mouth twitching open and shut as though the words were trapped inside.

Alarmed, Emily opened the cabinet drawer and laid the doll into it. 'We'll talk about it in the morning,' she murmured, angry with herself. She had been all kinds of a fool! 'I shouldn't have shown it to you,' she said, 'not now.' Sliding the door shut, she made to rise from the bed, but the fingers kept her there, pressing, restraining, and still the words would not come, the eyes stark and staring. 'What is it, Maria? *What are you trying to say?*' Emily had never been more afraid. She would have gone for the nurse, if only Maria would let go of her.

'*The . . . doll?*' She was struggling now, her frantic eyes glancing to the drawer, her voice rasping, painful.

'Tomorrow, Maria.' With determination, Emily bunched the

gnarled fingers in her fist, her free hand stroking Maria's forehead, sticky wet beads of sweat beginning to burst and trickle down the jutting temples.

Maria pulled away, reaching both misshapen hands to her throat, tugging at the fine silver chain. *'The key,'* she croaked, tapping the small barrel-shaped key at the end of the chain.

'All right.' Emily leaned forward and slipped the chain from Maria's scrawny neck. 'I'll put it here,' she said, 'on your bedside cabinet.'

'No!' The fingers closed round Emily's small fist, locking the chain there. 'Open the . . . chest.' She was gasping for breath, but nothing that Emily could say or do would stop her, not now, not when she could feel Death's cold breath calling her. 'Bring it, Emily . . . the chest.' Her eyes grew wider with every frantic word, until now they dwarfed every other feature. 'Can't sleep . . . *won't sleep.*'

Frustrated, Emily was convinced that Maria would not rest until the old chest that had belonged to her grandmother was beside her – something of the past, a treasured relic to give her comfort. 'Shh, I'll get it,' she said, 'but only if you will promise to rest then?' When the grey head nodded, Emily went to the place where she knew the old chest was kept. In a moment she returned. 'There,' she whispered soothingly, 'I'll leave it here, where you can easily see it, but don't you go trying to reach it, Maria, or I will have to take it away again.' She began clearing a space on the cabinet.

'NO!' The voice startled her. Pausing, she turned. Maria's expression was frightening. 'Take it . . . away!' she moaned.

Emily was astonished, especially when she remembered how closely Maria had always guarded the old casket. For now, though, she realised it was essential to humour the old one. 'All right, Maria, I'll take it downstairs.' And alert the nurse on the way, she thought. Tucking the object in the crook of her arm, she leaned down. 'I'll be back in a minute,' she said, her anxiety eased a little. Certainly Maria seemed much calmer now, a more peaceful look in her eyes, although the fear was still there – the fear

286

of dying, Emily thought bitterly. She did not want to leave her, not even for the few minutes it would take to carry the chest out of the room, out of the old lady's presence. The chest, or its contents, had seemed to disturb her. It would be better put away for now. She swept silently out of the room, purposely leaving the door partly open, her steps taking her immediately to the nurse's room. Emily had been terrified just now, it might be as well if the nurse kept vigil with her through the night.

In the semi-darkness of her room, Maria stirred. There was terror in her, the same terror that had driven her to bury the tallow image where she believed it would remain for all time. Nothing had changed. Not on that night fifty years ago, nor on this night. The lifetime between was only a single frantic heartbeat. It took every ounce of her dying strength to drag herself from the bed and struggle across the room to the doorway. Every faltering step was a new agony. For every second, every painful shuffling movement, she was in dread that Emily would come back too quickly. *Emily must not stop her!* Not now. Not when the chaos in her mind had begun to shift into a semblance of order. Not when the words were at long last piecing together, making a sense that was denied her all these years.

She whispered the words now, the very words that had issued from the icon itself. From the image, the black-eyed evil that had visited in the depth of her nightmares . . . '*Through the flames . . . eye to eye . . .*' The rest was lost to her, but it made sense now. *Eye to eye.* More than anything these words had haunted her. Now she knew the secret. *There was another doll! Another.* The partner, like right and wrong, black and white, young and old. Wasn't that what Emily had said? . . . 'similar . . . but old and ugly.' Fashioned by the same fingers, out of the same mould. Beauty and the beast. *The beast!*

Quickly now, Maria pushed the door to and turned the key. The cabinet was only a few steps away, yet it seemed a million miles. Slowly she fed her way across the hard flat carpet, her bare feet making a weird sound, like shuffling sand. She felt wonderfully old, bent at a peculiar angle, her neck arched upwards so she could see her way. Breathless, she paused, the tissue-thin skin stretching grey over her knuckles as she clung to the hard rail at the foot of the bed. The weight of her own head was suddenly unbearable. Sighing, she let it droop, digging her chin into the folds of her neck, hard blue eyes staring at the stiff dead flowers in the carpet pattern . . . *through the flames, eye to eye* . . . she smiled. At last, at last the fragments made a picture in her mind. Two dolls. Two tallow images! The thought stabbed her like the point of a knife. *The other one* . . . eye to eye. No matter. One was the other, the other this one, *the same*. What had Emily said? Oh yes. The other . . . 'old . . . ugly'. She chuckled. That was *her* now. She and the doll. Beauty and the beast. All part of the same intricate plan. She had paused for only a moment. It was enough.

When, having regained her breath, she started forward again, her eyes were inexplicably drawn towards the cabinet drawer. *It was open.* She chuckled again. She was not afraid. Not now. She would never be afraid again. Inch by inch, relentlessly she advanced; in the half-light a slight movement, only the slightest flutter, caught her eye. Her quizzical gaze swung from left to right, now it settled on the pillow where only a short while ago she had rested her head. Black malevolent eyes stared back, secretly smiling. *The doll was there.* Maria wondered whether her pillow was still warm with her scent. Her scent, musty, alive, mingling with the doll. There was a time when that thought would have struck horror in her. Now, it was a comforting thought. It made her smile.

'*Maria!*' Emily was at the door, afraid, bewildered.

'Tell him,' Maria called, a sudden strength surging through her, '*The doll is evil.*' Belying her old tired bones and with the deadly speed of a snake's tongue her arm shot forward, hard aged fingers locking round the doll's throat. The black eyes stared up, glinting brilliantly in the flickering light. As her bony fingers tightened, Maria felt it shudder, felt its awful strength. In the softest whisper she spoke to it . . . '*Through the flames.*' It knew. *It knew!* Roles were reversed. Triumphant, Maria reached into the drawer and drew out the box of matches. 'The other one,' she thought fearlessly, *'like me.'* She was momentarily startled by a low gasping sound.

Turning her head she roved her gaze about the room. 'Are you here?' she whispered. There was only an eerie silence. And above it Emily's voice calling, frantic, pleading. Hasty fingers fumbling with the lock, then the sound of footsteps running down the stairs. Banging fists now, tearing at the door. *'Tell him!'* Maria called. Then, 'Forgive me, Emily.' Without releasing her hold on the doll's throat, she shook a match from the box. With calm deliberation she struck the match alight. At once it was blown out as though by a draught, but there no draught, no open door, no window ajar, only the catastrophic silence and the presence of evil, of terror. But the terror was not hers. *Not Maria's.*

Drawing the matchbox closer to her body, she struck another match, quickly feeding the blue-yellow flame to the long flowing hair. It crackled and spat. She lit another, flaming the hessian garment and laughing defiantly when the doll squirmed and twisted in her stiff clutching fingers . . . *'Through the flames, eye to eye,'* the old one chanted, her vivid blue stare delving deep into the black hollow sockets, not pure black now, but alive, and lit from within.

When the flames licked at her hand, scorching the skin and devouring the loose folds of her nightgown, Maria feverishly chanted the words, her voice excited, shivering with apprehension, her old heart elated . . . *'Through . . . the . . . flames . . . eye . . . to . . . eye.'* It was screaming now, such awful screams, terrible to hear, and still Maria taunted. There was no pain, no compassion. Only a soaring sensation of joy. Her strength was indomitable. Soon, very soon, when the flames licked over her old dry skin, Maria's own screams would not be stifled. '. . . *Through . . . the . . . flames . . . eye . . . to . . .'*

'MARIA!' Emily's scream was one more. It might as well have been a whisper.

The tall straight-faced nurse regarded him with quizzical eyes. 'No, Mr Barrington, your son-in-law has had no other visitors.'

'I see. Thank you.' He followed her along the corridor, his emotions in turmoil. Strange, he mused, he had been desperate to find Cathy by Matt's side, and now, for no obvious reason, he was almost relieved. The nurse pushed open the ward door and peered inside. Satisfied, she whispered, 'How long do you intend staying?'

Thoughts of Cathy filled his mind. Cathy, out there somewhere. Alone and frightened. He felt so damned helpless. They would find her, though, he felt sure, and they knew where to contact him. 'For a while,' he replied now, 'I can't say how long.'

She nodded. 'I understand.' She touched his arm lightly. 'I'll get someone to bring you a cup of tea.'

'Thank you. Oh, and I would like to see the doctor before I leave.'

'We have only one doctor on duty, I'm afraid,' she told him, 'but I know he will spare you a few moments. I'll make sure he's aware that you want to see him. Just come to the desk when you're ready to leave.' She smiled and her features grew surprisingly lovely. When she pushed the door wide open, he silently brushed past. Behind him, the door slowly closed with a soft rushing sound, and suddenly he felt incredibly alone. A great sadness overwhelmed him.

Advancing towards the bed and the familiar figure of Matt so still and white, Bill had the feeling that he was not alone, that *they* were not alone, that there was someone else in the room with them. The feeling was so strong it made him call out, 'Who's there?' His head jerked sideways, his eyes scanning the room, widening to a fixed stare when the overlight suddenly flickered low. 'Cathy? Is that you?' His furtive glance was drawn to the window, to the curtains fluttering in the incoming breeze, wild grass and a profusion of multi-coloured blooms coming alive on a parchment background. Uneasy, he went to the window, thrust back the curtains and shut out the night. He shivered, a chill rippling through him, the flesh on his back was crawling yet his hands were clammy, the air unpleasant, cloying. Going to the bed, he stood over Matt, gazing down on the silent handsome face, his thoughts murmuring of things that were lost for ever, his every nerve-ending shrieking inside him. When the door was suddenly flung open, he almost clawed up the wall. Realising who it was, he made a noise, a sigh of relief, a distorted laugh. 'You gave me a fright,' he told the intruder.

'It's the quietness,' the nurse replied, coming into the room and placing a cup of tea on the bedside cupboard, 'it gets to you, I know.' Brushing shoulders with him, she took Matt's wrist between her finger and thumb, lapsing into a meditative silence while with her other hand she plucked out the fob-watch pinned to the breast of her apron, her head bent, her eyes following the tiny hand as it ticked away the seconds. Presently, she gently covered Matt's arm with the bedclothes and carefully checked the monitoring equipment. 'Don't let your tea go cold, Mr Barrington,' she said, thrusting both hands into her apron pocket as she brushed past him.

'Nurse.'

She stopped and turned. 'Yes?'

'Matt.' He swallowed hard and stole a glance at the bed. 'Does he know I'm here?' It would mean so much.

She made a wry face. 'Possibly,' she said, 'it's hard to tell.' When he looked away, she quietly departed, closing the door behind her.

Disillusioned, he pulled the stiff uncomfortable armchair nearer to the bed. Collecting his tea from the side cupboard, he sat with it cupped in the palms of his hands, its warmth permeating his skin, and with it a sensation of pleasure. Suddenly his arms felt like lead weights. He leaned forward, resting his upper body on the bed, his legs stretched out beneath, and his gaze carefully regarding Matt's face. 'Like a child asleep,' he murmured. Other than the features being thinner, more deeply chiselled, Matt was the same as always, the thick mop of earth-coloured hair darkening the pillow, tumbling attractively over his forehead. The same muscular neck and straight classic nose, the strong wide mouth. It was so easy to imagine him smiling in that familiar lopsided relaxed manner he had, so easy to see the dark eyes sparkling with laughter, so easy, too impossible. 'Oh, Matt . . . Matt, if only prayers could save you. If only I could take your place,' he murmured, the after-sigh rising from deep inside. He shook his head and closed his eyes, the tears spilled over. He was not ashamed to cry, only ashamed that he was so utterly helpless.

Shh! *What was that?* He stiffened, the hairs on the back of his neck prickling. He listened, inclining his head to one side, discreetly glancing over his shoulder. *Nothing.* Only the uncanny stillness and the ticking of the wall-clock. *But no! There!* A soft, unintelligible sound, like the rush of wind across a moor, or the purring sigh of a woman in ecstasy. *'Cathy?'* He was transfixed, held by a murmur of unearthly terror.

His nervous glance inched to the door. It was closed, like the window, like the room. There was only Matt, and him, and . . . *'Daddy.'* The voice was inside him, all around, trembling in the air, turning his heart over.

'Cathy!' The room was darker now. He strained his eyes towards the corner by the door. 'Is that you, Cathy?' He could hear his own voice quivering, could hear the tea cup shivering in his hands. Slowly, the apparition emerged, a spectral shape without substance, the awful sound of laughter, black threatening eyes locked into his. Mesmerised with horror, he stared as she came nearer, and nearer. He felt the sweat break out all over his body. He opened his mouth to speak but only the silence remained, brooding, violent, black merciless eyes mingling with his, the figure, tall and menacing, still far off, but growing in substance. *Icy cold fingers touched him*, making him slew round, sending the tea cup flying, the warm brown liquid spilling out to make an ugly stain on the bedspread. 'CATHY!' Her name was a scream from deep down inside. She stared down at him, madness, stark strident madness, grey-black eyes like hard dead things.

'I'm sorry,' she murmured, pressing the knife-point to Matt's throat. 'I have to do this. You know that, don't you?' Her smile was terrifying to see. The knife-point pressed further home – in his mind it was like slow motion, creating a sinister pleasure, the sight of first blood seeming to excite. He felt himself being drawn in, becoming a part of her.

'NO!' He sprang to his feet, reaching out, his arms unable to touch her, as though there was an invisible barrier keeping him from her. She was only an arm's reach away, yet he was on the outside looking in, watching her kill him, helpless. 'Listen to me, Cathy.' His voice was desperate, soft and persuasive. 'For God's sake, listen to me. I love you, Cathy. *Matt loves you!*' When she turned, just for the briefest second he thought . . . he thought. He saw the tallow icon where she had laid it, on the pillow, nestling against Matt's temple. Matt was stirring, uneasy, a look of excruciating pain on his face.

Something clicked in Bill's mind. Realisation dawned and he gasped aloud, his disbelieving glance darting to where the apparition had appeared. *It was the tallow doll!* Disturbing images rampaged through his senses . . . Cathy's violent attack on Matt when they were driving home from the airport . . . *The tallow doll!* Matt had related how Cathy had been taken ill in Australia, soon after they had visited the old lunatic asylum, where she had found . . . *the tallow doll!* And see how Cathy had begged him to bring it to her in the nursing home, how she seemed frantic to be parted from it. The black unpredictable moods, the horrifying and bloody hallucinations, the strange way she idolised and protected the icon. Oh, dear God! Edna had sworn that she had broken it, and he had thought her senile when he saw how it was unharmed! What was it she had warned – *'The bad things only started when that thing came into the house.'*

Excitement coursed through him, and fear, and a dark resentful anger. Snatching the doll into his fist, he spat the words out, startling her. *'Think, Cathy, think!* You told me once . . . you didn't want to hurt him.' He gripped the doll fiercely in his two fists, holding it up like a cross. 'You said there was badness in you, and you were right, Cathy, *you were right.*' He thrust his arms out, forcing her to look on the icon. In the corner of his eye he thought he saw a shadow, a substance forming, reaching out to him. 'This is the badness, Cathy,' he yelled, 'not you! *This . . . this is the badness!*' He had her. Grey bewildered eyes looking at him, but the knife-point still embedded in soft flesh, the trickle of blood meandering over the stark white pillow. 'Don't hurt him,' he pleaded, 'Matt loves you. We *both* love you. Put down the knife, Cathy. *Don't hurt him.*' His stark frightened eyes bored into Cathy's, watching them soften, her pain and confusion tearing him apart inside. 'You remember, Cathy, how happy you were? You and Matt, how much in love?' Softly, oh so carefully, he began to steal round the bed towards her, pausing when she pulled back, the knife-point sinking deeper into Matt's throat. 'Think, sweetheart,' he coaxed, 'think about how it was, you and Matt.'

'Me . . . and . . . Matt.' Her eyes swam with tears as she shifted her gaze to Matt's face, to the rivulet of blood creeping over her hand. Suddenly he groaned, his eyes opening to narrow slits, searching, searching.

'C . . . a . . . th . . . y.' Her name issued from his lips, soft and loving.

Startled, she bent towards him. In that split second, Bill sprang forward, the doll tight in his fist and his free hand seeking to snatch the knife from Cathy's grasp. Everything happened at once – the mind-splitting scream, the tremendous unseen force that sent him staggering backwards, and Cathy, laughing, shaking her head like a thing insane. Then the glow, the fiery blinding glow that encompassed her, the doll writhing in his hand, wailing like a soul in torment, burning his flesh, ebbing and glowing in a brilliant spherical light, the eyes scintillating, glaring at him, the hatred touching his very soul. Above the banshee screams he could hear his own voice calling out, yelling, growing desperate when no one came to shatter the madness. Dragging himself to the door, he banged his fist into it, over and over, each time louder than the last, his frantic screams rising above the mayhem. The voice was inside him, exquisite pain, burning, *like Cathy, like the doll* . . . 'They can't help you. No one on earth can help . . . you . . . now.'

The voice was faltering, the image melting before his eyes, and

Cathy, *Cathy!* He rolled his eyes upwards, crying out in agony when he saw not Cathy, but a wizened aged creature, like an old film flicking over before his shocked eyes. Cathy was there, then the doll, now the beauty, then the beast, and Maria . . . *Maria.* The room was on fire, the stench overpowering. *'Cathy, CATHY!'* She was burning, *he* was burning, the pain was excruciating, *and the laughter*, a wicked heinous sound straight from hell itself. He glanced down, into the black tortured eyes, bitter, empty eyes, long-ago evil, the voice filtered into his senses. *'They . . . can't . . . help . . . you.'* He felt the fingers tighten round his throat, he was slipping away into the blackness, deep down, into the furore of an overwhelming peace.

'It's all right.' He heard the voice inside his head, felt the strong hands urging him upwards. Like a drunken man he clung to them, his head splitting, the stench of fire still sultry in his nostrils. 'Okay. You're okay now.' His senses were in turmoil, his mind emerging from the darkness. With big disbelieving eyes he searched the room. A nervous smile shaped his lips; there was nothing here to alarm him. *But then he remembered!*

Beginning to tremble inside, he glanced down at the palm of his hand. 'Strange,' he murmured – there was no burn, no scorch mark, no indication of the intense heat that had melted through his skin. 'Cathy!' he gasped, struggling to clamber from the bed.

'Lie still, Mr Barrington!' The doctor was young, innocent. He did not understand. 'Your daughter is quite safe.'

'Where? *Where is she?'* Visions of fury and torment were still alive in him.

'When the nurse went back to carry out her normal checks, and found you lying unconscious with your daughter on her knees beside you, well of course she phoned the police. That was the instruction they gave only minutes before, to contact them immediately if we saw a young woman answering to your daughter's description.'

'The police!' He scrambled from the bed, his whole body feeling as though it had been forced through a mincer. 'The police took her? Is that what you're saying?' He desperately tried to gather his shredded thoughts.

'They were gentle. She gave them no trouble.'

'Was she all right?' He looked up, his head bent forward into the palms of his hands, his dog-brown eyes half-hidden beneath a heavy frown. When the doctor was slow to reply, he urged, 'For God's sake, man! Was she all right?'

'Distressed.'

'Harmed? *Was she harmed in any way?*' Try as he might, he could not thrust out the images.

The doctor pursed his lips and lapsed into deep thought. After a moment he shook his head. 'I don't think so.'

'Did they take her back to the nursing home?'

'I don't know.'

'I want to see Matt. And I need to call the nursing home.'

'Of course.'

On unsteady legs he followed the white-coated doctor down the narrow corridor towards that same small room. He found himself trembling. What would he find there? Dear God above, *what would he find!*

Chapter Fifteen

'Is Matthew Slater here?' The thin-faced, tight-lipped man sat upright in the chair, regarding Edna through serious eyes. 'I would very much like to speak with him.'

'No, I'm sorry,' Edna replied, politely offering the stranger a sandwich from the plate. When he gestured that he did not want refreshment of any kind, she went on in a small quiet voice, 'There's no one here but me, I'm afraid. You see, there's been a sadness in this family.'

'Oh, I am sorry,' he apologised.

She smiled wryly. 'We're all of us given a cross to bear,' she said, 'some crosses bigger than others . . . harder to carry.' Her smile broadened as she added in a lighter mood, 'But I've always said that if you trust in the Lord, you've nothing to fear.' She frowned. 'I'm sorry, too, about Laura. You say she was an old friend?'

He nodded. 'There was a time long ago when I had hoped we would marry.' He looked away, gazing at the open blue sky through the window. 'It wasn't to be. Laura was always a free spirit, not the marrying kind at all.'

'And now you're here on the sad errand of taking her home to be buried?'

'That's why I am staying overnight in Bedford, yes. All the arrangements are made. But I could not leave without seeing you. I have been made aware of the circumstances of her death, but I wanted to hear the account first hand. Is there anywhere I can contact Mr Slater? The stables do belong to him? He was her employer.'

297

'Oh yes. That's right, sir,' Edna agreed, 'but it ain't *Matthew* you need to talk to, because, you see, he weren't here two nights ago when . . .' She paused. The events were bright as day in her mind. 'When Laura was killed.' She might have added . . . 'When the other bad things happened . . .' but she chose not to.

'Who, then?'

'Why, *me*, of course, and my husband, Joseph. We did what was humanly possible, believe me.' She lowered her gaze to the carpet, unwilling to go on, not wanting to relive that awful night, a night like no other, a night when it seemed as though all the hounds of hell were let loose to wreak terror and carnage.

'Please, go on,' he urged. And, while she told him – of how she and Joseph were awakened in their beds by the unmistakable crackling and splintering of burning wood, when the wild leaping flames lit up the night like it was a brilliant summer's day – the man remained silent, his face moved in turn by a myriad of emotions, his small blue eyes never once looking away, though they were heavy with pain. 'Do you think she suffered?' he asked.

Edna shook her head, 'No,' she said gently, 'don't you go tormenting yourself with such thoughts. It was all over too quickly.'

He sighed, the faintest of smiles changing his features. 'That's what *they* told me,' he said, 'that the smoke would have rendered her unconscious before . . . before . . .' He could not go on.

'Like I said, don't torture yourself,' Edna entreated. She finished his sentence in her head . . . *before the flames burned her alive.* But that was exactly the way it did happen, she recalled with a riveting sense of horror. It was all too real in her memory. Soon after the nursing home phoned to say how Cathy had run away and they needed to contact Mr Barrington urgently, she and Joseph spent the best part of an hour just sitting and talking about so many things . . . how Slater's Farm used to be such a happy place with everybody part of one big happy family . . . how Bill Barrington was a tower of strength to them all . . . how everyone prayed for Matt and Cathy, agonised for them, despaired that they might never again be the same lovely, carefree souls. Joseph had declared sadly that it was 'as though a curse had been put on them' – although when Edna quickly agreed and spoke to him about the tallow image, he grew angry, almost afraid, she thought, dismissing her fears out of hand, and warning her never to speak of such things. 'Do you want folk to start thinking I'm married to a witch?' he asked, his amusement veiled in a more sinister mood. Feeling foolish, she had gone to bed, and besides, she reminded herself, that hideous tallow doll was broken into a thousand pieces! She had not regretted doing that. She never would.

Not long after, Joseph had climbed into bed and the two of them had fallen asleep. Some time later she was awakened with a start, thinking the house to be on fire, the dry acrid smell of smoke clogging her nostrils. Through the half-open window she was astonished to see the whole sky ablaze, illuminating the room, reflecting the crimson glow in the dressing-table mirror. Her shouts woke Joseph and the two of them threw their dressing gowns on, and ran full pelt towards the source of the fire. It was pandemonium!

The smoke was billowing over the stables, terrifying the horses and whipping them into a frenzy. Joseph screamed at her to 'Stay back!' but she knew he could never do it alone. Together they rushed down the yard, throwing open the stable doors and sending the frantic horses out across the fields. The heat was stifling, oppressive, choking them, impairing their vision, the spreading flames bent on devouring everything in sight. With the last horse free and galloping to safety, Joseph roared at her to, *'Get out! Get out!'* grabbing her by the arm and turning her away. But then the screams shocked them rigid. *'Jesus Christ! There's somebody trapped down there,'* Joseph yelled, pushing her on before swinging back to run into the thick of it. Undaunted and fearful for his safety, Edna followed, the corner of her dressing gown stretched over her mouth, her raw eyes streaming from the smoke and heat. The tack-room was hopelessly engulfed by the time they got there. Vivid red and blue flames leapt high into the air, the heat was intense, they could not come within ten feet of it. Dejected and realising how their own lives were in danger, Joseph hurried her away. Following a persistent instinct, Edna had looked back, just once, for the briefest moment, but long enough for her to see what would haunt her for all time. *It was the face a woman.* A woman, trapped and terrified, her two hands stretched wide and pressed against the blistering windowpane, her mouth open in a silent scream, the flames licking at her all around.

'*Laura!*' Edna's horrified scream caused Joseph to jerk round, his quizzical gaze following Edna's trembling finger as it pointed to the window. It was too late. Laura had slipped away. In the aftermath, when the fire crews had rendered the flames to embers and Edna stood with Joseph surveying the destruction, it came to her with a shock. *The woman!* The woman who had burned to death in the tack-room was *not* Laura. And yet it was. Edna had seen that tragic face with her own eyes and had instantly recognised Laura.

But there was something else. Something so strange and disturbing that she hardly dare let herself dwell on it. Certainly, she would never reveal what she imagined she saw. *Never!* Not to Joseph, not to a single soul. Yet she could not deny it to herself. In the pyre that had swallowed Laura's life, there had been another. A stunningly beautiful creature, long dark hair and wide black glowing eyes. In that instant before the scene was changed for ever and Laura slid away, she and the apparition merged as one. In the fervent belief that there may have been *two* souls lost in the inferno, Edna was mortally afraid for her sanity when it was later revealed that Laura and no one else had died there. And yet, Edna knew what she had seen. She knew. It was enough. Some things were beyond the understanding of mere man or woman.

What she witnessed that night was something to remember. *And something to forget.* That was why she made no mention of it now, to Laura's friend. He had come to Bedford to take her home, to where she had grown up and they had dreamed together, before he went his way and Laura went hers. Now, it was time for Laura to return. It would be a long and a sad journey. Edna would not add to his grief, and so she assured him, 'Laura would not have

300

suffered, please believe that.' When she saw the relief in his face, she hoped the Lord would forgive her.

Later, when Laura's friend had departed, she went down to the stable yard and stood before the devastation that once was the tack-room. In her mind's eye she imagined the face at the window . . . Laura . . . the black-eyed stranger . . . not two, but one. She turned away. She would never again willingly call the image to mind. It was too disturbing. *Too real*. She could never hope to understand.

Chapter Sixteen

The room was long and narrow, with tall arched windows high up in the wall, four on each side like silent sentries keeping watch. On the east side the morning sun poured in, bathing the room in warm brilliance. There was a hushed atmosphere, and a sense of great joy. There was peace, and there was hope. At the head of the room was a long mahogany table, each end bedecked with beautifully arranged flowers. Behind the table stood two people, a short bald and bespectacled man in a dark blue suit, and by his side a sturdy, somewhat handsome woman with an open book resting lightly in the palms of her hands, her soft invasive voice bringing the service to an end. Closing the book, she smiled and the smile revealed surprising beauty. As she walked away to sit behind a smaller desk to the right, she glanced back and her smile deepened. She had seen it all before, but each newly wedded couple brought their own unique glow with them. She watched fondly as the couple signed their names into the book. Afterwards they thanked her and she wished them well in their new life together. Quietly and with reverence the couple walked from the room into the glorious sunshine of a mid-October day. Outside on the lawn the guests laughed and chatted, spilling the coloured confetti over the heads and shoulders of the happy couple, while the photographer tried desperately to restore order.

'Oh, Emily, I do love you so.' Bill clasped her small fingers into his and bent his head to kiss her full on the mouth. The cheer that went up from all about brought a pleasant pink flush to Emily's face. Undeterred, he kissed her again. The photographs promised to be exceptionally good.

'God certainly smiled on you today,' said the photographer, blinking up at the clear blue sky, 'especially as it's been raining for a week.' He packed his gear, loaded it into his car and drove speedily away; he had a busy schedule today. Too busy, he thought. Was he getting too greedy, he asked himself.

'Are you all right, son?' Bill's warm brown eyes looked down on the man in the wheelchair, his heart brimming with love and gratitude.

'I'm fine. Stop worrying!' Matt laughed. 'I'm only sorry to be stuck in this damned chair.' He so much wanted to stand on his own two feet for this wonderful occasion, but he was not yet strong enough. There was a deep-down tiredness in him – 'debilitating effects of the drugs', the doctors had said. The couple on that barge were known addicts and the girl had a history of mental instability. Apparently it was not the first time she had endangered other people's lives. But Matt could only be thankful that they had dragged him from the river. Two of his spinal discs had been dislocated in the process, and he was still in considerable pain. Attending Bill and Emily's wedding had been in blatant defiance of doctors' advice, but his pleading had persuaded them, with the proviso that he report immediately back to the hospital where he should expect to spend at least another two weeks under observation.

'I don't want to take you back there, to the hospital.' The gentle loving voice was one he feared he might never hear again. When he lifted his gaze to her now, his dark eyes were bright with tears and wonder.

'I love you, sweetheart,' he murmured, reaching out his long, strong fingers.

'I love you too,' Cathy whispered, holding his hand and nuzzling her face against his thick shock of dark brown hair.

From a distance, Bill and Emily saw their own happiness mirrored in these two young people, and their joy was complete. For Emily this was something precious, this was her family. *Her family!* 'The nightmare is over,' Bill said quietly, though the memories were still alive in his eyes, in his deeper thoughts.

Memories too horrendous ever to leave him completely. The terror of knowing that Matt and Cathy were fast slipping away from him, the suffering, the evil that had infiltrated their very souls, even now on his wedding day and with the sun lighting all the corners, he was wary of every dark fleeting shadow. 'I still can't understand why Maria kept the truth of your background from you.'

'I thought about that a lot,' Emily admitted, 'and though I don't know why she kept it from me, I believe she had her reasons. We shall never really know.' Emily, too, had undergone a devastating ordeal. She had blamed herself for Maria's lonely and terrifying death. And yet, when the door was broken down and they found Maria there, it was as though she had left this world in a state of peace and grace. The room was filled with unique devastating calm. Maria was lying on the floor, her features lifted by the faintest of smiles, and her two hands clasped together, as though holding something, 'or like she was praying,' the nurse had said. There was nothing untoward, no indication of why such heart-rending screams had issued from the room. Only the absence of the doll made Emily wonder.

Later, the full extent of the horror of that night was revealed: the awful carnage that Emily 'imagined' she heard from outside Maria's room – and which the nurse did not! – the inexplicable events in Matt's hospital room, and the tragic death of Laura. It was incomprehensible that all of these things should happen almost at the same time, and yet they did!

Afterwards, when Bill and Emily talked of these things, it was agreed that somehow the tallow images so innocently brought from Australia were a source of unspeakable evil. Then, when Cathy gradually regained her strength of mind, and Matt also was on the road to recovery, they were obliged to see how Edna had spoken the truth when she claimed 'all the bad things started when that thing was brought into the house!' Maria's own records, and the findings of the private detective, confirmed their suspicions. There were other things too . . . Maria's family history so meticulously recorded in the Bible and hidden in the chest which had once belonged to her grandparents, Ralph and Maria Ryan . . . documented evidence revealing how Ralph Ryan was duty officer when a certain 'insane and murderous convict' was taken from the asylum to be hanged; there were even rumours that had filtered through the years in the halls of the prison establishment, as to how the witch had 'laid a curse on Ralph Ryan'. It was handed down also that this woman was skilled in the art of tallow moulding . . . a candlemaker 'like her hanged grandmother before her'.

There was talk that Rebecca Norman's wickedness sprang from a childhood where she had suffered terrible loneliness after being so callously deserted, first by one parent and then by the other. The child's unquestionable love for the father who cruelly abandoned her soon turned to a dark and seething hatred. It was said by those who remembered something of the truth that the father created in his child an evil that knew no bounds. And when they spoke of it, they only whispered, and prayed she was not somehow listening, marking their every word.

'Are you happy, Cathy?' Matt looked up from his wheelchair, smiling from his heart when her soft grey gaze mingled with his. It seemed a lifetime ago, he mused, when those lovely eyes were stricken with such pain, such dark loathing. Now, they shone with life and love, aglow with vitality and contentment. There had been times when he believed their lives, their love, was over. Now, it was the beginning again. There was so much to share, so very much to look forward to.

'Oh, Matt . . . Matt!' she sighed, but it was a sigh of pleasure. 'I could never find words to express my happiness.' They were alone at last. Bill and Emily had left for two weeks' honeymoon in the Channel Islands, and Edna had tactfully stolen Joseph away indoors, 'To make a fresh brew o' tea,' she promised, and the stable grooms had no reason to linger after enjoying the wedding refreshments so beautifully presented by the effervescent Edna. Now there was just Cathy and Matt, and a fleeting sense of sadness as they looked on the blackened corpse that once was the stables. Not for the first time, Matt wondered what could have brought Laura back to the stables so late that night. Had she forgotten something? Did she have a secret rendezvous? No one knew. Perhaps they would never know. 'Do you want to leave Slater's Farm?' Cathy asked now, hoping in her heart that he would not forsake this lovely place in spite of all the bad things.

It seemed an age before he spoke, but even so he did not give her an answer. Instead he continued to gaze on the ruins as he said in a curious voice, 'All these years, Cathy, and I never knew about Maria . . . that she was my great-aunt.'

He fell silent, shaking his head in astonishment as he recalled the revelations made by Maria's own hand, and which Emily had found secreted in the chest. It was all there, how Maria had survived many 'strange tragedies' in her family, and so, when her own sister and brother-in-law perished in a bush fire – which the children, a boy and a girl, survived – Maria put the boy into sakekeeping in an Australian orphanage. That boy was Matt's own father, who himself was later killed in a strange accident.

The surviving girl-child was Emily. The girl was injured, though, and left a cripple. Desperate and afraid of the ill-fortune that had so relentlessly stalked Ralph Ryan's descendants through the years, Maria gave the girl Emily to the homely couple who were employed by Emily's parents, and who adored the infant. With Maria's help and financial support, they left Australia for England, where they were to make a new life for themselves and little Emily.

Some fourteen years later, Emily's adoptive parents met a violent 'accidental' death, and Emily was taken into Maria's care, never knowing that she had been adopted, and unaware that Maria Hinson, the kindly but eccentric woman she came to love, was really her own aunt.

When, after Maria's death, she perused the contents of the chest and discovered to her astonishment that Maria's life history was also her own, her joy was mingled with regret. Regret that she and Maria had never openly shared her common heritage, regrets because now she knew that even in her most forlorn and solitary moments, she had never really been alone, without blood-kin. 'If only I'd known,' she confided in Bill, 'my life would have been so much more meaningful.' But she forgave Maria for that one mistake, after realising that the old lady had her reasons, and remembering fondly all the love and guidance that dear lonely woman had given her over the years.

'Penny for them,' Cathy murmured, kneeling on the grass beside him, and looking up to see how preoccupied he was. She saw too the hint of sadness in his dark eyes, eyes that had seen too much suffering, eyes which – like hers – had shed too many tears. Like her, he was still haunted. It was etched into his handsome features, thinner now, and seeming gaunt against the pallor of his skin. All of his pain had been her pain. In the dark confusion of her mind there had been only a shocking desire to hurt, to maim, to kill. Now, thank God, every day that passed was another step out of the darkness, away from the pain, until soon there would remain only the good things. *Only the good things.*

'I was just thinking of Maria, and Emily,' he said softly, *'my own kin.'* He stroked his fingers against her face and gazed down with the love of a man for his woman. 'All those wasted years after my parents were killed, and I searched the world for the old aunt my father had spoken of so many times.' He laughed with a mixture of anger and relief. 'And all the time she was here, in the home of our ancestors. Oh, and Emily! My father's own sister. If only he had known. Oh, Cathy, if only he had known.'

'Shh! Don't look back, Matt,' Cathy urged. 'There is so much to look forward to. You have Emily now. And me. We are all one family, with a family's ambitions and hopes for the future.'

He nodded. 'You're right, sweetheart. And I thank the Good Lord for bringing us together.' Suddenly his mood darkened. 'How could I ever live without you?' He was remembering, and the pain was intense.

Cathy put a finger to his lips. 'No, Matt. Don't think of what might have been. Think only that we're here together, you and me . . . and that my father and Emily have found each other.' She paused, looking back towards the cottage. 'You and I, Matt, we have so much. And I love you.' She looked at him now and he saw that she was crying.

He gazed on her a moment longer before clasping her in his arms. 'You are everything to me,' he murmured, his face lighting up as he declared, 'and we *won't* leave Slater's farm! We'll stay and build our lives here, just as we planned.'

'And it will be wonderful,' she answered, snuggling into him, *'just as we planned.'*

It was cold. The sky was grey and moody, heavy with the threat of snow. In a small hamlet some fifty miles from Liverpool, James trudged a path through the churchyard, a solitary figure, destined for ever to be lonely. Shivering in the bitter November day, he pulled the collar of his coat up around his neck, hurrying his determined footsteps towards the ancient cedar tree and the grave which nestled in the ground beneath its branches. He knew the path well; he could have walked it blindfolded. Every day for the past four weeks he had trod the same path. It was his love for a certain woman that kept bringing him back. And memories. And a deep burning regret.

After reverently laying the flowers beneath the tall marble headstone, he stood awhile, thinking of how things might have been, seeing Laura in his mind's eye, her auburn hair flowing in the summer's breeze the way it did on that day so long ago, when they walked across the meadow. A day so beautiful, yet so tragic, a day that was etched on his mind for all time. The day that he told Laura he was going away, that he had fallen in love with someone else. *It was a mistake.* What he felt for the other woman soon proved to be only a shallow infatuation. Over the years he had tried so desperately to make amends, but though she still loved him, Laura would not, could not, forgive him. And in all truth he did not blame her for that. What he had done was foolhardy and cruel. He had inflicted unnecessary suffering on a good and wonderful woman, who for all of her life had already survived so much tragedy.

'You do keep her grave nice.' The voice startled him from his painful reverie. The vicar was old, wrapped up against the chill wind. Peeping from beneath the lapels of his dark overcoat could be seen the white collar of his station. He came closer, looking down to where Laura was laid to rest. 'I remember her as a child,' he said, smiling with that confident dreamy essence of a man of God. He pointed to a neat row of grey granite headstones near by. 'Her parents too . . . and all their children. I knew every one.' An icy gust of wind buffeted him; he thrust his hands into his pockets and crouched over, taking the full force on his back. 'Laura's parents . . . two sisters and a brother.' He shook his head, saying sadly, 'All here in this churchyard. All taken too soon.' He sighed, straightening as best he could, but his old bones were too bent. 'All victims of a cruel fate,' he went on. 'Tragic. So tragic.'

James glanced meaningfully to a dark corner against the high wall. 'There are four generations buried here, I do believe that Laura was the last of the line.' He shook his head slowly. 'Strange, though, the violent manner in which they all died. None of them old . . . except of course the great-great-grandfather. He lived the longest, to a ripe old age. All the same, it must have been the cruellest suffering of all, to see your family leave you one by one in such a way. One wonders what that wretched man did to deserve such a fate. It is a strange thing,' murmured the thin-faced man, '*almost like a curse*. You're a man of God. Do you believe in such things?'

The old fellow pondered awhile, before saying in a quiet voice 'I think we all believe in the power of good, so it must follow that we believe in the power of evil. Goodness . . . and evil. There will always be a struggle for supremacy.' He glanced round the churchyard, before saying in a hushed voice, 'We can only pray that our souls will find everlasting peace.' He turned away and in a moment was gone from sight.

James lingered there, alone and silent, his thoughtful gaze stretching to that dark corner by the wall. The headstone was crumbling, the grave there was ancient. It was said that Adam Norman was a hard and selfish man, having heartlessly deserted